THE CLAIMING

Meghan's heart quickened with each impatient leap Rolf took up the stairwell. When they reached the landing, his arms tightened further, as if fearing she would break free and flee.

As if she could.

He thrust open his solar door and slammed it shut with the heel of his boot. Just paces from his bed, he halted to gaze down at her. A stiff breeze from the window opening enfolded them, and his arms tightened.

Her breath caught at the expressions flashing through his gleaming eyes. Triumph. Passion. Impatience. All were there, undisguised.

His gaze held her own as he lowered his arm beneath her knees to straighten her in his arms. Each inch she moved against him sparked hot fire through her flesh. Hard. All of him—his massive chest, the hard slab of his belly, that hot and eager part of him—until soft lips claimed hers.

RISK EVERYTHING

SOPHIA JOHNSON

ZEBRA BOOKS
Kensington Publishing Corp.
www.kensingtonbooks.com

ZEBRA BOOKS are published by

Kensington Publishing Corp.
850 Third Avenue
New York, NY 10022

All Kensington titles, imprints, and distributed lines are available at special quantity discounts for bulk purchases for sales promotion, premiums, fund-raising, educational, or institutional use.

Special book excerpts or customized printings can also be created to fit specific needs. For details, write or phone the office of the Kensington Special Sales Manager: Attn. Special Sales Department. Kensington Publishing Corp., 850 Third Avenue, New York, NY 10022. Phone: 1-800-221-2647.

Zebra and the Z logo Reg. U.S. Pat. & TM Off.

ISBN 0-8217-7883-8

First Printing: July 2005
10 9 8 7 6 5 4 3 2 1

Printed in the United States of America

For my husband, Gil,
who has the patience of an angel,
and in memory of my mom, Alice,
who taught me to love reading
while I was still a
munchkin.

With many thanks to Delle Jacobs,
my tireless critique partner,
whose frequent reminders
prodded me to show and not tell.

CHAPTER 1

Southeast of the Kyle of Tongue, Scotland, 1074

Meghan of Blackthorn slipped from her bed in the dead of night. She did not light a candle, for guards atop the battlements would note it.

Sprawling on the cold, wooden floor, her head beneath the bed, she pulled forth the clothing hidden there. A warrior's attire. She made haste to don them until she came to the last items. Helmet and chain mail. When her fingers touched their cold links, she sighed with satisfaction.

She soon sighed with frustration.

'Twas no easy task alone. After several failed attempts, she draped the mail on the side of the bed. She leaned over, her upper body level with the bottom links, and lifted them. She burrowed inside the armor much like a dog scrabbling through a tight tunnel, arms entering first, then head and shoulders. She gasped for air when her head and arms popped out their openings.

She grinned as she tied a coarse leather thong around her heavy hair, then stuffed its length inside a conical helmet complete with nose guard. Hidden beneath the armor, she would pass for a young warrior intent on carrying out Mereck's orders.

Simple blinked when Meghan lifted her from her perch, clasped her tight to her chest, then covered her with a dark cloth. She prayed the sparrowhawk would not take fright and expose her with loud, distressed chirps.

Casting quick, uneasy glances over her shoulder, she padded below to the keep's entrance and grasped the heavy door. Bit by bit, she opened it. She cringed when it made dull, scraping sounds. Why had she never noted it? She slithered through the narrow opening and raced down the castle steps. When she entered the dark stable, she released a long-held breath.

Happily for her, the warriors lodged their horses in a separate area. Working with quick efficiency, she readied Storm and mounted. As she rode out into the bailey toward the gathering patrol, her wary eyes did not miss a single detail.

'Twas still dark as midnight when she fell in line behind the last warrior. She kept her eyes lowered, her back straight. Had the moon been full, she would not have found an easy time of it as they passed by the guards at the gatehouse.

The horses' hooves made little sound on the thick carpet of damp leaves of the forest path. Half a league from Blackthorn, she lagged behind and guided her mount off the path.

Meghan had not felt this free in months. She dreaded the heated dispute she would have with Connor when she returned to the castle and he caught her.

Nay, no mere dispute. Her brother's efforts to rule her always turned into a resounding brawl. He would yell and bluster and threaten to beat her. She would react by screaming threats at him to even dare think on it. Never one to pass up a challenge, Connor would attempt to do just that. They would end up wrestling in the dirt like undisciplined, grubby squires.

Of course, if he appealed to their cousin Damron, the laird of Blackthorn, she would be in serious trouble. Knowing their cousin and his stern ways, she was sure he would blister her bare arse till she couldna sit for a sennight or more.

She shrugged. The taste of freedom was worth the punishment she might receive.

Mereck had taught her much about escaping. All manner of ways. The commander of Blackthorn's army would not be pleased that she used one of them now to thwart him. He had forewarned the warriors to confine the women within the keep.

He had cautioned them about one woman in particular.

Her.

Dawn's faint golden rays winked through the fluttering canopy of leaves when she came to her destination. After removing Simple's hood, she released her. "Fly, little one, but dinna think to prey on a plump hare," she cautioned.

'Twas not long after that she stalked her own prey, a buck making its hesitant way through the forest. He oft raised his head and looked around, then went back to his feeding. Slow and easy, she raised her bow and sighted down the arrow. Taking a deep breath, she drew the bowstring taut. A whoosh of air left her lips as she freed the arrow to zing its way to the target.

Moments later, she stood over the buck she had cleanly killed with an arrow through its heart. Simple swooped down to land on a bush and study the deer. The bird's small head twisted from side to side as if pondering how to strike. Meghan shook her head and clucked her tongue.

"Ye canna attack such a beastie, silly bird. 'Tis bad enough ye think to bring down cook's chickens and not the wee animals ye should be huntin', isna that right, Storm?" she said as she threaded her fingers through the horse's mane.

Warm and sticky now, she tugged off her helmet. Her hair tumbled down, and she lifted it, allowing the cool air to soothe her neck. How could warriors stand such confinement on hot days?

Simple swiveled her head, searching the woods on all sides. Meghan froze. The hair on her nape prickled. Her skin crawled, and shivers ran down her spine. How had she missed it?

She felt them.

Eyes. Everywhere.

As if hands explored her body. And not as a lover would do.

She lowered her head and peered from the corner of her eyes. How far had she strayed from Storm? Fleet as a hare, she spun around, took two leaps, and sprang onto her mount. As her bottom hit the seat, she kicked the horse into action.

Whoops of triumph rang out as men and horses burst through the trees. Guiding Storm with her legs, she whipped an arrow from the quiver and notched it. She bent low over

Storm's neck as she threaded him through a narrow opening in the trees that a warrior hampered with weapons could not manage.

Men raced to block her escape. To her thinking, one fool tarried too long when she charged toward them. He soon wore her arrow in his leg. Startled, he jerked back on the reins and strove to keep his balance. She streaked past, his loud curses ringing like music to her ears.

Who were they? So many of them. Deep within Blackthorn's borders. And falsely wearing the Morgan colors.

Sweat trickled between her breasts as she wove her mount through the dense forest.

Meghan ducked and swerved, dangling from the side of her horse to avoid low-hanging branches. Bushes and trees on all sides appeared to reach and grab for her, seeming to ally themselves with her pursuers. Her hair escaped its tie and flew free, whipping her cheeks with the leather strip that clung to small twigs and leaves caught in the tangled strands.

"Dinna let her get away!" a voice shouted behind her.

"Circle and cut the lass off," yelled another.

She veered to the right. A large brown steed pressed close. The rider's heated body reeked of pungent sweat. His fingers snatched at her left arm. She leaned far to the right. He overreached and grabbed his horse's mane to upright himself.

"Devil take it," he shouted, furious now. "Do I get my hands on her, I will tear her off that beast."

"Not afore I have the pleasure of teaching this warrior woman her place," bellowed a horseman bearing down on her.

She would bet it was the man she had injured.

"I will gut any man who harms her."

Meghan flinched. This man's tone was cold and hard. 'Twas surely their leader. Her heart lurched, then thudded in her chest as prickles of fear burrowed through her. His voice had a familiar ring, but she could not place it.

It was hidden, locked tight in her memory.

Lurking . . .

Teasing . . .

* * *

Rolf MacDhaidh had watched and waited for the opportunity to seize this foolish and intrepid girl, sister to the man he had once called friend. Meghan had done as he knew she would—entered the woods alone to hunt.

Now *she* became the hunted.

As surely as she had felled the deer, he would bring her to ground. When the chase started, he had spied her helmet on the grass. As he scooped it up, a faint scent of heather stirred his loins. He patted the hard shape of her headgear as he placed it in the bag tied behind his saddle.

For the moment, Meghan had eluded them. She had turned his men into hapless hunters. Baffled them with her skill. He shook his head as they crashed through the trees, searching for her. He could hear the thud of her horse's hooves fading in the distance.

One thing was certain. They had forced her farther from Blackthorn and toward the Morgan's southeastern border.

The men's tempers grew short. 'Twas no longer sport to them. They grumbled about what they would like to do to the woman who made a mockery of their skills.

Rolf whistled, loud and shrill. They cursed even harder at this signal to come to him.

"Return to Rimsdale."

Orders, abrupt and short. They stared at him, not moving.

"You canna mean it, Rolf. After the many hours we stalked this prey?"

"Alpin, your scowl willna change my words. Return and see your wound is tended," Rolf directed as he outstared his friend.

"We have not seized the girl." Alpin forced the words through gritted teeth. He hissed as he broke the shaft off the arrow lodged in his thigh.

"Go." Rolf frowned at the blood on the man's tunic and jabbed a finger in the direction of Rimsdale. "Bid Ede cleanse your injury and bind it." He turned to his first-in-command.

"Dougald, have the men dress the deer. Leave me enough for three days. Hasten all from Blackthorn's land afore they are spotted."

Alpin glared at him as he jerked hard on the reins. His mount whinnied and flung its head about.

"Are ye not coming, Rolf?" Dougald raised his brow, questioning his lord.

"A small matter is not finished as yet."

After the men were through dressing the deer, he watched them fade into the forest.

Rolf stretched and rolled his shoulders. A slight smile lifted the corners of his lips as he thought of this unexpected turn in their hunt.

He rode until he deemed he was close to where she hid, to keep guard though not be seen. Sliding off his mount, he watered the horse at a stream, then fed the beast. Working with quick efficiency, he gathered wood and built a fire.

While the meat cooked, Rolf washed himself. He grinned and nodded his head. 'Twas not long now. His blood quickened. He looked forward to the morrow with feral anticipation.

His prey would learn she could not run from him. He knew where Meghan would go to ground. She believed she had outwitted them. When she thought she was safe, she would learn she was not.

He would be there.

Waiting.

CHAPTER 2

Meghan raced Storm through a stream swollen with last eve's rain. Icy water splashed her face and soaked her leggings. When she deemed she had eluded her pursuers, she led Storm back into the forest. Half a league from the stream, the tense muscles in her face relaxed. She had not forgotten the cave's location.

A rocky lip overhung the entrance that faced a steep drop to a loch below. The ledge leading to it was but wide enough for Storm to walk behind her. Gripping his bridle, Meghan kept his head close over her right shoulder as she led him. He huffed softly, uneasy.

"Dinna fret, Storm," she whispered as she stroked the soft hair between his eyes. "I was proud of ye today. Why, ye were swift and slippery as an eel when ye wove between the trees and evaded the knaves."

Simple flitted from one tree to another as Meghan coaxed the horse through the narrow entrance. The bird acted with a rare bit of good sense, and her head bobbed as if agreeing.

The pleasant scent of pine drifted into the cave. Traces of sunlight filtered through the entrance. It was as she last left it. Ample enough for herself and Storm. She led him to the back and whispered, "Down." Storm snorted and shook his head, showing his annoyance with her, reminding her of Connor when he scolded her.

Simple landed at the entrance to the cave, then hopped over to her. Meghan held up her wrist, and the sparrowhawk alighted on the leather armband. Her fingers caressed the soft gray feathers on its wee head as she sat down to wait. Men shouted and horses crashed through the brush on the hill above. Hearing their vivid curses, she clamped a hand over her mouth, squelching a nervous laugh.

Men didna like to be bested by a mere woman.

When she heard the deep whistle of their leader, her heart skipped a beat. She coaxed Simple onto a small makeshift perch she had fashioned when she was but ten and three. Grasping her bow, she notched an arrow, ready to send it flying should she have the need. She stared, unflinching, at the cave's entrance. Muscles tense and ready, she listened and waited.

Did they ken she was there? Nay.

Again, a whistle split the air, sounding far behind the men above. She relaxed her taut muscles and returned the arrow to her quiver. 'Twas not long before all sounds of her pursuers faded into the distance. She settled down to bide her time.

The sun crept toward the horizon while she waited, but she was not so brainsick as to think it safe to leave her haven. No Scot intent on grabbing a hefty ransom was without a trick or two beneath his plaid. A trick not related to that other part of him that lurked there.

Nay, she could not leave. But Simple could.

Deep in thought, her fingers pinched her lower lip, pulling it forward. She studied the sparrowhawk. For the last fortnight, with guards aplenty around her, she had trained Simple to return to the mews without her. When the bird arrived, the head falconer rewarded it with a choice morsel. Never had they attempted it this far from Blackthorn. Still, 'twas worth the chance.

Her gaze darted around the small area, searching for what she needed. When the hair at her temple teased her face, she remembered how the leather thong whipped her cheeks. Though it was still tangled in her snarled hair, she worked it loose. After sliding the dirk from its sheath strapped to her thigh, she cut a strip four fingers wide. As she tied it to Simple's right ankle, she hoped the small raptor would remember its lessons well.

Coaxing it onto her wrist again, she padded over to the entrance.

"Well now, wee lovey. Fly home to Simon for a treat worthy of an eagle."

Simple blinked at her.

Meghan shook her finger much as she would when cautioning a youngling. "Dinna think to seek yer own prey, for I willna be there to soothe yer feathers if ye neglect to look where ye go."

Poor foolish bird that she was, she could likely forget her training and do herself harm trying to sink her talons in the arse of a Heeland cow. After a cautious glance, Meghan ventured a pace out of the entrance. Lifting her arm, she tossed the bird into the air. The sparrowhawk took flight, circled and climbed higher, then descended.

Meghan groaned. Simple circled again, then climbed and was soon out of sight. When the wee one returned to the mews without her, Simon would alert Laird Damron and her brother. She sighed as she stepped back inside. She had done all she could. After unbuckling the small sword strapped to her waist, she lifted the bow from around her shoulder, sat, and leaned back against Storm.

Cold seeped clear through to her bones. Could she better share the horse's warmth if she removed the chain mail? Nay. She needed its protection more than warmth. She huddled closer to the big horse to still the shivers racing through her.

She dared not close her eyes. Who were they? They wore Morgan colors to move with ease about Blackthorn lands. These were no homeless, marauding peasants, but men well mounted with weapons aplenty.

Her head jerked up with a thought. Why had they not brought her down with an arrow or sword? Neither had she aimed a fatal blow. For certes, had her aim not been accurate, the man who wore her arrow would not thank her for his life had he lost his own most pleasurable weapon.

Her teeth teased her lower lip. Had they known 'twas a woman they stalked before she removed her helm? She frowned, uncertain. All of Blackthorn knew of her preference for young men's clothing. She had ever hated needlework and womanly pursuits and had oft escaped, disguised as a squire, to learn the same skills as her brother and cousins.

The first time she had been found out was a disaster. A royal disaster. For she had been at the royal court in Normandy. Her nape prickled, remembering a hard, muscular arm grasping her waist and lifting her off her feet against an even harder body.

She rested her head against Storm's chest. His heartbeat soothed her. Ah well, 'twas long ago. . . .

She startled. Alert. Had she dozed? Light still shone through the opening. A soothing hand on Storm's neck warned him to keep silent. She held her breath and cocked her head to the right.

Listening.

She sensed, rather than heard, something. Of a sudden, someone blocked all light from the cave. She leapt to her feet, pleased to tease her brother.

"Well now, Connor, didna I tell ye Simple would learn such a useful trick?"

Meghan smiled and took but one step. And froze. The breeze carried the scent of the man standing there, his body tense with suppressed violence. A whiff of sandalwood and spices. A remembered scent. But 'twas not her brother's.

"A useful trick, to be sure," answered a dark voice.

Her head whipped around, and her gaze darted to the ground beside Storm where she had been so witless to lay down her weapons. How close was she to them? Too far. They would be no aid to her now. Her hand crept toward the dirk strapped to her thigh.

"Dinna even think it."

His lethal tone sent ice crystals shattering down her spine. It, too, was something half remembered. Heard long ago. Where? Her frantic mind searched for the memory. Her legs near buckled. She scowled. Did she turn coward? She dug in her feet, squared her shoulders, and stiffened her spine.

So large was he that naught but a glimmer of light found its way into the cave. He must needs duck to enter it. She tried to swallow, but her mouth turned dry as burnt feathers. Storm was sixteen hands at the withers. This man looked to be near three hands more. Though tall for a woman, her head reached no higher than his chin.

He stood with legs spread and fists on his hips. With a sneer, she adopted the same posture, daring him to approach her.

Her jaw set. She pitched her voice low, imitating a young man.

" 'Tis your death ye are wantin' if ye linger. The might of Blackthorn will be crashin' through this forest shortly. A guide will bring them straight to me."

"Guide?" The voice sounded amused. " 'Tis on this *guide* you pin your hopes of rescue?" He moved slightly. Far enough so the fading light behind him silhouetted his right side.

Meghan gasped. There was no mistaking Simple perched on the man's shoulder, content and swaying back and forth. The hapless bird rubbed her head against that granite jaw, acting for all the world like this man was her beloved handler.

Traitorous bird!

Fury swept through Meghan. What did he want? How had he known where she was? Her brain raced, searching for answers. She knew Simple could not have shown him the way. The bird would have done well to find Blackthorn, as big as it was, but never could she find her way back to this small cave. Why had he played this barn-cat-and-mouse game with her? His men could not be with him, or she would have heard them thrashing about.

"What do ye want of me?" Her chin thrust forward. He could not know who she was. "I am but a lowly squire, not worthy of a great ransom."

His harsh bark of laughter sent her hopes dashing.

"Are you now? A lowly squire? Aye, 'tis doubtful such would bring a ransom. Dinna think I am so mindless I canna know a woman hides behind a man's clothin'. Had I no nose to smell, no eyes to see, my tarse would have known the woman lurking there."

He took a menacing step forward. Storm nickered and stood as Meghan stepped back. She had no more room to maneuver.

"The woman who is sister to Connor and cousin to Damron and Mereck of Blackthorn is worth much more than mere gold." His voice grated over the men's names. He spit them out as if they were spoiled meat. Distasteful. Disgusting.

What grievance could he have against the men of her family?

"Ye talk in riddles, man. What is worth more than gold?" Did he plan to ask for precious jewels? She had no fear that Damron would deny Connor by opening his treasure coffers.

"Vengeance."

That one word anchored the pieces of her memory together. In the past three years, something had been happening in the background of the turmoil and excitement revolving around the marriages of Damron, Mereck, and Connor of Blackthorn.

She frowned. Tried to remember. A short time after Damron and Brianna's marriage, a systematic raiding of their outlying villages began. After each, someone brought a message to the laird of Blackthorn, which he tossed into the fire. She had walked into the solar one day, unexpected. The men were talking, their backs to her. Connor's tense voice read the missive.

Was it something like, "Ye have taken my deer" that he had said?

Nay, not that. She dug deeper in her memory. Ah. She remembered.

'Twas, *Ye have taken that which I hold most dear. Look to yer own.*

The men had seen her and had gone silent. Now it all made sense. The tighter security the guards kept on the women of her family. Someone always watching her. And Damron and Connor threatening to beat her if she went alone to hunt without an escort.

While she stood engrossed and staring at the cave wall trying to remember, he had moved closer.

She inhaled deeply. Her heart pounded. Remembering. Her legs turned to water as she stared at him. It couldna be! She opened her mouth to speak. He stopped her.

"Nay! Dinna say a word. Come peacefully with me or go trussed like a pig. 'Tis your choice." He grasped for her arm. Simple chirped and flew to land on the makeshift perch.

Meghan twirled to the left and kicked up with her right foot, landing a solid blow against his rock-hard stomach. Her sole stung from the contact. His hand shot out, grabbed her ankle, and twisted. She hit the floor. Hard. Face forward. She gasped. Dirt flew in her mouth. He pounced and straddled her back. Her breath shot out.

"I told you to come peacefully. Never have I hurt a woman apurpose, but to me you are not a woman. You are my vengeance."

He wrenched off the leather band that protected her from Simple's claws. "I dinna doubt you could free yourself by sliding from this," he said as he tossed it aside. He caught her wrists and bound them together.

"Devil's spawn! Lucifer's arse! Release me," Meghan cursed, and spit dirt out of her mouth.

"Still the gentle lady, are you?" He settled more of his weight on her buttocks.

"Ooof!" Did he intend to smash her like he would a beetle? Waves of heat from his body penetrated even the chain mail that covered her back.

She squirmed and arched. The mail bit into her flesh. She would not give in.

"Enough, woman," he commanded. He grabbed her nape and thrust her head against the ground. His legs gripped tighter.

She could not move. Though she could wrestle well with most men, she was no match for this one.

"Enough? Ne'er, you horse's turd."

As if offended, Storm snorted and stamped his hooves.

"Easy, Storm, easy," the man crooned gently. Storm quieted.

Not so with her. He forced her face into the soil and shoved it back and forth.

"Hmm, still scorning ladylike ways, are you? Mayhap another mouthful of dirt will hold your tongue."

He forced soil aplenty between her lips before he sprang to his feet. Raising her head, she spluttered and spit. She threw her left leg backward and twisted her hips to roll onto her back. She glared and eyed the distance separating them. 'Twould do her no good, for she could not reach him with a well-aimed kick. If the churl could read her mind, he would back away from her and cup his hands to protect that part of him that had grown and hardened, fit to rival a warrior's club.

Were her hands not tied behind her, she could rock forward and bounce up onto her feet. She seethed. Even the chain mail, twisted around her legs, held her down. Be damned if she would ask for his aid. Better she lay there until winter came, then spring, and even until the walls of Blackthorn crumbled from age. She wouldna make a gowk of herself and wallow and flounder about on the dirt floor like an upended beetle.

Meghan studied him in the faint light. Her gaze started from his feet and traveled up the menacing body standing there.

Black. He gave the impression of being as one with moonless midnight. His boots that enclosed firm calves, his breeches, a loose-fitting shirt tied at the neck with thongs— all black. No armor covered him. Was he so sure of his prowess he needed no protection? He wore a sword, though, belted about his waist. Mayhap not entirely assured, after all.

Slung about his shoulders was a loosely woven mantle of gray wool. A pewter pin shaped like the face of a beast secured it at his neck.

Her heart tripped as she blinked, then held her lids closed for a moment. It couldna be *him*. Nay. 'Twas too far from his holdings to be him. She swallowed. Forgetting about the dirt in her mouth and almost choked. She thought wryly that he had made her eat dirt for her words.

Thinking. Anything to keep from admitting who stood there and scorned her so thoroughly.

Hair, brown and near straight. Straggling and unkept, it framed his face and ended inches below his shoulders. His chin. Not clean shaven now. Close-cropped whiskers framed his hard jaw and above his lips. A nose, proud and strong, below silver-gray eyes, the shadows dark beneath them. Proof he did not sleep well. A broad forehead rose above straight brown brows that framed the hard eyes staring at her.

'Twas no mistaking or denying him now. Her heart had cried out his name. His scent had told her his name. The MacDhaidh of Rimsdale. Rolf. The man they now called the "Lord of Vengeance." Far away from his own lands just outside the southeastern borders of the Morgans of Blackthorn.

How could a man change so? Before she could clamp her teeth together, a soft whimper, one she regretted with all her soul, welled up from her parched throat.

"Aye. I am not as I was, thanks be to Connor." His lips thinned and his jaw clenched. "Come." He spat the word.

He wanted her to rise. She attempted to sit but could not. Her twisted mail held her on the ground. To turn onto her stomach and wriggle up on her knees was mayhap possible.

But 'twas unthinkable. She would not kneel, her back to him in such a position.

Instead, she opened her hands tied behind her so they would not grind the mail into the small of her back. Careful to keep her legs together, she stretched out and then wriggled her shoulders into a more comfortable position.

Defiant, she glared up at him. She wouldna grovel.

Her surprised squawk filled the air as her world whirled upside down as he slung her across his shoulder. Her hair dragged about her face. His arm clamped her knees tight to his chest. She strove to throw herself down. He reached beneath the mail and pinched her thigh. Hard.

He remained silent. She clamped her teeth together, grinding dirt between them. She relaxed her jaw. Dirt stuck to her teeth, coated her tongue. It tasted unpleasant, like burnt wheat.

Taking Storm's reins, he strode through the entrance. With each step, she bounced against his back.

"For God's love, Rolf, dinna be a fool. 'Twill be safer if I walk." 'Twould also be easier to dart off into the deepest bushes at the end of the path.

"Aye. If I trusted you." He snorted. "If? I dinna. We will be as safe if you cease flopping like a fish and cause me no misstep."

She wriggled a little as he ducked through the opening.

"Nettles and sharp rocks willna give you an easy ride to the bottom of this hill," he warned.

She stilled, knowing he spoke true. No easy ride, and before a body crashed to the bottom, it would no longer matter. After several steps, she raised her head to see if Storm was uneasy without the comfort of her hand. She need not have worried. The horse acted as if he sought to reassure her, for he nuzzled her with his great head.

Rolf's right heel slipped on loose stones. His knee bent and his body leaned toward the sheer drop. His hold around her legs loosened.

When his shoulders swayed sickeningly, Meghan couldna squelch a startled cry.

"Rolf, dinna!"

He chuckled, the sound evil amusement. The churl. He had not slipped on the stones. He had done it apurpose!

Helpless atop his shoulder, her pride seethed.

Bile surged to her throat. Not from fear of heights. Far from it, for she took delight in sitting high atop a tree to enjoy the unblocked breezes and scenery. This was another matter. She had lost control. Above all, she hated not to have mastery over a situation.

"By all that is holy," Meghan shouted, "ye will pay for this someday."

"Dinna count on it," Rolf warned. " 'Tis you who will do the paying if you dinna obey me."

CHAPTER 3

Rolf smothered the urge to sigh with relief when they reached the end of the dangerous path. To let Meghan of Blackthorn know he had been uneasy would be akin to placing a knife in her hand.

He couldna wait to dump her onto the ground. To put distance between them. When his friend Alpin suggested he steal Meghan away, he had not reckoned with the raging feelings she would wrench from him.

While he had lurked in the forest to learn her habits, he had been too far distant to see her clearly. He had thought she was as before. How wrong he was! The years had transformed her into a woman who would quicken even a blind man's desire.

On entering the shallow cave, before she realized he was not her beloved brother, her sea-green eyes had blazed with delight as she laughed up at him. How many times in the past had he seen her thus? The scent of heather floated about her. His body responded as if he were yet a callow youth. His pulse raced and darted blood to his tarse, lengthening and hardening him, causing his sac to grow heavy with need.

Meghan's tempting, generous lips lifted at the corners, inviting a man to kiss them. A small cut, still seeping blood, marred her broad forehead. Well-defined brown brows arched over eyes no longer lit with welcome but darkened with rage, once she had spied who he was. Chestnut-brown hair, with twigs and leaves strewn through it, spilled in wild disarray about her face. Did she know she looked like a woman fresh from loving a man on the forest floor?

Had it been so long since he had a woman that she could stir his blood so? Though wearing strange clothing, covered from head to toe in dirt, she still made his tarse as hard as the shaft on Beast, his battle axe. Anger built that it was so. His jaw hardened as he crushed any feeling for her, as surely as her brother Connor had stomped his life into the dust.

'Twould be better if he tossed her over the side onto the rocks below and have done with it. Unthinking, he stopped and faced the cliffs. When Meghan's body tensed like a drawn bow ready to speed its arrow, he realized he overlooked the craggy rocks below where gorse shrubs clung. Their bright yellow flowers sent their sweet scent up to him. He drew a deep, startled breath. His body shuddered at his thoughts.

Blessed Christ's blood! Could he do such a thing?

"If ye are thinkin' to kill me, be done with it afore I spew all I have eaten this day," Meghan gasped the words out. A breath later, she emptied her stomach on the tail end of his cloak.

"By all that is holy, do that again and I will see your face rubbed in it," Rolf shouted. Afeared he would cave in to his urge to dump her into the open void, he turned and shot forward like a startled deer, not slowing until he reached firm ground.

Three footsteps later, he felt a sharp pinch on his arse. The woman must be an eejit to bite a man through his clothing, much less someone holding her life by a thread.

"Lucifer's tarse! Cease, or ye'll feel the flat of my hand," he shouted as his long strides carried him to level ground and to his tethered horse. Startled, the steed snorted and sidled.

Rolf leaned forward to remove Meghan from his shoulder. She bit him again. He jerked forward and dumped her onto the ground. The tail of his soiled cloak followed her up from his back and over his head.

"What in . . . by God's . . ." he sputtered.

He twisted his head to the right to free it and glowered down at her. Clenched between her teeth was the wool of his cloak. He grabbed the material and shook it. Her head whipped back and forth, reminding him of a foolish, stubborn hound holding tight to a stolen boot. He gripped her jaw and squeezed her cheeks. Her gaze sparked defiance at him.

"Devil take it, woman. Open yer mouth," he muttered.

She refused to heed him and tried to jerk her head away. His fingers bit into her jaw until it opened. He relaxed his grip, only to have her nip hard on the soft flesh between his thumb and forefinger. Before he could stop the reflex, he slapped her cheek but winced when her head jerked aside.

"Have ye taken to beatin' women, MacDhaidh?" Meghan turned her face back to study him.

Meghan's gaze showered scorn over him. When had he come to this? Never before had he done such to a gentle-woman, but then never had a woman so challenged his patience. Gentle? Never would anyone call Meghan of Blackthorn a *gentle* woman.

She was a match for most men. But not him. Ten years past she had learned he was more than her equal. Today she would do well to remember it.

He sprang to his feet, putting distance between them to calm himself. Stalking over to her horse, he checked the bridle and saddle to secure them for riding.

The faintest of sounds drifted to his ears. He glanced over his shoulder to see she had rolled to her stomach and had drawn her knees up beneath her in an attempt to rise.

The mail pulled to each side of her legs, as it would for riding. The cloth of her breeches tightened across a slender arse. It revealed more than it hid from his eyes. She had been prudent not to attempt to rise in the cave when she knew he watched her. If she knew he spied her now, she would no doubt flatten herself onto the grass.

His blood thickened. As she wriggled her knees ever forward, his hands twitched with the urgent need to mold them against her firm flesh. Taking care not to alert her, he padded close. At last, her shoulders lifted off the ground. She knelt there.

"Going somewhere, Meghan?" He grasped her. Her shoulders jumped beneath his fingers. "Hmm, 'tis a shame to rise. Meghan of Blackthorn on her knees is much more to my likin'."

He nudged her forward, one hand on her shoulder, the other at her waist as if he would press her face back to the earth, her bottom upended to him.

"Nay, dinna!" Her head jerked back as the panicked words gasped from her throat.

Rolf snaked his arm around her body to lift her to her feet, her back to him. Grasping her waist with both hands, he swung her onto Storm's saddle.

"I canna ride with my hands tied behind me," she protested.

"Ha." After he grasped Storm's reins, he shoved her feet in the stirrups. "Do you think me so daft? After I watched you streak through the forest, bow and arrow in hand to bring down a deer?" He snorted rudely.

Rolf, one hand on the pommel of his saddle, leapt astride his own steed. He turned to where Simple waited on a bush, whistled to her, and signaled his horse into a canter.

Meghan's legs held tight to Storm as she cursed Rolf all the while.

"You pig's arse. What ransom will they pay for a broken pile of bones? I canna balance with my hands behind me," she shouted at him.

"You had best learn to." He did not deign to look back at her.

Drat the bastard. She wobbled a bit until she found her balance. No doubt, before they had gone a fraction of a league she would adjust. Huh! Why make things hard for herself?

"If ye hear a crash, 'twill be me. No doubt I will crush my head against a rock," she grumbled.

Two paces farther, she gasped. "Oh!" Through lowered lashes, she watched him glance back at her as she lurched in the saddle.

The men of her family would have laughed at her performance. All at Blackthorn knew Meghan was as skillful on horseback as the most agile Welshman, for a Welshman had taught her tricks neither Connor nor Damron could duplicate. Even as their breaths merged in the crisp morning air, rider and mount were as one, so attuned to each other Meghan needed but a subtle movement for him to respond. 'Twas as if Storm anticipated her very thoughts and wishes.

She had a plan. With her hands in front of her, she would have a fair chance to break away from him.

"Umpf!" she cried out. To appear convincing, she slid her arse half off the saddle.

Rolf swiveled around and tugged Storm's reins to fetch him closer.

Good. He believed her. Had he not, she had planned to dangle over the side of Storm to convince him.

"A mere woman after all, Meghan?"

The sneer in his voice rankled her, but she clamped her lips together. One day he would find she could do anything short of standing on one finger atop Storm's back.

Today was not that day.

Rolf grasped for her. A subtle adjustment from her cued Storm to back up. When Rolf neared again, Storm sidled away.

Irritation tightened his face as he slid off his mount to come over to her. He released her hands and retied them in front of her. After checking the knots, he turned his back.

Meghan kneed Storm. The horse bolted ahead, tearing the reins from Rolf's hands. As they galloped away, she grasped Storm's heavy mane and bent low over his neck. They crashed through the underbrush, gaining a good lead on him. Branches seemed to swoop down. She dodged them. Bushes forced her to swerve around them. Rolf followed. With each breath, he came ever closer.

"Fly, Storm. Fly so fast the wind from our passin' will knock the arrogant bastard off his mount."

Storm's stride lengthened as he charged onward.

The hoofbeats pounding behind her sounded like the devil pursued her. Branches grabbed at her long hair, scratched her face. Small limbs snagged in the chain mail, only to be ripped off the tree. Feeling his furious stare that bored into her, she felt the skin on her back crawl.

No man liked to be made the fool, this one in particular.

She glanced behind her and wished she had not. An icy rain of fear spread over her sweating body. Rolf's eyes were mere slits of determination; his lips snarled like a ravening beast. Hunger for vengeance crackled the air around him. Never had a man looked so ready to throttle a woman.

Ah, she well knew this region. She jerked Storm to the left. Hopefully Rolf was unfamiliar with the area. If an obstacle took Rolf unaware, she would have the time she needed to escape.

Soon after, she veered to the right at a fallen tree. Storm sailed over it without breaking his stride. Devil take it. She heard no comforting crash behind her.

Scant heartbeats later, she spotted a stream with water gushing over the smooth rocks. Storm shot over it and swerved to the left at the next sharp turn.

Rolf thundered closer. Dark curses rained over her body like scalding water.

He could not know of the deep furrow in the ground ahead. To swerve right would see him in trees growing so close together he could not pass. Surely, this hazard would slow him.

It did not.

She streaked left and squeezed between two rowan trees to avoid a large boulder, but Rolf was still hot on Storm's tail. She groaned. The woods thinned, and he inched up alongside her. She wouldna allow him to seize Storm's mane. By God's grace, she wouldna.

'Twas not Storm's mane but a fistful of her own that he captured as his horse drew abreast. He slowed his mount. She did the same, else he would jerk her off her saddle by her hair. By the time they pulled to a stop, he had coiled it around and around his fist.

She panted for breath. Her heart raced and pounded in her ears. Muscles in her back and thighs burned, her legs quivered like a newborn pup. For but a moment, she squeezed her eyes shut as she relaxed her fingers in Storm's mane.

Rolf's breathing was as harsh. Was he as drained as she was? She bolstered her courage and stole a glance at him.

Heavens help her. He didna look weary. The hairs on her arms tingled as if lightning had struck nearby. His lips pressed together so tight they almost disappeared. Likely, his teeth would break if he ground them any tighter. His eyes were mere slits shooting pure rage.

Neither spoke. Be damned if she would be first to break the silence.

Finally, Rolf took in a great breath of air and let it out in a slow puff as his furious gaze studied her.

"Pray tell, what did this game of run-and-catch prove?" His voice held an ominous quality.

When she did not answer, he jerked his hand. Her head snapped back.

"Answer."

"That I wouldna go easily."

"Aye. You will. From this moment, you *will* come. Easily."

Every bone in her body jarred as his arm lashed out and ripped her off Storm onto his lap. After unwinding her long tresses from his hand, he pinned her to him. Reaching for Storm's discarded reins, he secured them around the pommel on her empty saddle. He kneed his horse to canter, and the riderless Storm trailed behind, docile and obedient.

He wasted no time. He galloped his horse down clear paths, and Storm kept the pace. Rolf seemed to have no care of her. Yet, when they descended a steep hill he steadied her against him. When his horse's hooves skittered on stones near a cliff, his arm jerked, hauling her tight to his body.

Meghan did not attempt speech with him now. Whatever his plan, his purpose was clear. He gave her but one clue when she had asked what was more precious than gold.

Vengeance.

She mulled the word over in her mind. She tried to fit bits and pieces together from what she had heard over the years. One date was vivid in her memory, 1069, when she had heard

Rolf had unexpectedly married a young woman, a kin to Hereward the Wake.

Three years later, Damron and Connor had been at Abernethy on the Tay to support King Malcolm of Scotland, when William of England forced Malcolm to recognize him as his feudal lord. 'Twas there William demanded they meld a great Scottish family with one of England's. By his orders, Damron, the Morgan of Blackthorn, married the conqueror's ward, Brianna of Sinclair. A proxy stood in for Brianna.

Damron was furious but he obeyed. When he went to collect his bride, he did not find an easy time of it.

Meghan chuckled. Brianna was a kindred spirit. One who got into more trouble than she herself did.

"What sparks your humor?" Rolf's deep voice brought her attention back to him.

"What do ye mean?"

"Are you so daft you laugh for no reason?" He sounded irritated.

"Nay. 'Twas but an unexpected thought."

When she said no more, he did not press her.

Dusk crept over the trees, vanquishing the sun. By the time the next night fell, they would reach his castle at the northern tip of Loch Rimsdale. By then, she had to understand him. Why did the man she had once loved, who in days past had tender feelings for her, now show naught but hate?

Peddlers had told them of rumors that while Rolf rode with Hereward the Wake, the lady of Rimsdale had died. None knew how or why. Was it also after this when Rolf became marked as the Lord of Vengeance? Did it relate to his warring with Hereward? And why had he raided ever closer to her home? The men of Blackthorn had been reluctant to speak Rolf's name in her presence. Had they always known her feelings? Now, no doubt lingered in her mind that those *Look to yer own* messages had come from him.

These thoughts gave her no clue why hatred surrounded Rolf like a rank fog on a summer morn.

He moved about, restless, as if seeking a more comfortable

position. His left arm was clamped around her waist. It was well of him not to trust her. She would escape given the slightest opening. His harsh breath stirred the hair atop her head. She blinked and shivered at this enforced closeness but refused to look up at him.

Instead, she studied his fingers holding the reins. White scars crisscrossed his knuckles and the top of his hand amongst the fine brown hairs there. Had those hands been as rough with his wife as they were with her? She felt a pang of sorrow, for she doubted it.

His harshness was unlike the man he used to be.

Did he intend to ride through the night? She was thankful for the mail that covered her. At least she could not feel his firm, heated flesh as much as she would have without it.

Bad enough his scent surrounded her, tormented her. It did strange things to her. Things she did not favor, for they made her heartbeat surge like waves beating against a cliff. She shuddered and closed her eyes.

"We will stop soon." His voice was close to her ear.

She sighed with relief. She was bone weary. Hardier than most women, still she had carried the extra weight of the mail and had ridden hard most of the day. Not to mention the strain of eluding him, of her capture, then of her escape, only to be seized again. Blessed heaven! Even a man would tire after all that.

"Dinna stop on my account, churl. I can sleep as well sitting here as stretched out on the forest floor."

"Well now, I would be glad to ride farther, but the horses need rest." His arm loosened around her for the first time.

Thank the saints he did not force her bluff.

"To have Meghan of Blackthorn sprawled on a bed of soft leaves is an appealing idea." His voice held a sinister promise. "Ahead lies the spot I have in mind. We will spend a memorable night under the heavens. Be that to your likin'? Hmm?"

She gasped and lurched forward.

Oh, how she wished he *had* forced her bluff.

He jerked her back against him. She could not mistake that hard ridge felt even through her chain mail.

A deep rumble rose from his chest and ended with an evil chuckle.

Both were sounds of anticipation.

CHAPTER 4

Showers of ice flowed over Meghan, soon replaced by simmering heat. 'Twas better to pretend she mistook the implied threat in his words than to acknowledge it. Mayhap he meant other than what she thought by his forced intimacy and suggestions.

She reined in her emotions as they entered a heavily wooded area on the northern finger of Loch Naver. In the deepening dusk, little light seeped through a canopy of oaks. She spied the dark water of the inlet, but it looked far too cold, even for her.

Soft breezes cooled her face as she studied the tranquil scene opening in front of her. No spiny gorse grew here. Instead, graceful birch trees surrounded by crowberry shrubs, some sporting small purplish flowers together with black berrylike fruit, lined an intimate clearing.

She sighed, tired and conscious of the weight she carried on her body and in her mind.

His shrill whistle next to her ear startled her. Simple, who had followed above throughout the day, circled and came to rest on a birch tree nearby. Such a faithful sparrowhawk. 'Twas a shame the sweet little bird appeared to fancy Rolf.

His arm had fallen away. When? How long had they stopped?

"If you have had your fill of gawking at the sunset, 'tis time to give my mount a rest. The poor beast will be pleased to see the last of your weight atop his back."

Rolf's feet were on the ground before he finished speaking.

"Whose stubborn will forced him to carry me? If ye have forgotten, Storm's saddle was empty through no choice of my—"

He swept her off the horse and dropped her on her already aching bottom. Would she have permanent marks from that dratted mail marring her flesh?

"Umpf! Thank ye for being so gentle."

At her mocking words, his brows met above near-closed eyes, stabbing a warning at her. She huffed and scowled back.

Ignoring her now, he turned to his horse and loosened a double-headed battle axe and propped it against a stalwart tree. Never had she seen such a wicked weapon, for the axe had a shaft near as long as her legs and a grip of blackened leather wrapped with wire. One side of the axe head was a blade, its span more than a hand, gleaming sharp and evil. The armorer had plated the other side with bronze and shaped it like the face of a beast, its hair flowing onto the opposite blade. From its open mouth jutted a tongue with razor-sharp edges.

Rolf looked at her, his lips a mere slash in his face. "Lead your horse to drink, and be quick about it."

Though awkward still, 'twas easier for her to rise now with her hands afore her.

Ah. Would he give her another chance to escape?

"Dinna think to try it. I willna leave your side."

Drat the man! Could he read other people's thoughts like her cousin Mereck? Rolf walked his mount beside her, keeping so close that no more than a breath of air slipped between them. Storm drank his fill as she rubbed her face against his sleek neck, crooning to him all the while.

"Enough, woman. 'Tis a horse, not a man you are soothin'." Rolf tossed his head, freeing his face of his brown hair blowing across it. Dark ragged locks streamed out behind him.

"Are your women so unskilled ye canna trust them to trim yer hair?" Meghan eyed his unkept mane with distaste. "Give me a dirk and I will have it tamed in scant moments."

The baleful look he cast her way impaled her. She swallowed and fought for her usual confidence.

He secured the horses and dug through a large leather pouch, much like a lassie hunting colored ribbons. Meghan grinned, imagining Rolf, the Lord of Vengeance, sporting a silky red ribbon tied in a big bow. Instead, he brought forth a thick rope.

Still wearing a scowl, he untied her.

"Take off the mail. It ill-becomes a lass to dress in iron."

Arms folded across his chest, he waited.

She flexed her red and chafed wrists, reached down and grasped the bound links at the bottom. 'Twas even harder to lift than it was this morn. Determined, she raised them but halfway up her thigh and could go no farther. Her wrists refused to hold firm.

Sucking his teeth, Rolf brushed aside her hands and lifted the heavy mail to her chin. When the links came near her face, he slipped his hands beneath them to protect the tender skin of her cheeks. Her brows rose at this nicety.

Damp air seeped through her clothing, making Meghan clamp her thighs together. She had to use a force of will not to grasp herself like a child two years of age. She flushed when he eyed her, knowing her problem.

"Come." His steel-hard fingers closed around her arm to lead her a few feet into the line of trees, then released her.

He stood there. Waiting.

"Tend your needs." Curt orders.

Was he daft? "I canna."

Rolf's scowl spread.

The cursed man expected her to obey him. She felt her flush spread from her face to her chest.

"Please, Rolf. I need some measure of privacy."

"Privacy? You?" His brows shot up, fluttering the strands of hair falling beside his gray eyes. "This from the lass who didna give belted knights privacy?"

She glared at him. He had not forgotten that afternoon at the Norman court so many years ago. Because of him, Damron had deposited her at an abbey for the rest of the summer. Never had she had such vile punishment.

Mulish, she stared silently at the trees. He relented. Not wholly though, for he sucked his teeth and knotted the rope around her left ankle.

"Be quick about it." Holding fast to the end of the tether, he walked back to the clearing.

One thing was certain. She could move swift as a deer when necessary. A scant time later, her fingers tore at the knot.

"Are you done?" His voice sounded annoyed.

Meghan tossed her head. " 'Twas a long afternoon."

She clutched her lower lip between her teeth and doubled her efforts. Though the knot was intricate, it was one she had learned when her grandda taught Connor the art. Almost finished. Another loop and she would be free. Gone before he had a hint she was no longer there.

"But a minute more," she called out.

Heavy strands of hair falling around her eyes made her task more difficult. She shoved them aside.

Naught hindered her sight now. Not an arm's length away, black boots stood. Quiet. Menacing. How in all the saints' names could a man of his size move with such silence?

"Finish what you were about," he ordered. His voice was silky smooth. "I wouldna want your efforts wasted."

She swallowed. As she pulled the last bit free, he coiled the whole between his hand and elbow, watching her every twitch. Once done, he grasped her arm and led her back to camp, dropping the wound rope beside his saddle. Putting a hand on her shoulder blade, he prodded her toward the water. She half-feared he planned to toss her in.

"Cleanse yourself." He wrinkled his nose in distaste. "I heard the laird of Blackthorn's lady wife had aid from the women to dunk rose-scented, soapy water over the men as they came through the barbican." He eyed her distastefully. " 'Tis certain you didna join them. Is it your habit to wallow about in mud?"

Her nostrils flared and her hand itched to slap his face. How dared he accuse her of such?

"I had no dirt on my face until an overgrown eejit forced it there."

"Nay? Young Douglas of Altnaharra told a different story. He couldna run fast enough when he offered his suit and found the lady of his lustful dreams so covered in mud he was unsure of the color of her skin."

"Ha. After two days of rain, I grew weary of the fool blethering about his great prowess with the sword. I bid him show me his clever moves."

He looked at her as if she was beyond foolish and into the realm of brainsick. "Becoming a woman didna stop your ever wanting to best a man, hmm? How came you by the mud?"

"Best a man?" She sucked her teeth. "Only when such poor examples come struttin' and braggin' how great they are. Hmpf. Did I not say it rained for two days? 'Twas not the mud he disliked. After I cut the ties holdin' his leggin's, they dropped about his skinny shanks and bared his nether parts. He couldna run fast enough."

Rolf frowned, no doubt displeased on hearing the tale. Why did men believe they were God's chosen? If a lowly woman proved skillful, the dimwitted dolts wished to punish her for it. Not the men of her family, though. They took great pride in her skills. The fierce Blackthorn warriors treated her with respect.

This man made her feel the clumsy gowk at every turn. To Hades and back with him! No doubt he would dunk her if she said another word. Gritting her teeth, she cupped her hands to splash her flushed face and stinging wrists. She washed as much as modesty allowed and rose.

Rolf's hands on her shoulders forced her to sit with her back against a stately tree. He tied her around the waist, the knot out of reach on the other side of the massive trunk. Without a wasted movement, he gathered wood and kindling and prepared a fire. Dusting off his hands, he headed back to the water.

Hearing him splashing about, she envied him. In the fading light, she caught teasing glimpses of his imposing body between rows of spindly young trees. She swallowed. What she saw helped her piece together the whole of a picture of him. Solid. Hard muscle and golden skin formed chest and back tapering to an arse lighter than the rest of him. His legs looked hewn from trees. As did another part of his body. Her pulse quickened as she stared, wide-eyed.

A formidable male. Not a nithing. Not a braggart. She would have no easy time escaping him. Insight told her she must, for if she did not, his vengeance would destroy them both.

He returned, fully dressed. Water dripped from his face and ragged brown hair, darkening his gray tunic. Silvery gray eyes studied her, no doubt assuring himself she remained bound. When he pulled a helmet from a large sack, she knew 'twas her own. Stuffed inside it, wrapped in oiled cloth, was meat.

"Ye took time to dress the deer?"

"Nay. Others did the chore. I cooked it while I rested." His look was cynical. " 'Twas best to be prepared."

Cutting off a sizeable portion, he handed it to her. Her stomach grumbled at the aroma, for she had eaten naught since last eve. Never a fool, she didna scorn it. As they ate, her eyes strayed to the vicious-looking axe.

"You admire Beast? Best you fear him as so many hapless fools have learned." Rolf wiped his hands on the grass as she had done earlier and bounded to his feet.

As the last rays of light faded, he spread a wool plaid on the soft ground beside the fire. Its welcome heat held off the encroaching night chill. He brought Beast and thunked it, blade first, into the ground beside the plaid.

With slow, deliberate movements, he unclasped the large pewter pin at his shoulder. His mantle slithered to the ground at his feet. Through narrowed eyes, he studied Meghan.

Good. She looked uneasy. Best she felt fear of him, for he would soon lose patience with her headstrong nature. Not that he ever had patience aplenty. Though she would fight him every step of the way, he was determined to dominate her.

After all, she was but a woman.

"Come. 'Tis time we sought our rest. I would reach Rimsdale afore dusk falls on the morrow." Crouching behind her, he untied the knot and pulled her to her feet. She dug in her heels.

"I willna be your whore," she hissed with anger, and twisted and struggled as she tried to wrestle free of him.

"You flatter yourself. I dinna want a woman in my arms who reeks of iron and horse." He lied. He could smell her own scent, heather and spices, beneath the other. It inflamed his blood.

Earlier in the day as he waited near the cave, he'd had every intention to use Meghan of Blackthorn in any way he desired. Why did he hesitate? Surely not for the look in her eyes. Nor for the fatigue on her face.

He retied her wrists, leaving enough slack so the rope did not dig into her already sore flesh. The other end he tied to the leather belt at his waist.

"Sleep," he commanded as he pushed her down on the ground. He settled her between the fire and himself with Beast on his other side. He slung his mantle over them both.

Though he pretended to sleep, he knew her every twitch. He felt her eyes watch him. When she turned her back to him, his muscles burned, begging him to pull her tight against his heated body, her sweet female flesh handy to him. Damnation. His tarse strained and bucked, fighting his clothing to reach her.

Forcing his thoughts from his aching groin, he reminded himself why this woman was beside him. She was his vengeance. Nothing more. Connor would pay for causing Ingirid's death and that of his newly born son. His hands clenched, wanting to strike out, remembering the desperate look of fear in Ingirid's eyes as she lay dying.

So occupied was he with his thoughts, he near missed a smothered cry from his captive. Careful not to alert her, he sat up as silent as still water.

"Lucifer's warts! Are you brainsick?"

Startled by his shouted words, Meghan cried out as her flesh touched the white-hot coal against which she had been carefully rubbing the rope. With several burns for her efforts, all but a few strands remained to keep her tied.

"Ne'er have I seen a woman so heedless of the consequences of her actions." Rolf bolted to his feet and hauled her to the water's edge. He grabbed her arms and plunged them in the icy water, muttering as he did so.

"Fool woman. No wonder you have yet to find a man to husband you. What eejit would seek a woman so daft she would hold her hands over burning coals? Brainless. That is what you are."

"Let me go, dolt. I am not the brainless one here. Ye are the lackwit if ye dinna expect me to escape."

"Eneuch! Have you not learned by now 'tis useless to try? I will not let you go." He shook his head in aggravation. "Mayhap I should have trussed you like a pig after all."

He pulled his shirttail from his breeches, thought better of it, and grasped her shirt to pull it free.

"Stop. What are you doing?" She jerked and tried to move back from the water. His hand on her shoulder kept her there.

"I am making a binding for your burns. Mayhap if we keep them soaked in cold water the heat will draw from them."

He wet the cloths and wound them around each wrist. By the look on her face, he knew its coldness soothed her flesh.

That she would continue attempting to escape was a certainty. He must needs thwart her efforts before she did herself a serious injury. After they reached Rimsdale, he did not want to wait for her to heal.

When he brought her forward in his great hall to declare his intentions, he wanted Meghan of Blackthorn whole and hearty.

CHAPTER 5

Meghan gritted her teeth as she stared at the moving ground. "Did ye happen to note I am not a sack of grain but a livin', breathin' woman with two good legs to walk?" Meghan snapped her words at Rolf as she squirmed and kicked.

Simple flew down to hop along beside them, her wee head cocking from side to side as she studied Meghan. If only she could command her sparrowhawk to peck at Rolf's head till he had but a few strands of hair left atop it.

"Aye. I notice. Still, this living, breathing woman with two good legs comes with more ease if I dinna give her the use of her feet."

From the tone of his words, she could all but see his lips lifted in a snarl.

His arm tightened around her waist as he carried her against his left hip, dangling.

He did not drop her on the wool plaid as she expected but lowered her until she sat. Not binding her again, he pressed her down and turned her on her left side. His arm snaked around her waist and dragged her back against him, anchoring her there.

"'Tis no need for such closeness." Meghan stiffened and edged away from him.

"Be still, else you will find yourself beneath me."

She went as still as the skeletal trunk of a dead oak.

"Canna we declare a temporary truce? Until sunrise?" 'Twas worth a try. Anything was better than this forced closeness. "I willna attempt to escape while ye sleep."

His disbelieving snort answered her.

By all that is holy, 'twas worse torture than if Rolf had bound her raw wrists. His scent, so well remembered, tormented her senses. His hard body against her back tormented her memories.

She had forgotten neither over the past years. Nor did she forget he was not as he once was.

The Rolf of those yesteryears was not the man now pressed to her back. That early Rolf would never cause a woman hurt. Would never steal a woman from her home.

Mayhap he would for love. Now that was not his reason. If anything, he hated her. She was but a means to an end. His harsh treatment. His actions. All meant to remind her why he held her.

Not for gold, he had said.

Not e'en for anything more precious than gold.

For vengeance. What form would it take? Not to kill her. If that were his purpose, he would have strung her up on a tree while close to Blackthorn. She shuddered. What horror that would have been to her family to find her dead body in the woods! Nay. Rolf would never kill a woman. Nor would he ever beat a woman.

Would he? Could he have her tied to a post and flogged?

Nay. 'Twas not possible for him to do such. Nor did he plan to wed her. She had sensed that.

The downy hair on her nape stirred from his soft breath, tickling her there. His arm tightened, and he moved against her in his sleep.

"Ingirid," he mumbled as a calloused hand slid up to gently cup her breast.

She froze. What would he do if he awoke to find himself so aroused? She kept her breathing shallow, for every intake pushed her hardened nipple against the palm of his hand. Heat streaked down to pool between her legs, dampening her there. Never had any man caused her body to take such interest. Only him. It had ever been thus, though he never knew of it.

This vengeance. She could think of only one that would destroy both her and Connor. Sweat beaded her forehead.

If Rolf made her his leman.

What better revenge than to render a loving brother powerless to protect his closest blood tie? To shatter a woman's pride. *Please, sweet Jesus. Not that.* Better he flay her back raw and dump her on Blackthorn grounds than break her in that way.

Meghan prayed for dawn. She had to find a means to escape. For her sake as well as for Rolf's. Whatever he intended would break his soul, his pride, as well and truly as it broke hers.

She was sure of it.

Finally, exhaustion claimed her.

Rolf slept soundly, comforted by dreams of holding his sweet Ingirid close. As he roused, his hand stole between her legs, ready to take his ease from the soft body pressed against him. Instead of a soft smock, he confronted trews! A boy? He jerked his hand away, moved back from her, and rose up on an elbow. He shook his head to clear it.

In the breaking dawn, he remembered who lay there.

And why she did.

Meghan's face was gentle in sleep, her long lashes shading the dark circles beneath her eyes. She had not slept well. Her soft inviting lips parted slightly, and little puffs of air escaped. Brown hair tumbled about her face, unkempt, giving her the look of a woman who had been well loved between the sheets.

She likely missed his warmth, for she scooted back searching for that small comfort. Upon not finding it, a soft, forlorn sound escaped her lips and she stilled.

Slowly he rose and quietly slipped away into the trees. Not once did he take his gaze from her. He did not trust her, though she still slept. When he returned, he rekindled the fire.

"Rise, woman, if you wish to freshen yourself afore we depart." Even to his own ears, his voice sounded harsh. 'Twas not the way to awaken a sleeping woman.

She did not respond as his warriors would. He nudged her rear with his boot.

"Churl!" Meghan pushed up with her hands. And gasped. Her teeth clamped tight while she rose to her feet.

She looked stiff and sore from head to toe. Shame nudged his conscience. He dismissed it. Certain she sported a mass of bruises beneath her clothing, he would have to leave her unbound this day. The thought did not please him. Unlike no other woman he had ever known, Meghan's strong will and determination to elude him drew his grudging respect.

He would have no easy time breaking her.

"Come." As he had the day before, he led her a short way into the bushes.

"Give me your ankle," he ordered as he dangled the length of rope. He stared her in the eye, warning her to behave.

She did as he expected. A slight move to the right, then a twirl to the left, her right foot aimed high for his jaw. He clamped her ankle in a viselike grip, holding it shoulder high.

"Ah, such eager obedience. But you didna needs be so swift." When Meghan wobbled and waved her arms about, he nestled her foot between his legs and squeezed it tight. Against his sex. A flush began at the neck opening of her shirt and rose to her cheeks.

What? Meghan blushing? He wouldna have expected it. Her gaze fell to where he clasped her. What she spied caused her eyes to widen. He ignored the hot bulge that strained against his clothing. Before this sennight was through, ease would be available for the ache that plagued him.

"You have till a count of twenty and five. No longer." He turned his back, trailing the line out as he went but keeping it taut enough that he felt resistance there.

"One. Two. Three. Four . . ." Her curses filled his ears. Some were passing strange. No one had ever called him a "rat-eyed weasel," or a "wart on Satan's arse."

Before he could say twenty and four, she charged back through the trees. If looks were weapons, he would be bleeding aplenty.

Rolf tossed her a small bag of oats and motioned to the fire where steam rose from an iron pot there.

"Prepare the porridge if you would break your fast."

Her chin stuck out defiantly, her eyes narrowed. His narrowed back, and he put his thoughts there of what he would do if she did not mind him. She read him aright and turned to do as he bid. She added a handful of oats to the bubbling water.

Prior to arriving at Rimsdale, she would obey him. He would not have his people think he could not control a woman. In particular, not this young woman, isolated from her family and without a champion to defend her.

Meghan's teeth ground together. By the saints! She likened the changes in the man Rolf had been and the man he now was to the difference between a piglet and an enraged boar.

Treat me like an animal on a lead, will he?

Demand I fix his porridge, will he?

She watched as the pot bubbled away, the smell of porridge causing her mouth to water. She was hungry. What a shame to waste good gruel on such a harsh man.

Her eyes lit. Once, Mereck's bride Netta had told her what mischief she had done during their journey from Northumbria to Blackthorn. On preparing Mereck's food to bring to him, she had put worms in his stew.

She glanced down at useless rocks and leaves. Mayhap a little sand from the water's edge would do the trick? She had slack enough in her lead to reach it.

"I go to bring fresh water to drink," she called out to him. At his nod, she took her flask, went to the water, and filled it with one hand. With the other, she palmed a small amount of sand.

She strolled to the fire and darted glares at his back as she took a wooden spoon and scooped gruel from the pot onto a trencher of stale bread. Adding the sand to the porridge left in the pot, she stirred it well. She grinned as she emptied it onto the second trencher.

She felt him watching her. Had he seen?

"Come. Your food grows cold."

She ambled a short way from the fire, then sat cross-legged on the ground and took a large spoonful of her gruel. Eyeing him over the spoon, she blew on it till it cooled enough to eat. 'Twas heaven to eat something warm.

He filled his wooden spoon and thrust it in his mouth, then frowned. He did not seem to savor his mouthful as much as she did her own. His gaze lifted to her face. The next spoonful he clasped between his lips to rub it there. His hand swiped it away. He gulped a mouthful of water and rinsed it. He knew.

His gaze scoured her face. She shrugged and scooped up another large spoonful. The spoon went flying to land in the leaves. He snatched the trencher from her lap and placed it next to him.

"Did your aunt Phillipa not see you taught in womanly skills? 'Tis best you learn. Now."

His big hand clamped her jaw, forcing her to open. He filled her mouth with his sandy porridge. She tried to jerk away.

"Eat it, witch." His hand covered her mouth so she could not spit the food out. "Your efforts must have been the best you could do. You wouldna dare prick my wrath by such a lowly trick as to spoil my food . . . would you?"

She flashed hate at him. He pinched her nose shut. Like a person drowning, she lashed out, fighting for air. He held tight to her face, wrapped his legs high around her, pinning her arms to her side as he toppled her on her back and straddled her.

"Swallow." The word ended on a snarl.

She felt her face turning purple. The horrid man would hold on until she passed out. Her throat worked, trying to swallow. It wouldna go down. Frantic, she tried again. He released her nose at the last moment, and the porridge slid down her throat.

He leaned over, his nose near touching hers.

"Ne'er try such with me again, Meghan of Blackthorn, else you will eat naught but wormy bread for a sennight."

His words exploded out with such force they made her head ring. He unclasped her mouth and shot to his feet as she gasped for air. She was still breathing deeply as he threw their food into the fire and rinsed the pot. She winced, hearing her stomach grumble.

Drat the man! She brushed at the dirt and leaves clinging to every inch of her. 'Twas no easy job, for her hair was full of snarls, and she had no comb. She did the best she could with her fingers. What did it matter? She cared not what he thought of her, and if she had her way, she would escape him afore they reached Rimsdale.

"Dig your sharp elbows between my ribs again, and I will tie them together," Rolf threatened.

"Let me ride Storm and ye will be free of my presence." Meghan twisted her head to look back at him. Hmm. He did look a bit on the surly side at that. Good.

"Ha. Daft I am not," he muttered.

Meghan's muscles screamed. She sat in front of him, straddling his horse and sharing the saddle. Cradled between his legs, her bottom rested against his hot groin. Every time she tried to shift to a more comfortable position, she felt his tarse respond. She inched forward and stiffened her back, straining to bend as far from his heat as possible. Had she not been an excellent rider, she would have long since fallen from his damned steed.

Her slight movement made him curse beneath his breath.

"By what name do ye call yer mount?" Mayhap talking would occupy her mind and turn it from his closeness.

"Horse."

Irritable, was he? Ha. What reason did he have to be aggrieved? She was the one carted off against her will.

"Horse?" She gave a disgusted huff of air and again poked him with an elbow. "Ye mean to tell me ye order the stable boy to 'saddle Horse' and he brings this particular one?"

"Why would he not? He knows 'tis my mount and no other's." He slipped both his arms under hers and held tight to her body.

Meghan shuddered as she felt his hard muscled arms

against the sides of her breasts. Each breath she took seemed to rub her breasts against him. She tried taking shallow breaths. It did not help, for she soon felt starved for air and took one too deep.

" 'Tis a lass's way to name every living thing that abides within a castle's grounds," Rolf added.

"A woman's way, is it? Nay. Not so. Damron calls his warhorse Angel, though Brianna says he should bear the name Lucifer. Mereck's destrier is *M'Famhair*, for the horse is for truth a giant. Bleddyn's huge black is Thunder." Her chin lifted. "No lass but a man named each of them."

She twisted around and glared up at him. Seeing his baleful expression, she turned back. Her frequent movements were done apurpose. Her dirk rested in a sheath strapped to his right boot. If she could steal it away, she had the means to escape the next time he tethered her by the ankle.

"Be still. For the love of Christ, hold your clack! I dinna remember you ever running at the mouth as you are this day."

When she squirmed around and looked up at him again, he grabbed her shoulders.

"Eneuch!" His shout caused Simple to give a startled chirp and take to the sky.

"Look what ye have done. Poor Simple will get lost for sure now. It will be your fault, ye dratted man."

She squelched a chuckle when an explosion of air blasted past her ear. Rolf was vexed. No doubt about it.

Well, she was none too happy herself. They had not stopped, not even once. By the looks of the sun, they were well into the afternoon. If she didna make her move soon, they would be within leagues of Rimsdale. If they were not already that close.

She stretched her hands far in front of her, then high over her head. Though it caused her breasts to brush against his arms, she ignored it.

"Cease," he demanded.

"I canna. Every muscle stiffens. Soon I willna be able to move at all." She twisted to each side and moved her arms around.

"We will stop but a short way ahead. Rimsdale is but three leagues distant."

So close? How had they covered so much ground today? By hard riding and not stoppin', ye foolish woman. By the saints. Now she not only talked to herself but also answered.

"Then you willna mind my stretchin' a bit afore we stop." She leaned far to the left, then to the right, her arms stretched with her. He grabbed her waist, no doubt thinking she would topple over.

She straightened and grinned in triumph. Her dirk was where it belonged, in the sheath strapped to her leg, hidden beneath the folds of her overlong shirt.

'Twas in its rightful place.

CHAPTER 6

Meghan could not sit still. Never had she been forced to ride with a man since she was a babe. When she was but four years of age, she became adept at escaping her nursemaid and making her way to the stables. There she would climb atop the gate of a stall and coax the horse to come to her. The stable hands near died of fright when they found her jabbering to the steed while patting and kissing his huge neck.

No amount of paddling her wee bottom had kept her from returning to the stable and doing it again whenever she wanted. The stable master pleaded with the old laird, her grandda, until he gave her a Highland pony and taught her to ride along with Connor.

Now she wanted off Horse. She rolled her eyes skyward and grimaced, thinking about Rolf's neglect to name his steed. For certain, this beautiful animal deserved a worthy name.

"By the cross, woman, are you ne'er still?" Rolf's impatient huff of air tickled her cheek.

"I can be when the mood strikes. I am not used to sittin' and doing nothin' when on a horse."

He turned deeper into the woods and stopped beside a waterfall that near overflowed the banks of the stream beneath it. As it raced over good-sized rapids, the air filled with sounds she likened to music. He swung his leg over the horse and sprang to the ground. When he reached for her, she ignored his gesture of aid. She, too, jumped down.

Her feet hit the ground, and she winced as the jolt shot

through her sore body. Until this lout had caused her such stress, she had been quite graceful. Not so today.

While the horses drank, Meghan cupped her hands and splashed icy water on her face. She stood, waiting. Rolf raised one brow in a questioning slant. She held up her left foot.

"How far will ye count this day?" She waited, her foot in the air.

Rolf's eyes hooded as he watched her. Did he think her so foolish as to attempt to strike him again? She had other plans.

"Well now, my leg grows tired." Meghan shifted and scowled at him.

He made a loop and tightened it around her ankle.

"Nay, I willna count. Best you hurry, though, or your modesty will suffer," he said as he dropped her foot.

"Ha. Worse than it has already? Ne'er have I seen a more impatient man," she muttered as she wove her way through the trees until she felt the rope grow taut. Keeping tension on it, she backtracked to secure it around a tree. As she did so, she felt him tug on the other end.

"Do ye think to topple me into the brambles?" she called out as she cut the rope from her ankle. Her footsteps silent and swift, she circled the area until she stood by their horses. His back was to her. She grinned, for he looked up at the sky as if asking God for patience.

After snatching up the horses' reins, she jumped astride Storm and set him into motion. "Come," she shouted at Horse and tugged his reins. Soon they were galloping away.

"Meghan! Get you back or you will regret it," Rolf shouted.

"When Lucifer freezes his arse, churl," she hollered back.

A loud, shrill whistle rent the air. Saints, she hated that sound. Horse skidded to a stop. The jolt on the reins near pulled her off the saddle until she let them go.

She need not look behind her to know Rolf would soon be breathing down her neck.

"Misbegotten monster," she grumbled as she leaned forward and urged Storm to fly as fast as possible. "He didna bother naming the horse, but sure as Lucifer's horns, he taught him enough commands."

This was her last chance. Once they entered the grounds at Rimsdale, she would have not only him, but also every one of his people to evade.

Horse pounded close behind her. A quick glance at Rolf's face caused cold dread to grip her throat.

"Lucifer's wretched teeth. Can I never best the man?"

Storm pricked up his ears. Was he listening to her, or was he paying heed to the other horse charging ever closer? Mayhap the rivalry between the two steeds would aid her.

"Dinna let him near, Storm. Did he not try to nip yer ears this morn?"

Storm surged forward. Horse followed suit.

Rolf also leaned into his mount's great head, urging him as she did Storm. From the looks of him, he meant to throttle her.

Damnation. He must have said something dire to Horse, else the steed had wings to reach such speed. Before she could count to ten and two, Rolf pulled alongside, crowding Storm until he forced him to stop.

Meghan panted for breath. The horses snorted and stamped, and Simple called from above. Poor confused birdie. Ne'er had she been left so long on her own.

Rolf's saddle creaked as he slid off Horse with deliberate slowness. She squeezed her eyes shut and swallowed. Mayhap he would end it all now and be done with it? She opened her eyes just as his hands reached up for her. Her own hand lashed out. With a low cry, she jerked it back a hair's width from burying the blade in his neck.

When had she drawn her dirk? She did not remember doing so.

He seized her wrist and near crushed the delicate bones. She screamed in pain, for rope burns and blisters circled there.

"Damn you, Meghan," he shouted as he jerked her from her saddle. Her quivering legs gave way and she fell to the ground. "At peril to your life, ne'er do such again. Had you drawn on me in front of my men, I would be forced to have you whipped. Are you so lackin' in brains you dinna know when to yield?"

Rolf raised his hand to strike her. She stifled a flinch. She would not cower. His arm quivered with strain as he held back the blow. Both hands fisted time and again. He took several deep, rasping breaths as he fought for control. Reaching beside him, he jerked the coiled rope from his saddle's pommel and began making a noose.

Did he mean to hang her? A wave of panic swept over her. She desperately tried to hide her fear from him.

"Ye would kill a woman, Rolf? Ha'e ye sank so low?" If she lived to be ten times ten, she wouldna think he could do such.

"Get up!" He stepped back, allowing her room.

She stood, and he slowly circled her. She gasped when the noose fell around her neck. He could not do it. Could he? She thought it best to keep her mouth shut and her body still. He would come to his right mind soon. She grimaced. Or would he?

"I gave you every chance to come easily, but you wouldna. I canna trust you on your horse. I canna trust you seated with me. I canna trust you on foot if you are not within my reach." He wrapped the end of the rope around his left fist, secured Storm's reins as he had done before, and then sprang onto his saddle.

He sat and waited. She stood and waited.

"Walk," he said in a voice fraught with rage.

Meghan squared her shoulders and strolled in the direction he intended for them to go. He followed close behind, letting the rope dangle so it did not tighten around her neck. She lengthened her stride to get the greatest distance, not knowing how many leagues she would have to trudge. Her last attempt to escape had led them away from Rimsdale, perhaps half a league more. Thank all the saints her boots fitted quite well over woolen hose.

To occupy her mind, she enjoyed the closeness of the plants around her, something she couldna do while riding. Nestled close amongst the trees, she spied some of the herbs they kept in supply at Blackthorn.

She did not recognize many, for she had left the healing arts to the other women of the castle while she trained to help defend them. Were they ever invaded, the varlets wouldna expect a "mere" lass to be guardin' the ladies.

She spied clusters of feverfew for its white flower and golden center, and valerian for its small white, pink, or lavender flowers and its pleasant scent.

One herb she knew enough about to be leery of was mandrake. Its pretty greenish yellow flowers belied its deadly power. She had remarked to Damron's wife that its branched root brought to her mind the shape of the human body. Brianna had made sure she recognized it and knew how dangerous it could be.

"You dawdle," Rolf said as he flicked the rope behind her. She had not realized she had stopped to stare at the plant.

"Do I, now? I thought 'twas a pleasant stroll I was takin' through the woods."

A jerk on the rope paid her for her sarcastic remark. She deemed it prudent to keep one hand up to hold the noose out from her tender flesh.

How many leagues had she walked? Looking for herbs no longer occupied her mind, nor did watching for the wee forest creatures hiding from them. Her feet burned and her heels stung. By Lucifer's ragged toes, she wouldna limp!

"Turn left at the tall pine ahead. We will stop to water the horses," Rolf ordered.

His voice still held the rasp of anger. Because a woman had dared continue to defy him? What had he expected when he came to the cave? That she would throw up her hands in fear and follow, timid as a scullery maid?

Rolf glared at Meghan. He wanted to strangle her for forcing him to take this position. At times she became so engrossed in her thoughts, she forgot to hide behind stalwart behavior. When she did so, he grimaced each time she limped. Rimsdale was yet a league away at the far end of this woodland. For the last league, they had traveled parallel to the northern tip of a finger of water nestled between two woodlands.

He led them to the water's edge and stopped. Meghan dropped to her knees and plunged her head below the surface, and he knew 'twas to shock her body into a spurt of energy. She came up gasping and shaking her head. Her wet locks whipped about her, flinging droplets of water that caught the sun like tiny rainbows.

When she threw back her head to lift her face to the sky, eyes closed as she fanned her hair back and away, desire burst through his control. His stomach muscles tightened, then lower yet, heat spread through his groin. Her full, sensuous mouth glistened from water still resting there. He fought the urge to lick her lips dry before nibbling them between his teeth. His aching tarse urged him to take her. His iron will forced his body to ignore his desire. Even with her snarled mane and her clothing covered with dust and mud stains, he couldna deny his attraction.

Meghan was the most desirable woman he had ever beheld. The hellcat! How he despised her for it.

Did she ken what she did to him? He couldna look at her but that his groin flamed hot enough to burn through his clothin'. Since he had captured her, he was in a constant state of arousal.

Not much longer to wait, he promised himself as he tamped his feelings down.

He knelt and splashed his own heated flesh, rubbing his eyes to rid them of her image. Both drank their fill. Once done, they tended their needs. He stayed close, he on one side of a bush, she on the other. When she returned and he saw her face abashed and red, he grunted, satisfied.

" 'Tis of yer own makin', Meghan." He knew she understood when she stiffened her shoulders and glared at him.

Several times after they continued their slow trek, he would have stopped and lifted her up in front of him had she asked. She was too stubborn, too proud to yield. He was too determined to tame her to offer. So be it. She could no longer mask her limping. He tried to smother any feelings the sight of her distress stirred.

To him, Meghan of Blackthorn was more precious than gold. Not as a desirable woman, but as a means to his vengeance. Why should he feel shame? He silenced those bygone dreams he once had of her as his bride.

The ground sloped downhill now. Through the thinning forest, the gray stones of Rimsdale Castle appeared. The fortress occupied an island linked to the land by a stone bridge. A gatehouse guarded the entrance to the bridge. At its end, another defended the island with a drawbridge as added protection. The castle itself sat sideways on the land. The entrance was at its midpoint in the shortest and most sprawling part of the structure. To the left, the walls rose four stories high. Behind was another much larger and taller portion.

His lips lifted in a slight smile when Meghan halted and stared. Rimsdale was far different from Blackthorn. Her home crowned the edge of the cliffs overlooking the Kyle of Tongue.

On the right side of his island, a grove of apple trees grew amidst purple and white heather that sweetened the breeze blowing toward them. In front sprawled a field ample enough for several practice areas. Behind the island, the loch swelled to the foot of a mountain on the far side.

Hmm. Her study of the island was calculating. Not only was she trained in unusual skills, but he knew she was also knowledgeable in castle defense. Her gaze darted over each part of the bridge, the gatehouse, and the drawbridge. She squinted as if to judge the depth of the water, then studied the land leading up from it. She gave an almost imperceptible nod.

It brought a scowl to his face. What had she seen?

"You dawdle." He flicked the rope again.

With head high, Meghan stiffened her back and sauntered down the hill. Pride showed in every footfall. His people had gathered at the opposite end by the time they reached the first gatehouse. Storm stomped and balked at the bridge. Rolf gathered the gelding's reins. A sharp tug brought him in line.

The guard raised the portcullis, its iron bars sharp and lethal.

"Can ye no' take this noose from my neck now? 'Tis certain I canna do ye harm on yer own bridge."

She swallowed and glanced at the gawking crowd.

"'Tis certain *I am* if I keep you tethered you willna cause me further trouble. 'Tis for your own good. I willna have a lass defy me afore mine own people."

Clearing her throat, she raised her head. Pride stiffened her body. Surprisingly, she pretended to swipe off an insect as she brushed the dust and grime from her clothing.

She began to walk as fast as she could. From the set of her jaw, he knew she labored not to limp in front of these people who were strangers to her.

"No need to race, lass."

Meghan ignored him. He could hear the surprised voices of those awaiting them as they speculated on the identity of his captive.

"It canna be a lass, no' in men's clothing," said a cook's helper.

"Nay, the MacDhaidh would no' tether a lass," answered a washerwoman.

"Hmpf. 'Tis a lass, right eneuch. Did I no' tell ye the girl rode and fought like a mon?" This came from a warrior who had been with Rolf outside Blackthorn.

"Aye. Too shapely fer a lad. This'uns locks would tease a man's body did she ride him."

A loud screech floated from a tree on the land side of the bridge. Meghan stopped and turned to watch Simple fly to her.

"Ah, little feathers, ye look afrighted," Meghan murmured, then whistled softly. "Come, ye silly creature," she called out. Simple slowly circled above her, and Meghan lifted her left arm in invitation.

"Dinna!" No leather band covered her wrist, and Rolf could see the red, angry flesh there. The bird's talons would be agony.

Meghan shot him a scornful look. "She is frightened and needs me." She squared her jaw as Simple landed. Talking and soothing the sparrowhawk, she coaxed it closer to her elbow. She continued to walk until they reached the next gatehouse.

The guard had raised the portcullis and lowered the draw-bridge. Meghan stared ahead, ignoring everything around her.

"Do ye see that? The lass has no gauntlet." The head fal-coner's voice sounded admiring.

"'Tis well you arrived." Alpin MacKean glanced up at him, then he turned to glower at Meghan. He rubbed his thigh where her arrow had entered. "I see you found her." He moved close beside her right side, peering at her as if assess-ing her physical value to a man.

Alpin's gaze lingered far too long on the swell of Meghan's breasts for Rolf's liking. His friend's hand fondled and squeezed the lass's bottom.

Meghan whirled and swung back at Alpin, striking him in the neck. Gasping and spluttering, he grabbed his throat.

"Why, you fashious bitch," he shouted, and raised his hand to cuff her.

"Dinna dare!" Rolf's command stopped Alpin's hand inches from Meghan's cheek. "Move away," he ordered as the crowd surged closer to see the spectacle. Rolf halted. "Listen and listen well," he shouted so everyone could hear. "Meghan of Blackthorn is mine. *Mine alone.*" He paused and glared around him. "No man, no woman, no youth may discipline her but me."

They had reached the entrance to the castle walls and had passed through into the front bailey where more curious peo-ple swarmed around them.

Simple chirped, distressed, and Meghan cuddled her close so she could smooth the dainty little head.

"Be she a slave then, brother?" called a voice that cracked between a youth's and a man's. Garith shoved through the crowd and stood in front of Meghan. His right arm hung list-less by his side. Upon seeing the chafed skin of Meghan's neck, he frowned.

"Nay, she is to be our guest," Rolf answered.

Laughter rang out from the people crowding around them.

"If she be our guest, Rolf, 'tis a mean way of showing our hospitality, draggin' her about by a noose," a woman's angry voice said. She looked fit to lay a pan about his head. She reached to lift the rope away, but Rolf stopped her.

"Leave it be, Ede. The lass is lacking in proper respect for men. I will say when to remove it."

Putting her hands on her hips, Ede flipped her red tresses with a jerk of her head. Blue fire spit from her eyes. "I canna believe you are my cousin. No MacDhaidh has e'er treated a lass so."

"No MacDhaidh has e'er had Meghan of Blackthorn to deal with," Rolf answered. "All of ye, go about your business. 'Tis no spectacle for your amusement. Begone."

The crowd murmured, some hostile now that they knew 'twas a woman of Blackthorn who stood there. Others darted furtive looks of sympathy toward Meghan, but soon they all moved away. Not to go about their business, though. They fiddled around, trying to look busy while watching Rolf's every move.

Only Alpin, Garith, and Ede refused to heed his command.

"We go to the stables, Meghan."

She glanced about and spied the structure at the right side of the bailey. Without a word, she headed toward it.

He well understood why they called her the "Warrior Woman of Blackthorn." Not once did her shoulders slump, nor did she show distress in any way. He knew her mortification was deep. The blow to her pride must cost her every bit of control she possessed.

Would her humiliation soften her, or would it make this proud woman even more defiant?

Knowing the answer, he sighed.

So be it.

CHAPTER 7

Rolf waited beside the stable door until the stable master and his helpers appeared.

"Garith, see the grooms take special care with the gelding. His name is Storm." He pointed at one young stable hand and ordered, "Bring me a soft leather strap fit for a woman's neck and a lead no more than three paces long." The boy took off on a run. Rolf frowned at the other grooms. "Ne'er leave the horse and this woman alone. She has trained him well."

Meghan sucked her teeth and glared at him.

Rolf handed his own reins to the stable master. "See Horse has the same treatm—"

Meghan's loud scoff interrupted him.

"His name be *Luath*," she informed the stable master; "Speed is his finest feature. As your master has neglected to give him a proper name, I have."

The stable master looked quickly at his master. When Rolf made no protest, the man nodded to Meghan.

The newly named Luath nudged her back, then nickered and tossed his head, making his silky mane fly. Looking proud of himself, he gave a few excited stomps before settling down.

"Ye dinna have to thank me. Ye deserve a noble name," she said gravely.

The woman was daft! She talked to the horse as if she believed it knew her words. Barely within his castle's walls a heartbeat in time, and she ordered his people. Yet the name suited. Why had he not thought of it? He wouldna countermand her.

The head falconer stood in the background, his head tilted to the side and a smile on his face as he waited. His kind eyes peered at Simple, then searched Meghan's face.

"The little feathers will be fine with Malcolm," Rolf said.

Meghan watched the falconer for a few moments, then seemed to decide. "Come, love." She ran her hand over Simple's head, soothing her, then offered Malcolm her wrist.

The falconer placed her fingertips atop his hand and laid his gauntlet-covered arm alongside her own. Rolf winced at the falconer's glare on seeing raw skin and burns there. As the man murmured to the bird, Simple looked at him, back at Meghan, and took one tentative step.

"'Tis fine ye will be. Malcolm will see ye have a proper feedin'." She whistled softly. "Go now."

Simple hopped onto Malcolm's wrist and waited while he placed a hood over her head and tied it.

"Dinna ye worry, I will take fine care of the wee birdie." He left, whispering encouragement to the nervous sparrowhawk.

Rolf turned to Alpin and Ede, who stood side by side, Alpin's silvery blond hair near mingling with Ede's own fiery red. "I will meet you in the great hall after I finish with Meghan of Blackthorn."

Alpin smirked, his icy blue eyes flashing satisfaction at the rope around Meghan's neck before he left. Ede refused to budge. Flames spit from her deep blue eyes, making them even more striking.

"Go! Dinna question how I handle this woman."

With a huff, she turned, muttering to herself as she went out into the bailey.

Rolf took in an irritated breath, then regarded his captive.

"You will stay here," he informed her as he led her inside the stable and looked around. He still seethed that she had dared draw a weapon on him. Should she show him such foolish defiance afore his warriors, he couldna do else but have her whipped. His stomach churned at the thought of a lash striking her soft skin. How should he secure her? He couldna leave her arms free. She would slip from her binds and be out the door in a trice. Her wrists were too sore to bind them. Not her upper arms, though.

The young boy returned with a small strap that would chaff Meghan's neck less than the harsh rope. Rolf led her to the side wall where they had embedded an iron ring to tether the horses. She stiffened, sensing his intention.

"I am as an animal to ye?" The air between them crackled with sparks, and her face grew red with anger. Before he removed the noose, he placed the leather strap around her neck and tightened it only enough that she could not slip it over her head. He attached the leather lead to an iron ring on the strap.

He noted her hands clench and didna doubt she wished to claw his eyes. His jaw set, determination was in each movement as he pulled the lead through the ring and knotted it.

"Turn around." She stood, unmoving. He spun her to face the wall and freed the noose from around her neck, then looped a long piece of leather around her right arm at elbow height and secured it there. Grasping the other elbow, he did the same, leaving the width of four hands between her arms. She could neither lower the leather to her wrists nor raise her arms to release the strap around her neck. He didna doubt her resolve to escape, though. A guard at the door would be added assurance.

He left her and returned with a small crate and placed it against the wall for her to sit on.

"Why do ye not put me in a stall, throw some straw about the floor, and oats in a pail?"

Her chin quivered before she clamped her teeth together and turned her back to him. By the cross, she was right. The horses the men curried and pampered were in better shape than she was. How had he become so hardened to a woman that he would treat her thusly? Hearing his brother talking to Storm gave him his answer.

Treachery had hardened him to *this* woman.

Because of Connor, his young brother had little use of his right arm.

Because of Connor, his wife and son had died.

Outside the stable door, Alpin and Dougald awaited him. His mind quickly filled with the happenings of Rimsdale during his short absence. After he reached the great hall, he rebuffed all questions about Meghan. His hard face and steel-hard eyes spoke more than words. He wouldna speak of her. As evening fell, tension grew. Cook's helpers carried in bowls of steaming food, but not even their mouth-watering aroma lightened his mood.

He noted that the deer Meghan had brought down graced the savory stew. Halfway through his meal, he felt Ede's aggrieved glare.

"After you are done with your meal, Ede, see the Blackthorn woman is fed." Ede shoved her trencher aside, more troubled with his captive's hunger than with her own.

"Dinna untie her. Feed her with your own hand." His mouth tightened into a hard line.

Ede grabbed a tray from a serving girl, a trencher filled with stew from another, and a cup of ale from a third. The whole time she filled the tray, a frown marred her sweet face. "What have we become that we would treat a woman of gentle birth in such a way? No good will come of it. Just you wait and see." She shook her head, her worry evident in the frown lining her brow. "When all is said and done, Rimsdale will suffer."

"Rimsdale suffers now because of Connor of Blackthorn. Had he not tried to capture my sweet Ingirid, she and my son would yet live. Had Garith not sought to defend my wife, his arm would yet be whole. Ne'er speak to me of my care of Connor's sister."

Ede turned her back and headed out the door. She had the last word as she shouted at him, "Meghan of Blackthorn isna Connor. She wasna on that raid. 'Tis wrong to make the lass pay for her brother's deeds."

He winced. Before he could reply, she was gone.

Tethered like a wild animal within the stable, her hair snarled, Meghan's resolve hardened with every breath she took. Never had she been so tired, so full of aches from her bruised head to her blistered feet.

Aye, she had been this tired, she corrected her thoughts. The first time her cousin Mereck took over her training with the quintain. Before the day dimmed, her mistakes had left her with bruises over most of her back. She had been un-horsed so many times she couldna sit for the evening meal. But she had not minded the aches and pains, for she had learned much that day. That eve, Mereck's praise in front of all in the great hall made up for every twinge.

Not so this day. To be honest, 'twas not her sore wrists or the bruises over much of her body that caused such distress. Nor was it hunger and weariness as she fought to keep her back straight and her shoulders level.

'Twas her pride that suffered the most.

Had she been daft to take refuge in the cave? That *particular* cave? Had she any idea who pursued her, she wouldna have gone there. Rolf was the one who showed it to her those years ago. Back when she believed he would ask Grandda for her hand. Afore things had gone so very wrong.

Now he treated her as he would a raving beast.

Someone spoke to the guard outside the door. As it squeaked open, she stiffened her posture. She blinked and her mouth watered as the smell of well-cooked stew floated on the air. The woman who carried the heavy tray was the same red-haired lass who had scolded Rolf earlier. He had called her Ede. She was short and softly formed, round in all the right places. The guard waited several paces away, his arms folded across his chest. So, Rolf didna even trust her alone with his cousin.

"Meghan, I have come to help you eat." She turned to the guard. "Bring a pail of water and a cloth so I may cleanse her face."

"Nay. The MacDhaidh said she was not to receive any comfort but ale and victuals." He frowned and his shoulders twitched.

"If you be afeared of Rolf, I am not. I will get them my-self." She went over and thrust the tray at him.

"Nay, lady. Do ye do so, I must needs tell him of it." He backed up and refused to accept the tray.

"Ede, please dinna fash yerself." Meghan forced a smile to her lips, acting like she was in the great hall at Blackthorn. Ignoring her state of disarray, she lifted her head with pride.

"Well now, the least you can do is bring somethin' I may place the tray on," Ede said as she scowled at the man.

He nodded and brought forth a short barrel from the first stall. Plunking it down in front of Meghan's crate, he returned to stand beside the door.

Meghan sat and stifled her unease at being fed like a bairn. Though 'twas degrading, she needed the meal to keep up her strength. After several mouthfuls, she couldna force down another.

"Nay, 'tis kind of ye to tend me, but I be more thirsty than hungry. If ye please, I am content to finish the ale." When Ede held the cup to her lips, she forced herself to swallow it all, then smiled at the woman. "Thank ye for yer kindness."

Ede flashed her a smile before she turned and stalked to the sleeping quarters in the rear. "Prepare a fresh pallet and bring it to me," she ordered two young stable boys. After they carried one out to her, she plumped it up and placed it near the wall. "'Tis not the best, but it will give you some ease." Having done all she could for Meghan's comfort, she flashed her an apologetic smile and left with the guard.

Meghan sighed and relaxed her shoulders. Her efforts to appear unfazed had taken a toll on her strength. She sat on the crate and waited until she heard naught but night sounds, then she knelt on the floor and eased her tired body onto the pallet.

Sometime during the darkest hours, she heard whispers on the other side of the door and the sound of coins changing hands. Though usually agile, when she tried to rise to her feet, she stumbled. With catlike movements, a man entered and waited for his eyes to adjust, giving her time to steady herself.

He crept closer.

A hand reached out and grasped her arms. After he forced her close against him, he jerked her head back. The stench of sweat and urine from his unwashed body choked her. Though she twisted and jerked like a wild woman, she did not scream. 'Twould shame her more to have another see her so helpless.

His sex hardened. Hard, cruel lips clamped down on hers, grinding against her softness until their teeth clashed together.

A beefy hand on her jaw forced her mouth to open, and his thick tongue plunged deep, gagging her. She bit down. Hard. Then let go. He gasped, released her, and swung a fist up to cuff her across her lower cheek. The blow split her lip.

Still silent, he spun her round to face the wall.

What did he want now?

His clothing rustled, then one arm looped around her waist and pulled her against his naked sex. He forced her right hand around a shaft as hard and as hot as steel warmed o'er a fire. She tried to open her fingers, but he didna let her. He dragged her imprisoned hand up and down his shaft.

Meghan relaxed. Let the accursed dimwit think she savored it. He was but a hand taller than she. She snuggled herself to him, and he reached up to rip her shirt open and fondle her breast. She bent her head forward till her chin touched her chest, then whipped it back as fast as she could to crack it against his face. Ah, the sweet sound of a pummeled nose.

"Lucifer's bitch!"

Footsteps sounded in the gravel leading to the door. He slung her against the wall and lumbered down the dark row of stalls. As she slid against the rough wood planking and landed on the pallet, she heard him wrench open the back door and flee into the night.

"No needs to check the lass. She couldna move from where Lord Rolf tethered her," she heard the guard say.

"Since when have we no' checked what we guard at the beginnin' of a shift?" his replacement replied.

The door creaked open, and a man entered holding a rushlight high above his head. Meghan, silent still, kept her back to him. He stood there a moment, then left, taking care to close the door quietly.

She sat against the wall for the rest of the night. Her heart raced at each sound, and she dared not sleep.

As the faint light of dawn filtered between the cracks of the barn door, the relief guard entered and held his rushlight close to peer at Meghan. After one quick look, he jerked back and yelled loud and furious, "Get Lord Rolf and be quick about it."

From the open door, Meghan saw dawn's golden light beginning to creep over the tops of the castle walls. Blessed saints, she was tired. She guessed she looked a fright. Ha! As if she hadna already appeared like a badgered hound.

The guard hesitated, then reached out a hand. She couldna stop herself from flinching away from it.

"Nay, lass, 'twas only to steady ye," he told her.

Heavy footsteps pounded outside.

"What goes here?" Rolf's harsh voice demanded as he burst through the doorway.

She forced her chin up and glared at him. 'Twas Rolf's fault. All of it. Had he not treated her as an animal, his man wouldna have thought her fair game.

Rolf's gut lurched with a sickening feeling. Meghan leaned back against the wall, looking weary but ready to fight. If looks could kill a man, he would soon bleed from wounds aplenty.

Her lips were swollen, split on the left where her face darkened from a bruise. Her torn shirt barely concealed her breast. His gaze swept over her. Her breeches were intact. Whoever had dared enter to batter her had been frightened off.

"Who allowed this?" His shout was not meant for her but at the men who were set to guard her. He wanted to pummel someone.

"Ye did, gowk," Meghan answered, daring to call him fool. "What did ye expect? That yer men would treat me with kindness when ye set my value as less than the horses in yer stable, the pigs in yer pens?" She turned away, refusing to look at him.

Rolf reached out and stroked her swollen jaw. Anger and

regret roiled through him in hot seething waves. She jerked her face away from him. He didna blame her.

Careful not to scrape her neck, he loosened the strap and eased it off her neck. The sight of her flesh, raw and sore as her wrists, made bile surge to his mouth.

"Every last man who guarded Meghan of Blackthorn is to report to me." His cold voice was quiet, lethal, as he spoke to the men around him. "You had best be prepared to account for yourselves."

When he grasped her shoulders, she stiffened. As he turned her back to him, she struggled.

"Easy, lass. I want only to free yer arms." Her flesh quivered beneath his touch. Freed at last, he turned her to him to pull her shirt together. She leaned away from his hands.

"Come." He stepped back and offered his arm for support. She ignored him. His arms ached to carry her, but he knew 'twas best to leave her be.

They entered the bailey, and Meghan spied the crowd gathered there to see why their lord had been in such haste. She halted. Not for long. With each slow step she took, Rolf's heart lurched, knowing he was the hateful churl she so oft named him.

Alpin stared, aghast at her swollen lips and bruised cheek as he fell in step with them. Rolf glanced at his lifetime friend, whose icy blue eyes showed shock that anyone would dare usurp Rolf's authority and touch the woman.

Fergus, Alpin's man, lagged close at his heels. His face didna show sympathy. His hand stole up and felt his nose. It was swollen and red. The common warriors were forever brawling over the favors of a wench. Forsooth, this one couldna long stay from fighting.

Would they never cross the bailey and reach the doorway into the main castle building? Never had the distance seemed so long as it did now as Rolf watched each painful step Meghan took. Why had he not bid Ede to tend her feet? No doubt blisters burst with each footfall. Whene'er she faltered and he reached to help her, she spit nay at him with such loathing he held back.

How came a lass by such pride? Pride belonged to a man. 'Twas hard earned in battle with deeds of bravery. What reason had a woman to hold herself so high?

Garith interrupted his thoughts when he ran up to him.

"Best ye hurry if ye dinna want a soakin'," he said as he pointed behind them.

Rolf had no need to look. Fat drops of rain plopped into the dust of the bailey, forming tiny mountains with craters filled with water that rapidly seeped through the earth below.

He scooped Meghan up into his arms, ignoring her protests. They didna last long. She looked at his face and must have read his determination there, for she kept her tongue behind her teeth. Would that she kept it there more often.

They reached the protection of the castle nary a moment too soon, for the heavens opened with a vengeance.

"Ede, our *guest* has needs of your skills. Fetch your healing herbs." He hurried past everyone and took two steps at a time up the stairway to the floor above, barking orders to the servants gawking at him. "Bring hot water and clean cloths to my solar."

Someone had already set flint to a peat fire in the room. The meager flames fought to dry the damp air. Tallow candles, so wide around they held four wicks, chased the shadows from the corners.

"Put me down, drat ye." Meghan pounded her fist on his shoulder. "I can verra well walk the length of this room."

Rolf ignored her as if she were a bundle of dirty linens he carried. The thing was, he was very much aware the bundle in his arms was not something he could disregard. The feel of her woman-soft flesh and a whiff of heather teased his senses.

She kicked her legs and pounded her fists against his chest. He staggered and bumped into a large war chest to the right of the door and all but toppled the frame holding his chain mail and helmet standing next to it. He stomped past his worktable and a carved wooden chair that occupied the space beside the window.

"Be you still or I will put you down right enough. Out yon window," he grumbled. His stride was determined as he headed toward his bed. It sat far enough from the warm fire that he was ne'er hot of a night.

"If ye dinna heed me, I will let loose a bloodcurdling scream that will have yer men thinkin' 'tis a banshee ye brought to yer solar."

He looked down to see her face set, ready to let loose a vigorous scream. He raised her high in his arms. And dropped her.

Onto his bed.

"Umpf!" She sank into the pallet filled with down, her arms and legs grasping about.

"Bloodcurdlin'? A banshee?" His eyes gleamed as he lifted one brow. "Garith's birthing cry would be more impressive."

Meghan sucked in air to fill her lungs, closed her eyes, and let loose a scream fit to raise chill bumps on a man's nape. The solar door slammed shut with a loud bang. It muffled her scream. She opened her eyes and frowned. Ede, her face scrunched tight and hands clasped over her ears, stood at the foot of the bed.

"Wretched hound from hell," Meghan muttered as she glared at the door. "He scampered off afore he could lose an argument."

CHAPTER 8

Mereck, Damron's bastard half brother, was commander over Blackthorn's warriors. The castle baileys swarmed with patrols coming and going, the men looking like ants scurrying over an oatcake slathered in honey and left in the sun.

"Mereck has returned. By the set of his face, he knows who has taken Meghan." Damron's deep voice was calm as he peered out his solar window to the ground below.

He watched as Mereck dismounted, stretched his neck, and rolled his shoulders to rid himself of tension building there. All who were familiar with him realized Mereck held himself in check, for when he loosened his temper, he became the berserk warrior that had earned him the name *Baresark* among his enemies.

"The MacDhaidh has taken the lass," Damron murmured. "He left warnin's aplenty of what he intended."

"When I get my hands on Meghan," Connor shouted as he paced the solar floor, "she'll soon find herself wed to a man who will beat her each morn for the things she but thinks to do that day."

Both men spun around as Mereck strode through the doorway.

"Do ye think beatings would stop Meghan?" Mereck asked, his expression wry. "Rolf rode her to ground. She took refuge in the cave at Beinn Stumanadh."

"What happened there?" Fear of Mereck's answer caused Connor's voice to quaver at the last word.

"I found Storm's prints and a few of Simple's feathers.

'Twas proof she was there. Her short sword was on the ground, deep in the shadows."

Mereck did not tell them he had seen where Rolf had pressed her face against the soft earth of the cave, for as he had sifted through the soil, strands of dark brown hair clung to his finger.

He placed her sword on the oak table in front of the window. The noonday sun shone in and glinted on a small crystal set low on the handle. 'Twas Meghan's only concession to an adornment. Connor put his hand on the blade, his face stricken.

"I dinna think Rolf will harm her." Damron grasped his cousin's shoulder, comforting him. "The mon has been dafty o'er her since she was a wee'un. He was ever ridin' over on some unlikely excuse. Didna ye note his eyes sought her out?"

"Aye, but that was afore some varlet caused Rolf to believe me responsible for his tragedy." Bitterness rang in Connor's voice. "Do I but find that man, he will breathe his last."

"By the timin' of it, 'twas likely the treachery of Rollo, Eric MacLaren's man. Didna we find he had stolen yer garments to pose as ye on raids?" Damron clasped his hands behind his back as he paced the sunlit room.

"Aye. Guardian made quick work of him when he harmed your Brianna," Mereck said. "The man didna have time to scream afore the wolf's great jaws clamped his throat."

"No note for ransom has arrived," Connor interrupted as he resumed pacing. He ran agitated fingers through brown hair so like his sister's.

"I dinna think 'twas for ransom he stole her." Damron eyed Connor before continuing. "Mayhap he knew Meghan wouldna forgive him for not askin' Grandda for her hand instead of weddin' another. She wouldna go with him easily now."

Mereck kept silent. Rolf had not behaved as a lover would when he forced Meghan's face in the dirt. Damron had ordered Connor to remain in Blackthorn, for his wife, Elise, carried their first bairn. She was a timid woman, though Meghan had done much to strengthen the Saxon girl's character.

Of a sudden, Mereck smiled. Bairns. The castle nursery was

filling with babes since the three of them had married. His little Donald had arrived at the end of 1073, and one month later, Brianna birthed Douglas. With little Serena, the child many believed Damron fathered on his leman, that made three wee ones. Now Elise looked forward to her own babe.

"I have ordered another foray into MacDhaidh lands. 'Tis time we learn what he demands." Mereck ran a hand over his unshaven jaw and frowned. "Damron, 'tis best the missive comes from you as laird of Blackthorn."

"Aye. I expected to do such." He handed a small parchment to Mereck. He had prepared the note earlier, even as far as addressing it to the MacDhaidh of Rimsdale.

Not many heartbeats after Mereck left the room with the message, a dozen warriors galloped through the barbican and headed into the woods toward their southeastern borders.

A savage-looking Mereck rode at their head.

As Rolf entered the great hall at Rimsdale, he was certain the people gathered there didna expect him. His warriors had turned into quarrelsome, clacking women.

All because of Meghan of Blackthorn.

The men who had gone with him in his abduction of her were the most vocal. Alpin urged that Rolf toss Meghan in the dungeon, arguing they had seen firsthand how the woman was as skilled as any one of them.

"Are ye daft, Alpin?" A battle-scarred man laughed. "No lass could ride a horse like a seasoned warrior and disappear into the mist as ye say. Ye must have been tippin' from a keg to break yer fast."

"You think naught but an image put the wound in my thigh?" Alpin shouted. He purpled as it dawned on him how foolish he was to remind them the lass had bested him.

"Why did ye no' use yer own *weapon*?" A man cackled with glee. " 'Tis the proper one to use on a lass, if ye want her soft and pliant."

"Mayhap he did, and the lass found his tarse wanting." A

burly man with a great red beard and but a few strands of red still gracing his shiny dome, slapped his leg with glee.

"Should she be beneath me, the lass willna find my tarse wanting. I warrant Rolf will have gold aplenty when he sells her back to Blackthorn." Alpin hastened to steer the discussion away from his nether parts. " 'Tis said they call her the 'Warrior Woman—the Pride of Blackthorn.' Let us see how much they will pay to have their Pride restored to them."

"Eneuch!" Rolf's blood boiled at the image of Meghan beneath Alpin. Beneath any man, for that matter. "When we sit for the evening meal, ye will all know full well why I have brought the lass here. Until then, I suggest ye all get about yer duties."

The warriors stirred, some not moving fast enough for his liking. He shoved his fists on his hips and glared at them.

"If ye dinna have enough duties to occupy yer time, I think ye might find cleaning the cesspit a worthy chore."

None lingered a moment longer but scrambled out the door. So fast did they leave, the door fair hit the last man on his arse when he scurried through. Alpin and Dougald grinned watching the men's hasty departure.

Rolf's young brother Garith sat on the floor in front of the fireplace. The fingers of his weakened right hand stroked the long, scarred ears of the most fearsome, ugly dog ever to click toes against Rimsdale's floors.

Meghan had taken him to task for his mount's lack of a proper name. When she dubbed his steed Luath, he had to admit she did right by the horse, though he hated to admit it even to himself. Simple was also an apt name. Secreted high atop a tree, he had watched Meghan when she accompanied Blackthorn's hunters, her guards trailing her. He could still hear her bubbling laughter at the bird's hapless antics. She did not bring the bird to hunt food, for her bow and arrow did an admirable job of providing meat for the cook pots. Simple was her pet.

Days later, when he waited for Meghan to feel safe hiding in the cave, the hawk flew low overhead. He watched as the bird swooped down, her talons grabbing a large hare by the hind end. As she labored to fly away, so absorbed was she with keeping her struggling, coveted meal, she neglected to notice a tree in her path. She met its trunk. Head on. When she plopped down, near senseless, her prey darted away. The sparrowhawk wobbled about as if she had been tipping one ale too many.

Aye, Simple was a proper name for the bird.

Meghan would have to admit that "Ugsome" was also a fitting name for the hapless dog.

"What has brought a smile to your face for the first time in many moons? Is it thinkin' on your revenge? What do you plan to do with Meghan of Blackthorn?" Alpin, his pale hair gleaming about his face, sat with one hip on the end of a table. Angry still, his knuckles whitened as he gripped a cup of ale.

"Ye will know when I announce it to one and all this eve." Rolf did not hold back a frown. Alpin presumed on their friendship if he thought he would be privy to Rolf's plans.

Especially to this plan.

"Come, Dougald. 'Tis time to find who battered the Pride of Blackthorn."

"Aye." The big man scratched his head and cursed beneath his breath as they crossed the bailey. "I chose my best men to guard the lass. Each denies any knowledge of the lady's mistreatment. Until this morn, I ne'er had reason to doubt any one of them."

Rolf was determined to punish the man who had defied his orders and accosted Meghan. The men stood, heads close together. Did they hatch excuses to give him? His anger mounted as his mind flashed back to the dark bruise beside her split lips and the torn shirt that had barely covered her.

When he had turned her back to him so he could release her arms, his gaze wandered over her shoulders and spied two lovely, firm breasts. Breasts not pale but as golden brown as Meghan's face and arms.

Sweet Jesus! How came she by the color?

His lips pressed together. How much more of her flesh had seen the sun? Far more disturbing was, who had seen her when she bared herself to its heated rays?

"Rolf?" Dougald looked puzzled. "Is aught amiss?"

How long had they stood there? Rolf realized his teeth were grinding together and tried to relax his jaw.

"Nay." Mayhap it was good he had stopped, for now the men awaiting him appeared even more anxious to prove their loyalty to him.

He walked closer and hesitated in front of each man in turn. Silently, he watched their expressions. All would need strong ale when he was done, by the looks of them. Never had he seen that knot of cartilage in a man's throat bob so often as his men now swallowed.

Slowly circling them, he studied each in turn. He had assigned guards to change at every hour of the Divine Offices, one at the stable door opening and one at the rear. At Vespers when the sun set, at Compline when everyone else sought their pallets, at Vigils marking the end of one day and the beginning of another, and at Matins as dawn broke.

Eight men in all.

Rolf ordered them to stand in line according to the time each man began his watch. They fidgeted even more. He moved ten paces away and called two men at a time to come to him. He didna want them knowing what the others said. The men from Matins were first, for 'twas when they discovered his captive's bruises. He dismissed them both since they had been new on the watch. They wasted no time in leaving.

He motioned forward the two men from Vespers, the beginning of the watch. His eyes narrowed and hardened as he demanded an accounting for every hour the men stood duty. He queried each whether the man had left his post unguarded, perhaps to piss. Both swore they had no need to leave. The grass around the stable provided what was necessary. He next asked whether they had checked their captive at the end of their shift. Satisfied with each man's answers, he released them.

Rolf felt an uneasy presence and turned slightly. Alpin and

his man Fergus stood there. Alpin appeared normal enough, but Fergus stared, his eyes squinted and mean, at the guards he had yet to question. Rolf couldna tell who drew Fergus's feral regard. Suspicious, he shifted to keep both him and his men in sight.

Next came the men from Compline. Both denied leaving their post. The front door guard confirmed the lass looked none the worse when he had cracked open the door to check she was there.

Rolf watched Fergus. The man didna change his attention to the men from Compline but stared at the remaining men assigned for the hour of Vigils. Rolf motioned to the men he had just questioned and bid them return to their training.

The man assigned to guard the back door of the stable darted glances at his partner, then stared at the dirt at his feet. His shoulders hunched. Wary eyes on Fergus, the other man approached Rolf with lagging feet.

Aye, both hid somethin'. Rolf spread his legs wide, folded his arms across his chest to keep from lashing out at them, and glared at each one in turn.

"Two of ye together and still ye were no' able to best the lass?" He slowly walked around them, his muscles tensed with the need to pummel them. "One puny young lass with her arms tied behind her? Her neck tethered to a ring in the wall?" He watched Fergus. The man didna take his glare from the front door guard. So, why did the back door guard also look afrighted? He stopped in front of this man.

And waited, silent.

"I didna think the lass could escape. I but closed my eyes to rest them," he blurted. "The next thing I knew, someone hurtled out the door, his booted foot landin' on me chest." He pulled up his shirt to reveal bruised ribs. "I thought 'twas the girl. I started after her, but then clouds moved from the moon and showed it were a man. He got away."

"Did you go inside to check on the lass?" Though Rolf wanted to shout, he kept his voice quiet. As quiet as a soft breeze.

His head bobbed. "She leaned against the wall. The lass didna cry out. I thought 'twas but a curious intruder who wanted to see Blackthorn's Warrior Woman up close."

Rolf clenched his hands and turned to the last guard. Sweat beaded the man's face. His gaze met his master's. Disgrace and guilt lay like a heavy blanket, weighing his shoulders down.

"I be the man ye should punish, Lord Rolf. Me wife be sickly, and her due with her fourth birthing." He raised shame-filled eyes and straightened his back. "When offered the coins, I kenned it would pay for help with the birthing and caring of the other bairns. He said he wouldna harm her. She gave no outcry. I heard him leave soon after he entered."

Reaching in the pocket of his trews, he pulled out three pence and threw them at Fergus's feet.

Fergus flew at him. His hands grasped the guard's neck, and they toppled to the ground. Astride him now, Fergus tried to throttle him. "Ye stupid, whining fool." The words erupted from deep in his throat. His lips lifted in a snarl. "'Tis yer word against mine. None can prove 'twas me."

Alpin fisted his hands together and slammed them into Fergus's head, knocking him near senseless.

Rolf studied Alpin and rubbed his jaw. "Mayhap the lass will know if 'twas him that struck her or no'." He motioned to several warriors who ran to them. "Take Fergus to the dungeon."

Rolf glared at his own two guards.

"Ye will be whipped. I will wait to have the punishment settled until I have spoken with Meghan of Blackthorn." His eyes narrowed. He must needs know what had happened to her last eve afore he decided the severity of the lashing.

"After a good soakin', Ede, I will be glad of yer help to tend my wounds." Meghan stood beside the bed and looked down at her dirty clothing. Her family had long formed the habit of a bath when possible. "We have learned at Blackthorn that wounds dinna fester if kept clean."

She stripped, quick and efficient, dropping her clothes in a heap on the floor beside the tub. She stepped into the hot water and steeled herself not to cry out.

Bruises covered the bottom of her feet, and her heels wept with blisters. Her shoulders and arms screamed from being held at such an odd angle all the night. Merged with the burns, raw spots ringed her wrists where the rope had rubbed her flesh. 'Twas not all of her problems. It did not include her rope-burned neck, swollen jaw, and split lips or the scratches on her chest where the man's nails had dug when he tore open her blouse.

She was a mess.

Meghan's smile held a touch of irony. If her family could see her now, she would be in for one of Damron's furious lectures and Mereck's quiet scolding that meant even more. Not to mention Connor's livid curses and threats of the dire beating he'd ask Damron to administer on her posterior because she had put herself in harm's way. He couldna bear to do it himself. She shrugged, then winced for the effort.

The picture of Damron, Mereck, and Connor's wives filled her thoughts. She would get no screaming and posturing from them. They would put their heads together with her and help her plan a means to retaliate for each ache. One ache she savored. The back of her head where she cracked it against the bastard's nose.

"Please. Let me help?"

Meghan looked at Ede and saw nothing but kindness on her plump face. When she nodded, the woman smiled and started to wash Meghan's hair. Oh, it felt so good to get the grime off. 'Twas much more than she had ever had on her body, thanks to Rolf cramming her into the dirt at every chance.

"How come you by such beautiful coloring o'er your body, Meghan?" Ede's voice was shy.

"I dinna hide from the sun." Meghan shrugged.

"Are you not afeared the sun will blemish your skin?"

"Nay. What matter if it did?" She looked up and frowned. "I am more than just a body. My worth is not in my skin. 'Tis in my honor. My mind. My skills."

Ede had finished rinsing Meghan's hair and helped her finish her bath. When done, she poured warm rinse water over her. She held up a huge drying cloth, and Meghan wrapped herself in it.

"I will bring fresh clothing of my own for you once we have tended your wounds," Ede told her.

"Nay, thank ye, Ede. I will wear my own." Meghan's chin lifted proudly.

"But dirt covers them, and your shirt is torn. The laundress will wash and return them to you. We will mend them together. You canna go about in a drying cloth." Ede looked serious, then giggled. "Though 'twould cause an uproar fit to bring down the walls if you did."

How could Meghan escape if hampered with yards of cloth tripping her at every turn? "Then I would ask for breeches."

As Ede tended Meghan's wounds, they slid into an easy, yet tentative, peace.

After she was done, Meghan pulled the heavy chair closer to the window. Hearing men yell and scuffle about in the bailey, she stood cautiously on her bandaged feet, clutched the cloth tight to her breasts, and stared out the window.

"Ye should not be standing," Ede scolded as she looked over Meghan's shoulder. " 'Tis good Rolf hasna Beast at his hip or blood would flow, from the looks of him. See. His hands keep fisting like he yearns to throttle the men. Mayhap we will learn why at the noon meal."

Meghan stared hard at the warriors. After they had hauled up the knave who tried to throttle the other, she caught sight of the knave's swollen nose. She reached up and rubbed the back of her head, tender still from crashing it against her assailant last night. She smiled. She had spied the man this morn but wanted to be certain. Now she had no doubt. She would recognize his face until Hades turned cold as a loch in winter.

"Speakin' of the noon meal, I think I can find breeches and a shirt that will do." Ede stood back the better to judge Meghan's form, then turned on her heels and left the room.

When she returned, she helped Meghan into soft brown breeches and a white cotton shirt tied at the neck with a white ribbon threaded through three holes on either side. Over the top went a dark brown tunic that came below her knees. Meghan looped the rope belt around her waist, letting it ride lower in front than in back. She could put no shoes over her bandaged feet, but Ede gave her thick wool stockings to cover them.

"Why do you not want to wear women's clothin' within the castle? I will be pleased to lend you any of mine," Ede asked.

"I ne'er wear skirts if I can help it. Why should men have the comfort of breeches when we must drag a mountain of cloth about our legs?" Meg raised her brows at Ede.

Ede put her fingers to her jaw and studied Meghan. "I never thought of such. Hmm, you do have it aright about them dragging around our legs. This past winter, I kicked at mine and ended on my back deep in the snow." She grinned at the memory and beckoned to Meghan.

"Come, sit, and I will work the snarls from your hair. I canna ken why Rolf did not bring you into the castle." She shook her head and muttered, "Never have I seen him treat a woman so."

Neither had Meghan. When she was but a lassie, Rolf had treated her with kindness. He had oft praised her skills when she proved as proficient as the fostered lads who trained at Blackthorn. But later, never had he treated her gently as a woman. Now, she didna know the reason for his hatred.

She had but one great fear kept hidden deep but sensed Rolf knew of it. Many years ago, his father had brought him to Blackthorn while he sought the help of her grandda, old Laird Douglas. That noon, Meghan escaped her nursemaid and hid in the storage area at Blackthorn Castle to play with a kitten.

When he went there to drink from a small cask of wine stolen from the laird's table, the blacksmith's cruel son found her. Afraid she would tell, he lifted her high and shook her till she spewed her porridge over his head. After he slapped her hard and she cried out, he clamped a hand over her mouth and crept through the shadows of the castle to carry her to the dungeons below. After tossing her in a slimy cell, he slammed the door shut.

It was darker than the deepest night and she couldna see. She found her way to the door, but she was too small to budge it. Sure that Lucifer lurked, waiting to pull her into a deep pit, she huddled against a wall and cried the night through.

The next day, Rolf, with a frantic Connor following close behind, found her. She never revealed how she came to be there.

'Twas after that that she determined to learn the skills to defend herself.

Once Ede combed the last tangle from Meghan's hair, Meghan stood and looked about the room. She shuddered. This was Rolf's lair. She had tried hard to ignore that fact. His chain mail hung on the stand, his helmet perched atop it. A black robe hung on a wall peg, with a clothing chest sitting below it.

Earlier when he had dropped her on the bed like he couldna abide her touch against his body, the soft sheets of the bedding had enveloped her in a sensual cloud of his scent. As if he joined her there. She couldna rest in that bed.

"If he doesna chain me in the dungeon, where am I to sleep this night?"

"Why, with me, Meghan. Now that I no longer have my Angus to share it, I have space aplenty on my bed." Ede's hands caressed a soft wool cloak she had folded and placed atop the table. "'Tis his clothing you wear. He was not comely or big like Rolf, but he was the only man in the world I would share myself with."

"Oh, Ede." Meghan put a hand on the woman's shoulder. "Are ye sure ye would have me wearin' his clothin'? I know not why, but Rolf treats me as his greatest enemy. I would think ye would feel the same."

"Nay. Never think it." Ede frowned and would have spoken further, but the armed guard posted outside their door rapped his sword against it and then threw it open.

"Lord Rolf orders the Lady Meghan to come below." He scowled and jerked his hand, motioning for her to hurry.

"I ken 'tis time I be carted to the dungeon." Meghan swallowed her fear and forced her body to stand tall and proud. She wouldna give Rolf the pleasure of seeing her cowed.

CHAPTER 9

"Unhand me," Meghan ordered. Though the guard's harsh fingers dug into her bruised upper arm, she ignored the pain. "Do ye think I can escape ye with my feet bandaged and no boots to cover them?"

"I heard tales of how ye can disappear at will. I will take no chances and have me back flayed like he is about to do another's," he muttered as he shoved her ahead of him.

Meghan gulped. So, Rolf would tie her to a post and whip her? Why did he bother having Ede tend her wounds if he was about to create more? It didna make sense.

"Hold, guard." Ede deftly slipped in front of him. "Lord Rolf can wait but a few moments more for you to allow our legs to keep up with yours."

Meghan knew Ede slowed her steps to make it easier for her to walk with dignity, instead of stumbling about like a drunk varlet. Saints help her. She must look a fright with her bruised face and salves and bandages from head to toes. Thankfully, much of it was hidden beneath her borrowed clothing.

As the guard led her out into the bailey, she feared her heart drummed so loud a toothless old man sitting on the ground could hear it. Ede walked alongside her. Feeling the stares of Rolf's people, Meghan was comforted by the kind woman's support. Several faces she recognized from yester eve's crowd, but those seeing her for the first time looked surprised, as if she were a strange apparition. What tales had they heard? Not all looked askance, though. Many studied the dirt at their feet, appearing shamed.

She caught her breath. The guard led her to stand not twenty paces from the whipping post. Rolf, his back to her, talked with his silver-haired friend. Alpin, by name, she remembered. Garith stood on Rolf's other side. Alpin spied her first and trailed off into silence. His pale blue eyes widened as he studied her.

Rolf spoke to him. When he did not answer, Rolf turned to see what distracted his friend. A scowl soon covered his face.

"Bring the woman and be quick about it."

Rolf's angry face boded ill for her. Her scalp crawled. Would she be able to remain silent after the first stroke of the lash? Or would she scream, shaming herself?

"I knewed he would be angry for havin' to wait," the guard hissed at her; then he shoved her the last few feet to his master's side.

Without the added height her boots provided, Meghan was a finger width from reaching Rolf's chin. She stiffened her back and stared up at him, eye to eye.

Rolf stared back. Slow and deliberate, his gaze left hers to travel over her hair flowing about her shoulders and down her back. He studied her face. His gaze stopped to examine every mark. When his silvery eyes looked at her neck, she pulled the top of the shirt to cover more of the nasty rope burns there. That drew his stare lower, for her sleeves had fallen back and bared her bandaged wrists. She lowered her hands so the shirt again covered them.

Saints! She could do nothing about her feet encased in the bulky wool stockings, other than to hunker down on her heels to hide them. Hell. She was twitching as much as her sister-by-law Elise did when Connor glowered at her for some slight misdemeanor. Be damned to Rolf. She firmed her jaw and straightened her shoulders.

"If ye think me such an unsightly mess to look at now, ye will find me far worse if that whip is meant for me," she warned.

Garith gasped and looked at his brother. Rolf graced her with an even bigger frown. "Nay. Not for you."

His eyes narrowed and he added, "Yet."

He must have remembered her taking her knife to him. Aye. 'Twas that for sure, for he stared into her eyes to force her to acknowledge she understood. He fixed her with a glare until she nodded at him.

Three men stood there, each with a guard behind them. They were the same men who were with him in the bailey earlier when she and Ede heard the commotion. To guard them? She spied the lout who accosted her during the night and scowled at him. Hard. Unwavering. She would ne'er forget his face.

"I have summoned you to tell me what befell you last eve. What did this man take by force from you?"

"Is he not Sir Alpin's man?" Had Rolf not seen her bound and tethered, no man would have tried to force himself on her. Even hampered as she was, she had stopped him from taking that which he had been intent upon. She would fight her own battles. One day, she would avenge herself.

"Aye, but you have not answered the question." Rolf waved his arm toward the man, irritated.

"He took nothin' from me." She glared up at him. "No man will take aught from me by force and live to see the sun rise the next morn."

"Then how came you by the bruise on your face, the cuts on your lips?" Impatient, he shifted as he awaited her answer.

"I fell against the crate."

He did not believe her, for his eyes narrowed, his lips thinned in anger. When he reached to feel over the crown of her head and found the swollen lump there, she winced.

"Aye, and sure you did. I ken you gained this lump when you bounced back against the opposite wall, hmm?"

"Somethin' like that." She shrugged and refused to look away. "Though not against the opposite wall. Ye well know yer tether gave me but a few paces to move."

Ha! Was that shame that flashed through his eyes? His jaw twitched, and his brows near met in the middle of his forehead.

"How can I mete out fair punishment if I dinna have the truth?" he shouted.

"The truth is that ye thought me so loathsome ye bound and tethered me in a stable and left your guards to see I didna slaughter all in their beds," she yelled back. "By yer actions, ye made me helpless. Fair game. I willna help soothe yer soul by placin' the blame on another."

She turned her back on him.

He twirled her around and lowered his face until his nose touched hers. His voice lowered, ominous in the way he spoke through a jaw held so tight he forced the words through his teeth. "Ne'er turn your back on me, Meghan of Blackthorn, unless ye want to feel the flat o' my hand on your proud rump." Each word came out deliberate, careful, a slight pause between them.

Before she could reply, he stalked over to Fergus. His right fist flashed out to blacken the man's eye, his left streaked to slam into his stomach. As the lout began to fall, Rolf grabbed his tunic to hold him upright and pummeled him until Rolf finally grunted with satisfaction. He hoisted Fergus higher, sucked in a deep breath, and his right fist sped up from low on his body to crack against Fergus's jaw. He toppled like a fallen tree and was out like a candle's flame held afore a brisk evening breeze.

"Alpin, if Fergus ever again dares enter Rimsdale's lands, I will see him whipped back across the borders. I want him gone. Now."

Alpin winced at the roar of Rolf's voice. He beckoned to several men, who hauled the senseless man over to a waiting horse and threw him over its back. They tied him there, then mounted and led the horse out Rimsdale's gates.

The horses' hooves striking the stones as they crossed the bridge sounded like an ominous message. No one moved until the horsemen disappeared into the woods. Rolf turned a grim face toward his own two warriors.

"I should turn you from my service. I ken how you thought 'twas no vicious captive you guarded but a woman. Ten lashes for falling asleep while on guard," he said to the first man, then turned to the next.

"Ten and five lashes for taking money to shirk your duty. Had your woman not been expectin' her fourth, I would see you gone from here. In all conscience, I canna deprive her of your help."

"Not deprive her of his help?" Meghan asked in disbelief. "What aid do ye think he will give if he isna able to move about for the next sennight?" She shoved her hands on her hips.

"Barbarian! Neither man deserves to be whipped. At Blackthorn, we have not the need of the whip. Had ye better treated yer men, one wouldna been so worn he fell asleep. Had ye provided for them, the other wouldna have taken coins."

"Not content to strut about attired in men's clothing, are you? Now you wish to direct me on how to discipline mine own men?" He folded his arms and eyed her as if he thought she had lost her wits. "So. Tell me how *Sir* Meghan would mete out fitting discipline."

Her eyes scanned the bailey as she rubbed the side of her nose, thinking. She noted the various structures built against the base of the curtain wall and nodded.

"If a warrior sleeps durin' guard duty atop the gatehouse or battlements, around a camp or siege site, I wouldna haggle with whippin'. Were he under my orders in *those* circumstances, he could verra well lose the skin on his hide," Meghan allowed.

The warrior's face blanched and he gulped. Fear flashed in his eyes as he stared at Meghan. She looked at him and frowned.

"Such lack of discipline could cause the death of his comrades or the defeat of a castle." She paused for a moment. "But this man guarded a woman rendered helpless, one he knew was powerless to do harm. For a sennight, set him to cleanin' the cesspit. I doubt he would sleep afore the chore was done."

"Yew!" Garith wrinkled his nose in disgust.

As Rolf watched the man, the warrior's face showed emotions that ranged from abject fear to revulsion. The duty was one a common varlet would do. Degrading. Aye. This discipline the man would remember.

"What of the guard who took coins?" Rolf raised a brow, curious as to what punishment she would mete out.

"If ye flog him with ten and five lashes, he wouldna be of use to his wife and bairns for the next fortnight. Did he for certes take the money to aid his family, then he should be put to tasks for a fortnight to earn his needs."

Still thinking, she squinted her eyes. "On Saturdays, he will carry his family's clothin' to the laundress and help her wash them." Hearing the shocked mutters of the warriors, she glared them to silence and took an aggressive stance, legs spread wide. "Each weekday after his warrior's practice, I ken the cook could use his help preparin' the noon meal. In return, she will give him an extra crock of food to take to his family."

Garith snickered and brought a hand up to cover the sound.

When Rolf spied his man's eyes bugged wide and his head shaking as if to deny what he had heard, he held back the beginning of a smile. Humiliation was a deadly penance. Were his own plans for Connor not built on such?

Forgetful of the bruises there, Meghan tapped her finger to her cheek, then winced. "Ye have a weaving hut, do ye not?"

He nodded and waited, more curious now to hear what Meghan would devise for the rest of the discipline. He soon found out. She looked up at him and continued.

"At Blackthorn, a man of advanced years works with the looms and helps with the weavin'. I see no reason this man canna do the same. Late in the day from Monday through Friday, he will make any repairs on the structure or looms, clean the floors, and carry the completed cloth to the storage room. On the hours he is doin' these chores for them, the women will work on weavin' blankets and cloth for his wife and children."

"You forgot Sundays, *Sir* Meghan." Rolf kept his face iron hard, though he longed to laugh aloud. The men's eyes beseeched him to take the whip to their backs. By the devil's tarse! Not one of his warriors would e'er dare incur his wrath while Meghan of Blackthorn was about.

Meghan looked at him and huffed. "Why, he will attend mass, of course, to give prayers of thanks for yer sparin' his life. Wounds from the whip often fester. He could verra well succumb from infections after a lashin'."

"So be it," Rolf decreed. He walked over to stand in front of the two guards. "You will start your duties this next morn. Until then, think long and hard on this. My first intent was to turn you from my service after the whippings. Know you this! Should you ever fail me so again, that will be your fate."

Seeing the men blanch satisfied him.

"Come." He motioned to all around him. "Our meal will soon be cold if we dinna soon sit to it."

As Meghan started to limp away with Ede, he moved close and offered his arm. She looked down at it but did not place her hand there. He straightened his arm and held it in front of her, halting her. His eyes told her she would not move another step until she accepted his proffered courtesy.

"I dinna need yer escort," she grumbled.

"E'en so, you will take it." So light was her touch on his wrist, it held no more weight than a butterfly.

Meghan hated the way her pulse raced and her knees weakened when she felt Rolf's heat. He had bathed, washed his hair, and shaved all but the bristle framing his lower jaw and upper lip. The clean smell of soap scented with sandalwood drifted to her on a light breeze. Her stomach tightened and her heart skipped a beat. His clothing was clean and neat in shades of deep gray. The feel of crisp hair covering the hot flesh of his wrist felt too intimate, making her want to jerk her hand away.

"Dinna move it, Meghan of Blackthorn," Rolf cautioned.

Ah, so he had felt her wish to put distance between them.

"You know, do you not, that after hearing of those shameful duties, they were ready to beg for my punishment?"

"Shame is a harsh master, but they will both remember this next fortnight. Ne'er again will either shirk their duties." She frowned as she thought of the man's three children. "Ye will allow the food and clothin' for the bairns?"

"Did you think I would not?"

She shrugged and did not answer. She fixed her gaze on the ground and forced one foot in front of the other, her jaw tight against the pain. At last they entered the great hall, and he led her to a stool where she sat. Ede was to her left, Garith to her right, beside his brother. Alpin and Dougald occupied the seats on the other side of Rolf.

Savory aromas drifting from the trencher of stew placed in front of her reminded her how long she had been without an adequate meal. The men laughed and commented on the unusual morning's events. She looked up and noted a hint of respect mingled with curiosity in some eyes. Others were wary. All eyed her unusual clothing.

"I have heard tales that you stand atop the gatehouse and pipe the greetings and farewells with your clan piper." Ede's face was full of curiosity. "They said the music traveled twice the distance, sounding as an echo one to the other."

"I enjoy the pipes, and Laird Damron doesna object." For the first time, Meghan felt the need to defend her love of the pipes.

"I should not think he would. We laid our own piper to rest but two months past. 'Tis unfortunate none other play near to his equal." Ede sighed.

Beneath the table came the distinct clink of an animal's nails on the floor as it padded closer. Meghan's nape prickled, warning her of danger. Low, rumbling growls, followed by a feral snarl sounded nearby. At her feet.

She stiffened. Had blood seeped through the heavy bandage and hose she wore? Little did it matter. The beast would smell it even had she worn stout leather boots.

"Nay," Garith shouted as he stuck his head beneath the table. "Come, Ugsome." He grasped a large, hairy head by the nape and coaxed the animal out into the open. "Dinna be affrighted. He will not bite unless I let him," the young man informed her.

Meghan clasped her hands under her chin and tried to look properly afeared. Not an easy task when she fought laughter. She knew her face must be red with the effort to hold it in. Mayhap they would account it to fright.

"I approve of the name for your dog," Meghan gasped. "His ugliness makes him mighty fearsome. Why, he must have been in many a battle and won out, what with half an ear on one side and the other so battle scarred."

"Aye. He has known many battles. Like a true warrior, is he not?" Garith's chest puffed up with pride for his dog.

"Aye. Indeed."

She looked the dog over, noting his other features. A long scar ran from his left eye to his jaw, causing his face to look lopsided. His tail lacked hair, the skin there ravaged from burns. When he bared his teeth and growled at her again, her eyes widened in surprise. She covered her mouth. The act would doubtless make her appear witless with terror. God's truth, it was the only way she could hold back loud, boisterous laughter. The "fearsome" creature lacked three upper front teeth.

"Ye willna let him attack me, will ye, Garith?" She kept her voice a solemn plea.

Rolf, about to leave the room, stopped and watched the exchange between her and his brother. He rubbed his chin for a moment before he returned to them.

"Lady Meghan, you may move about within the castle, but dinna think to escape. Ugsome willna allow you past the front door. A guard will be close by." He turned to the dog, pointed his finger at Meghan, and issued a stern order. "Stay. She isna to leave." He watched as Ugsome snapped his teeth, growled, and stalked close to her side.

Ede gasped and backed away from the creature.

Rolf motioned his brother forward. "Come, Garith. Father Mark awaits at the chapel to teach you your letters."

As they left, Meghan walked close to the hearth. The dog growled and snapped his teeth at her heels.

"I dread to leave you alone with this monster of a dog," Ede said as she trailed after Meghan, "but last eve Rolf requested a special meal for this night. I must plan with the cook."

"Nay, Ede. Have no fear. Ugsome and I will deal well together."

"Deal well? Mayhap if you sit very still and cause him no alarm, he will leave you be." Seeing the cook waiting for her, she cast Meghan a sympathetic smile and hurried to him.

Meghan spent an interesting afternoon testing the dog. She hid her grins, though, for she knew not who watched. Blackthorn had their own four-legged guard. His name was Guardian, a very beautiful and very large gray and white wolf. The difference between the two was striking. Guardian had not one hair of bluster on his whole body. He was every inch a menace to anyone threatening his adored Brianna and Damron or to the rest of the family as well. One fateful day, he had torn the throat from a man who had harmed Brianna.

Nay. Beneath this dog's scruffy exterior lay a lonesome soul begging for love. She kept her body between Ugsome and the door so she could work with him. When no one watched, she had pocketed choice bits of meat from her trencher. With a few soft commands and lavish praise, coupled with a treat from her pocket, he soon responded to a few hand signals. Firm but friendly strokes on his head showed the dog she did not fear him.

To test how well they understood each other, she stood. Her right forefinger lifted to touch her chin. Ugsome rose and followed her. She ignored the man set to watch her at the door to the great room. As if warding off a cry of fear, she placed two fingers to her lips. The beast growled and acted fearsome.

Rushes stirred with each step she took. Thanks be to the saints, they were clean and not fouled with debris from dogs and men alike. 'Twould do her harm if they soiled her bandages. As she neared the stairway leading above, she felt eyes following her every movement. Her flesh tingled and heated.

Someone stripped her flesh bare with his eyes.

Someone teased that flesh with his carnal thoughts as surely as if hot, callused hands stroked every inch of her.

Meghan did not turn, didna acknowledge he stood there. She would not give him the satisfaction of knowing she felt fear.

Not fear of Ugsome. Not fear of his men.

Fear of him—of what was in his thoughts.

Rolf. She sensed what he planned for her.

She, too, wished he had lashed her at the stake and been done with it.

CHAPTER 10

Heat infused Rolf as he watched Meghan, graceful despite her bruises and cuts. Hers was the fluid grace of a woman born to tease a man with every move of her body. He lost himself in the sway of her limbs, as he envisioned stripping her clothing away, baring her pliant, gleaming flesh to his eyes.

Eager, his tarse stirred beneath his trews, and the thought of his hand on that sweetly curved arse made every inch of him restless with anticipation.

Ugsome followed close at her heels, snapping and snarling. The dog had been queerish in the head after tangling with two wolves several winters ago. A pang of guilt shot through him for setting such an unstable creature to guard Meghan. Still, he couldna back down. Meghan would see such an action as a sign of weakness.

Nor would he relent in his plans. How alike they were. Each knew shame and humiliation as the worst of all punishments.

'Twas because of their pride, their sense of honor, of course.

The punishment she elected for his men did not shame them so much for honor as 'twas a blow to their manliness.

With the Pride of Blackthorn, his plans struck to the root of her honor. Through her, he would deliver an insult to Connor he couldna ignore. When he learned of it, he would come for her. When he did, Rolf would wreak vengeance on his family's killer. He refused to think on what would happen to Meghan because of it.

In 1072, he had returned to Rimsdale and found his Ingirid near death after birthing his son. The tiny bairn did not live out the day and passed just moments afore Ingirid.

Garith told him 'twas one of the men wearing a Blackthorn tartan that pushed Ingirid down the stairs. If only Alpin had arrived sooner. His friend told him the raiders fled as he and his men approached. Rolf felt some satisfaction, though. Alpin and his warriors overtook several raiders and killed them. Unfortunately, their leader escaped. When Alpin's patrol entered Rimsdale, with wounds to prove 'twas a hard-fought battle, they brought the bloodied tartans back with them.

Nay, no vengeance was too severe for leaving his Ingirid paralyzed and unable to speak. So soon to die. He hardened his heart to images of Meghan when he was done with her. Not until he avenged his wife and son's deaths would his own honor settle again about his mind like the familiar cloak it had been in the past.

"Rolf, you have eyed an empty stairway nigh on minutes now," Dougald's harsh voice gentled with amusement.

"I have just entered." Rolf turned to frown at his commander.

"Aye." Dougald nodded his head solemnly. "For what reason then does a servant await your answer to a question she has thrice asked?" Dougald shook his head and clucked his tongue much like an old nursemaid, to Rolf's way of thinking.

"Aye, lass?" The young girl's blue eyes grew round as she looked up at him. Her red hair had come loose from a braid tied with a ragged yellow ribbon, and a lock fell over her left eye. Without conscious thought, Rolf brushed the strand back from her face. Her eyes widened and her arms quivered, almost dropping the bloodied plaids she carried. Behind her, a squire carried a hauberk, tunic, and helmet, all marked as Blackthorn's.

"Master, what did ye want we should be doin' with these?" The girl's voice squeaked out her request.

Rolf motioned over a sturdy male servant. "Attach these"—he pointed to the tartans the girl carried—"behind the high table and to the walls at either side. I want them visible from the doorway and from seating at the table."

He clenched his jaw and stared hard at the soiled garments. "Bring a frame from the barracks and place the hauberk and tunic on it. The helmet goes atop where it belongs."

Where should he have them stand it? Not where Meghan would see it right off. He would save it for his announcement. 'Twould be fitting to have it brought to face her seat at the table at the right moment. As if Connor bore witness to what he had to say. That brought a flicker of satisfaction. Bit by bit, his vengeance would build until the cloth of his honor was whole again.

In Ede's room, the hours dragged for Meghan. Ede hurried through the doorway, cautious to make a wide arc around Ugsome. Meghan asked for a bucket of warmed water. After it arrived, fearful that her foray into the dusty bailey had dirtied her wounds, she removed the bandages and put her feet into the water.

"I dinna understand Rolf." Ede shook her head and looked baffled. "He insists everyone but the guards atop the walls are to attend the great hall for the evening meal. He ordered a feast more likened to a celebration. I know not why."

"A feast?" Meghan's brows knotted. "Is it his saint's day or mayhap Garith's?" She could think of no other reason for such festivities at this time of year.

"Nay. Garith was born but a sennight before Christ's Day."

"'Tis yet the middle of September." Meghan examined her sore feet to make sure they were clean. To escape Rimsdale, her wounds must heal so she could wear her boots. If she could not spirit Storm away, she must needs run long and hard to avoid capture.

"Never have I known Rolf to care what meal is placed afore him. Only that it be untainted and plentiful."

Meghan took a deep breath as the pleasant steam wafted from the water, calming her. It was her favorite scent. Why had she not noted it that morning? She smiled, for it was the one vanity she allowed herself to enjoy. That someone at Rimsdale also liked heather pleased her.

"Did ye order the soap scented with heather when they made it?" She was curious, for Ede's clean scent was more like spring roses.

"Oh, nay." Ede brought an extra drying cloth. She pulled a stool close within Meghan's reach and placed the cloth on it.

" 'Tis unusual for the soap maker to do such on her own." Of a sudden, Meghan remembered Ingirid. "Oh, 'tis sorry I am I mentioned it. Rolf's wife likely preferred heather."

"Nay. She also favored the rose." Ede shrugged and looked puzzled. "Many months ago Rolf ordered the soap made and stored with the linens. He permitted no one to use it till now. Yesternight he bade me fetch it."

Meghan dropped the bathing cloth she was wringing dry. It made a small splash as it plopped into the water. Her heart pounded. Did he recall those many years ago whispering how her heather fragrance pleased him? For certain he did not. Not the hardened and bitter man she knew today.

She willed her thoughts to cease. As she snatched the cloth up, droplets flew out and landed on Ugsome beside her. He snuffled and grumbled deep in his throat, affrighting Ede to the other side of the room.

Meghan dropped her hand down to her side, opened flat to the floor. The dog quieted and put his head on his paws, his soulful eyes watching her.

"This night being special for some reason, would you not wish to wear soft clothing against your body?" Ede's hesitant voice sounded hopeful. In her earlier visits, she told Meghan to make free with her Angus's clothes. She eyed the fresh shirt and breeches Meghan had folded atop the bed.

"I dinna wish to appear weak and womanly afore Rolf. I would be more vulnerable if attired in gowns and such."

He hated her boyish attire. She would wear nothing but such clothing as long as he kept her here.

Ede clucked over Meghan's still-swollen lips and applied

salves to her scraped neck, tending the wounds Meghan could not see. Meghan took the small jar of salve to care for her feet. If she wore heavy woolen hose over them, she would not need wrappings. Still, she could not wear her leather boots.

"He has even ordered the rushes changed." As Ede braided her hair, a slight frown wrinkled her forehead. "And sprinkled with meadowsweet and rosemary. Never can I recall him noticing rushes," she murmured. Her eyes widened as she glanced at Meghan.

Meghan shrugged and, without a wasted movement, donned the breeches and shirt that were on the bed. As she strapped the wide leather belt about her waist, she frowned, missing the dirk and short sword that always rode against her thighs. She narrowed her eyes and determined that afore the sennight was over, she would again feel their weight as she made her way back to Blackthorn.

"What brings such a look to your face, Meghan? Do your feet pain you?" Ede hurried over, ready to offer aid.

"Nay." Meghan smiled and reassured her. "It is but disgust that I canna wear my boots."

Ede picked up a wooden comb and tapped it against her chin. Her eyes lit with an idea. "You have such thick hair. 'Tis a lovely deep brown, and my hands itch to try something. Will you allow me to fashion it?"

"Aye. 'Twould please me."

It would do no harm to give this kind woman her way. Ede had looked distressed that she would not wear feminine apparel, and it was relaxing to have someone manage her heavy tresses. She felt Ede take sections from each temple, bring them to the back, and start to braid them together. As she worked her way down the back of Meghan's head, she added more sections of hair. After she was done, Ede sighed and clapped her hands in delight.

"Oh, Meghan. You look like a lady of Malcolm's court." Ede held a polished sheet of metal for Meghan to peer at.

The face Meghan saw reflected there startled her. If she didna take into account her swollen jaw and split lips, the woman looking back at her appeared soft and feminine. Curly wisps of hair brushed the sides of her cheeks, and the rest had been drawn back into a braid that accented the delicate bones of her face.

Delicate?

Her mouth gaped open with shock. How could she, Meghan, the Warrior Woman of Blackthorn, look delicate? She swallowed and studied the image again. Mayhap it wouldna be a bad thing to look soft and feminine. In their male ego, the men at Rimsdale would think her helpless and resigned to be their captive.

"Lady Ede," a voice called outside the door. "Lord Rolf would have ye and the Lady Meghan come below."

Meghan stood and rubbed her right forefinger against her chin, as if she tested it for soreness. Ugsome jumped to his feet to follow her from the room.

"I dinna see why Rolf must needs have Ugsome guard you." Ede trailed behind, wary of the huge dog. "You dinna need both a guard and the beast as well."

Meghan stopped in front of the guard, put two fingers on her lower lip and hesitated, acting unsure of where she was to go.

Ugsome began to act fierce. His growls and snarls made the guard grip the hilt of his sword.

"Oh, Saints help me, dinna let us upset this fearsome dog," she beseeched him as she allowed her voice to quaver. 'Twas not hard, for she wanted to laugh at his uncertain look.

Why did the man study her as if he had not seen her but hours ago? By the way he offered her his arm, she realized Ede's handiwork was responsible. She gave his sleeve a light tug to remind him they were to go below to the great hall.

"Dinna ye worry. I will see to yer safety." He blinked at her and led her down the stairs. Ugsome growled with each step as he followed behind.

Below, Rolf studied the room, approving of the clean and sweet-smelling rushes on the floor, the cloths upon the high table, and the silver cups placed there. His eyes scanned the walls. The Blackthorn plaids drew the eye as one came into the room. She wouldna fail to note them.

Hearing Ugsome's growls before the dog even came into view, Rolf turned his gaze to the stairway. Meghan allowed Jamie to aid her. Rolf stiffened. She fought him, denied *him* that same courtesy, yet she smiled sweetly up at her guard, her hand on his arm. Rolf's lips tightened and his hands fisted.

Devil take it! Where came she by that clothing? The overlarge shirt should have looked manly on her. It did not. Flowing to just below her knees, it resembled a wide-sleeved tunic. Even the leather belt that rode low on her hips in front did not look out of place. 'Twas unusual to see Meghan of Blackthorn without weapons at her side.

To his eye, she appeared dressed in but a loose-fitting tunic with woolen stockings cross-gartered up her calves. He caught a glimpse of breeches beneath the hem of the shirt. Hearing the restless moves of his men behind him, he glanced around to find his men studied his captive with as much interest as he had. His brow lowered and his temper stirred.

Meghan and the guard reached the last step, and she dropped her hand to her side as Rolf came to meet her.

"I trust you have rested since noon?" he asked as he offered his arm. When she clenched her fist and refused to take it, he stiffened.

Ugsome shoved between them and started to bare his teeth and snap at the hem of her shirt. He reached down and tugged on the ruff of the dog's neck.

"Quiet. I will take o'er from here." Ugsome paid him no mind. Irritated, he turned and motioned to his brother, who looked nervous as he eyed the Blackthorn trophies. "Garith. Quiet this beast so I may hear myself think."

As Garith reached them, Rolf noted Meghan wiped her hand on her shirt as if the dog had made it sweat. Ugsome snapped his teeth together and stood, quiet, until Garith led him away.

"He has taken a dislike to you. Never has he been so fierce with anyone." Rolf watched her face to see her reaction. "Mayhap 'tis because he knows you hail from Blackthorn."

"Like as not he mimics his laird's evil temper," Meghan replied. She gazed up at him and waited.

"Evil temper? Rolf?" Alpin sounded surprised as he came to stand beside them. He looked from one to the other. His gaze dallied overlong on Meghan's form, building Rolf's ire.

"'Tis best you beware of my 'evil' temper," Rolf snapped. To which one he sent the warning, he did not know. Both perhaps.

He studied Meghan and noted the soft look of her face. Ah, 'twas her hair. He approved of the style. It drew attention to light eyes the color of spring leaves, and full, luscious lips. Those lips that could fire words of ice, yet made him yearn to trace their outline with his tongue. Would they taste of the coolness of mint if he were to nibble and suckle their softness between his teeth?

More likely of fire, from the looks of them now as he led her to the high table. She spied the Blackthorn tunics. She did not speak. He could almost hear her thoughts: *Where came he by them*? He would bide his time till she asked. Connor would not have admitted to her he had attacked a woman, helpless with her body swollen with a babe.

He motioned with his hand for her to take the seat to his left, but she hesitated. His firm hand on her shoulder persuaded her to sit. Garith settled between her and Ede, the ever-present Ugsome at their feet.

Rolf poured wine from a flask into the silver cup between them, then filled the trencher they would share with the most succulent of the roast pig, salmon, and lamb. Meghan was a hearty eater, but her manners were ladylike and dainty. Much more so than any woman at Rimsdale.

How could she be anything else, for she had spent many months at the court in Normandy? She and Connor were orphaned at the same time as raiders killed Damron's father. Her aunt, Lady Phillipa, took all three children to spend the summer months in Normandy with her family for courtly training. Mereck was left behind, for his grandda wanted to keep him close. Anyone who dared call Mereck bastard, though he was, would find himself trounced into the ground, be he prince or varlet.

Alpin, Dougald, Ede, and Garith tried to bring him and Meghan into conversation, to no avail. He could feel her tension build with each passing breath. Still, she did not ask. Tension seemed to spark from her and spread around the room. His people started to twitch on their benches, to look toward her with expectant faces. He watched out of the corner of his eye to assess how long she could contain her temper.

She began to shift about and refused to look at the walls. Her body started to give off a heat and caused her heathery scent to float and surround him. His loins heated, as they always did, whenever he smelled heather. On her. Ever since that summer in Normandy, it never failed to excite him.

Ah. He sensed she was now coiled so tight she was ready to spring from her seat. He counted in his mind as she picked up the wine and took a healthy swallow. One . . . two . . . three . . . four . . . five . . . six . . . He did not make it to seven.

Meghan could no longer hold herself back. She slammed the cup on the table and sprang to her feet. Wine sloshed over the rim and splattered like droplets of blood on the white cloth. Faces turned toward her, their expressions alert.

"How came ye by bloodied Blackthorn plaids?" Meghan clenched her teeth and stared down at him, awaiting his answer. Her heart beat faster. No raiding patrols had gone out in the short time she was at Rimsdale, and he had not fought anyone from Blackthorn afore he overtook her.

"When they raided here those two years past, Blackthorn men led them." Rolf's gray eyes narrowed as he rose, slow and deliberate.

"Raided? Never has Blackthorn raided into Rimsdale lands." How could he tell such a lie? "Ye well know a bargain was struck between yer father and Old Laird Douglas. Laird Damron would ne'er break it. 'Tis ye who raid deep into Blackthorn's villages. Ye leave missives to prove it."

They faced each other, both so tense that if a spadeful of peat lay between them, it would ignite.

"Aye, we leave them. Do you ken what they say? Or was Connor too great a coward to show you?"

"If Connor ne'er showed me the notes, he didna for his own reason. He has not a coward's bone in his body." She grasped the belt that rested on her hips, else she would strike him for saying such about her brother. Rolf's written words had made no sense. *Ye destroyed that which I loved most. Look to yer own.* "The Morgans of Blackthorn have taken naught from ye."

"Aye, they took from me! What they took I held most dear."

"What? They have taken nothin' from ye," she shouted. "If one of our men broke the agreement, he did so without Connor or Damron's knowin'." She smacked her hand down on the table so hard it rattled the cups nearby.

"My wife!" Rolf struck the table with his fist. Cups flew. "My son!" He struck again, so hard she heard a board crack.

"Nay!" she screamed. "Ne'er would Connor do such."

Rolf turned and nodded to a squire who stood close behind him. While Meghan watched, the young man brought a heavy stand that held armor. His body was between her and the stand until he placed it on the floor across from her and drew back.

Meghan caught her breath. It held a helmet, a hauberk, a tunic. Blood stained them, the tunic's sleeves as well. Bile surged to her throat, almost choking her. There for all to see was the elegant Gaelic letter for *C* on the front of the helmet and the bloodied tunic. She could not speak.

"Because she refused to yield to him, your 'honorable' brother pitched Ingirid down those very same steps that brought you to the great hall." He spit the words at her with icy venom.

"Ye are wrong! He couldna." She denied him. "When did this ghastly thing happen? I will prove to ye it wasna him." Never would Connor do such to any woman. Women made their way unbidden into his bed. That is, until Elise entered his life.

Rolf's hard stare cut through her. It was then she realized the silence in the room. All held their breath as they watched and listened to what passed between their lord and his captive.

"I was with Hereward the Wake. In 1072, leagues outside Abernethy, King William's patrols came across us. In order for Hereward to get away, others and I led them in an opposite direction. They captured and held me. I escaped and made my way home. I entered hell!" He reached for the flask of wine and drank straight from it, his expression bleak with his memories.

"Do you ken what it is like to return home to find someone you love unable to move even a finger? Unable to speak?" His jaw hardened, his hands clenched. "Naught but her eyes could move. They filled with a terror so horrible it burned my soul to see it. My bairn lay beside her. Too small. Too helpless."

Tears filled his eyes. Meghan near cried out seeing his pain.

"The midwife had just delivered my son. I held him and begged God to help me find a way to aid him. The bairn took but two short breaths. Ingirid didna last the night."

Meghan held on to the table edge, for her legs were ready to buckle.

"God in heaven, Rolf, Connor *couldna* have done that."

"He did!" Rolf roared back. "Ask Garith. He tried to stop him. Connor twisted his arm behind him and left it near useless." His fists twitched, looking impatient to strike out again.

"It had to be another disguised as Connor," Meghan insisted. "How can anyone tell who is behind a helm with a nose piece? My brother wouldna have been here at the time. He was with Damron at Abernethy. Go to Blackthorn with a flag of truce, and we will prove neither he, Damron, nor Mereck could have done this."

"Alpin recognized his clothing when he pursued them." Murmurs spread throughout the room, though they had heard the story many times already. "The smell of so much blood must have sickened Connor, for he was fool eneuch to throw down his helmet and armor." Rolf smoothed out the tablecloth where he had bunched it in his fist.

"So, it comes to this. You insist 'twas Connor. I insist it couldna have been. Connor was at Abernethy as ye were. From there, he went to England with Damron to bring Brianna of Sinclair back as Damron's bride." Meghan shook her head. How could she prove it to him? Cold dread ran down her back. What *did* he want from her? He had said 'twas not for ransom. What then?

Ye destroyed that which I loved most. He had explained that.

Look to yer own. She, obviously, was the answer to that. Her gaze met his.

"What do ye want from me, Rolf?" What could he want? Not money. Not jewels. No ransom of any kind. He would have already sent messengers about such. She dreaded his answer.

He motioned to the squire, who turned the armor's stand to face them. Rolf folded his arms and spread his legs wide in a battle stance. His jaw tightened, his face hardened to punishing stone.

"What do I want from you?" He raised his brows, his voice silky. "Have you not guessed?" After a long, deliberate pause, he added, "*You know*."

She shook her head. Slowly. She wouldna e'en think on it.

"A son." His chin lifted. His expression became unyielding, arrogant. "I want a son."

"Ye wish to wed me? Sister to the man ye believe caused the death of yer wife and child?" His words astounded Meghan.

"Nay, Meghan. Not wed. You will be my leman until you birth a healthy son." His eyes burned stark with misery. "After I know the bairn will live, I will release you."

She could not speak. His leman? He wanted a son? A bastard? By her? Yet he would send them back to Blackthorn after the babe was born?

As hot rage sparked through her like blinding lightning strikes, Rolf spoke again.

"The bairn stays with me."

CHAPTER 11

His leman! He wanted to couple with her as he would breed a stallion to a mare? Without thought to consequences, Meghan's hand cracked across Rolf's cheek with all the force she could muster.

"Ye cold-hearted whoreson." The words hissed through her teeth. "Ye would breed me like an animal and take the bairn from my breasts?" She paid no heed to the hand that whipped up and clamped her wrist with fingers of steel. He twisted her arm down and around her back.

"Ne'er do such again, Meghan, lest ye wish mine own hand to return the favor," Rolf shouted. "And ne'er call me whoreson."

She felt the force of his words resounding through his chest as they sprang forth, for he held her crushed against him. His eyes blazed down at her, daring her to defy him.

Ugsome barked, then snarled as he tried to shove between them. He became ever more aggressive when he could not separate them. Not with Meghan, though. He clamped his jaw on Rolf's booted ankle. Rolf shook his leg, and the dog let loose only to circle behind Meghan. He braced his paws against her hips, and his teeth tugged the sleeve of Rolf's arm that held her in such a cruel grip.

With Ugsome's weight pushing against her hips, Meghan's stomach made forceful and shocking contact with Rolf's groin. Each time Ugsome snapped and tugged, the hot hardness there grew to alarming proportions.

"Begone, beast," Rolf growled out the order as he released her wrist. "Garith. Control him."

Meghan sprang back from Rolf. Her left hand darted out to grab the wine flask from the table. She slammed it against his chest. Wine trickled down his clothing as the flask bounced its awkward way to the floor.

Rolf went as still as a well-built cairn. His lips thinned, his eyes narrowed to slits. His soft voice commanded everyone in the room. "Leave us."

They needed not to hear his words. Rolf's lips pressed together, and his nostrils flared with fury. 'Twas enough to make grown men charge from the room, some scurrying like mice before a hungry barn cat. Alpin, Garith, and Dougald did not move until his wintery gray eyes turned to them.

Meghan took a deep breath to calm her rage. It didna help. Her hand twitched at her hip. Oh, how she missed her dagger! Were it at her side, he would have felt its prick against his throat.

Not to kill. To warn. No man would treat her as a baseborn slattern. Not even the king himself could command her to his bed. She would die first.

"I willna play the whore for ye," she blazed at him.

She backed up and started to circle the tables. Her eyes searched over each. Mayhap in their haste, someone had left their eating knife behind.

Rolf followed. One slow step at a time, he stalked her.

"Heartless, churlish swine." She spied a pewter tankard and threw it. It bounced against his waist. Ale sloshed onto the rushes. When the tankard clanged to the floor, the noise rang out in the empty room. Grasping a soggy trencher, she hurled it at him. To her great satisfaction, it landed against that hard bulge that was ever more apparent. The veins in his forehead bulged. His jaw twitched harder, and she heard him grind his teeth together.

"Ne'er will I bear a babe and discard it like offal that means nothin' to me. Ne'er," she shouted. How could he know so little of her that he believed she would agree to such a terrible deed? She could not understand this man who had changed so.

He remained silent as he stalked her. She bounded onto a bench and was on the other side of the trestle table afore he could blink. He followed just as quickly.

She somersaulted over the next table. Her hair escaped its bounds to fly about her face. It almost blinded her. He was hot on her heels. Silent still. He came after her, the veins in his neck pulsing and swelling, his face tightening, becoming ever more grim, if that were possible.

She had made a foolish mistake. In her rage, she failed to note he guided her so that solid wall stood behind her. She twisted to run. His hand darted out to grab a handful of hair and pull her up short.

When he hauled her around to face him, his eyes were no longer the gray of a winter's sky but the hot ash of a well-stoked fire. Hard arms encircled her, pinned her own against her sides. His demanding mouth cracked down with such force he ground her lips against her teeth. Holding her with one arm, he grasped her jaw and forced her to yield and open to him.

His hot tongue invaded her defenses and tasted of wine and passion. He left no part of her mouth unexplored. She could not move. The hard length of his sex pressed against her stomach and felt like a thick, white-hot poker taken from the fire. Her mind rebelled at a hideous thought.

Did he intend to take her here on a table strewn with food? A shameful whimper escaped her throat.

His lips gentled and feathered across hers, soothing them. Her heart slammed against her ribs as he relaxed his harsh grip on her face. Calloused fingertips smoothed as soft as a butterfly's wing over her cheek as he stroked her jaw and then made their way down her neck to linger on her collar bone.

She gasped and drew her head back. "Dinna."

"Dinna what, Meghan?" His voice growled low in his throat as his hand wandered down to caress her breast. In her efforts to escape him, the ties at her neck had come undone, and the material gaped wide to expose her enticing softness. His heated eyes delayed there. "Dinna beat you?" He glanced up at her. "Hmm?"

His hand stilled as he studied her face. "Nay. You dinna fear a man who throws you to the ground and grinds you in the dust. Often enough I spied you hidden beneath your squire's clothin', wrestlin' with Damron and Connor."

"I ne'er hid. Grandda knew I trained." She gasped for breath.

"You have not answered me, Meghan. Dinna what?" His arm around her moved lower and tightened to grind his arousal against her soft flesh.

"Ye well know. Dinna shame me by raping me. That is the only way ye'll have me. I will ne'er yield to ye as yer whore."

"I dinna need your yielding. Whether you do so or not, I will have a bairn of your body." His eyes changed to cold slate again. "Connor of Blackthorn tore my son from me. Meghan of Blackthorn will breed me another."

"I swear to ye, Rolf," she said slowly, clearly, "force me to accept yer body and I will kill ye."

He shrugged his shoulders, no doubt dismissing her words.

"Dinna think I wouldna. Mayhap not this day. Not this night. One day, when ye least expect it."

"Do you think I would be fool eneuch to allow you a weapon?" He slanted a cynical brow at her. "Or allow you to attack me in any way?"

"Ye need not *allow* anythin'." Deep sadness filled her that he would force her in such a shameful and sinful way. "If I canna stop ye takin' me, I *will* stop ye from keepin' me. Some way. Somehow." She gazed hard into his eyes. He had to understand. "When no one expects, I will cease to be. Many stairways lead to the parapets. Many window openings are high above the stones. Dinna think ye will always be there to stop me. Ye willna."

His eyes registered shock, and his arms fell from her. "You wouldna do so. 'Tis sinful to think such thoughts."

"'Tis the shame that ye would pile upon my head that causes them."

"We will talk on it no more." His eyes hardened with new grimness as he took an abrupt step back. "I will grant you two days to accustom yourself to amending your brother's wrongs."

When she would speak again, he clamped his hand over her mouth to silence her.

"Nay. Not another word." He looked down at the wine and food splattered on his clothing and shot her a ferocious frown. "I should beat you for this alone. Be glad I have not."

She glared at him, defying him to even think on it. With slow, deliberate movements, she backed away from him as she retied the ribbons at her neck. Raising her chin in defiance, she swept the tumbled hair from her face and turned.

"Bastard," she muttered low in her throat.

He brought her up short. A hand on each of her arms pinned them to her side. "You tempt me to change my mind and forgo waiting to have your body beneath mine." He pressed himself against her back and ran the tip of his tongue along the outline of her ear. "Tempt me not, lass. Anger me not. Your defiance heats my blood and makes my tarse ache and throb. 'Tis eager to ram its way into your woman's heat." He lowered his face to stroke his cheek against hers.

She felt the stubble of new growth there. It sent prickly chills down her neck to her chest, to pool at her breasts. They tingled and grew heavy. She knew he could see her nipples harden and press against the cloth there.

"'Tis for this you stoke my anger? Hmm?" The husky growl of his voice unnerved her.

"Release me, fool. I want no touch from ye."

Rolf lowered his mouth to her neck, avoiding the chafed flesh there. His teeth nipped, then suckled strongly. When she shuddered against him, a chuckle rumbled from his chest. Suddenly, he released her.

With head held high, she strode from the great hall. The urge to run to the highest point of the castle consumed her. No one would know how hard it was for her to keep her stride even, to walk out of that room and into the crowd of people who lingered outside the doorway.

" 'Tis well-kissed she be, by the looks o' her lips," snickered a laundry woman.

"Did he give her a taste o' the lovin' to come?" The blacksmith's helper grinned at her.

"Nay, lad. Seems to me he took a taste o' her neck," the blacksmith replied.

"Did he beat her, do ye think, Da?" the tanner's son asked, his voice worried.

"Had he, she wouldna be walkin' so easily."

The man's pungent odor made Meghan hold her breath as she swept past.

" 'Tis a mistake he didna," muttered a battle-scarred warrior. "Beat 'em and bed 'em. 'Tis how ye show a lass her place."

Meghan's leg muscles twitched, longing to strike out at his groin. Had she worn boots, he would be crouched over holding tight to his shriveled manhood as he spewed his meal onto the rushes.

"Enough," Dougald ordered. "Go about your duties or return to your meal." He made no move to hinder Meghan's progress.

Ugsome barked. Garith tried to hold tight to the ruff of his neck, but the dog shook his head and freed himself. He bounded ahead of Meghan, causing the crowd to scatter. Much to her relief, several long strides later she reached the stairwell.

Rolf smelled the scent of heather that lingered in the air where she had walked. He steeled himself not to bound after her, throw her over his shoulder, and carry her to his solar. He would have her, whether she willed it or not.

He grimaced. If she remained unwilling, could he force the woman he had once loved?

Had it not been for Connor, never would he have thought to treat Meghan in this way. In his dreams, she was always willing and pliant, ready to meet him thrust for thrust. He doubted she was virgin still. Not after that time at the royal court.

He had sat at table three seats from her during the evening meal. The women had retired to the solar, leaving the men privacy. Meghan protested that it was a silly thing to keep secret what they did. Not long after, squires came into the room to be of service to the knights. One youth seemed new to the task, for he hesitated, though he mimicked the other squires.

"Here, boy," a comely young knight called out and crooked a finger at the squire.

The boy took an earthenware pot shoved at him by a page and went up to the knight. Once the man untied his leggings and released his formidable tarse, the squire looked startled. A lock of chestnut hair slithered from his cap and down his back. The knight had a difficult time with his aim, for the pot trembled and wavered.

"Hold steady if ye dinna want piss on yer clothing," the knight grumbled.

Suspicious, Rolf had moved closer to see the squire. 'Twas Meghan. Her green eyes furrowed in concentration as she tried to keep the man from soaking her purloined clothing.

As soon as the knight finished, Rolf hauled Meghan from the room like a sack of grain, his arm around her waist. She shrieked and kicked like a wildcat. He dumped her at her brother's feet. She bounded up and clawed Rolf's face.

Connor had given over the duty of tanning her arse to Damron. From the screeches in the next room when he did so, 'twas clear Damron was well used to it. The next day, Damron sent Meghan to an abbey to spend the rest of the summer months.

She had not changed over the years. He had heard of other incidents when she masqueraded as someone else and ventured where she should not. She was still determined to have her way and obey no man. She would him, though. He would train her as he would a prize stallion. 'Twas yield or break. Either way, he thought grimly, he must have her.

He removed his food-spattered tunic and shirt. Bared to the waist, he wore tight black trews that left no doubt of his aroused state.

"You would make her your leman?" The man's voice was hard and angry as he confronted Rolf.

"Aye. My leman. Dinna think to interfere, Alpin."

"How can I not?" Alpin scowled and slung himself onto a bench beside him. He scowled at Rolf's engorged sex. "It displeases me that you would flaunt a leman when Ailsa arrives."

" 'Tis naught to do with her."

"Naught? She will deem it an insult to find you swiving a leman. She will be much aggrieved."

"What matter if I swive my leman, a serving wench, a woman of the keep, or any other?" Rolf raised a haughty brow at Alpin. "Does Ailsa think to interfere where she should not? 'Tis not her right. I willna allow it." His words issued a warning.

Alpin fell silent. His ice-blue eyes squinted down at his booted feet.

"Come, Dougald." Rolf gestured, impatient. "I have need of a good workout."

"Ha, 'tis more than a workout you will be needin' to rid you of that battering ram." Dougald laughed and shook his head. "Methinks you had best visit a doxy afore you do yourself an injury."

"You will be visitin' the rushes if you dinna heed me." Rolf turned to his squire and ordered, "Bring Beast to the practice yard. Put the heavy cover o'er the blade. Dougald, be glad I bid the armorer make the safeguard. Carry your staunchest shield, for I dinna mean to hold back my blows."

He turned on his heels and stormed out of the room.

Meghan hurled past Rolf's solar, her hands fisting so tight her nails dug into her palms. Ugsome padded beside her. She heard Ede running to catch up with her long strides.

"Meghan, where do you think to go?"

"Up, Ede. Just up." Meghan swiped at her eyes, startled by the moisture that brimmed there. "I want to feel the air on my face, to see the sun set on this miserable day."

"Milady," called a man behind her. "You canna go upon the battlements. Lord Rolf willna like it." The warrior hurried to plant himself in front of her.

She halted afore she stepped on his toes. "What is your name?" she asked bluntly.

"Jamie, lady." He shifted and eyed Ugsome as the dog started to growl low in his throat. After he backed up, the animal quieted.

"Well, now, Jamie. You can escort me to the battlements or you can report to your master and tell him I said he can stick his head in horse shite. 'Tis your choice. Either way, I am going out into the air." When he appeared reluctant, she strode around him and was up the stairway afore he could blink.

"Lucifer's hindquarters," he muttered, "never have I seen a more stubborn woman." He huffed and cursed under his breath and pounded up the stairs behind her. Arriving at the rough-hewn door to the battlements, Jamie reached around her and pushed the door open. He followed close on her heels. Cold air whipped the clothing tight to her body and tugged at her hair.

Oh, how she wished to be alone. Just a moment to herself to regain her composure. She walked over to an opening notch in the crenellated battlement, where Jamie hovered so close she felt his arm twitch in readiness to grab her should she decide to plunge to the ground below.

She took deep, slow breaths and looked out over Loch Rimsdale, so peaceful in the early evening. They were at the rear of the castle. No land stretched out below, for they had built the castle close to the eastern tip of the island. Just enough room remained for a small grassy area and a stone wall set above the big boulders that formed there.

No way to escape by that route, for not a single tree graced the line of wall. Not even a child could explore it unseen. Upon hearing the clatter of swords and shields, she moved farther along the walkway at the south side of the castle. Below was a large practice area, fenced off with wooden railings. Rolf and Dougald battled there, surrounded by cheering men and gawking women.

Sweat glistened off Rolf's back and chest as he circled his

opponent. When he struck, his muscles flowed and surged
with his movements. His breeches looked filled to bursting
as the muscles in his buttocks and thighs tensed with each
lunge and parry. His arm rose high as he swung his great battle axe in a wide arc.

"Rolf's usin' Beast. If Dougald isna fleet, 'tis a broken rib
he'll be sportin'." Jamie shook his head in sympathy.

Light flashed off the steel shaft as the axe crashed into
Dougald's shield. The man rocked from the blow and barely
had time to balance himself afore Rolf struck again.

"Mayhap Rolf will get as good as he gives." Meghan eyed
the combatants as she appraised their skills. After several
minutes, she saw what she would do if she were in Dougald's
position. "Watch. Dougald will strike low on the next swing."

"Nay. He willna have time to duck then raise his shield
for the following blow," Jamie muttered.

True to her thoughts, when Rolf next struck, Dougald took
the blow on his shield and allowed the weight of it to bend his
knees enough to attack Rolf's legs with his own blunted
sword. Both men tumbled to the ground.

Rolf's hearty boom of laughter surprised her. He lay
sprawled on his back, arms outstretched, sounding as if someone had apprized him of delightful news. Meghan had not
heard him laugh since she was ten and five years of age. She
stared, engrossed. For the first time, he was much as he used
to be.

Strands of sweat-dampened hair clung to his forehead and
cheeks as his body shook with mirth. Her gaze strayed over
the impressive breadth of his shoulders, down his sweating
chest, and lingered on the taut muscles of his abdomen. The
hair there narrowed to meet the heavy leather belt at his waist.

Her eyes did not stop to linger. Nor did she want them
to. The slenderness of his belly and his widespread legs accented the bulge of his manhood beneath his clothing. Interesting. Did her eyes play tricks with her? That part of
him seemed to change. She frowned and wondered. Did
laughter arouse a man?

That couldna be. He no longer laughed. He lay outstretched. Not a muscle moved. Had Dougald injured him? Startled, her gaze flew over his body, seeking a wound. Once she spied his face, she knew the source of his stimulation.

His hot stare seemed to bore into her eyes. He had sensed her on the battlements watching him. Had felt her gaze rove over his body. Lucifer's pointy ears! Did the man have the sight of a hawk? He lifted his hips slightly. A bold invitation for her to fill her gaze with him.

"Hmpf!" She frowned and slanted her nose into the air as if she had spotted something unsavory. As she swung around to leave, his laughter rang out again. Had she a stone to throw, he wouldna be laughing long. If Jamie dared to utter even the thought of a snicker, she would lay him flat with a kick to his chest, sore feet or not. Just see if she wouldn't.

"Displayin' his wares fer all to see," she muttered beneath her breath, then whirled around and stomped off.

Jamie held the stairway door open for her to pass through. She made her way down the steps, mumbling as she went. "Mayhap he can impress the scullery maid, but it takes more than an ample tarse to catch my eye."

When she reached the landing and approached Ede's room, the hair on her nape prickled. Booted footsteps clambered up the stairwell at the far end of the hallway.

CHAPTER 12

"Demented fool." Meghan grasped Ede's door, wrenched it open, and slammed it behind her. As she dropped the latch, Rolf's footsteps pounded to a halt on the other side.

"Do ye wish to change your mind, lass?" his voice purred. "Two days is a looong wait to quench your needs."

"I would as soon jump from the parapet, dolt."

"Aye. You looked ready to jump but moments ago." A wicked chuckle sounded on the other side of the door. "Right atop o' me. Be that your favorite way for bedsport, hmm?"

Meghan gritted her teeth, grabbed an empty wooden bucket beside the clothing chest, and slung it at the door. The loud clatter gratified her; the half-moon mark in the heavy wood satisfied her even more. But seeing a crescent on his forehead would have brought a smile to her face.

When Rolf next spoke, Meghan scowled at the door.

"Oh, aye. I know you think of mating with me." His voice deepened in laughter. "Had you not, you wouldna be so aggrieved."

"Get you gone, oaf. I would as soon mate with a bandy-legged swineherd," Meghan spat out the words in contempt.

"Two nights, Meghan. A *lonely* two nights must you wait, but not one hour more."

"Surely he will break it down now," Ede's shocked voice whispered in her ear. "Never has he allowed anyone to defy him."

Meghan turned and frowned at her. "Ha! Ne'er have I allowed any man to speak such dishonor to me afore this day and not put a knife to him."

"You have killed for such?" Ede's shocked eyes opened so wide they looked like blueberries resting in a spot of milk.

"Nay, not killed. 'Twas unfortunate they didna die. I but pricked their throats to remind them to keep such words behind their teeth."

As Rolf's footsteps faded, so did the sound of his laughter. She gritted her teeth, wishing she could stamp her foot like an angry child, open the door, and hurl the bucket at his back.

She did not. She was no fool.

"'Tis unlike Rolf to force a woman. And never have I known him to take a leman." Worried, Ede paced around the room, wringing her hands. "He has ever been careful where he spilled his seed. He has sired no bastards."

"None that ye know of, mayhap." Meghan huffed in disbelief. "From the looks of him, he is far too randy not to have a stream of women for his bedsport."

"Aye. He has no lack of willing lasses. But a fortnight ago, he returned late of an evening and entered his solar. Not a minute later, I heard a woman wailing in his room."

"He is cruel with his lovemaking?" Meghan shuddered at the thought. The man was far too large, in body and in his male organs. If not gentle, he would hurt a lass in mating with her.

Ede looked shocked at the question. "Oh, nay. Never have I seen him be cruel to a lass." She stopped and her face flushed. "Not until he brought you to Rimsdale."

"If not for pain, for what reason did the lass wail?"

Ede blushed. "I opened my door but a crack. Enough to see she stood on the landing bare as the day she was birthed."

"He threw an unclothed lass out of his room?" Meghan's lips curled in disgust. Had she been there, Rolf would have felt the flat of her sword across his nether parts.

"He didna ask her there." Ede shrugged as she pulled back the bedcovers. "From what I could hear, he was bone tired from his vigil in the woods waiting for . . ." Her voice trailed off, and her face flushed fiery red.

"Aye. He spied to learn my habits." Meghan's eyes narrowed to slits as she eyed the door, wishing she had belted him a good one.

"He found the lass in his bed. She has tried to entice him to mate with her ever since his wife, uh, died."

"Did he not find her bonny?" Meghan was curious now.

"Oh, aye. She was pretty enough. Mayhap he was too weary for play between the sheets."

"Ha. From the looks of his bulging breeches, he's ne'er too weary." Meghan shrugged. "More likely she smelled rank. He has a dislike of unclean women."

Once, at the Norman court, she had seen Rolf back away from Lady Delphine who always smelled sour and wore clothing that needed more than a day or two of airing. Meghan's chest ached recalling how he had taken every occasion to put his face close to her own hair and inhale deeply, thinking she didna note it.

As they prepared for bed, they fell silent and were soon fast asleep.

Rolf did not sleep, though, but paced the floor in his solar as he rubbed the back of his neck. He had underestimated Meghan's courage that day. 'Twas not often he misjudged a foe. Strange he should think on her as such. In his dreams, she was far from an opponent. Nay. He deluded himself. She was an opponent rightly enough. Though not one of the killing kind. One he pursued with cunning and vigor, who eluded him until he brought her to heel. Naked. In his bed sprawled beneath him, his weight pinning her there. Where she belonged.

Such thoughts caused him to fidget and ache with longing. Had he a smidgeon of sense, he would ease his tension on one of the willing lasses asleep below. He would but for the fact they would not do.

None but Meghan could ease his lust.

Guilt gnawed at his soul. His heart ached for what he was about to do. She bore no guilt in her brother's treachery. Why had he chosen this form of revenge? Mayhap 'twas because of Meghan herself? To have her as his own? He willed the cold room to soothe his heated flesh. It didna work.

"Satan's puckered arse!" He stomped across the chilly floor to the window opening and peered out at the star-filled sky. Puffs of air stroked over him like icy fingers. His gaze lowered, and he cursed again in disgust. Instead of withering in the frigid air, the moon's pale light showed his rampant tarse stood erect as a warrior's pike.

Meghan would not succumb with ease to his plans. What a battle he had on his hands. Pride wouldna let her be any man's leman. He must break her as he would a fine-blooded destrier.

Aye. A destrier. Never a placid mare but a rare and high-strung battle horse. He would hold tight to the reins, keep her locked between his legs and ride her until she became resigned to him as her master. Unease swept him. After all was done, would she be a woman honed to be a perfect mate? Or would she be but an empty shell of herself?

Of all the women he had met in his travels, he wanted only Meghan to birth his bairn. His seed planted in her body would yield a son even kings would envy. Her courage, her honesty, her intrepid personality, her honor, the way she challenged him mentally and physically, all these qualities made him admire her more than any woman on earth. For all these traits, he chose her to replace the bairn her brother took from him.

Recalling a time when all he wanted from Meghan was love, a sharp pain shot through his chest.

Bile scorched his throat. To give him what he demanded, he must needs break her. She would never bend. When all was done and she learned everything, would hate for him destroy her? Grasping a flagon of ale, he drank deep.

'Twas a long night.

Afore first light, a rough scraping sound roused Meghan. 'Twas something with four legs, not two, outside their door. Sliding from the bed so as not to wake Ede, she opened the door enough for Ugsome to squeeze through. As he whined and licked at her hand, she stroked the coarse hair on his battle-scarred face.

"Shh, now. Ye dinna want to wake everyone. Sit while I dress," she whispered. Ugsome sat back on his haunches and thumped his tail on the floor, a happy look in his eyes.

"Meghan? Is someone there?" Ede's sleepy voice came from across the room. The bed ropes squeaked as she climbed out of bed.

" 'Tis my four-legged guard." Meghan put two fingers to her lips and Ugsome obliged with a fierce growl. *A pity you couldna so easily train a man. But then, such a man wouldna be worth the trouble.*

They dressed and were ready to go below when a sharp knock sounded on the door. Closest, Ede opened it. She stepped back, her brows lifted in surprise.

Rolf's powerful, larger-than-life body filled the doorframe. His gaze swept past her to stop on Meghan.

"Come. I would have you break your fast with me." He snapped the order at her.

Meghan frowned. *Why was he so irritable this morn?* Dark circles rimmed his eyes. *If he scowled a bit harder, his eyebrows would blend together.* Eyeing her, his lips tightened. *Good. If men's clothing made her unappealing, all the better.* Expecting him to demand she change, he surprised her and did not say a word.

She nodded and passed through the doorway afore Ede. He courteously waited until Ede also exited. Placing her right forefinger on her chin, Meghan signaled Ugsome to follow her and hastened down the stairwell. Her lips pressed tight together trying to stifle a grin.

Entering the great hall, she ignored the curious looks and whispers. *Had everyone in this blasted castle heard him pound up the stairs last eve? From the giggled remarks about his words outside her chamber door, they apparently all had ears like elves too.*

"Good day to ye, Garith," she said. "If ye have time, mayhap ye could walk with me outside this morn? I fear Ugsome will attack me if I attempt to go alone."

Garith drew himself up to sit tall beside her. He nodded, solemn, and spoke to his brother. "Rolf, do you approve?"

"Aye. She may walk about, but you will not let her out of your sight." He stared hard at the young man and waited until Garith nodded. He filled a wooden bowl with porridge and placed it in front of Meghan, along with a pitcher of cream and a small pot of honey.

Meghan studied him through lowered lashes as she murmured her thanks. Rolf was being considerate. Why? When he placed a hot bannock beside her bowl, her eyes narrowed. What was he up to? Last eve he had treated her like a common slattern, now this morn he played the chivalrous knight?

"How spent you the night?" Rolf took a bite of his scone, and honey glistened on his lips.

Meghan spotted the sweetness spilled here. She remembered the feel of those lips on her own, hard and punishing, then soft and soothing. The tip of her tongue came out to dampen her lips. She noted the corners of his mouth twitch.

She glanced up. The gleam in his eyes told her he had dribbled the honey apurpose!

She thrust out her chin and glared at him. "I slept very well. Ye dinna look to have done the same. Yer conscience botherin' ye, mayhap?"

His eyes blazed with heat as his gaze swept over her, slow and intimate. "Nay. Not a whit. I spent the night thinkin' on the bedsport we will have. After a night of hard ridin', I doubt not you will sleep late each morn."

"I doubt not *ye* will sleep *verra* late the first morn." She sniffed and her eyes flashed as she added, "Mayhap never to awake again." To her disgust, he chuckled.

"You prefer to do the ridin' then, Meghan? Were your lovers so inept you had the need to set the pace?" He sighed and shook his head in mock sympathy. "Let it not be said I dinna allow a woman her pleasure, but first we will do it my way."

He had not said lover, but lovers! How dare he talk to her

like she was a trollop? Her gaze spied the closest thing to hand. The pot of honey.

He captured her hand. "Dinna think on it, Meghan."

"Release me," she demanded.

"When you behave as I wish. Not a moment before."

Meghan ignored his enticing scent as she tried to yank away. His grip tightened on her hand and kept it clamped to the table. She could not move it even a wee bit.

"Horse's arse," she shouted. She grabbed for the cold pitcher of milk with her free hand.

Rolf captured it also and shifted to face her. His expression darkened. The veins in his neck stood out in livid ridges. He switched both her hands to his own big, steel-fingered one. He did not speak but narrowed his eyes to glare into hers. Of a sudden, the room was deathly quiet.

"You will *not* call me a horse's arse or any such thing again." He ground out the words between clenched teeth as his face flushed red with rage.

"You tell her, Rolf. The lass needs tamin', she does," a man shouted from across the room.

"Ye are breakin' my hands." She tugged hard to no avail. "Let me go or so help me, I will bury the first blade I find in yer chest." Her eyes blazed murderously at him.

He bounded up and jerked her to her feet, then pinned her arms to her side and pressed her tight against him.

"Not until my own weapon is buried deep within you. 'Tis what you are lackin'. The fight will soon go out of you then."

The hall echoed with hoots and hollers of advice.

"Show the lass that wearin' a man's breeches will do her no good when she is spread beneath ye, Rolf."

"Keep her abed, man. There be nothin' like a good swiving to tame a lass." Another man chortled, an avid gleam in his eyes. He hitched the belted plaid at his waist higher.

"Keep yer tongues behind yer teeth, churls," Meghan blazed at them furiously. "I am a highborn lady, not a common serf to be taken at the master's will."

"Highborn or no, you will be my leman in one night's time."

Rolf lowered his head to capture her lips. Meghan's knee came up and slammed into his groin. Not as hard as she had wished. He held her too close. Hard enough, though, that he released her. She tore out of his grasp and ran, making it to the door.

Rolf whirled her around with such speed her hair flew about her.

"Ne'er will you get away with that again." His steely glare held her gaze prisoner. "If you dare try, I will swive you on the spot. Here. In everyone's sight."

His probing kiss showed her she had failed to dampen his ardor.

He released her at last. Meghan's eyes flashed with defiance as she scrubbed her sleeve across her mouth. Wordless, she spun on her heels. Her long strides carried her to the door of the castle with Ugsome padding beside her.

Garith, his face red with shame, caught up to her in the front bailey. Though he was ten and three and could not be an innocent about carnal matters, his brother's behavior to a lady had surely challenged his ideas of chivalry. She felt pangs of guilt knowing she contributed to his distress. The young man had endured enough turmoil in these last years. He should not need to question his belief in the rightness of Rolf's decisions.

She swallowed and took a deep breath, wanting to calm her racing heart. "Though we have not met in many years, yer brother and I have had many clashes afore, Garith."

"Aye. I felt that between you." He kicked a pebble and sent it skittering across the ground. His face flushed, and he chewed on his lower lip.

"'Tis why his actions are so harsh now. Had I been any other lady, he wouldna treat me thus."

She raised her hand, beckoning Ugsome, who scurried over to pad along between them as they walked into the outer bailey. She reached down and patted the beast's head, urging it closer to Garith's hand. The faithful dog nuzzled the boy with his wet nose.

Garith chuckled and tugged the dog's ear. "I think Ugsome likes you." He grinned up at her.

"Likes me? Aye. Sure he does. And when he growls and snarls, 'tis affection he is showin'?" Meghan smiled down at the boy.

They were fast approaching the small huts built along the outer curtain wall. Her eyes searched until she spied the long building where the blacksmith worked with the armorer and where the bow maker and fletcher combined their work areas. Did they store weapons there of a night, awaiting their attention the next morn?

Garith raised his right eyebrow. "I have noted these past two days that Ugsome snarls whene'er you touch your lips."

"He didna snarl when I wiped my lips but minutes ago, did he?"

"Nay." The boy chuckled. "You wiped them with your sleeve. You didna touch your hand to your lips as you did on times afore."

Meghan grinned. "What else has yer quick eye told you?"

"That each time you and my brother, uh, quibble, he canna keep his hands from you."

"Anger sometimes stokes a man's appetites, be it from the belly or below." Meghan frowned at the sky. " 'Tis why after battle, men filled with bloodlust fall upon any woman within their reach."

"Is it not their right?" His voice faltered. "They have conquered their enemy and 'tis a way to show possession." Garith watched her, his gaze intent.

"Ha. 'Tis a way to make the conquered people hate them even more." She clenched her hands, thinking of the women she had tended from burnt-out villages surrounding Blackthorn.

Ugsome stalked around her, baring his teeth and snapping at her ankles. Garith burst out laughing.

She looked at him in shock. "What amuses you?"

"You."

She scowled.

He grinned back. "When you clenched your fist, the beast responded. What other signals have you taught him? Do you think you could teach me the skill?"

She stopped dead in her tracks and shook her head. "Ye are far too clever for a young man. Will ye promise not to tell anyone? Not even yer brother?"

"I dinna see it as disloyal to him." He nodded. "Aye. It will be a secret betwixt us."

While the sun rose high in the sky, she and Garith whiled away the time beneath the apple trees growing in the inner bailey. She chose a spot toward the far end that provided the most privacy from prying eyes, for older trees grew there, their branches heavy with leaves drooped low to the ground.

Meghan spent a good while talking with Garith to learn how much use he had in his arm and hand. The arm didna look to be completely useless. Not having a proper healer at Rimsdale, he had worked with no one. At Blackthorn, a Welshman of indeterminable age named Bleddyn, who came to Blackthorn with Damron's wife, taught them much about healing. Meghan chewed her lip. Mayhap with exercise and training, Garith could regain some of his arm's former use.

Without saying why, she urged him to learn the signals with his right hand. At first, she worked with his stiff hand, exercising it and helping him make a fist. She cautioned him to be patient. It would take days of working the unused muscles, but she assured him he could do it if he tried very hard.

Keeping their backs to Ugsome, they formed Garith's hand into a fist. When he turned toward the dog and brought it to his side, the dog looked from him to Meghan, confused. After Meghan coaxed him several times by bringing her own fist from behind her back while Garith did the same, Ugsome ran around them acting as if he would tear them both apart.

Garith burst into delighted laughter. They laughed so hard Rolf was upon them afore they heard his shouts.

"Down, Ugsome. Damnation, dog, have ye gone daft?"

Ugsome stopped in midsnarl, his scarred ears drooped beside guilt-laden eyes blinking up at Rolf.

Meghan pulled a long face at Garith, who snickered. She turned to Rolf, her demeanor serious. " 'Tis good ye appeared, Rolf. I dinna ken what set the beastie off."

"Were you arguing with Garith?" Rolf's stern gray eyes studied Meghan.

"Nay." With affection, Garith thumped the ugly dog on its side as he answered for her. " 'Tis not the dog's fault. When I swatted a bug off Meghan's arm, I ken I confused him."

Eyeing her from head to toe, Rolf frowned. "Wear proper women's clothin' when you come to the noon meal, else ye willna eat," he snapped as he turned and left.

Her temper surged back to life. "Hmpf," she huffed. "I think not."

His stride halted but a heartbeat in time.

Meghan spent time praising both Garith and Ugsome until Father Mark came to collect the young man. Already Garith's knowledge was greater than all but Rolf and Alpin here at Rimsdale; at Blackthorn, the boy would not be so unusual.

Her grandda, old Laird Douglas, had seen to it that all his grandchildren could read and write, do sums so they could keep a proper eye on the accounts, plan dimensions for a new building, and even defend the castle. Damron's mother, Lady Phillipa, saw to it they learned to speak fluent French, German, and Spanish.

Meghan was not slighted because she was a female. She studied along with them. When it came to their physical training, they were so used to having her with them that they treated her as they would have a younger brother.

More than once, they had cause to regret it. Connor gave up in despair that she would ever obey him. When she became too much for him, he turned to Damron and begged him to discipline her.

Now Rolf thought she would be docile? Bow her head and do as *he* wished? Not while she had strength in her body to defy him. She would be no man's whore for his bedsport.

When time for the noon meal, Rolf watched the doorway as the cook's helpers began to carry in the meal. He expected Meghan to appear, and when she did not, he turned to Ede.

"Does Meghan sulk in your sleeping chamber?"

"Nay. She was not there when I came below," Ede said. Her worried eyes strayed to the trencher in front of her.

"What?" Rolf bolted to his feet. "Garith, did you allow her to leave the castle grounds?"

"Nay, Rolf. I wouldna do such. Afore I joined Father Mark, I saw her safely within the castle."

Rolf turned to Jamie. "Go atop the battlements and see if she is there. Dougald, look about the grounds. Mayhap she went out another opening." He turned to his friend. "Alpin, help me check within to see if she mistook the time."

Facing the room, he ordered everyone to go about their meal. He charged up the stairway two steps at a time and thundered down the hallway. He slammed open the door to her room, but one quick glance showed him she wasna there. He threw open the other doors in his path. After he recalled only the cook's helpers had appeared to serve the meal, a thought struck. Going below to the kitchens, he stormed into the room.

Meghan sat at the end of the table eating from a trencher filled with mutton stew. She and the cook were intent on discussing the merits of different spices to vary the taste of fish and fowl. She jumped when the door crashed back against the wall. The cook's wooden spoon flew from his hand and splattered gravy on the floor.

"Are ye tryin' to ruin a delightful meal, Rolf?" She looked up at him and frowned.

"Why are you not at the table in the great hall where you belong?" He stalked across the room to tower over her.

"Can ye not tell? Or is yer thinkin' as feeble as an ancient man and ye dinna ken the reason?" She smirked and raised her brow, awaiting his answer.

"My memory is keen. 'Tis your own that needs help, lass."

"Oh, and how is that? Ye said I was to wear proper women's

clothin' when I came to the noon meal." She gestured around the room, reminding him they were not in the great hall. "As ye see, I dinna wear yer proper clothin', and I didna go to the noon meal."

"You do not remember all of it, Meghan," his voice purred at her. Seizing her trencher, he tossed it to the floor. "I also said if you did not obey, you would not eat."

"What a waste of good food. Are ye so thoughtless ye dinna care for the needy?" She pointed to the mess on the floor. "That would have fed two hungry children." She could hear his teeth grind together.

"You willna eat in the kitchens or elsewhere dressed as a lad." He thumped a finger on her chest for added emphasis. He hauled her up out of her chair and shoved her ahead of him. "If you want food, you will do as I say or else go without," he shouted as he herded her past the great room and up the stairs.

"Ye prig. To hell with ye," she shouted back. "I would as soon go hungry as sit at table with a nithing of a man."

"You will obey me, Meghan, one way or another," he bellowed as he shoved her into her chambers. "When hunger gnaws at yer belly, you will dress as a proper woman." He banged the door shut behind her.

" 'Tis not as a proper woman ye are treatin' me when ye will me to be yer leman. Yer whore." Her yell strained her throat.

She slung the wooden bucket, gratified by its resounding crash. Afore many moons, the bedchamber door would be amply decorated with half moons.

CHAPTER 13

Late that evening, Ede, her eyes wary, laid a forest-green tunic, a leaf-green smock, white silk hose with ribbons to garter them, a silver girdle, and an earth-colored cloak atop the bed.

"Dinna tell me," Meghan ground out through tight lips, "Rimsdale's lord and master expects me to tuck my tail betwixt my legs like a good hound and do his biddin'?"

"He willna relent. Never have I seen Rolf so determined to gain his way." She looked down at the clothes and blushed. "When you did not come to the evening meal, he said to remind you hunger oft makes commands easier to abide."

"Whose clothin' are these, and why would they allow me to borrow them?"

"Dougald's wife was near as tall as you. She sickened from a fever but two years past. He said 'twas a shame that no one wore them." Ede's smile brightened as Meghan caressed the soft fabrics, but it faded slowly when Meghan spoke.

" 'Twas most kind of Dougald, but I willna be wearin' them."

"Rolf vowed you will have no food till you dress as he orders. After, he was too vexed to eat himself. Mayhap he will be missin' some meals of his own?"

"Ha. Once his anger wanes, he will eat his fill." A thought brightened Meghan's spirit. All was quiet. She would go to the kitchens and find bread and cheese.

She got no farther than the door. Jamie lounged outside, his shoulders propped against the far wall. He smiled and waggled his fingers at her. She rolled her eyes and waggled her own back at him. As she closed the door, she heard him laugh.

Rolf was determined to make her obey his every word. He wouldna care if she grew weak with hunger but would still force her to become his leman in another day's time. Locked in this room, she would find no way to escape. A compromise was in order.

"Ede, Blackthorn 'trophies' adorn the walls below. Will ye bring me what plaids and tunics ye can manage?" Meghan pressed her lips together and thrust out her jaw, determined to be as stubborn as Rolf. "If he insists I dress in proper women's attire, it will be in Blackthorn's tartans."

"Most everyone is abed." She drew her lower lip between her teeth, worrying it, then added, "You canna wear them as they are, for the, uh, stains."

Meghan squared her shoulders. "Bid a servant fetch a bath. I will wash the blood from the clothin'. If I hang them out the window opening, the breeze will dry them. If they dinna freeze."

Time flew past. Ede brought what would not be noticed if it was suddenly gone. She helped Meghan, and when they were done, they tore the most damaged tunic into strips. They tied these strips to a washed garment, hung it out the window opening, and secured the other end to a handle on the bathing tub.

Satisfied with their work, they slept peacefully.

The next morn, as the first rays of sun lit the sky, Rolf waited in the great room for Meghan to appear.

"The lady will soon arrive," Jamie said as he came over to him.

"She isna dressed in breeches? She has donned proper clothin'?" That she had readily given in surprised and disappointed Rolf.

"Well, now"—Jamie did not meet Rolf's eyes—"she has not donned trews."

"Leggin's?" Rolf shot to his feet. " 'Tis best you not let her out of that room if she wears pants of any type."

"Nay, no leggings," he said. The corners of his mouth twitched.

Meghan breezed through the doorway looking rested and cheerful. The room quieted, then the men started laughing, and the women hid their smiles behind their hands.

"She got ye there, Rolf," the blacksmith choked out.

"Aye," said someone else who sounded disappointed. "I liked the breeches better, man."

In the middle of the room, Meghan pivoted slowly. She wore an oversized tunic, tied at the neck with strips of plaid. Gathered around her waist were yards and yards of tartan. A man's tartan. Blackthorn's tartan. So much of it she looked fat as a portly pig. To secure it about her waist, she had pulled it up under her breasts, then wrapped a leather belt twice around to hold it. Her hair lay tangled about her like she had stood in a high wind, and dirt smudged her face.

"Do I look more the woman to ye, Rolf?" She turned to face him. "'Tis as ye ordered, for yer own lasses wear the tartan. I willna don MacDhaidh colors. Since I dinna have my own, I wear what ye claim belonged to my brother's men."

Rolf clenched his hands and beat them against his thighs. Why did Ugsome snarl and snap as if he were in a brainsick frenzy, not knowing where to attack? Garith choked on his laughter as he grabbed the beast around the neck and calmed him. Meghan's mouth twitched with amusement.

He took a deep breath. He couldna deny her food, though in truth she wore men's clothing. He nodded. Bit by bit, he would force her to his hand.

"Well, now, goin' without eatin' seems to make me fatter." She chuckled as she tried to sit.

"Allow me." Garith grinned and pulled her stool farther away from the table.

Rolf watched as she tried to lower her added bulk to it. She couldna. Finally, she grasped the bulky cloth on each side and lifted it so her legs could bend and her sweet arse sat on the stool.

Strange. Why had he thought he would be less drawn to

that portion of her if he couldna see her fetching curves? Now he pictured her beneath the yards of wool.

Soft. Rounded. Made for a man to kiss and nibble.

Would the skin there on her nether cheeks be as golden as the silky breasts he had glimpsed?

The thought of her stretched naked beneath the sunlit sky quickened his heartbeat. None but him would see her thus again. His heart thumped as he imagined swiving her beneath a canopy of trees. Gentle beams of golden sunlight would filter through the leaves to caress her naked skin. The image hardened him near to bursting.

Never had there been a woman any man would admire for so many traits. Her intrepid personality and the way she thwarted his attempts to rule her made Rolf unsure whether to laugh or bellow at her. Every step of the way, she defied him. But at least she wasna wearing trews.

While Meghan settled her cumbersome bulk on the stool, he placed the morning's fare within her reach. She ate slowly, careful to dip but small spoonfuls of porridge so she wouldna spill it on the cloth. Never once did she look at him.

"Come, Dougald. We work on the eastern sea wall today." Seeing him stand, the men gobbled the last of their meal and tore off hunks of bread to munch on as they hurried to go about their duties.

He stopped behind her and ran his hands down her arms to her wrists. Clasping her hands firmly in his, he pulled her close as he brought her arms around her bulky middle.

"Tonight, Meghan," he whispered in her ear while he rubbed his cheek against hers. "Tonight you will lie beneath me. Think on it. I will set my brand on you. You will forget any man who came afore me. Any who come after will be found lacking."

"Forget? Ne'er! Ye willna match the men in my life."

He held tight to her struggling hands as he nuzzled his lips on her throat. He nipped her gently with his teeth, then soothed the skin with his tongue afore trailing it across her jaw and up to her ear.

"Release me. Ne'er will I be yer leman." She jerked her head to avoid his lips.

"Aye. You will. This eve. I will taste your breast, your soft belly—all of you." His voice grated with passion. He gloated in triumph as tremors rippled through her.

He released her and had strode halfway across the room by the time a pewter goblet thunked on the floor behind him. He smiled, satisfied.

All morning Meghan feigned being subdued and resigned to her fate, until even Ede seemed to relax. Several hours later, seeing no one watched her, she carefully approached Rolf's solar. Bending, she pretended to retie her shoe so she could glance at both ends of the landing. Seeing no one watched, she entered and eased the door shut. The man was neat, she had to give him that. Nothing laid about but a wooden comb, a pot of soap on the washing stand, and some cloths for washing.

A heavy lock secured his weapons chest. No doubt her own dagger was within. With the right tool, she could open the lock in a trice. Throwing open the unlocked clothing chest, she searched through it. Nothing. Not even an eating knife. With hands on her hips, she sucked her teeth at the offending chest. Noting the pegs on the wall held a cloak and several pairs of breeches, she patted them down but found the pockets were empty.

The drone of many voices and the noisy clatter of cart wheels coming across the bridge echoed in the stone walls. Meghan crossed the room to peer out the window.

'Twas market day. The perfect time for her to escape within a crowd. Carts carrying cages where chickens squawked and protested, children shouting and laughing as they herded sheep through the gatehouse—all added to the confusion. An old woman pulling a trundle of vegetables drew her interest. Even from where she watched, Meghan could see the soil had not been kind. The turnips looked small, as did the onions and carrots. Her spirits brightened and she smiled. Though she could not take Simple, or ride out on Storm, she would leave the castle.

Returning to the clothing chest, she rummaged through it. A short time later, she put her ear to the door and listened. All was quiet. She opened it enough to see her way was clear afore she left the room.

Ugsome, forever close when duties took Garith elsewhere, loped up the stairwell and padded over to her. His tail wagged so hard it nearly toppled him as he followed her into Ede's room. She changed, and when ready to leave, commanded the beastie to lie quiet and stay. He stretched out on his stomach, his battered head on his paws, and turned sad eyes up at her.

Every man Rolf could spare worked on the sea wall, out of sight from the north barbican that led from the castle and the bridge on the west.

In the bailey, Meghan strode toward the well, warily watching from the corners of her eyes for anyone who might recognize her. Seeing no one noted her, she dabbed her hands in the wet ground beside the well. When she again stood, mud splattered her face and clothing. She looked like a common lad who worked hard in the fields. Weaving in and out of the milling crowd, she avoided Rimsdale's servants and waited until a boisterous group of village merchants gathered their empty baskets and carts. As they headed back through the gatehouse, she mingled in with them.

Drawing abreast of the weary old woman struggling with the empty trundle, Meghan deepened her voice and spoke. "Ma'am, I be strong and restless. Me da saw ye needed help and sent me. Let me push yer cart for ye." To strengthen her story, Meghan glanced behind her to wave and flash a grin at an old swineherd many paces behind. Puzzled, the man waved back.

The woman sighed. "'Tis thankful I be fer yer help, lad." She shook her head and gave a sad smile. "The master, he be a good man. After me auld man passed, the master said I was not to be afeared to bring what I could grow. Ne'er has his cook turned me away, e'en tho me wares be not the best."

"Oh, aye," Meghan agreed. "The MacDhaidh is like no other." She kept her head lowered.

Halfway across the bridge, the old woman stumbled, and Meghan dropped the handles of the trundle and put her arms around her. "Oh, ma'am, let me help ye sit in the cart. 'Twill anger me da if I let ye get hurt." She eased the frail woman over to the cart and made sure she was securely seated. Meghan felt her hat begin to slip. She tilted her head to hold it steady, and when her hands were again free, she righted it.

"Fer a lad with so much dirt on yer face and clothes, ye do smell fresh as the mornin's air."

"Ma makes me bathe afore comin' to the castle. I fell in the mud this morn. No doubt, she will thump me heid fer ruinin' me clothes." Meghan, pretending her da had already cuffed her, settled the cap over her secured hair. She judged the woman weighed less than a hundredweight. How had the poor soul managed her loaded cart this morn?

Once they reached the village, Meghan saw her settled securely in her broken-down cottage. Bidding her a good day, she hurried down a path in the heavy woods until she was out of sight of the villagers. Rolf would not discover she was gone for a while, and by the time they searched the castle and grounds, night would fall. She would have a good start. She broke into an even-paced run. If the weather held, the moon would guide her until she had to stop and rest.

It was cool in the forest. Even so, Meghan began to sweat after she had gone about two leagues. She stopped and listened. No sounds of pursuing horsemen disturbed the utter quiet. Pulling off her cap, she shook out her hair, then lifted it to cool her neck. She knelt down and tugged at the clothing on her legs.

She was thankful that she wore two pairs of heavy wool hose. Hose pilfered from Rolf's chest. She had donned one of his gray tunics and a pair of breeches too. They were far too big, but she had rolled the waistline of the breeches and pulled the drawstring tight to hold them. She bunched the tunic up and over her leather belt. Since she had left the clothing borrowed from Ede folded in a neat pile on the bed, Rolf would look for her to wear what she'd had on that morn. She hoped Ede wouldna notice that the Blackthorn tartan and tunic rested between the pallet and the ropes of her bed.

Hearing water nearby, she left the path, careful to lift branches aside and not break them. Each step she took, she glanced back to be sure she left no clues behind. She found a small stream, and after splashing cold water on her face and drinking her fill, she studied the position of the waning sun. If she continued northwest, she would come to the Naver, the river that fed Loch Naver. 'Twas at the northern end of the forest, a league or two within Blackthorn lands.

With any luck at all, she would meet up with a Blackthorn patrol sometime late in the next day. She pressed on throughout the afternoon, walking in streams whenever she could to throw off any hounds Rolf might bring with him. Long after night fell, she trudged down a stream and was so weary she feared she would fall on her face. She must stop to rest and start fresh at daylight.

Meghan looked about her. Best not sleep on the ground. A perch high atop a tree would give her an advantage. If his warriors were to stumble on her path, they would be studying the ground and never look up to find her. An added boon was she would see them coming. She spotted a large tree where a good-sized branch hung out over the water. 'Twas perfect. In a scant bit of time, she was hidden high in the tree so thick with leafy branches she could barely see below. Good. If she could not see them, they would not see her.

Straddling a stout branch, she took off her belt and wrapped it around herself and the trunk and buckled it. She leaned back against the trunk and sighed with relief. She swayed back and forth, testing it. The belt kept her from moving more than two hands' span in either direction. If she slept, she had no fear of plunging to the ground. Her eyes grew heavy and soon closed.

* * *

At the first light of dawn, a hearty yawn coaxed her awake. She yawned again and reached up to rub her stiff neck. Again? Wait! Her body stilled. She slapped a hand over her mouth and held her breath. She had but yawned once. Wary now of disturbing any branches, she peered down past her right side to the ground below.

Steely gray eyes stared back at her. Rolf lay on his back, arms folded behind his head, his gray cloak flung over him. From his rested look, he had not only spent several hours there, but he had also slept well while doing it.

"Well now, I would enjoy the view more if ye were clothed as a proper lass. Still, no proper lass would spend the night tied high in a tree, would she?" He waited. When she kept her lips pressed closed and glared her hatred at him, he stretched and threw off the cloak.

"Come down, Meghan." His voice was hard.

"Nay. This view far surpasses the offal littering the ground."

"Come down, Meghan," he repeated. His voice softened.

"Go away. Find another lass willin' to be yer whore. Do ye not know when a woman scorns ye?"

"Well now, if you dinna come down, then I must come after you." His gray eyes hardened, and his voice grew even softer, more ruthless. "You willna like it." He stood and watched her as he shook out his cloak. "Have you e'er made love beneath a tree? Hmm? Did you like the feel of the sun on your bared breasts, warming them for a man's lips?" He dropped the cloak and put his hands on his hips. His hot gaze never left her eyes. "Have you felt a warm breeze caress between your widespread legs? I am told it heightens a lass's pleasure tenfold."

"Bastard!" A shoe struck him on the shoulder. He picked it up and studied it, as if it was a curiosity, then continued as though he had not stopped.

"I will count to ten. If you are not down by then, I will come after you. Dinna make me, Meghan. If you do, 'tis on your hands and knees you will serve me." He put his hands on his hips and stared at her.

"One . . ." She didna move. "Two . . ."

"Whor—" She stopped herself, remembering his threat to beat her did she call him whoreson again. "Lucifer's spawn!" The other shoe went crashing down. He sidestepped it with ease.

"Three . . . four . . ." He stared into her eyes, daring her to thwart him.

"Five . . ." He started to unbuckle his belt. "Obey me, Meghan, and I will wait until this eve to couple with you in the comfort of my solar. Else, I will do as I said."

She swallowed bile, for she knew he was ruthless enough to do it.

"Six . . ." The belt slithered to the ground. When he reached up to pull off his tunic, she knew she had best give in.

"Halt, ye slatherin' beast." Furious now, her hands fumbled at the buckle of her belt. A cold knot closed off her throat, stifling the curses forming on her lips. So close to her own lands! She should ne'er have stopped to sleep. Her throat ached with the lump there.

When she at last released the buckle, she replaced the belt around her waist to keep his breeches from falling off. She had some slight satisfaction seeing his eyes widen. He recognized his clothing. After he retrieved his belt and put it on, she worked the stiffness out of her arms and legs. In a flash, she scrambled down the tree as fast as she had gone up.

She clamped her teeth together, for if she spoke, she knew her voice would waver and give her away. She *wouldna* yield to tears like a weakling of a woman.

CHAPTER 14

Rolf stifled a rumble of satisfaction as Meghan swung down, as supple as a youth, from one branch to the next. As she released the last one, he caught her around her thighs, her hips held tight to his chest. Her buttocks rested against his forearms. She glared down at him; her fists pounded his shoulders.

"Lucifer's poxed arse." She spit out the words with contempt as she glared down at him. "Release me."

His arms tightened, and he nestled his face against her stomach. "In due time," his muffled voice answered.

"Now!" Every inch of her body tightened with resistance. Every hair on his head challenged her angry fists as she grabbed them and tugged to force his face away.

"Aye, *Sir* Meghan, I am at your command." Of a sudden, he opened his arms. Her fingers released their grip. With arms flapping like a bird taking flight, she tried to steady her balance. She plopped on her bottom to the crackling sound of the dead leaves that carpeted the ground.

She scowled up at him, and he raised his brows in question. "Did you not demand I release you?" He reached out a hand. She ignored it. He watched her as intent as a hawk spying a field mouse. She didna disappoint him.

Meghan bounded up and struck out at him with her fists. His arms deflected each blow. He did not strike back. Never would he beat a woman. She would soon tire herself and know she could not fight or wrestle him to the ground. His strength was far greater than her own.

Damp whorls of brown hair fell over her forehead. As she

peered at him through the strands, he saw defeat lurk in the sea-green depths of her eyes. Her resolve would not waver, not until she suffered the last blow of his vengeance. He grimaced at the wrongness of it, and his heart lurched. He must build a steel cage of memories around his mind and heart with pictures of Ingirid's terrified eyes as she passed and the feel of his tiny son in his arms as he breathed his last. They braced him.

He gripped Meghan's shoulders and forced her to stand quietly. "You can strike at me till you drop, or we can wrestle together on the ground all this morn, but in the end you will return with me to Rimsdale." His harsh voice grated in the quiet of the woods. Her shoulders slumped beneath his hands. "Come. Luath waits but a short way back."

"How did ye find me so quickly?" Her voice was little more than a whisper of air.

Had Rolf not been so attuned to her every move and sound, he would not have heard her. "I returned to my solar and knew someone had been there. I ken when an object is moved but a mite. When I went to your room, I found Ugsome shut within. I knew Ede was too afeared to be near the beast. That left only you."

"I covered my tracks. Even froze my feet in streams to throw ye off."

"Aye. You did." Should he tell her he had learned her secrets each time she rode out with her escort? Why did he debate with himself? "I have watched you climb the highest trees when you hunt. You wouldna sleep on the ground. If not for the moon, ne'er would I have seen where you rested."

He tossed her atop Luath and mounted behind her. Meghan didna speak again. He admired the lass. She had well-nigh eluded him with her cleverness. For near a league, Ugsome had searched both banks beside the stream and could not find her scent. Rolf rode far upstream and looked back. When he noted the large branch overhanging the water, 'twas then he knew he had her.

She had covered more ground than many of his warriors could have in the same time. He didna tell her Laird Damron had an endless pattern of scouting patrols crossing his borders. Half a league more and she would have been free. Lost to him.

He also kept silent about his strict orders that whenever messengers arrived from Blackthorn, the patrols were not to allow them within half a league of Rimsdale.

Mereck had arrived yester eve. When Rolf met with him, Mereck had insisted Rolf name the ransom he sought for Meghan. Rolf replied that he did not hold her for ransom. She was a *guest*. Not a prisoner. She would return to Blackthorn when she concluded her *visit*.

This night, she would begin to make amends for what Blackthorn's men had done. He did not have the sense of satisfaction felt on earlier days. Instead, knowing he could not waver from his plans, her coming humiliation caused him pangs of distress so harsh he near cried out. He shook his head, trying to stifle his thoughts. He could have captured Connor's bride, a Saxon. She would not do. He did not want her to bear his son.

Only Meghan would suit.

Neither spoke until they rode across the bridge. He felt her stiffen further. Her eyes studied the water with longing.

"Dinna think on it, Meghan. Even did you someday again elude the guards and make it to shore, I would be there as you came from the water." His arm tightened around her. He would not allow her to flee from him again.

Though all at Rimsdale noted their arrival, they went about their business. That did not stifle their curiosity. While pretending to be occupied with their pursuits, they watched from the corners of their eyes.

Meghan felt her tension ease when he stopped at the castle steps. He did not intend to again imprison her in the stable like a horse to be broken.

"I have not seen Storm or Simple these past days. I would that you take me to them now."

"On the morrow I will take you to see the wee hawk and Storm. This day you will keep within and prepare yourself for me."

Prepare herself for him? Was the man daft? She would as soon prepare to meet the devil!

Meghan ignored Rolf's outstretched hands and sprang from Luath. He near stepped on her heels all the way to Ede's room. She gripped the door, ready to slam it in his face, but he was too swift for her. He sent it crashing against the wall.

"Get out," Meghan shouted. "Ye dinna have the right to invade another's room."

"Aye, I do. No door in this castle may be closed to me." As he sauntered into the room, his eyes scanned everywhere. Spying the trunk in the corner, he strode over to it and threw back the top. Seeing it held male attire that had belonged to Ede's husband, he shouted for Jamie.

"Take this and store it with the clothin' in the warrior's barracks."

"Ye have no right to remove Ede's possessions." Meghan's hands tightened into fists.

His sole response was to quirk a brow at her.

Jamie left the room with the trunk balanced on his shoulder. Rolf latched the door and turned to her.

"Take off your clothes."

Meghan folded her arms across her chest and stared at the wall.

"I dinna want to tear my own garments. If you force my hand, you will repair the damage." His lips twisted in a bleak, tight-lipped smile. One meant to freeze the viewer.

Meghan planted her feet; her chin lifted higher.

"I know how much you dislike womanly pursuits, Meghan." His voice purred as he stepped closer. "Did I not watch you steal out of the women's solar whene'er Lady Phillipa set you to the task of sewin' Connor's garments?" He rubbed his jaw as if recalling an incident. "Hmm. Did I not also hear a tale of a certain tapestry you made to welcome Damron's bride?"

Meghan felt herself flush. All on the tapestry was done right enough, except for the figures that represented Damron, his bride Brianna, and Connor. They were stick figures.

"Brianna loves that tapestry. She had me help her take down the one hanging in their room and set mine in its place."

Of a sudden, Rolf's hands flashed out to remove the belt around her hips. She tried to shove at him, to pull away from his grasp, even to hit him with her fists. She failed to thwart him. Never had she been so quickly divested of her garments. That the clothing was overlarge was part of the reason. In a mere trice, his pilfered breeches were the last thing covering her.

Her efforts brought her bare breasts in closer contact with him, and she gritted her teeth and stood still. One quick flip of his eating knife, and the breeches fell to puddle around her ankles.

He released her. With as much dignity as she could muster, she stepped out of the breeches. She turned her back on him and walked over to the bed. Every inch of her felt his heated gaze as she snatched a blanket and draped it around herself.

Taking all he had stripped from her, he tossed them out the door, then turned back to her. The heat from his narrowed gaze added its own threat.

"You will wear none but womanly attire till I return you to Blackthorn. Dinna again stoke my ire on this." He waited for a response.

He would roast in hell's fire afore she gave him the satisfaction of hearing "aye" from her lips.

Rolf had not wanted to leave her. What he had wanted was to bar the door and explore her intriguing body inch by beautiful inch. Every beautiful, *golden* inch. His mouth went dry and his manhood strained so mightily against its confines that he near expected the cloth would split.

He glanced down at the throbbing bulge centered there between his legs. Mayhap he should wear naught but a tartan when Meghan was about. He shook his head and grimaced. Even so, the obvious effect she had on him would be nigh impossible to hide.

Once he had begun to strip her, he thought she would be

affrighted. Nay. She wasna. She stood as proud, as regal, and as defiant as any queen.

By God's grace! She was magnificent.

A feast for his eyes, even though mud streaked her face. How could a lass so enthral him, standing with her lovely breast bared yet with her lower body still clothed like a man?

She would never know how hard he fought to keep his face impassive as he bared the rest of her. It had taken all of his hard-won control not to snatch her back against him when she turned and walked to the bed. His hands twitched, wanting to stroke that beautifully curved back, to squeeze those firm rounded nether cheeks.

The sound of his boots striking the steps leading below disquieted him. From whom did he run? Meghan? Himself? A growl rumbled up from deep within him. He prickled with impatience. He must needs wait for evening. His revenge, planned with such care, called for the witnessing of her surrender. He glanced out a window opening to judge how many hours remained in the day.

Too many.

The sun crossed low in the western sky as Meghan prepared herself to go below. She handled the white silk hose with care as she gartered them above her knees with white ribbons. When she held up the pale leaf-green smock, she noted it was near transparent. As it slithered down her body, it floated soft and luxurious against her skin.

Earth colors were her chosen favorites. She admired the deep hue of the forest-green tunic. In some lights, it appeared near black. The silver girdle would lend a beguiling contrast.

"Ede, dinna linger for me. I would have a minute of quiet afore I go below." She peered in the polished metal, pretending to take one last admiring look at the artful way Ede had arranged her hair.

After the sweet woman left the room, Meghan yanked the pins from her hair, ran her fingers through her tresses until it flowed, untamed, as wild as racing storm clouds. Minutes later, she settled the silver girdle about her hips. Satisfied, she threw the brown cloak about her shoulders and jerked open the door. Jamie jumped to attention.

"Thank you, sir, for your escort," she said as she smiled up at him.

The closer they came to reaching the great hall, the more her skin crawled at what awaited her.

At the entrance to the room, Meghan squared her shoulders. Lady Phillipa had trained her well. She could grace any royal court with dignity.

Rolf waited in front of the great table, clean-shaven with his hair neatly tied back. He wore a white shirt with the red, green, and black MacDhaidh tartan about his waist and up over his left shoulder. She fancied she smelled spice and sandalwood. For the first time, he looked as he had so many years afore. Her heart ached for what had been lost between them.

Standing in the middle of the room, she held a steady gaze on his eyes. With slow, deliberate movements, she released Jamie's arm and stepped forward. Out of his reach. She let her hands drop, shrugged her shoulders, and the brown cloak slipped to the floor to lie there like soft earth among the rushes.

Her chin shot up. Cold air struck her on every side. She fanned hair from about her shoulders to cover her breasts.

She wore naught but white stockings and the sheer green smock. The silver girdle rode low on her hips, its heavy clasp accenting the dark triangle at the apex of her thighs.

Rolf was too stunned to move or speak.

Not her, though she didna have much to say.

"Ye would make me yer leman? Then 'tis a slut ye desire."

As greedy eyes from every corner of the room roved over her, she steeled her flesh to not quiver.

Rolf stood as if frozen, unable to move. Not a muscle twitched. Had she misjudged him? Could any man have so changed his character in a few short years? Cold heartache struck its fist into her chest. Her breath caught with the pain of it.

Could she call forth the Rolf he had once been?

CHAPTER 15

Meghan twirled in the center of the great hall. She fought the burning muscles in her legs that wanted to turn and flee up the stairway to hide in the darkest corner she could find. A lifetime had passed since she had entered the room. She again faced Rolf and threw back her head.

Defying him. Challenging him. Would he allow her to so degrade herself and not move to stop it?

He would not. He exploded into motion.

The veins in his temples stood out in livid ridges as he stormed over to her. "Are ye brainsick?" he yelled at her.

He lunged down, grabbed the robe, and sprang up so fast the garment swooped through the air like a giant brown bird, its wings swirling and dipping, scattering bits of rushes high to float down and sprinkle through her tumbled hair.

"Dinna ye ken ye are near to naked? As any common trollop?" His nostrils flared in a face taut with anger. "Not an inch of yer body is hidden from any who care to gaze on it."

Rolf, his face a hot mask of rage, yanked the robe tight about her neck. She flinched, fearing he longed to throttle her.

"Ye would do well to fear me," his voice rasped. "Ne'er have I felt such a great need to beat a woman."

Still silent, she squared her shoulders, stiffened her spine, and shot him a hand gesture that Brianna, Damron's unusual wife, had said meant a man should swive himself. How that was possible, she could not say.

"You goad me to violence, Meghan of Blackthorn." Rolf glowered at her and slapped her hand down.

Sparks of tension flew from him, prickling her skin. His teeth ground together, his hands clenched as he fought to control his anger. Sorrow seeped through to an already burdened heart as she fought tears that threatened dishonor. She blinked them back.

"Beat me. Go ahead," she taunted him. Her fists pounded on his chest with each word. "'Tis better to take a thrashin' than be made a whore afore all the world."

"My leman," he bellowed. "Not a whore. None would dare call ye such."

"Nay. Not to *yer* face," she shouted. His hands slackened. She pulled from his grasp and clasped the robe close around herself. "Nonetheless, 'tis a whore I would be."

She stepped back, away from his scent of spice and sandalwood that played havoc with her heart and mind.

Both were locked in a war stance, neither willing to give in. She meant what she had said. Why did he not accept it?

As he studied her, Rolf read her determination, for his eyes narrowed. Finally, he nodded. His shoulders relaxed as he stepped back.

"We will handfast," he offered.

Her gaze searched his eyes, his face.

With arms crossed and legs spread wide, he nodded at her. "We will pledge to each other this—" he stopped as a shout interrupted him.

"You canna." Alpin surged from his seat and stormed over to them. He grabbed Rolf's shoulder.

"Hold your tongue." Rolf glared at the fingers gripping his shoulder, then back at his friend. His eyes narrowed. "Remove your hand." As Alpin's hand dropped, Rolf's steely eyes blazed at Ede, Garith, Dougald, and Jamie, who had jumped up from the high table. His warning was clear. Keep silent.

Garith, about to protest, sucked in a breath and parted his lips.

"You will abide by my words, else seek your room." Rolf glared at the young man, then gestured to the doorway.

Garith clutched Ugsome's ruff in his hand and plopped down on his stool. Silent.

Rolf's attention returned to Meghan. Her eyes studied him, probed into his soul to find her answers there. He nodded, forced his face to a gentler expression, and continued as if he had never been interrupted. "We will pledge to each other this evenin' and begin life anew."

She did not respond, but he sensed a softening in her stance. "I want you, Meghan. Though you fight against it, you canna gainsay this thing that lies between us."

She started to counter with a denial.

He held up his hand to bid her to silence. "Nay, lass. 'Tis there and well you know it."

Meghan lifted her hands and shrugged, implying her own puzzlement. His hands darted to pull her cloak about her as it started to slip and reveal again what he wanted no other man to gaze upon.

"Ye agree to handfast with me?" Meghan's face could not hide the disbelief her mind fed her.

"Aye."

"Ye are not plannin' to deceive me on this?" She frowned at him as she mulled it over. "A year and a day I will be as yer wife? If at the end of that year ye dinna want a weddin', what then, Rolf?"

When he did not answer, she continued. "If ye refuse to wed me then, the child will stay with me?" She lifted her chin and dared him to defy the unwritten rule.

"Aye. 'Tis the way to resolve a broken proper handfast." His voice slowed on the word *proper*. "You canna pledge yourself in this clothin'." Meghan bit her lip and frowned. He lowered his voice and added, "Please. Go above." Her eyes opened wide. His voice gentled. "When you return, all will be done aright." He turned her toward the door.

She peered over her shoulder at him. He watched entranced at the changes that fell over her face. Her forehead smoothed. Large sea-green eyes no longer glared at him but glowed with shy warmth. Slowly, her cheeks and jaw relaxed. Warm, full lips were the last to surrender. They softened and lifted at the corners. All her icy scorn, her hot anger, her stubborn defiance seemed to melt away.

Meghan looked . . . vulnerable.

Never had he thought to see this proud lass with her guard down. Pangs of guilt ripped their sharp claws through the vengeance guarding his heart, leaving hurtful, gaping rents.

Though it near felled him to do so, he must have his way.

Pandemonium broke out after she disappeared up the stairwell.

"Eneuch!" His stare raked over the people there. His order brought the tumult to a quieter din. He strode over to the high table and spoke to no one in particular. "Hear me well. Dinna argue with me on this."

"But, Rolf"—Garith's eyes looked puzzled—" 'tis not a knightly thing you propose."

" 'Tis more knightly than for the lass to believe herself a whore."

"Is it, now? What will she deem herself later?" Alpin's face still showed his anger.

Rolf did not answer but turned instead to Ede. He steeled himself against her accusing eyes. "You will not interfere."

"What you do is wrong." She jumped up from her bench. Ugsome growled at her, and she scowled at him and raised her hand flat out over the table and slapped it. "Be quiet, beast." Ugsome settled at her feet. Ede's eyes grew round with surprise.

Rolf glared at her. "You will keep your thoughts to yourself. Was your husband still with us, he would tell you 'tis none of your affair. You will abide by my will." His voice softened. "Go above and help Meghan, but keep your tongue behind your teeth." He frowned and scowled around him.

Dougald had not spoken a word. He had no need. His thoughts were there in his eyes, plain for Rolf to see.

Disappointment.

* * *

Meghan stood in the bedchamber, uncertain, and glanced around. Never would she be Rolf's leman. But to handfast with a man was honorable. For the lack of a priest, couples often practiced it. She frowned. Father Mark was within the castle. Why did Rolf not want a proper marriage? Slowly, her frown eased. Nay. He was right. 'Twas better this way. If wed by a priest, they would be sealed together through eternity. This way, if they couldna resolve their differences, either could reject the other with no dishonor to her or their child, should she prove fertile. He had agreed that by proper custom, should he not marry her, the child would stay with her.

Her spirits lifted. The door opened, and she was pleased to see Ede. The sweet woman was fast becoming like a member of her own family.

"I am sorry I ruined the beautiful work ye did on my hair, Ede." Meghan made a face and lifted her hands to shake her long hair. Bits and pieces of rushes mixed with heather, crushed rose petals, and rosemary floated to the floor. "Mayhap we should leave it loose?"

"Your hair is beautiful." Ede's soft smile looked forced. "I am sure Rolf prefers it thus."

Meghan nodded. What was the matter with her? She never blushed, but now her face was fiery hot as she remembered Rolf once whispering how he longed to feel her hair on his naked loins. 'Twas disgraceful. She had blackened his eye for saying it.

"Come. Remove the girdle so we can redress you." Ede stood, the green tunic held aloft, awaiting Meghan's arms.

In but a short time, they again dressed Meghan as a noble woman should be. Fastening the girdle around her hips, she wondered why Ede seemed reluctant to meet her gaze.

"Do ye dislike the Morgans of Blackthorn so much ye dinna want me as a member of yer family?" Meghan studied Ede, for the woman puzzled her. Before this, she had been open and far friendlier than she could expect.

"Oh, nay," Ede hastened to reply. "You are a most welcome addition to the castle. 'Tis more honor you hold in your hands than most men have in their massive bodies." She reached out to hug Meghan to her. "Ne'er would I not want you as part of my family, as my friend."

"Ah, such a pleasant feelin'," Meghan murmured against Ede's neck. "I have missed the comfort of arms about me."

"If ever you should need me, I will be here for you." Ede released Meghan and stepped back. "Now, I will comb the twigs from your hair. You will be the most beautiful lass ever to walk down those stairs."

Finally, she felt Ede give the last pat to her hair at the same time they heard Jamie outside the door. Why did she feel so twittery? Uneasy? 'Twas not that she was afeared of what happened between a man and woman. She had learned at an early age about those matters, for other than her Aunt Phillipa, the other members of her family were men.

Blackthorn had many happy lasses who sought her brother and cousins for their favors. Their *more than ample* favors, she had learned. In their early manhood, they had been too eager to be discreet. After she tripped over Connor's legs one dark night, she placed a well-aimed kick at his bare arse. The happy lass he was with shrieked with pleasure. He groaned. Whether from pleasure or not, she wasna sure.

Meghan chuckled at the memory. Had she been so occupied with her memory she did not realize they had entered the doorway of the great hall? Rolf's head was cocked to the side, listening, his eyes heated. Noticing everyone looked at her, she put a hand over her lips to quiet her nervous laughter. Connor had oft said it was much like his own. Deep and throaty. For the first time, she was conscious of it. Embarrassed, even.

"Ah, 'tis the first I have heard you laugh in many years, lass." Rolf's voice was a husky purr close to her ear. "Were you in a room with as many people as leaves in a forest, I would know you there with but a single laugh."

She hesitated. Unsure. Why? Never before had she been beset by such foolish women's notions. She took the arm he held out to lead her to the high table. When they reached it, servants bustled about bringing in steaming platters of food. They had awaited their meal for her? 'Twas an unexpected courtesy.

Everyone watched her. Some seemed open and friendly enough, while distrust radiated from others, fear from a few, and some merely looked curious. One could expect that with people who knew nothing about her but what they learned from hearsay.

Garith was silent and seemed to need comfort from Ugsome. Alpin looked as if he had swallowed a foul brew. His pale blue eyes darted ice slivers at her. If he pressed his lips any tighter, they would disappear. How had she pricked his anger? What worried her most were the intercepted looks of what suspiciously looked like pity from Dougald. Why pity? 'Twas not dishonorable to handfast. Uneasiness crept up her back.

Rolf was attentive, but she sensed tension he tried hard to conceal. It matched her own. If she had her way, they would dispense with the food and get on with the pledgin'.

"I ken you prefer your wine not be watered?" Rolf offered her the goblet they would share. He waited for her to take a hearty sip, then drank himself.

" 'Tis good. Not bitter or sour." Lucifer's toes. She sounded like a fool making small talk with someone she hardly knew. 'Twas not far from the mark, for this Rolf who had captured her was as a stranger.

This eve he looked more like the Rolf she remembered. No doubt he had taken great pains with his person to remind her of how he once was. But the bitter lines beside his lips could not be smoothed with soap and the scraping off of his whiskers. Nor could he sit for long afore his forehead creased in a frown. More and more, she felt as if she should dash for the door.

"Why do you study me? Am I not the same man you have known since you were a skinny sprite?" His mocking voice startled her.

"Nay. Ye are not." She shook her head and frowned as she

studied his eyes. "'Tis not age that marks ye. Nor battle scars. Though the white slash through your right brow is new to me." She quirked a brow at him, and her lips twitched. "Did ye mayhap forget to duck?"

Rolf shifted in his seat, looking ill at ease. A memory flashed through Meghan's mind. "Aye! Ye did." She burst into laughter. "Now I remember." She grinned at him. "Ye should have kenned better than to dally with Meridene de Anjou while Henri yet lived. Aunt Phillipa didna take kindly to ye cuckolding her brother."

She took a long swallow of wine as she watched his face turn from pink to bright red.

"Tell me"—she leaned close and whispered—"did Aunt for truth strike your bare arse with the flat of a sword as ye made a dash for the door?" At his shocked look, she giggled. "'Tis the reason ye hit yer head on the door's opening, is it not?"

"How came you by such a tale? You shouldna be privy to such happenings," he blustered.

"Ha. No tale. 'Tis truth." She poked his hard-as-rock arm. "Connor and Damron came to visit me at that desolate abbey Damron forced me to when ye betrayed me after the feast. They told me of it." The memory of her miserable summer made her scowl at him.

He shifted in his seat and shoved the wine back close to her hand. She took another sip.

"Mayhap had they confined you for a longer period, suitors aplenty would have bid for your hand when you returned. Had they found you changed to a gentlewoman, you would long ago have bairns clinging to your skirts."

His words were splashes of ice pelting her. She narrowed her eyes, then turned away. What knew he of her suitors? Plenty had come to bid for her hand. A poor lot they were too. Why, she had bested most of them at the quintain. She was more adept than many with a blade, a bow and arrow, and even throwing her dirk. No. He knew nothing of her suitors.

"I had suitors aplenty." Angry now, she turned back to him.

"Aye? Why then are you not wed?" he mocked her.

"I didna *want* a nithing of a man." She glared at him and hit her fist on the table, almost upsetting the wine. "All were weak in some way. None strong enough to be a fitting husband to me."

He said nothing. His eyes deepened to smokey slate as he studied her face.

"Aye. No weakling could control you. You will not find me so easy, Meghan." He drew out her name slowly, softly. "You are like a wild stallion that must needs be, hmm, tamed, by a firm hand."

Each time Rolf had brushed against her, she felt his tension mount. His body tightened, seemed ever more firm. His breathing became rapid, and she sensed his need building to a pitch.

He bounded to his feet and ordered the servants to clear the tables. Though he wore a tartan belted around his waist, she spied the telltale signs of a manroot fully engorged.

She tried to swallow, but her mouth had gone dry. Instead, she took a quick gulp of the wine he had been coaxing down her since they started their meal. He was more subtle than most, but she knew when a man tried to soften her.

When all was set aright again, he didna need to call for silence. He grabbed her wrist and hauled her to her feet. Impatience sparked from him. Within a few scant breaths, they stood in the cleared center of the great hall.

He scanned the room, then looked down at her.

" 'Tis time." Thick lust made his voice husky.

Meghan looked around and did not see Father Mark. "Wait. Though 'tis not necessary, I would pledge afore a priest."

Rolf's voice lowered. "He was not able to attend."

She frowned, for those within their hearing looked at each other.

"We need no priest," he continued. "All here will witness our pledge to each other." He turned her toward him and clasped her hands. He took a deep breath and spoke loud and clear for all to hear. "Know all ye that I, Rolf, the MacDhaidh of Rimsdale, pledge myself to Meghan, a Morgan of Blackthorn. I keep myself only to her *for as long as we are one.*"

He waited but a scant second afore he squeezed her hands, impatient for her to cite her pledge. She hesitated, still uneasy. Her teeth nibbled her lower lip.

"Come, Meghan," he murmured, his voice laden with passion. "I am no nithing of a man who will let you escape me now."

She blinked. Her heartbeat quickened, for she had longed for this union for so many years.

'Twas the reason no suitor could win her hand.

"I, Meghan of Blackthorn, pledge myself to Rolf, the MacDhaidh of Rimsdale. I keep myself only to him . . ." Her voice faded. What had he said? Had she not heard all he said? Mayhap the wine made her forgetful. She started over. "I keep myself only to him *for a year and a day, as long as we are one.*"

She felt his hands jerk at her words. Before she could worry further, his hard muscled arms surrounded her, and he kissed her so thoroughly she was in grave danger of forgetting her own name.

Where the room had been silent before, it erupted in bedlam. Men were men, alike everywhere. They hooted, banged their fists on the table, and yelled advice. When Rolf released her at last, breathless and weak-legged, she clung to his shoulders for support.

His hot gaze probed her face. Why was there such triumph in his eyes? He swooped down and effortlessly lifted her in his arms, and she gasped.

"Come. I have waited overlong for this night," he whispered. He kissed her again, hard and fast this time. His impatient strides took them from the room and up the stairwell to the landing above.

The clamor below faded to a faraway murmur.

CHAPTER 16

Meghan's heart quickened with each impatient leap Rolf took up the stairwell. When they reached the landing, his arms tightened further, as if fearing she would break free and flee.

As if she could.

'Twas not only his undisguised anticipation, but the drumming of his heart beneath her ear that weakened her. If she needed further proof of his eagerness, she could not doubt the flaming hardness that throbbed against the side of her waist.

He thrust open his solar door and slammed it shut with the heel of his boot. Just paces from his bed, he halted to gaze down at her. A stiff breeze from the window opening enfolded them, and his arms tightened.

Her breath caught at the expressions flashing through his gleaming eyes. Triumph. Passion. Impatience. All were there, undisguised.

His gaze held her own as he lowered his arm beneath her knees to straighten her in his arms. Each inch she moved against him sparked hot fire through her flesh. Hard. All of him—his massive chest, the hard slab of his belly, that hot and eager part of him—until soft lips claimed hers.

She wrapped her arms around his neck, afeared she would slither to a puddle on the floor. His ardent tongue traced the seam of her lips, demanding she open to him. She did. He probed her mouth, explored her, tasted her. Hesitant at first, she welcomed him and opened wider. A growl rumbled up from deep in his chest. She shivered, for it reminded her of a ravenous wolf about to devour a deer.

He raised his head and looked at her, studying her face and seeming to hesitate. What did he seek there? She grasped his cheeks and brought his lips back to hers. This time, it was she who ran her tongue over his lips, shy and reticent. He opened, slowly at first, teasing, until she became bolder and demanded entrance. He tasted of sweet wine and mint, a heady mixture.

"Ah, Meghan lass." His whispered breath tickled her lips. He held her motionless with his gaze as he unfastened the silver girdle. The links tinkled together, a merry tune, as it fell to the floor. Her tunic followed, soundless.

He slid his hands down her arms and over her hips, then he stopped to kiss her again. So engrossed in what his mouth was doing to hers, when his lips released her, she tried to follow them, unwilling to be parted. He grasped her sheer smock, lifting it to her shoulders and over her head.

No longer within his arms, she felt the cold air float over her, startling her. Naked, all but for stockings and shoes, she stood there. Heat flushed her face and traveled down to warm her neck.

Rolf chuckled. A wicked, enticing sound.

"Such a lovely sight, Meghan lass, with your face flushed." He stroked his fingertips down her cheeks. "Your neck." His gaze traveled over her, following his fingers as he caressed her. "Ahh, even your breasts. Golden and rosy at the same time."

For a moment, his gaze hardened, then heated again. He rained damp kisses from her jaw to the tops of her breasts. "I would know how they came to be so sun-kissed. Later," he breathed the word, then caught his breath as his lips found her nipple.

Shock rippled through her as he took it between his teeth. He released it, and it thrust toward him and begged his attention.

"Ah, so sweet, like sun-ripened cherries." His hot, wet lips swooped over it to draw it into his mouth to suckle.

Lightning traveled to the pit of her stomach. She grew heavy there. Fiery. Dewy.

He grasped her hips and lifted her to rub her aching flesh

against his hardness. She gasped and moved against him, seeking to quench the need growing with each breath.

"Ah, sweetling." He chuckled, triumphant. His hand dipped between her legs to cup her, and now it was he who surged against her; he who strained and ground against her flesh.

"So fiery. So moist." Sliding a finger into that tight heat, he took a deep breath. " 'Tis eager you are."

Rolf began kissing her again, harder now as he guided her back till her legs bumped the bed. Grasping the edges of the soft green blanket and white sheet covering it, he whipped them back and lowered her onto the downy pallet. He removed her shoes and peeled her stockings from her, then left her but long enough to near tear his own garments off and toss them atop his clothing chest.

With the moon's light streaming in from the window opening, Meghan spied his bare flesh as he stripped. Her mouth went suddenly dry. She was no innocent as to how a man was made, for the men of her family were known for their masculine prowess, their ability to please a woman. Yet, Rolf's size surprised her. She knew a woman's body was made to accommodate a man. Too, she was no wee slip of a girl. Even so, her eyes widened.

The moment his hot flesh spread over every inch of her, she caught her breath at how he made her feel. She was enveloped in the scent of him, which tripped her heart and heated her flesh. Fully aware of his massive power now, she, who had always prided herself on her courage, was as other women.

Weak. Helpless. Powerless.

Her heart beating wildly, she grasped his shoulders.

He nibbled her ear as his fingers roved over her. He reached her center and found her legs locked together. "Ahh, nay, lass."

Rolf's knee urged her legs apart though she would have kept them together. He settled his body there between her thighs, and the feel of his hot, hard shaft resting against her thighs worked magic over her swelling flesh. She jerked as his fingers threaded through her damp hair and found her nub, swollen and throbbing.

"Mmm, 'tis but a small bit of pleasure now, lass." His finger again entered her, teased her.

Too tight at first. Her body gave around it, surprising her. He stroked and tantalized as he drew on first one nipple then the other. She tried to force her hips to stillness. She could not.

Rolf's breathing became heavy, labored, and he again growled deep in his chest. He nestled his hips against her, and the blunt tip of his tarse nudged at her opening, hot and turgid. Startling.

"Nay, Rolf, please, 'tis—"

"Shh, Meghan mine." He entered, restrained at first as he eased into her. She started again to tell him he was too large, but she realized with each thrust that her body sought to keep him within. She gasped at how his entering made her feel. Complete. She had waited these many years for him. For the rightness of it. He lowered his hips, withdrawing and entering, each stroke easing deeper into her. She gripped the hair at his temples. He lifted his head from her breasts, his passion-glazed eyes staring into hers.

"Look at me, Meghan. Know that it is the MacDhaidh that possesses you." With that, he surged forward, halted a moment, then broke through to bury himself deep.

She tried to draw away, unable to stifle a soft cry. Her hands jerked hard on his hair. His eyes cleared. For a moment, he looked grim.

Shock held Rolf still. When he had found her so very tight, he kenned she had been without a man for some time. Reaching her barrier, he dismissed it as fancy. One powerful thrust and he claimed her as his own. Once he broke through, he could not deny it.

Meghan had been a virgin.

Elation soared. Only he had lain between her legs. He studied her face. Her lower lip was clamped between her teeth, her eyes pressed shut. He held still until her body began to relax as her pain ebbed. Lust filled his sac near to bursting. Its weight rested there against her nether cheeks.

He placed soothing kisses on her chin until her lips relaxed and he could capture them. He moved only after she began to respond. Slow at first. Ever cautious of her. His thighs clenched as he sought to control the desire that surged like a ship driven afore a storm. She tensed, and he lifted to smooth a hand over her skin. Quivers began low in her stomach. He raised higher. His fingertips sought her hot slickness to rub and tease her flesh.

Her first release exploded through her, and he rumbled with satisfaction and clasped their bodies close again. His pace quickened as he plunged and retreated, until she was in the throes of her climax. She clawed his back. She whimpered. Cried out. Only then did he allow his own release.

Never had he experienced such. Never had a woman matched him in passion. Eager with each spasm from within her, his tarse responded until every drop of his seed burst into her.

Rolf rested his forehead against hers until he caught his breath. Neither spoke. Finally, she surprised him with a wry chuckle.

"Ne'er did I expect such. 'Tis no wonder lasses smile so after they couple. I have missed much, it seems." She grinned up at him. "Years to make up for."

Anger exploded through him. "Why didna you tell me?"

"Tell ye what?" She tilted her head, puzzled.

He moved to her side and pointed at her bloodstained thighs. "What?" he repeated her word, becoming angrier. "That you were virgin. I could have made it easier for you, you daft woman," he shouted.

"Did ye ask?" she hollered back.

"I didna feel the need." His voice shook the bed.

"Didna feel the *need*?" She sprang to a sitting position. Winced. Her eyes widened, realizing what he inferred. She struck him hard across his cheek.

He was too surprised to react.

"Ye thought me a trollop? A woman who spreads her legs for any well-hung male?" Her eyes glared lightning flashes at him. "If that is what ye kenned, why did ye wish to handfast with me?"

Rolf refused to answer. Her mouth turned grim. Shame flushed her face, and she grabbed the sheet and covered herself.

"If that be what ye believed, then I ken I lack experience." Her fingers twitched, then clenched. She looked mad enough to tear his eyes out, sitting there clutching the material around her breast. "I have no doubt men aplenty will be happy to supply the schoolin'."

At the thought of Meghan sprawled beneath another man, hot fury erupted from the depths of his body and roiled up; his face and neck felt twice their size. He grabbed her shoulders and shoved her back on the bed to straddle her, locking her hips between iron-hard thighs. He grasped her face and forced her to look at him.

"I have branded ye *mine*. My property. My possession." Each word was harsh and cold as he rocked her face back and forth, then brought his own close to hers. "Ye belong to me now. Ne'er will ye lie beneath another man."

She clawed at his wrists and twisted her head until he let her chin go. "I am no man's property. No man's possession." She spit the words at him. "Get off me."

Suddenly, she went still. Her head whipped to stare at the corner to the right of the heavy door, several paces from his clothing pegs. Shock widened her eyes. She blinked several times, then turned back to him.

He had no need to see what had startled her. 'Twas her brother's stained clothing upon the stand, his armor and helmet atop its holder. At first glance, it appeared like a man who stood there. A man who observed them.

Rolf grunted. His lips thinned. He answered what he knew she asked without words.

"Aye. It stood as witness that you were in my bed. In my arms. My body between your legs." His eyes narrowed, and he added, slow and even, "My tarse embedded in you."

"Offal," she shrieked. She tried to claw his face. He was too quick for her. He grasped her wrists and forced them back beside her head. She surged and bucked beneath him, fighting with all her strength. Finally, exhausted, she quieted. Seeing the anguish in her eyes, he rued every brainsick word he had uttered. How could he have said such to her?

Meghan's eyes appeared like a wounded doe. Haunted. His heart cried out in pain, and ice-cold regret ripped at his soul. What they had shared was beautiful. Unique. She had given him a most priceless treasure, now forever gone. On planning his revenge, he had not thought he would take an innocent.

Now, he viewed her early escapades in a different light. In Normandy he had believed her keen to tend a man's needs. What he judged was eagerness to dally was naught but curiosity. His heart twisted, remembering the wonder in her eyes when she exploded around him. Would she ever feel the same again?

Meghan fought the pain in her chest. A lump formed in her throat. His eyes burned like frozen ash as he stared into hers.

Rolf had deemed her a trollop. A whore.

She had deemed him a man of honor. Equal to her brother, her cousins, this man who had held her heart for a decade or more.

When she had news of his marriage, she had escaped into the forest and wept till no tears were left. From then on, no suitor appealed to her, no matter how handsome, how worthy. She found fault with them all. They didna measure up to Rolf. Or to the Morgans of Blackthorn.

Later, when she learned of his wife's tragic death, she grieved for him.

All that time, he had thought basely of her. Shame filled her. She swallowed the lump in her throat and fought for control.

"Move from me, Rolf." Her voice sounded huskier than usual, but at least it didna quaver overmuch. To account for the little it did, she added, "I canna breathe." She tugged her arms, trying to free herself from his grip. He did not release her.

"Nay." His cheek rested against hers. "Nay, lass," he

repeated. "We have said our vows. You are mine now. I willna release you." He nuzzled his lips against her neck, then trailed them down and across her collarbone.

Her flesh tingled, and she jerked her head aside. "Cease. I willna play the whore to give ye ease. Go below to any who pant for yer favors." Again she jerked hard to dislodge him.

Breasts still swollen and tender rubbed harshly against the crisp whorls of hair on his chest, and she bit her tongue at the streak of pleasure that shot through her.

He sensed it, for he glanced up at her. His eyes gleamed as he again lowered his head, and his hot mouth closed around a nipple, and his tongue stroked roughly over it. She caught her breath and shrank back from him, thinking to pull away. He did not follow but held firm, stretching the nipple. Surprise made her gasp, for it increased her pleasure. She stilled.

Finally, he lifted his head and ground his hips against her. She bucked and writhed beneath him. She had wrestled often with the men and now did everything she could to dislodge him.

"Offal! Horse's arse! I want none of ye."

"Nay?" He crooked an eyebrow at her. "I think ye will." He went on to prove it by tormenting her other breast.

Heat shot down like a bolt from her nipples to the pit of her stomach. "Lucifer's tarse," she shouted. "Leave me be."

He chuckled. The vibration sent even more pleasure through his mouth to her breast. "Nay. Not Lucifer's tarse, Meghan. 'Tis Rolf's tarse. Mine." Fully aroused, he lifted his hips. The wet tip of his penis stroked against her thigh. To give her added proof, he nudged it against her opening.

Meghan bucked again. The movement caused him to enter her. He stilled and watched her. She went rigid.

"Umm. Go ahead, Meghan mine. Challenge me." His eyes grew smokey. "I would have you no other way. 'Twould not be like you to give in easily."

She gritted her teeth and glared up at him. Determined not to move. Not a single muscle. If she did not aid his pleasure, would he tire and leave her? Now that she had stilled, every sensation heightened. His scent filled her. His hair against her breast tormented her with each breath they took. The deepening color of his eyes showed that his pleasure also increased.

Saints help her! His tarse swelled with each heartbeat. She could not turn her mind from the feeling. 'Twas as if her body willed her to accept him. Her wet sheath turned to liquid fire. She stifled a groan when her muscles contracted around the head of his tarse.

Nay! Her traitorous body tried to pull him in. He laughed. Deep and exultant. Though he did not move his hips, he grew longer and entered deeper. How long had she held her breath? She gasped and her body moved downward, enveloping him more.

A cry of disbelief left her lips as her body continued to betray her. Her stomach jerked, her hips quivered.

With a shout of triumph, he plunged into her. She squeezed her eyes shut and arched her back. He angled his hips and followed.

A sob tore from her.

"Open your eyes, Meghan mine." He gripped her chin.

"I am not yers." She accented each word as she panted and glared at him. With all her strength, she fought for control.

"Aye, you are," he whispered. "Mine." His head swooped down, and he kissed her hungrily. "Mine," he repeated as he increased the tempo of his thrusts. "Yield to me."

"Nay," she cried.

"Yield, Meghan mine," he repeated as he thrust harder, deeper. His gaze would not release her.

She shook her head, gritted her teeth, and waged a futile war against herself.

"Yield!" His voice was a demand. He plunged deep. Filled her near to bursting, then held still.

He throbbed within her. Fire coursed through her. Lights burst before her eyes.

Wave upon wave of tumultuous ecstasy shook her. A wail escaped her lips. His back arched. Every muscle in his body quivered as he held still through each spasm of her body.

Finally, he threw back his head and freed his own stormy climax.

Meghan panted, exhausted. Tears slipped between her closed lids and slid down her cheek. Mayhap she was a strumpet that he could force such an unwilling response from her?

He pressed his face there between her neck and shoulder and gasped. Moments later, he took a great breath as his tarse slipped from her. He rolled to his side, put his arms around her, and pulled her tight against his sweating flesh.

Rolf pulled her head to rest beneath his chin. Tears slid from her tightly closed eyes to fall on his chest. Pangs of remorse snaked their strangling arms around his heart. Her defiance had so aroused him that he had determined to have her desperate and begging for release.

She had fought him valiantly. She had not begged.

He had fought her, had given her no quarter.

She was no match for him, for his experience.

"Shh, Meghan mine. 'Tis no shame you should feel." He thought back on the years afore. "Always we have had this between us. Something has sparked and driven us both to fight it. You couldna win against it."

With gentle hands, he rubbed her back while her body shook with silent sobs. She who never cried.

He kissed her and sought to soothe her anguish.

"Shh, love." He squeezed his eyes tight to deny the sudden moisture spilling there. Murmuring words he never thought to use, soothing words, nonsense words, he nuzzled his face in her hair and clutched her tight to his heart.

CHAPTER 17

The feeling of triumph eluded Rolf. Long after Meghan slept, he held her. The night air turned chill, and she burrowed closer. Her hand searched up his chest to the side of his head till her fingers felt his long hair. She grasped it tight, then stilled. She sighed, satisfied.

A cold gust of wind caused her to shiver. Reluctant to wake her, he could not rise to reach the wool blanket at the foot of the bed. With his foot, he rooted around until he caught the edge of the blanket on his toes. Moving slow and easy, he bent his leg. When his knee neared his chest, he spied smears of blood on his thigh.

He needed no reminder she had come to him a virgin. How had he been such a fool to believe she was not?

He answered his own question—her bold behavior in Normandy had deceived him.

But Normandy was not the first time Meghan had engaged in untoward escapades. She was but ten and three the spring he had visited Blackthorn. He and Connor had come in from the training field and joined the warriors in their quarters. As Rolf stood in the doorway and looked over the room, something seemed odd.

He eyed a squire who edged backward toward him. He frowned, for the lad's shoulders were too narrow, the legs slender, and shapely hips rode below the belt. The squire's soft body bumped back into his own solid mass. The lad squealed.

Squealed?

The youth froze and seemed to think he had backed into the doorway. A hand reached back to search the wood frame. What it found was Rolf's hard thigh. The lad snatched his hand back and tried to edge away. Rolf propelled the culprit through the doorway and out into the bailey. He guided him to the foot of the stairs and spun the youth to face him. 'Twas the first time he had seen Meghan in pilfered clothing.

"Bloody saints! What are you doing mingling with the men? Nay, dinna bother to answer." Eyeing her frightened expression, he pointed to the castle stairway and shouted, "Go."

She sprinted away so fast she needed to grab the hat confining her long hair. Rolf returned and motioned Connor to follow. By the time they reached Meghan's room, he had told Connor what he had found.

She did not deny she was curious about the men and how they lived. In fact, she turned to her brother and whispered.

"Why do they strip off their clothin' and strut about afore each other?" She frowned, looking puzzled. Then her eyes lit. "Is it to judge the size of those things?" She pointed at Connor's groin. His mouth gaped open, and she flushed.

They took turns yelling and lecturing her until they were both hoarse. Her small chin lifted stubbornly, and she had tried hard to hide the fear in her eyes. 'Twas only their threat to tell her grandda that brought a subdued look to her face.

From the earliest days he had known her, he admired her for her total honesty, her courage. And her pride.

Meghan was everything and more a man could want in a woman.

He snuggled the covers about her back and shoulders, and she murmured and burrowed her face closer under his chin.

Nothing had ever felt so right.

He could not sleep. A ragged tear appeared in the cloak of vengeance wrapped so snug around his heart. An ache formed in his chest. What an agonizing dilemma revenge had brought him.

'Twas too late now. He squeezed his eyes tight in a grimace.

Two vows.
One he must honor. The other he must forsake.

Meghan ran faster than any time in her life. Fear nipped at her ankles. She did not dare spare scant seconds to look over her shoulder. Heavy footfalls crashed closer. Her very soul screamed for her to be wary. Of a sudden, a man's punishing hand caught her long braid and tossed her to the ground. She lay sprawled on her stomach. Her legs twitched and jerked, her fingers clutched the ground. Far away, someone called her name.

Wrenching herself from her dream, she panted. Her heart raced as faint wisps of man and sandalwood jolted her senses. Rolf.

Alert now, she knew she was in his bed. Naught but the scent of him accompanied her.

"Meghan?" 'Twas Ede in the doorway.

"Aye?" Meghan sat up, controlled a wince of pain, and glanced at the bed. As she thrashed about in her dream, she had tossed off the covers. She tugged the pillow over to hide the bloodstained sheet.

Ede looked toward the fireplace, embarrassed. "Rolf ordered a hot bath for you. I was not to awaken you, but I thought I heard you cry out."

"Mayhap I sneezed." Meghan rubbed the tip of her nose. She felt hot shame that she had showed fright in her dream.

"Surely 'twas that I heard," Ede agreed.

"A bath would be most welcome." She stayed in the bed and waited until the bath arrived and the servants left.

"Would you like help?" Ede's eyes shone with sympathy. "Mayhap someone to talk to?"

"'Tis not necessary, but thank ye." Meghan sighed with relief after the woman left the room. She looked at the bed and grimaced.

When Rolf had taken her to his bed, he had believed her

sullied by other men. Unchaste. Even after learning his thoughts, she had responded to him like a wanton. She stepped into the hot water and scrubbed, then scrubbed again until her flesh was red. Not until the water turned cold and she began to have chill bumps did she leave the tub. But no soap could wash away that shame to her pride. Wrapped in a large drying sheet, she looked for her clothing.

Someone had entered while she slept, for last eve's raiments hung on a wall peg. That horrible stand, bearing the bloodstained clothing and Connor's armor and helmet, was gone. In its place, she spied a small trunk. Folded atop was a pale pink smock and a deep rose tunic.

She draped them over her arm and opened the lid to peer inside. All that a woman needed rested there—a wooden comb, a polished piece of metal to peer in, jars of ointments, ribbons of various colors, stockings, and other clothing. All were soft and feminine. None were in rich browns, or deep forest colors.

All his trunks now bore locks. Irritated, she ground her teeth together. Sure that he had picked out what she was to wear, she placed his selection inside. Delving through the rest, she found a fawn smock. At the bottom of the clothing lay a tunic the color of rich earth after a summer's downpour.

She dressed and left the room. Jamie awaited several paces down the landing. His curious gaze swept her from head to toe. Meeting her eyes, he had the grace to blush. She nodded and started to go below. By the looks of the sky as she passed the arrow slits, she had best go to the cookhouse to break her fast. It was long past the sun's rise.

She did not hear Jamie's steps follow her. Had Rolf posted him there to see she didna wear breeches? She huffed.

At the cookhouse, she ate sharp cheese and hot bread. She glanced back at the main castle building. Theirs was an unusual handfast. Surely Rolf wouldna follow custom too closely. If she spied the bloodied sheet displayed atop the ramparts, she would tear it to shreds.

Just see if she did not.

Thankfully, no such sight greeted her, and she sighed with

relief. People hurried about their duties, some smiled at her, others appeared sheepish and turned away.

No one was about but the usual servants when she went to the great hall. Hanging on the far wall near the fireplace was the bagpipe left by the clan piper. She shook her head. A pity no one had taken over the job after his passing.

She missed her own pipes, for 'twas her custom to join the Morgan piper atop the battlements to play. She enjoyed the musical salutes, gatherings, and laments as well as the merry tunes of welcome that burst through the air as visitors approached the barbican.

She inspected the pipes and found them in good order. She inflated the bag, and soon emotions flowed from her body to the pipes as she played. The room vibrated with wild and abandoned music, the music she preferred.

Far at the end of the castle grounds, paired men spaced wide apart honed their skills in the practice field. The deafening clang of metal to metal, metal to shields drowned out speech.

The tumult failed to erase Rolf's memories of Meghan in his arms. Her eyes had looked up at him with trust when he broke through her barrier. Never had he felt such triumph. Nor such shame. Afterward, intense pleasure, more than any before, flooded him as he brought her over the brink to ecstasy. His own release had been unsurpassed. It shook him to the core of his heart.

All night he had held her.

Triumph. Regret. Victory. Each had flooded him in turn.

Leaving her bed before dawn was not what he had wished. Had things been different, he would have spent the day—nay, days—abed with her.

Cautious not to wake her, he had moved from her soft warmth. Before throwing on his clothing, he grabbed the hateful stand bearing Connor's armor and thrust it out the door. His cruelty on using it in such a way sickened him.

God's grace, Meghan was beautiful. Her slim, golden back

was bare down to the slope of her rounded hips. Dark hair spread across the pillows, and a long wavy hank streamed down her supple spine. He had hardened and became heavy with need. He forced his eyes from her.

Her clothing lay where he had stripped her of them. Leaning down, he picked up the sheer smock and the dark green overdress and breathed deep of her scent. He set things to right in the room, then turned to look at her once more; sorrow at what might have been near bent him double. He opened the door and left.

The clang of a claymore against his shield jolted him. He felt, rather than saw, that someone awaited his attention.

"Hold, Dougald." His man lowered his claymore, and Rolf turned to see Alpin stood there.

His friend's fist beat a slow, steady rhythm on the wooden beams of the fence separating the practice areas. His body was taut, his jaw thrust forward, hostile. Ah, he must needs get over his anger at the handfast. His friendship didna give him the right to dictate Rolf's plans.

Jamie stood beside Alpin and looked embarrassed with his duty. He held an armload of rumpled bed linen. "Do you want me to display proof the lass was pure when she came to your bed?"

"Nay."

"You would brand her impure?" Jamie looked displeased with the thought.

Rolf glanced at the sheet with distaste and frowned. " 'Tis not for Rimsdale that I had you retrieve it."

Alpin's eyes lost some of their glare. "For Blackthorn," he said with certainty and nodded his head.

"Aye. For Blackthorn."

Dougald came closer. "Do ye want me to send the *gift* with the next patrol? I can have my best man place it close within the Morgan borders. Their men will spy it soon enough."

"After the night deepens, hang it from the tallest tree," Alpin suggested. "They canna let the insult ride for long."

"Nay," Rolf said. "It goes to Laird Damron, along with my

missive that Meghan and I have handfast. They will not dare attack to gain her back. She is as a wife to me."

The thought of using Meghan's virgin blood in such a way made his stomach lurch. But it could not be helped.

"You canna," Alpin's shout caused nearby warriors to pause in their practice and stare at them.

Dougald frowned and motioned them back to what they were doing.

"Ne'er dare say what I can and canna do." Rolf's voice was so soft, so lethal, that Alpin's eyes widened. "I wouldna have them the wiser until Meghan takes with my seed." He motioned them away and resumed practice with fervor. After a while, Dougald laughed and begged respite. Rolf lowered Beast and leaned on the long shaft. He stared about him. Something was amiss.

What had seeped into his awareness?

"Cease." Rolf's bellow sounded above the clamor of weapons. The warriors stilled. Moments later, sound drifted on the wind.

Soft. Plaintive. A lament.

Someone played the pipes. Nay, not someone. Meghan. None but she could call forth such pain. Nor such joy. A new tune started low, with each note rising higher, faster, until it became a lure that caused every footstep to hurry toward it. From the empty looks of the bailey, she had played for some time.

Did she wear the rose tunic he set out for her? He lengthened his stride, kicking up whirls of dirt in his hurry. Close to the castle, wild abandoned sound greeted him. His blood raced as if forced by the music.

Meghan played, her eyes closed, and she let the music carry her atop the Blackthorn battlements where she saw the lands of her home sprawled far below her. How long she swirled the music through the air, she didna know. Tired now, she allowed the last note to fade and squeezed the bag free of air. Relaxed, she pulled off the mouthpiece to clean it.

"Rolf told me you used to sneak the Blackthorn piper's own

instrument until your grandda gave ye your own," Garith's voice said behind her. "Was he not angry?"

Meghan startled, not realizing until now that she was no longer alone. People had been drawn to the sound of the pipes. From the looks of the crowd, they neglected their work.

"Angry?" She looked at his earnest face. "Who? Angus or Grandda?"

"I guess 'tis about Angus I wondered."

"At first, aye," she answered and grinned. "The poor man went to play a greetin' for the laird of the MacLaren. The pipes were not where he stored them. I had taken them deep in the storage rooms of Blackthorn so none would hear my sorry attempts." She shrugged her shoulders and rolled her eyes at him. "Angus found me, but 'twas too late. The MacLarens were already within the castle drinking ale with Grandda."

"From Damron's tale, you didna sit for your meal that eve," Rolf's voice came from behind her.

She stiffened. "Nay, I didna."

"Angus beat you?" Alpin stood beside Garith. He sounded shocked that the man would dare.

"Not Angus. Grandda. A fortnight later he called me to his room. I kenned he knew about something else I had done, so I padded my bums." She grinned at Garith when he chuckled.

"You had to do that often, I ken." Alpin's eyes lost some of their hardness, and his tall, lean body visibly relaxed.

"More oft than I care to recall." She shrugged and made a face. "Grandda didna summon me for a thrashing but to give me my own set of pipes. He had Angus trade three fat sheep for the pipes to a man some leagues away. My lessons on the proper method of piping began that very noon. Those pipes, my sword, and my dirk are my only treasures."

"Have you no jewels, no baubles?" Alpin looked surprised. "Ailsa forever bemoans the fact I do not supply her with enough trinkets. Had she her way, she would wear a ring on each finger."

"Your wife?" Meghan was surprised a man would tell of such greed from his mate.

"I have no wife."

"On her last visit, she wore so many gewgaws I thought mayhap she adorned her toes," Garith piped up.

Alpin glared him to silence.

Wanting to distract attention from the young man, Meghan spoke again. "I found adorning my hair and fingers sometimes caused an injury." She glanced at a scar on the middle finger of her right hand. "The bowstring caught atop an ornate ring. When it tore the decoration off, it ripped my finger from knuckle to knuckle. I willna wear rings to this day."

At the mention of a bowstring, Alpin frowned. Too full of his own maleness, she decided. The Blackthorn warriors did not resent her skills. They sought her out for practice or asked her aid in teaching a squire the proper way to throw a knife.

She turned to Garith. "Where is Ugsome? I havna seen his comely face this last day."

The boy chuckled. "'Tis the first time anyone has called the hound comely," Garith said. "Not even his mother kept him close for long."

"Even as a pup?" Meghan asked. He shook his head. "The poor thing. Did no one think him worthy to cuddle, to give him love?"

"Oh, aye. Rolf made a pallet from an old tunic. He brought it to my room, and we took turns feeding the pup milk and porridge. Later, we chewed meat for him until his teeth were strong enough. 'Twas a long and tiresome task."

On hearing the hardened warrior had taken such pains over the dog, Meghan felt a pang of longing for the man Rolf used to be. "Ye ne'er said where he is," she reminded Garith.

"Hunting. Now and again he goes off on his own. More often than not, he returns bearing new scars," Rolf spoke up.

She couldna look at him. Thankfully, he smelled of weapons and sweat, not the heady stuff that was his usual scent. Even so, every inch of her was aware of him. His hands drew her eyes. She blinked and willed herself not to look at them. 'Twas futile. Her breasts tingled, remembering how those calloused thumbs had rubbed over her nipples.

A sound, animal-like, rumbled from Rolf's chest. Startled, she peered up at him. And wished she had not. A rush of heat rose to her face, for he stared at her nipples pushing against the soft material. His gaze did not stray. Her breasts swelled and grew heavy. She crossed her arms.

"Now that we are handfast, do I have freedom to roam the grounds, Rolf? I would see Simple and Storm this day."

"I have not the time to escort you."

"Escort? I am no weakling that must needs have a warrior to show her the grounds."

"I would have someone with you." He frowned at her.

"If that be so, I am prisoner still, not a helpmate as was sworn last eve." She stiffened her back.

"I will accompany her, Rolf," Garith spoke up.

Rolf nodded and turned to Meghan. "You will not stray outside the gatehouse or to the weapons' room. You may exercise Simple. The wee birdie hasna the sense to aid you."

"My steed also needs exercise. If kept confined, he will kick down the stall door and take out on his own."

"I ride him twice daily."

"Ye have not the right! Storm is mine own."

Rolf's brows shot up in surprise. "Not the right? You forget, Meghan mine, we are as man and wife. What was yours is now mine. You will ride when I say you may." He stared down into her eyes.

"Lucifer's bloody toes." How dare he take her horse from her? "If, as ye say, we are as man and wife, why then may I not come and go at will?" she shouted.

"Because I dinna trust you."

Meghan fisted her hands and clamped her lips together, fighting her anger. She lost. He knew it. She opened her mouth to shout further at him, but his arms closed around her, and he kissed her until the reason for her anger flew from her mind. His arms slowly released her. She wobbled like a newborn colt. Rolf's eyes gleamed with triumph, and a slow smile spread across his face. Long strides carried him from the room afore she was again steady on her feet.

Drat the man!

Day passed quickly from bright sunlight to the dim rays of early evening. Garith's was a bright and sunny disposition, so unlike the darkness lurking in his brother's soul. She laughed at his quick wit and enjoyed exploring his clever mind.

Through the evening meal, Rolf plied her with the finest offerings, from juicy bits of lamb to a steaming apple pastry with melted cheese atop it.

Finished with their dining, warriors gathered in groups to swill ale or play rowdy games. Their blaring voices echoed off the stone walls, making conversation nigh impossible.

Several times, Alpin opened his mouth to speak, then closed it. Finally, he leaned close. "While the knotty-pated fools rattle their brains, would you play the pipes for us, Meghan?"

She frowned at the unruly warriors across the room. "'Tis sorry I am, Alpin, but I dinna feel the urge to make music."

"Perchance 'tis another type of music that calls to you?" Rolf whispered in her ear. Puzzled, she peered up at him. He added, "Do you not know your cries of pleasure are the sweetest music to mine ears? Do you wish to sing such a heady tune? Hmm?" His lust-filled eyes gazed down at her as he grasped her wrists and hurried her from the great room.

CHAPTER 18

Meghan was hard-pressed to match Rolf's eager strides. His need fired her blood, though her mind told her to be wary.

Man and wife. He had said such. She would respect her vows. Her honor demanded it. Though it aggrieved her that he would guard her still. By the time they reached the bedchamber, her ardor cooled.

Breathing hard, he drew her into his arms the moment he slammed the door behind them. She twisted her head aside when he sought to kiss her, and his hot mouth brushed her chin.

"Rolf, I swore the words that I would keep myself to ye for a year and a day. I wouldna dishonor them."

He rocked his bulging sex against her and kissed her cheek. Hungry lips and gentle teeth nibbled along her jaw and made their way back to her mouth. She sighed and avoided his hot kisses. Before he befuddled her mind with lust, she would have this out between them.

"Storm can carry me to Blackthorn and back in but a five-day span."

He jerked his head up and stared at her. "What are you suggesting?"

"'Tis right my family should know I am safe." She strained back to see his face. "I wouldna have them believe me in a dungeon. Or food for carrion."

"They dinna." As though that was the end of it, he clutched her tight and attacked her mouth with renewed vigor.

Ne'er had she believed a man could fire her blood with but a kiss. Nay, he didna need even a kiss. Her face close to his skin kindled her blood. She inhaled, slow and deep. A sigh escaped her as she opened her lips to his eager tongue.

She was no stranger to kissing. Her most ardent suitors had been clever in waylaying her, much to their later dismay. If they tried to thrust their tongue into her mouth, they found her knee in their groin. Not even her shadow remained by the time they straightened. Yet Rolf had but to dampen her sealed lips and they yielded to him.

Her eyes flew open. Had Rolf used his drugging kisses to still her arguments? She shoved his shoulders until they stood apart.

"They dinna?" Her narrowed eyes studied him. "Ye had word from them and didna tell me of it?"

"Nay. I sent Laird Damron a missive of our handfast."

"They will not believe ye. It was not written in my own hand. Why did ye not tell me?"

"You think to question me?" He stiffened, overbearing now.

"Aye." Hands on hips, she stared back at him.

"Learn now, Meghan, you are but a woman. You dinna question me. You dinna gainsay me." As she took breath to form a heated reply, his finger on her lips forced them to stillness. "You will do as I say, when I say it. Do you ken?"

"Aye, I ken what ye say, but it will be a long, hot day in the dead of winter when ye think to rule me." She huffed and headed for the door. As she lifted the latch, his hand slammed down on hers and closed it again.

"Think again, Meghan mine," his voice purred behind her. He grabbed her wrists in one hand and held them high above her on the door. Pressing her against the wood, he cradled his hot groin against her buttocks as he nibbled and sucked at her ear. The more she wriggled to free herself, the more she excited him.

Rolf's hand pressed between them to release his rampant tarse from his leggings. Knowing what he did, she heaved back attempting to turn around. His fingers snaked the hem of her clothing up above her waist.

Meghan's sex was naked and vulnerable to him. He bent

his knees until his hot tarse rode against the seam of her nether cheeks. He rubbed himself back and forth, then lowered still farther. A foot nudged her legs apart enough that his tarse burrowed between her thighs. The curls nestled there dampened as her body readied itself for him.

Rolf's big hand cupped her. "Ah, Meghan mine," his husky voice murmured as he nipped at her shoulder. "So hot." She shook her head, denying him.

"You would fight me still though your body craves mine?"

"Aye." Her voice sounded strangled as she fought down the hot lust that fired her body.

"How long, Meghan? How long can you deny me?"

His fingers combed through her damp curls. Ever so slowly, one slid into her and stroked.

Her body quaked. Her muscles convulsed around him, trying to draw that lone finger deeper. She shook her head, resisting it.

"How long? Hmm?" He traced the slick opening and had to use considerable strength to keep her pinned against the door, his knees against the back of her legs.

She shuddered again, then gasped when he licked her ear and whispered into it.

"How long, Meghan mine?"

She clamped her teeth together. Fought herself, fought him.

"Now, Meghan mine. Now," he commanded before his mouth clamped down on the side of her neck. He plunged his finger back into her and stroked the hardened nub of her sex with his thumb.

"Rolf," she gasped. As she arched back against him, she moaned and squeezed his hand between her thighs as she climaxed.

He held her there, his hand tight against her pulsing flesh. As the last spasms faded, he turned her and lowered her to the floor. Her eyes closed. Shamed. Her legs were like a newborn colt. She could not keep him out, had she wanted to. She did not.

Settling himself between her thighs, he thrust into her. Her body welcomed his fullness, was eager for it.

At first, he rode her, slow and easy, seeming to savor each stroke as she rose to meet him. Her own movements soon became frantic, and he quickened his thrusts, rocking fast now and holding tight to her shoulders.

"Again, Meghan mine. Again," his voice demanded. Of a sudden, he reached down, wet her clothing with his mouth and suckled a nipple. When it hardened, he took it between his teeth and tugged.

Her body tensed tight as a Welsh longbow. Wrapping his arms tight around her as she bucked and writhed with violent orgasms, he rode her as if he were breaking a mare to his thighs. With an outcry of pleasure, he released his iron control and his seed spurted into her.

Neither moved for long moments as they fought to regain their breath. Finally, he knelt beside her. Without speaking, he lifted her in his arms and carried her to the bed.

"Mayhap we should have a servant lower the covers afore the sun sets." He gave her a wry smile and stood her on her feet before he tossed the linens back. After he helped her remove her clothing, he shrugged out of his own.

"'Tis sorry I am I was too eager to take you to the bed." Rolf turned her so he could study her back. His hand floated over her skin, seeking any discoloring.

Her flesh quivered. He stroked her again. Gentling her. Gratified, he lowered her to the bed and stretched out beside her, propped up on his elbow as he studied her.

"Why didna you wear the rose this day?" His question was slow, lazy. She would be even more lovely with such a warm color against her golden skin.

"I would choose my own clothin'." She lifted her head and rescued the hair trapped beneath her. "Ye know I dinna like linens flapping against my legs. Why can I not wear what is comfortable to me?"

He fondled her hand and studied the scar on her finger.

"Because you have no need for them. Had you not been

wearing them, you wouldna have caused this hurt." He drew her finger to his lips and kissed the scar.

" 'Twas not the clothin' but the bauble that caused it."

"Aye. Were you not playin' at being a man's equal, you wouldna have challenged the warriors at archery."

" 'Tis not playin' to prove a skill. I bested all but Damron and Mereck." She stopped and added, "Mereck is like no other with the Welsh longbow. He didna use it to outdo me."

"What of your brother?"

"Equal." She grinned up at him. "He, Eric MacLaren, ten other warriors, and I scored the same."

He lifted a lock of hair, brought it to his nose, and inhaled. "When the heather is in bloom, 'tis like you are close beside me." He wound the curl around his finger to rub against his cheek. "At what other feats do you think to shame the men?"

"Shame?" Surprised, she stared up at him. "I dinna *shame* any man at Blackthorn. Most have had a hand in teachin' me the skills. They boast they have taught a 'mere' woman such feats."

He studied her face and nodded. "Aye. I remember well your first attempts at the knife. Did Mereck succeed in perfecting your aim?"

Meghan smiled lazily up at him. "If ye return my dirk, I will show ye how accurate my aim is." His burst of laughter made her grin.

"Do you think me so beguiled by your beauty I would do such a brainless thing?" He moved to cover her with his hard body.

"Are ye afeard I will impale ye with my wee shaft?"

"Nay." He shook his head and grinned. "Are ye afeared I will impale ye with mine own shaft?" he teased. His hardening manhood stirred against her thighs.

"Shaft? Nay. 'Tis much more than that." Meghan chuckled.

"What amuses you, Meghan mine?"

"When Mereck brought Netta to Blackthorn, he had not yet bedded her. The Saxon girl knew naught of men. She asked one day by what name was the thing that dangles in front of a man."

Rolf rumbled low in his throat and spread her legs with his knees.

She giggled, then went on. "I told her when it be small and pitiful like, it goes by the apt name of prick or pintle."

"Um?" Slow and deliberate, he rubbed against her hot center as his sex swelled and lengthened. "Prick or pintle, eh?"

Meghan gasped and wriggled beneath him. Her body caught fire with each teasing movement. "If it be long, ye do like to call it a tarse, a rod, or a shaft."

As his wet tip entered her, she lifted her hips to better seat him firmly. Her breath quickened. "When hard and strong, it became a ram, um"— she wriggled beneath him, urging him to move—"a dabbler . . . a weapon."

"What pleasures ye now, Meghan mine?" He held still within her and watched her eyes darken with passion. "A pintle?"

"Oh, nay."

He rotated his hips, and she gasped with surprise.

"A shaft?"

"Nay."

He surged into her, seating himself until his hips ground against her.

"What, Meghan mine?"

She grasped his shoulders and held her breath.

"Hmm? Tell me." He nibbled her earlobe. "What impales you now?" He pulled almost out, then thrust into her, filling her with heat and power.

She wrapped her legs around his hips, meeting his fierce thrusts with eagerness. Her blood surged so hot she could think of naught but the building tension that filled her.

"What brings you such pleasure, Meghan? Tell me!" When she would not answer, he again went still.

Her nails dug into his flesh and she gasped. If he did not continue, her body would explode from unreleased tension.

"Rolf!" She clawed at his back. Her hips and legs tried to draw him deeper within her.

"Tell me."

"Weapon," Meghan gasped. " 'Tis a weapon ye use against me."

Rolf clamped his lips over hers. Though the night was cool, his efforts to bring her to untold heights of rapture covered him in sweat. Never before had he craved a woman's pleasure response.

With Ingirid, he had not unleashed his passion for she had not cared for bedsport. Was this urgent desire to couple with Meghan fueled by his need to quickly get her with child? The urge to conquer her, physically and mentally, overwhelmed him.

Once he mastered her, it would sate his passion. Not until then would she be forever his. Not until then would he be satisfied.

He gained little rest that night. Each time he woke, his shaft was hard and throbbing, his sac full and urgent. Even after he filled her with his seed, he did not want to leave her.

'Twas well past nightfall at Blackthorn. Damron, along with Connor, had waited in the solar since dusk, for they expected Mereck to return afore the midnight bells of vigils. As warriors clamored over the drawbridge, Brianna and Netta barged into the room, their babes held at their shoulders.

"Is Meghan with him?" Brianna asked, breathless.

She hurried to the window opening to peer out. Her delicate, small body belied the strong will housed in it. Whenever Damron stood his massive body toe-to-toe with his wee wife and glared green daggers at her in an attempt to intimidate her into obedience, he fought a losing battle.

"Nay, wife. Mereck carries somethin' under his arm. Here, give me wee Douglas afore ye upset the lad with yer frettin'."

"Fretting? Ha. It's Connor who has his bowels in an uproar," Brianna huffed as she handed the babe to his father.

"Not any old man will do for her." Connor ignored her odd teasing and nodded his head as he raked his fingers through dark brown hair so much like Meghan's. His mouth, which was forever lifted at the corners in a smile, now turned down with worry.

"Eric MacLaren's uncle Angus has need of a wife. As big as a bull and twice as mean. Meghan wouldna dare thwart his orders."

"'Tis too late now for finding the lass a man to husband her," Mereck said as he strode into the room. The air crackled with his energy. The wolf, Guardian, followed close at his heels.

Mereck was a giant of a man and would appear Damron's twin except for the laird's dark hair. Mereck's long and wavy hair, neither brown nor golden, flowed wildly about a face painted blue on one side. A hide tunic covered his sculpted torso to just above the knees, while wolf skins framed his massive shoulders. Pewter armbands circled muscular arms. His attire brought out the wild Welsh side of his heritage.

The first time his Netta had seen him thus, she was so frightened of the wild savage called Baresark that she had run away to hide at her friend's castle.

"Did Guardian lead ye to her scent, brother?" Damron asked.

Netta near threw herself at Mereck, so relieved was she that he was home again. He put an arm around her and kissed her with enthusiasm before he nuzzled his son Donald's head. Without speaking, he tossed a white bundle to Connor.

"Aye. Guardian led us to the base of a tree but a league inside MacDhaidh borders. Meghan must have covered her tracks in the water, then spent the night in the branches. I found signs she had tied herself high to escape notice, but Rolf spied her out."

"Were there signs of a struggle?" Connor's face blanched as he caught the white bundle tight to his chest. 'Twas apparent it was a sheet, but he hesitated to open it.

"Nay. No struggle." Mereck looked down at Netta and put a stern look on his face. "Unhand me, wife. 'Tis unseemly ye would fondle my body in sight of my family."

Netta gasped and drew back in preparation to strike his chin with her fist. He forestalled her.

"For shame, Netta." He wagged his head in disbelief and

clucked his tongue. "Now ye would fight with your husband in front of our son?"

"Hell's bells, Mereck. Where's the ransom note?" Brianna demanded. No one raised their brows at her speech, for they had long become accustomed to her way of speaking.

"Well, now that Netta has stopped pawing over my body, I can give it to ye. I found the missive and sheet attached to the tree I spoke of. He knew we would track her to it." He reached beneath his wolf pelts and drew forth a rolled parchment. As he did, his eyes lost their teasing glint and became deep emerald, cold as the jewels they resembled. Unfolding the message, he spread it flat on a small table beside a fat, tallow candle.

Brianna pounced on it and began reading aloud.

I, Rolf, the MacDhaidh of Rimsdale, did this day handfast with Meghan of Blackthorn. She is in my keeping and will remain so. Her virgin's blood gives proof we consummated the union.

Until such time as I allow, she will have no contact with her former family at Blackthorn. Any forays onto my lands will be met with force.

Netta snatched the bundle from Connor's arms and flapped it in the air to open it. There for all to see were the telltale red splatters. She scowled up at Mereck as if her husband was responsible for the news he brought to them.

Damron's eyes narrowed and his back stiffened. "If 'tis a handfast, why then does Rolf forbid her contact with her people?"

"Likely he remembers she is nigh impossible to control?" Connor cleared his throat. "I like it not that he forbids us to see to her welfare." He could not keep the worry from his voice.

"Well, to hell and back with him." Brianna took the sheet and balled it up. "I don't trust the man. Mereck, how difficult will it be to snatch one of his men to question?"

Mereck frowned, not understanding. "Snatch? 'Tis a word you have not used afore. I ken it means to kidnap?" Seeing her nod of agreement, he added. "Not hard. I will take none but my squire Dafydd with me. If their patrols keep their pattern, they will be well within our southeastern borders this sennight."

"Bleddyn will return from Wales soon," Damron said. "Mayhap Cloud Dancer will carry a message to Meghan. I would that she knows we will aid her if she wishes."

"The mystic, his great eagle, and your gift of hearing people's thoughts, Mereck, will all be of great help." Pride lit Netta's eyes as she looked at her husband.

"I remember the time you were affrighted by my 'gift,' wife." Mereck grinned as he hugged her to his side.

"Hmpf! What woman wishes a man to read her every thought?" She looked up at him, wrinkling her nose.

"'Tis settled then." Connor squared his shoulders, his face bleak. "If we find Meghan has not spoken her promise freely, we will besiege Rimsdale and bring her back to people who love and understand her."

"Dinna worry so, Connor," Damron said kindly. "Ye know the lass has loved the man since she was no higher than my waist. If I read him aright, he favored her even then."

"Aye. But is Rolf the same man he was afore?"

None had an answer for him.

For the next fortnight, Rolf was content for the first time in his life. In his sleep, he drew Meghan close in his arms. During the day, he forgot his duties and sought her out. With Ingirid, he had never felt a need to have his wife beside him.

His mind spoke to him, taunted him. It couldna last.

His honor nagged him, warned him. It couldna last.

He ignored them both.

What would happen when 'twas over?

Leggings and breeches became objects of irritation. He took to wearing a shirt with his tartan belted about his waist. To free his manhood. He had but to shove the clothing aside and his tarse was readily available.

If Meghan came within sight, he found reason to call a halt

to whatever he was doing, overtake her, and hurry her to a secluded area.

He tried to put her from his mind. He could not. If he did not see her, he found himself seeking her out in the middle of the day. He ignored the knowing looks and told himself he would soon sate his lust for her.

Who did he think he fooled? The more he had her, the swifter his body responded to the slightest reminder. A whiff of heather, the sweet sway of a lass's hips, her throaty laugh when Simple caused Garith to chuckle—all thickened his blood.

Never had he known a woman so responsive to his slightest touch. She caught fire from a single kiss. Sometimes, he had not yet kissed her. If she burrowed her face beneath his chin and breathed deeply, she moaned and tilted her head back to offer her sweet lips to him.

Ede became her stalwart friend. She cast him accusing glances whenever he drew Meghan to him. In his leisure time, Garith sought her out. The women of the castle no longer looked at her with fear but went out of their way to be friendly.

"When are you going to stop this lackwit behavior?"

Alpin's voice interrupted Rolf's thoughts as he entered the stable. He meant to order Storm and Luath to surprise Meghan with a ride on the mainland.

"Lackwit? Why think you I behave foolishly?" His brows lifted to challenge Alpin.

"All comment on your easy manner, your ready laughter." Alpin's pale eyes held no warmth of friendship but blazed with something else. Resentment? Jealousy? "They say the hardened warrior plays the lapdog sniffing after a bitch in heat."

Rolf stiffened and clamped his lips together.

"Nothing is secret in a manor. You canna wait to reach the privacy of your solar but thrust yourself into her on the spiral stairwell, behind the stable, or e'en against the sea wall." His haughty face became scornful. "You constantly rut with the Blackthorn strumpet."

Rolf's hand flashed out to grab Alpin's tunic tight about his neck. He brought his nose to almost touch his friend's. "Ne'er, lest you wish an untimely end, call Meghan of Blackthorn a strumpet. You well know she was pure when I handfast with her."

"Aye. Yet you have taught her wanton ways." He jerked back. Rolf released his hold on him. "Ailsa has long awaited this upcoming event. She willna abide your swiving—"

"Ailsa has no say in what I do." Rolf's shout interrupted him. "She is but a woman. 'Tis my right to have any lass within this manor, and she willna interfere. Nor will you." Out of the corner of his eye, he saw someone approach the stable, then retreat. His blood told him 'twas Meghan.

"Eneuch," he warned Alpin. He left him and went to see both steeds were readied. His blood still singing with anger, he vaulted onto Luath, took Storm's reins from a stable boy, and rode out into the bailey.

Meghan decided to find Ede and ask why Rolf and Alpin argued about this Ailsa. Today wasna the first time she'd noted the name. More often lately, she heard it whispered. Always, the voices hushed when she neared. Was Alpin's sister elderly? Was that why they prepared so carefully to please her? It would gladden her to meet someone else who held Rolf dear.

Hearing a horse advancing fast behind her, she whirled to see Rolf astride Luath and leading Storm. He stopped beside her.

"Come. I deemed a ride along the beach would be to your liking this day." He grinned down at her.

Meghan laughed with joy as Storm huffed and bumped his cheek against her shoulder. She put her arms around his massive neck and hugged the beast. Some women might think the smell of a horse disagreeable, but Meghan found it a familiar memory.

"A ride?" She turned her head enough to see Rolf. "'Tis a lovely day for it." Afeared he could change his mind, she dashed a quick look around, hiked up her skirts, and was astride Storm afore Rolf could dismount to aid her.

She felt his heated gaze on her bare legs and pulled her

clothing down to cover them. "Ye have seen them aplenty, Rolf. Dinna stare as if it were the first time."

He cleared his throat before he answered. "Aye. But now I picture myself, not Storm, gripped tight between your thighs as you ride me." His nostrils flared.

Meghan grinned at him. She knew the first chance they had she would be astride him. As they crossed over the bridge, she looked forward to reaching land where they could let the horses have a bracing gallop.

Something in the woods along the shoreline caught her eye. She caught glimpses of warriors paced far apart among the trees. He didna fully trust her. He was no fool and had planned ahead in case she bolted. He didna believe that once she had said her vows with him, she would not run from him.

The minute Storm's hooves hit the sand, she hollered to Rolf, "Race you to the curve ahead." She leaned close over the horse's neck and urged him to run free. As Storm thundered ahead like a bolt shot out of the sky, she laughed for the sheer joy of the wind rushing against her face.

Her skirts whipped back from her legs, freeing her skin to the sun's warm touch. The wind combed her hair, flying it about her. She knew Rolf was close behind by the pounding of Luath's hooves. Soon he drew alongside, boxing her between the water and himself. He would not let her easily win. He, too, leaned far forward and urged his mount to greater speed. When they reached the bend, Storm led by the length of his nose.

At a slow walk, they cooled the horses down. As they neared the bridge, he grinned at her.

"Come. A pool lies within the woods. I go there often to bathe in the summer months." He led her into the woods, and the man closest to where they entered trotted his steed farther down the beach.

Lacy birch trees grew at the pool's edge and dipped the tips of their green leaves into the clear water. Others stood majestically offering shade. At the left end, a large flat rock overhung the water. 'Twas there Rolf led her.

Within a dozen heartbeats, both were naked and plunging into the cold depths. When Meghan came up for breath, she saw Rolf's dripping face watching her. He had no need to speak. His face showed his intentions. A laugh escaped her. She hunched her back and dove deep. She could feel him behind her. Could feel him as he hovered above her. Followed her. She grew out of breath and headed for the surface, but he remained still. His fingertips traced her body as she pulled upward through them until she reached the open air.

He was not through with his play but swam beneath her. Slowly, sensuously, like a living Neptune, his body slid under hers, his lips nipping like little minnows at her flesh. He kicked her ankles apart, and by the time he surfaced, he impaled her on his eager shaft.

They loved with passion and then swam again, never speaking a word. Meghan because she didna want to break the moment; Rolf because he wanted to hold back time. They made love again until both were satiated. Tired now, they lay on the large rock until dry enough to don their clothing.

"Thank ye, Rolf. Now the days are warm, mayhap Ede and I could enjoy coming here to bathe?" Meghan asked.

"You canna come unguarded; 'tis not safe. Besides, I like not the thought of your bathing nude where warriors could see you."

"The escort can be within the woods, their back to us." Seeing he still looked ready to say her nay, she worried her lip. "Ugsome returned this morn. Poor beastie has yet another notch on his ear. Ugsome would not let anyone near. Garith and he can guard us close by. I doubt not the lad will keep his back turned."

"I will think on it."

By the soft look on his face, she knew she could look forward to lazy swims on warm days.

As the days passed, more work than seemed usual kept everyone busy about the castle and grounds. The servants cleaned and aired pallets. They changed the rushes often, while carpenters mended any trestle tables that needed it.

Meghan became more concerned, though, for more often, if she drew near, conversation halted. She didna think the cause was dislike. More unnerving were looks of sympathy. Heaven help her, she even glimpsed pity. Why would they look thus? Was Alpin's relative so ill-tempered as to dislike Meghan on sight? It made her uneasy, and she took to spending more time out of doors.

The practice fields drew her, and Meghan studied the men at their warrior's training. Soon, they began to take her presence as an added help. Her aid in developing their skills didna trouble her, for she knew at the end of the year she would wed Rolf. While she was at Rimsdale, there would be peace between the two castles. Dougald grew so accustomed to having her there that if she but raised her hand, he came over to speak with her.

A horn sounding atop the battlements warned of someone's approach. Meghan stared as a handful of horsemen rode across the bridge and into the outer bailey. She had no need to see the colors on the banner to know they were messengers from Alpin's castle, for he and Rolf rode up to meet them.

Curious, she followed along with Garith and Dougald. They drew close, and Ugsome hugged tight to her legs, rumbling deep in his throat. He didna like the men.

The warriors smiled and looked friendly enough. From what she could overhear, Alpin's relative would arrive within a fortnight. He appeared most pleased, for he smiled and thumped Rolf on the back. 'Twas strange, though. Rolf didna return the smile. He looked much like someone who had eaten rank meat.

Dougald's big hand patted her shoulder. The motion caught Rolf's eye. He studied her standing there, and though she smiled at him, he didna meet her eye.

CHAPTER 19

Meghan did not see Rolf until the evening meal. Though courteous and pleasant, he studied first Garith, then her. His eyes filled with pain, and he squeezed them tight as if to vanquish memories lurking behind them.

"Have you thought of another riddle for us this night, Meghan?" Dougald urged.

Oft of late, she had been called on by the warriors to play the pipes or tease their minds. She glanced at Rolf to judge how much note he paid to his surroundings. Seeing he was deep in thought, she nodded.

It swings by his thigh a thing most magical!
Below the belt, beneath the fold of his clothes it hangs,
a hole in its front end, stiff-set and stout, but swivels about.
Levelling the head of this hanging instrument,
its wielder hoists his hem above the knee:
'tis his will to fill a well-known hole
it fits fully when at full length.
He has often filled it before. Now he fills it again.

"What?" Rolf bolted up and came to jerk her to her feet. "I canna believe you learned that at Blackthorn." His face darkened, and the heat of his anger wafted his scent to her. "Did you hear such hangin' around the men's barracks?" He stood toe-to-toe and scowled at her.

She did not back down from such obvious bluster but frowned back and poked him in the chest with her finger. "I can well see where yer mind lies." She huffed in disdain. " 'Tis in the cesspit."

Alpin laughed heartily. "Aye, Rolf, she has that aright. A key is the answer. 'Tis an old riddle. Did you read more and were less scornful of the Saxons, you would know of it."

It was the first time she had seen Alpin laugh. It brought glowing color to his pale face, his blue eyes sparkled, and his lips softened. For the first time, she kenned he was beautiful. But not in a way that appealed to her. Though Rolf's dark features were not as comely as Alpin's, she far more favored them.

After that evening, Alpin often sought her company. He brought her the pipes and politely requested she play. At first, she would pipe Blackthorn's battle song to pry Rolf from thoughts that seemed to sadden him. Once she had his attention, she played all the ancient tunes and the wild music she loved.

Rolf oft took Meghan to the swimming area, and if he could not, Ede and Garith accompanied her, as did six "protective" warriors. After the first day that she and Ede went, they kept their tunics on and invited Garith to join them. He wore his breeches for modesty.

When Meghan learned he could not swim, she remedied that lack. At first, he was fearful for he had little strength in his right arm. As he learned to swim, the exercise firmed the muscles in his weak arm, and he started to use it more often.

One day as they came from the water, Meghan felt a man's eyes. She talked to Ede as her hand ruffled through the grass at her side. Closing her fingers around a chestnut-sized stone, she positioned it. Her hand whipped up, and she hurled the missile some ten paces away. The man who lurked in the bushes ran, holding his forehead and weaving through the woods like a tippler in his cups.

A guard called out, and Garith hollered back through choked laughter that 'twas no cause for alarm.

"Meghan, are you as accurate with the dirk as with that stone?" His eyes lit with interest.

"Aye. Though the dirk is far more deadly."

"Would you teach me?"

"A dirk?"

He nodded eagerly.

"Mayhap. Yet not until ye learn to hit a mark with a stone. Help me to gather some. We will start this day."

They began a regular training ritual of Garith first swimming and then firing stones at picked targets.

The exercises increased his strength, and Rolf questioned him about it. Garith kept their secret even from him. 'Twas easy to do as Rolf was often distracted by the frequent arrival of messengers. Meghan asked about them, and he said they brought reports from the village, missives from Alpin's family or messages from neighboring allies. Now and again, Rolf rose before the hint of a new day and was gone when she awoke.

'Twas the middle of the week, and Rolf had said he would work on the south wall for most of the day. Before she trained Garith, Meghan made sure Rolf was occupied elsewhere. Using an old shield as a target, the young man's progress with the dirk delighted her. His aim was accurate and lethal.

"Come, Garith, I would show ye what distance ye can stand from a man and still be deadly." She set the makeshift target at a longer distance.

"If the blade strikes, would it not be deadly?"

"Nay. It must cut deep and hold. If 'tis but the tip that enters, the man will yet come at ye."

He stood by her side to hand her the blades. Meghan hurled one after the other until all five quivered, embedded in the target. She backed up five paces and waited till he retrieved the knives.

"At this distance, I canna stop a man."

She used all her strength to throw the first three. True to what she had told him, they did not lodge deep enough. Some fell to the ground after the tips entered the wood, and the knife wobbled about. She had made her point.

"Er, Meghan," Ede said behind her.

"Hmm?" She took the next knife and added power from her body by stepping forward as she threw the knife.

"Uh, I think you should stop now," Ede whispered.

"Aye. One moment. Watch closely, Garith. Ye must get your weight just so," she said as she released the last knife. Thunk! "See? Not a killin' blow but one that will give ye an advantage."

The hairs on her nape tingled. Her nostrils flared. 'Twas his scent. She knew who stood behind her.

On his way to the pool, Rolf's blood had stirred. He had planned to dismiss Ede and Garith so he could be alone with Meghan. He pictured her naked, sliding up and down his body in the cool water. Mayhap today he would show her a pleasant and exciting way to float—with him between her thighs, firmly embedded in her supple body. Sounds much like those made on a practice target broke his blood-stirring fantasy.

Thunk! Thunk!

Devil take it! 'Twas Meghan. How long had she practiced with the knives? She had little need, for she had been as accurate as himself for many years.

He stalked close. Ede spied him and murmured a warning at Meghan. He slitted his eyes at her, and she pinched her lips closed. He didna want Meghan to turn on him with a knife in her hand. Did she know of the forays between Blackthorn and Rimsdale, she would be highly aggrieved. A pang of guilt struck him, for he could not tell her.

At last, the final blade struck, quivering but embedded in the makeshift target. Ah. Good. Meghan stiffened. She knew he was there. He grabbed her shoulders and spun her around.

"Lucifer's warted buttocks." His bellow caused her to blink rapidly. "Where came you by the knives?"

"She did nothing wrong, brother," Garith cut in.

"Wrong? You know I forbade her the use of them. Do you not ken she throws as well as any man?"

"Are ye saying I would use a blade against yer brother? Or Ede?"

Her shout was admirable, he had to admit. "Nay, not against them. But what is to stop you from pilferin' one to use later?"

"Against ye?" Her eyes opened wide in disbelief.

Rolf did not answer. Did she learn the reason for the arrival of the "elderly" lady from Alpin's family, she would very likely use it on him. He would not blame her.

"By your very silence ye give me your answer." Hurt flashed through her eyes before they turned cold and scornful.

"You warned me aplenty that you would escape given a chance." His nose near touched the tip of hers. "Mayhap you wouldna use the dirk against me, but what of my men when I am away from the castle? What would stop your use of it then?"

Like an angry cat, she stiffened and near hissed at him. "What would stop me?"

Had she claws, it would not surprise him if she raked them against his cheek.

Meghan took a deep breath and raised up on her toes to glare at him, eye to eye. "What would stop me?" she repeated. "A vow! On my honor I promised to be with ye a year and a day. Do ye know so little of me that ye believe I would break my vow? If naught else, my pride wouldna let me."

"You are but a woman," he said savagely. "Dinna prattle to me of vows taken and manly pride."

Rolf's conscience tore at him like a freshly honed blade. He well knew Meghan would honor any vows she spoke. And he well knew he would break those selfsame vows to her.

"Go. Get you back within the castle walls and dinna let me hear another word from your lips." He forced himself back, though he yearned to clasp her tight and beg her to forgive him for what he had started in motion and could not stop.

"Come, Meghan," Ede pleaded and tugged her arm.

"Aye, let us tend Simple," Garith suggested. "Dinna forget you promised to show all the young'ns what a gowk the wee birdie is. They will be waitin' by now, for we have been gone overlong." Garith turned a cold eye on his brother and took Meghan's hand.

Rolf's gut tightened at this added look of disappointment

in his brother's eyes. As they disappeared down the path, he speedily tossed aside his clothing and plunged his heated body into the cool water. He dove deep and did not surface until his lungs screamed for air.

His mind's eye filled with the memory of Meghan's naked body gliding through the water while he followed with but a ripple of current betwixt them. He heard the phantom of her throaty laughter when he had surfaced beneath her, enticing her to ride him like a mermaid. How had she the power to fire his blood at will? To make his rod swell with but a few words?

Lucifer's withered balls! With powerful strokes, he made for the shore, pulled on his hose and boots and vaulted onto Luath. His wrenching dilemma grew with each step the horse took.

He didna want to crave her.

He didna want to ever let her go.

He didna want any man to touch the golden skin that was his.

His. She belonged to him. How could he live knowing another man's body covered hers? That another pleasured her and called forth such stormy passion to the surface?

Luath's hooves sent mud flying. Rolf paid no heed to the startled curses of the chandler who approached the castle entrance. The man held a pole across his shoulders with the uncut wicks of two dozen fat candles strung across it, and his sudden movements to avoid Luath's hooves set the candles to swaying as if in a summer's gale, some falling off the end into a muddy puddle. Rolf felt a twinge of regret, for he knew the chandler had taken extra pains in making them for Meghan.

Sun flashed on Cormac's bright red hair as the squire sprinted up to grab firm hold of the reins. The horse tossed his head, snorted, and would have bit him had Cormac not been wary. He thumped the beast alongside his head and held tight as Rolf jumped off and bounded up the stairs.

Meghan heard the sounds of cursing and the thunder of a horse's hooves outside as she crossed the hall to the stairway. The massive door to the castle stood open, for servants were busy removing stale rushes they had swept from the floors.

Rolf burst through the doorway like a conqueror intent on raiding the castle. Seeing her, he stopped but a second.

'Twas enough for her to gauge his mood. Her eyes opened wide. She had thought the sounds impatient? Nay. More than that. Determined? Hungry? Both those and more, from the looks of him.

Why, he may as well have been as the day he was born. His wet leggings were a gray skin that hugged his taut hips and strained over his burgeoning sex. She forced her eyes upward over the dewy whorls of hair covering the sculpted muscles of his chest, until her gaze swept across his broad, scarred shoulders.

When she glanced up at his face, the smoldering flame in his eyes made her tense with anticipation. He waggled his brows at her and licked his lips, and even at this distance, she heard a hungry hum well up from his chest much as one would do on seeing a banquet spread before him. He looked ready to take her here against the stairway as if it mattered not who watched.

"Ho, Rolf," Alpin called as he came up behind him. "A word with you, please."

It distracted Rolf. One small step at a time, Meghan inched back so he wouldna notice. The first step touched the back of her heel. Whirling, she sped up the spiral steps. She giggled, excited. She would hide from his sight.

He ignored Alpin's surprised calls and came after her, his boots ringing out on the first steps. She shrieked with laughter and fled. Her woman's skirts hampered her, and she grabbed handfuls and tugged them above her knees. Her bare legs flashed as she flew up the stairway.

He pounded ever closer. Not a word passed his lips.

Knowing he gained on her, she tore in a gasp of air. His footsteps resounded with a furious ring. She reached the landing and fled to the door of Garith's room. She yanked it open. Darkness welcomed her.

He would not seek her here; he would mayhap search the other rooms. Slipping under the heavy covers on the bed, she slid against the far wall and made herself small.

The door opened, slow and quiet. Somehow, the lack of sound was more ominous than if he had crashed it back against the wall. 'Twas like he stalked a hapless prey to ground.

Rolf did not see her, but his eager tarse knew where she hid. In the bed. He untied his leggings, and his turgid flesh sprung forth. Ready. 'Twas like Lucifer's own tarse, or a hunting dog pointing to her whenever she was near.

He padded over to the bed, his ragged breathing the only sound in the room. Prickles of expectant tension swept over Meghan. His hands burrowed beneath the covers, then struck swift as a snake as he grabbed her ankles and tugged.

She shrieked, feeling as small as a newborn pup and as helpless. While he pulled her down to the edge of the bed, she fought her clothing and the covers that bunched up over her waist to her head. She dissolved in laughter when he tickled her ribs and lapped his tongue around her navel.

Cold air spread over her naked legs as he pulled her ever closer to him. She tried to fight the tangled mounds of material. Then she felt the heat of him on the insides of her calves, the insides of her thighs. One more tug. Cold air warned her that her body was open to him.

His heat moved closer to her exposed center, and as she thrashed about, he grasped her hips in a steel vise and twisted just enough to brush against her. The hard length of him sent bolts of heat through her.

He thrust into her. She cried out. He grunted, withdrew, and entered slowly. Each time she took him more fully until he filled her near to bursting.

"Wait, you rutting beast. Free my arms," she hollered at him.

He ignored her. The more she flailed about, the more entangled she became in the bedding and the faster he thrust into her. With a hoarse shout, he surged again and again as he spurted his seed into her, filling her.

Spent, he collapsed atop her, his heart pounding through the covers. She beat against him, trying to dislodge him.

"Ye misbegotten goat." The material muffled her voice. "I canna breathe."

He lifted enough to thrust the covers off her.

"Ye great randy oaf, dinna—"

She got no further. Hard at first, his lips softened and gentled until they urged a response from her. For a moment, she no longer knew why she protested. Just for a moment. Then she remembered the covers and tugged great handfuls of his hair.

"Dinna e'er do such again, or Christ help me, I will maim ye. Ye will need the aid of a stout tree branch tied to yer prick to make that part of ye rise again."

Rolf raised up and stared hard at her. "Humpf," he muttered, then nibbled at her lower lip while he began to strip her of her clothes.

"What do ye think ye are doing?" She grabbed for her smock, but he soon had her naked beneath him.

"'Tis simple. You gained little pleasure from the coupling. I will give it to you now." He sounded so sure that her reason for protest was that he had not gratified her.

"Do ye think ye can have me any time? At yer own will?"

After talking with the women of Blackthorn, she knew neither her brother nor her cousins would take their wives for granted thusly. Well, mayhap Damron had on first marrying Brianna. Ne'er after she set him straight on it.

"Ye dinna wish to swive?" He rocked his hard tarse against her and waggled his brows in disbelief.

"Dinna dare think to thrust into me again." She glared up at him.

"Nay?" After studying her eyes, he shrugged. "Still, I would give you pleasure, if but from the sound of my voice, the scent of my body, as I tell you of all the things I want to do to you. And *will* do to you. If not this day, then another."

Pinning her hands above her head, he whispered of his fantasies of them together. He rubbed his cheek against hers, spoke softly in her ear. His scent quickened her heartbeat. His breath against her ear caused her to shiver. His words made her twitch. He nuzzled her throat, her breasts, lapping the nipples. All the while, he told her of every erotic pleasure he knew until she squirmed and panted.

Never once did he caress her with his hands or kiss her. He played her body with words, the deep timbre of his voice and the powerful aid of his body's scent. He knew of that power, for the hint of heather that wafted from her was all he needed to thicken his shaft.

Feeling her stiffen, he knew she was on the brink of surrender. He reached down, latched on to a nipple, and sucked greedily. Meghan reared and exploded. Wave after wave pulsed through her, each more intense than the last. He did not release his hold on her breast until he felt her final tremors.

Meghan lay stunned. What had he done to her that she would respond at his will? Was he a mystic that he could call forth a response any way he desired? She lay limp and exhausted.

Rolf sprang to his feet, pulled his leggings over his stillraging tarse, and tied the strings at the waist. He chuckled and pulled the door closed with a snap, the sound as arrogant as the man who caused it. His footsteps retreated down the landing.

By all that is holy, she was more furious now than ever before. At herself. It tore at her soul to have a man control her very emotions. Never again would she allow him to prove his mastery over her body.

No sooner had his footsteps faded than they approached the door again. She jumped up, still naked and her flesh heated as she stalked to the door. Jerking it open, she prepared to slam it in his face when she'd had her say.

"Ye stupid lout—" Her shout died to an embarrassed gasp. She had spied who stood before her.

CHAPTER 20

Alpin MacKean stared at Meghan, looking stunned. More than stunned. Turned to stone—but for his eyes. Their intense gaze roved from her head to her toes, appreciating every exposed inch of her.

Heat rose to Meghan's cheeks, but she did not flinch. With regal composure, she stepped aside to use the door as a shield.

"'Twould be best if ye had announced yerself," she said.

"Did you give me the chance, I would have. You opened to me afore my lips could speak the words." His eyes twinkled with humor she never thought to see there. "'Tis gratified I am that I did not."

"No doubt. What is it?" She cocked her head and waited.

"Hmm? What?" He stumbled over his words as he forced his gaze back to her face.

"For what purpose did ye seek me out?" Meghan wished he would get on with it. The cold wind swirling up the stairway made her doubly sorry she had not a stitch of cloth on her body.

"Oh, aye." He blinked, then cleared his throat. "While you were, uh, occupied, word came of a raid to the north."

The whimsical smile on his lips told her he did not as yet have his wits about him.

"And?" Her eyes narrowed. Did they judge Connor responsible?

"Uh, Rolf thought mayhap you would join us and help calm the village women?" When she hesitated answering, he added, "We believe masterless louts have preyed on the help-less crofters."

"Why didna ye say so right off?" As she started to push the door shut, he wedged his boot between it and the door frame.

"You will come?" His voice sounded hopeful.

"If ye will remove yer hulking body, I will be down afore ye are on yer steed." Her naked toes reached around to nudge his ankle. He took the hint and removed himself. She heard him laugh as he clattered down the stairwell.

Without a lost movement, she threw on her clothing and raced out into the bailey as Jamie led Storm over to meet her.

"Thank ye, Jamie." She took hold of the pommel and started to spring onto Storm's back, but a gust of wind lifted her skirts. "Lucifer's toes," she grumbled in disgust. "Look aside, man, if ye dinna want me to blacken yer eyes."

Meghan gave him but a few moments to turn his head, then she gathered her skirts and mounted. "Devil take it. Storm isna used to foolish women's skirts flappin' at his sides."

"Is it your wish to return to the castle and sew on a tapes-try for the great room?" Rolf's stern voice said behind her. Luath snorted and stomped, but his master tightened his reins.

"Ye should geld that misbegotten destrier." She pulled Storm out of the mean-tempered horse's range.

"Nay. He obeys me well. Always have I used firm con-trol o'er rebellious souls. They soon learn who is master between us."

Looking expectant, Rolf studied her. She knew he dared her to disagree. She could not stand it.

"Huh! He is but a dumb beast with no brains to reason."

"Should we return above where I may again prove who is master?" His voice was soft. Promising, yet sinister.

Meghan flashed him a disgusted look and shot forward on Storm. The gelding soon caught up to the men riding across the bridge. Rolf's satisfied laughter floated to her as he closed the distance between them.

"Stay within the center of the warriors," Rolf ordered as he streaked forward to lead the line of men.

Meghan sucked her teeth. Since she had no weapons to defend herself, she had no choice but to obey him. Would he have armed her if he had thought any danger lingered?

They rode hard for several leagues. Of a sudden, Meghan sensed they were not alone. Rolf's gaze darted to the trees and scanned their branches, looking for hidden archers. He grasped Beast and brought his shield to cover his left side. At a soft command, his men closed in around Meghan.

"Jamie, give me a weapon," she whispered.

"I canna." He shifted in his saddle, his broadsword at the ready. His wary eyes scanned the woods on either side.

"Dinna be a fool, man. I dinna ask ye for yer sword, but for a dirk to protect myself." The skin on her back prickled. She knew eyes watched her. They were not friendly. She felt helpless, useless, as drawn swords rasped shrill against their scabbards.

Suddenly, arrows flew from the surrounding trees. Behind her, a man cried out. Moments later, Alpin pulled alongside her.

Men swarmed from the forest like a mass of angry bees. They screamed and slashed out with rusted swords, too close now for the bow and arrow. She watched, anxious, as a man hurtled toward Rolf, his weapon lifted high. Before he could bring it down, Rolf swung Beast in a vicious arc. The man's head toppled to the ground afore the body joined it, with lifeless hands still clutching his sword.

A gnome of a man in a thick cloak of animal pelts darted between several horses and grabbed for Meghan's leg. Locking her hands together, she slammed them down on his head. She wheeled Storm around and signaled him to rear up and strike out at the varlet. Shrieking, the man disappeared beneath stomping hooves.

The battle raged around her. Men and horses cried out as they were struck. She cursed Rolf for keeping her weapons from her. But for him, she would be as much help as any man.

After what seemed an eternity, the battle waned. The horse beside her screamed in outrage as a stray blade pricked his flank. The steed reared and dumped the rider to the ground.

'Twas Alpin who fell so hard it knocked him senseless. Meghan noted a lout racing toward him, and she leapt from Storm, bent over Alpin, and whipped a dagger from his boot.

An evil grin split the man's ugly face. A rusty, nicked sword sliced the air as he came at them. The bastard. She read the thoughts in his eyes. He would skewer Alpin as he lay helpless. Then, believing she was but a weak woman, he deemed he could disarm her and haul her off into the woods.

More fool he.

As the dagger left her hand in a blur, Meghan was aware of an eerie silence. Entering with a dull, grating thunk, the blade embedded in the base of the man's throat.

Surprise bulged the lout's eyes. His mouth gaped open. Blood spurted with such force it splattered her clothing and coated Alpin's mail in a sickening design. Time slowed. The dying man's knees buckled, and he sprawled across Alpin on the ground.

All was quiet except for the moans of wounded men and horses snorting. The battle ended mere moments afore her blade flew.

"Addle-pated woman," Rolf roared behind her. "Had you missed, he would have gutted you."

"Missed? Are ye blind, man?" Meghan blinked in disbelief. "Ne'er would I miss such an easy target."

"Killin' is for men." His shout ruffled her hair. Grasping her shoulders, he spun her to face him and shook her. "Where did you get the blade?"

"Stop yelling at the lass and get this carrion off me," Alpin's strained voice intruded.

Jamie was closest. He grasped the dead body by a shoulder and a leg and tossed it to the side of the road. Alpin pushed himself up and shuddered. He bent over to stifle a gag.

Meghan wanted to cosh Rolf alongside the head with her fist. She did not, for his helmet would cause her more hurt than him. His gray eyes scowled at her from either side of his nose guard. She glared back. His hard jaw worked as he ground his teeth behind narrowed lips.

"What matters where I got the blade? Do ye think me such a lackwit that I would cower while he killed Alpin?" she shouted. Bile surged into her mouth, leaving her throat raw. "Tend yer men and let me be." If he did not unhand her, she would spew what little she had in her stomach on his boots.

"Are you ill?" His hands softened on her shoulders as his eyes probed her face.

"Nay. Let me go." Shudders swept over her, near making her knees fold. When riding out on patrol with her cousins, she had been in more than one battle. Fortunately, she had need but for her bow and arrows. Never had she been so close to someone she had been forced to kill.

Just in time, she broke away as Rolf's fingers loosened. No sooner had her urgent dash taken her behind the nearest tree than she grasped her stomach and heaved.

Rolf's strong arm snaked around her waist to support her. She wanted to groan in shame. Gentle fingers pulled her hair out of the way, afore his hand braced her forehead.

"Ah, lass, 'tis sorry I am for yellin' at you," he whispered.

She grasped the hand that near spanned her stomach and clutched it as a lifeline. She was so dizzy that she would crumple to the dirt if he did not keep her tight against his body. Tears ran down her cheeks as she heaved and could not seem to stop. Never had she been so sick; never had she been so shamed.

"Mayhap this will help," Alpin's voice said nearby.

Meghan moaned as Rolf's hand released her forehead. A moment later, it came back to wipe her face with a cold, wet cloth. It felt wonderful.

"Thank ye, Alpin." Her voice croaked like an old armorer's who had been too long afore the fire pits. She grasped the cloth and covered her face as she straightened. Rolf did not take his supporting arms away, and for that she was thankful.

She leaned against him and took deep breaths of cool air. As the dizziness waned, she ventured to open her eyes. Alpin stood there, dripping pink water. He had splashed himself to spare her the gory sight. The nicety surprised her.

"Come, we are but half a league from the village. I ken we surprised the varlets who were about to attack it again." Rolf led her to Storm and took special care to lift her onto the saddle and arrange her clothing around her legs. She glanced at the bodies laid in a neat row beside the road. Thankfully, none were Rimsdale warriors.

At the village, the hours passed in a cloud. Rolf sent several villagers back to bury the dead, while he and his men helped the rest. The women were grateful for Meghan's no-nonsense advice for them to join together. The eldest were asked to care for the children, while the younger women helped set the huts to right and aided the men as best they could.

Rolf promised them much-needed food and grain. The marauders had carried off most of the villagers' foodstuff, some of which was destined for the castle as their rent.

Hearing a child's laughter, Meghan stood in the doorway and watched as Rolf swung a wee lass high in the air. His eyes were merry and crinkled at the corners as he whirled her around in circles, laughing all the while. He looked to enjoy the play as much as the bairn. Such sweetness and longing covered his face that she wanted to run to him and vow they would one day have all the children he could desire.

Someone cleared his voice beside her. Surprised, she saw Alpin stood there awaiting her notice, looking uncomfortable.

"Rolf was on his way to collect you when the little one caught his eye." The sun glinted off Alpin's pale hair as he, too, studied his friend.

Rolf brought the child close to his chest, and her little arms grabbed his neck in a hug. After Cormac brought his helmet and shield, Rolf kissed her head and seemed reluctant to hand her back to her mother.

Turning to spy Meghan beside Alpin, he gestured with his hand for her to come. 'Twas time to leave.

A league from the village, they approached a fork in the road. Meghan still mulled over the soft expressions on Rolf's face while he played with the child, but when men gathered around her to hurry her to the left, it got her attention.

Something on the opposite path caught her eye. 'Twas a traditional warning to unwelcome visitors. A pole with a crosspiece stood planted in the ground. Atop it perched a skull, complete with a helmet. On the crosspiece, a draped plaid warned men of that tribe to keep distant.

Recognizing the plaid, suspicion and shock worked their sick way from her mind to her stomach. She clasped a hand over her lips to keep from retching again.

'Twas Blackthorn's. She near screamed with fury.

"Rolf, ye lying bastard." Meghan fought the roiling sickness as she hurled her furious words at him.

Rolf's back stiffened, but he did not turn to face her.

She used Storm to press the man to her right out of the way so she could approach the hated warning and study it closer, but more warriors hedged around her and forced her forward.

"Are ye so vile a man ye canna face me and tell me the truth?" Still he did not answer, though she knew he heard her shouted words.

"I gave ye my missive to Connor telling him of our vows. Ye said my family was content that I had handfast with ye." She fought back a sob. "Lucifer's spawn! Why is there such dire warning for Blackthorn warriors not to approach Rimsdale?"

Rolf pulled to the side of the trail. His iron-hard face and taut body shouted his displeasure. She pulled abreast of him. He swept his hand in the air and jabbed to the back of him. His men fell behind, giving them space. Her anger transmitted to Storm, who sidestepped and tossed his head about, snorting and looking as peeved as the woman on his back.

"Control Storm or I will do it for you," Rolf snapped at her, and stretched to wrench the reins from her hands. She backed the gelding farther away and glared her defiance at him.

"Dinna think to take the reins, ye nithing of a man. If my family knows we are handfast, ye need no such warning. Never would they raid the lands of a man I am as much as wed to."

"They know we are handfast. I sent them notice when I first told you I had." His cold eyes accused her as if she was the one in the wrong. "The warning was necessary. In the last sennight, several of my men have gone missin' when my patrols returned. 'Tis likely more treachery from your brother."

"Never. If Connor knows our handfast is legal, he wouldna dishonor me by kidnappin' men who are now part of my family." She glared at him, daring him to say she believed wrongly.

A strange look flickered across his face. In her heart, she knew something was terribly wrong. Ready to send Storm crashing through the woods, she searched for an opening. Even as her muscles tightened, he sensed her intent. He jerked the reins from her and started out at a fast pace. Cursing him with each breath she took, she grabbed Storm's mane and tightened her legs around the big horse.

Bleddyn ap Tewdwr, the Welsh mystic who was as a brother to Brianna, returned to Blackthorn. Thunder, his eighteen-hand destrier, merited his name as his hooves pounded over the drawbridge and through the barbican.

Of the same great height as Damron and Mereck, Bleddyn was as broad of shoulder but with a fearsome demeanor. His hair, black and long, was shaggy around his face. His eyes were as black as a storm-filled sky. They were mysterious eyes that saw more than any man had a right to see. A high, chiseled nose and firm, well-defined lips added distinction to his face.

As was his custom, he had painted the left side of his face blue. On the right, a ragged scar painted a vivid red ran from his hairline down across his eye to end at the corner of his lip. He wore a brilliantly colored, feathered mantle over a black tunic and leggings. His great eagle Cloud Dancer perched on his shoulder, its eyes always watchful to protect him.

As fearsome as was Bleddyn's mien, a stranger would be startled to see even the smallest of Blackthorn's children eager for his attention.

Damron allowed an ample time to pass until everyone greeted the Welsh mystic. After the women left to tend their bairns, it was a fitting time to discuss what needs be done for Meghan without Brianna or Netta demanding a say in their plans.

"Come, we have need of ye," Damron said as he led the way to his solar.

" 'Twas no surprise Meghan did not greet me with her pipes as is her habit. I know of her plight." Bleddyn's voice was soft and reassuring. "She is at Rimsdale. Though she will suffer for what he has done, Rolf will never harm her."

Damron dropped the latch on the solar door and hoped the men could finish their talk afore the women tracked them down. He brought the Welshman up to date on Rolf's curt demand that they stay away.

"Since then, we have trailed their patrols and taken the last man in line to bring here for questionin'." Damron grinned wryly. "Five men are 'guests' below, but not in the dungeons. In separate cells."

"None would tell us anythin', but Mereck's gift has told us all." Connor's voice sounded heartsick.

Bleddyn looked at Mereck and waited.

"Aye. They knew not that I could read their thoughts. I asked if Meghan and Rolf were handfast, and they answered aye soon enough. When asked if 'twas done in proper fashion, they agreed. Their shamed minds told me different."

"Cloud Dancer will take a message to Meghan to let her know we watch and wait." Bleddyn gripped Connor's shoulder, comforting him. "Rolf will not harm her. After all is done, he will know of his great love for her. Still, 'tis best she does not know his plans aforehand. She will come to understand what is inevitable. Though it will be painful, she will gain from it."

Loud thumping and banging sounded at the door, the first obvious kicks and the second pewter tankards striking the sturdy wood. 'Twas their three wives.

"Dammit, let us in. Now," Brianna's voice ordered through the thick wood. When it did not spring open, she yelled louder and kicked the door again. "Demon, open the door. Don't force me to make you sorry you ever woke up this morn."

"Mereck." 'Twas Netta's voice, accented with a sharp whack of pewter against the wood. "If you read my thoughts rightly, you will let us in even if all others say you nay."

Mereck and Damron looked at each other and shrugged. Both knew their wives would think nothing of denying them their beds. Both men knew they could do naught about it. None but Bleddyn's sharp eyes saw who was first to reach the latch.

"Well, now. I'm glad that's settled." Brianna swept into the room and eyed Damron with a you-had-better-listen-to-me look. "I think Cloud Dancer should take a message to Meghan."

"We thought of that by ourselves, love." Damron grabbed her around her waist to lift her high for his enthusiastic kiss.

She returned it with such vigor that when she pulled back, her eyes were dreamy. Shaking her head as if to clear it, she sighed. Leaning back in his arms, she smiled at him.

"Ha! I'll bet you won't think to tell her we will have someone waiting at a certain spot. Just in case she should want to leave that overbearing lout who won't let me visit her." She frowned her displeasure and turned to Bleddyn.

"Rolf had the colossal nerve to write that he 'will not allow the Lady Brianna to visit Meghan until Meghan becomes accustomed to her new station in life.' Whatever that means. Even I understand a handfast is like a marriage."

"My little one, Rolf grows more possessive of our Meghan by the hour. As for having someone watch for her, we planned to tell her that also." Bleddyn smiled at the loving touches the couple failed to conceal. "The tree where she escaped him and hid the first time is a likely spot. 'Tis close to our borders, and she knows the way. Mayhap you will write the message? It will give her added comfort to see it in your own hand."

"Let me down, you great hulk of a man." Brianna put her hands on her husband's shoulders and leaned back.

Damron nestled his face between her breasts and whispered, "Mmm, 'tis enough milk ye carry to feed wee Douglas and still have enough to share with his da."

Brianna boxed his ears.

"Ow, wife. Are ye tryin' to scramble my brains like ye are wont to say?" He grinned as he lowered her inch by inch to the floor. By the time her feet touched solid wood, her face was flushed with need. "This word *hulk* ye used. Is it another of yer strange names from that time afore ye came to us?" His head tilted as he studied her face. While she hesitated, he scowled until his brows near met in the middle. "It isna a compliment? Think well, wife, afore ye answer."

"Hulk? Did I say that?" Brianna put her finger on her chin and scrunched up her face at him. "Remember when I used to call you a lumbering Neanderthal or an obnoxious lummox?"

"Aye." He glowered and took a threatening step toward her.

"Well, it's nothing like that." She put her hands on her hips and stood her ground. "When I was a girl, there was a story about a man who turned green and changed into a veritable giant when he was angry. Hmm, like when I used to call you Lord Demon because of your own anger."

"Are ye sayin' I look green to ye?" He held out his arm and stared hard at it. Seeing nothing but a healthy golden tan, he waited expectantly for her to continue. How could he be angry with his wee wife when she was trying so hard to explain one of her memories. Stories of her previous life from far in the future never failed to fascinate him and his family. It was a well-kept secret from all but them.

"No, love. But you are a giant to me. We believed the tallest men of today were about up to here on you." Her hand lifted just above her head to give him an idea of the height.

"That isna a man," Damron huffed. "Yer people had little reasonin'. If we had but the strength of a lad, how did ye think we could wield a broadsword as tall as ye, wear gambesons, chain mail, helmets, short swords, shields, and other weapons?"

"It's too much to explain now." She shrugged and marched over to the table where he kept his parchments and writing utensils. "Let's get word to Meghan, and then I'll tell all of you the story about this hulk who turned into an avenging green giant."

Soon after, the missive was ready and tied to Cloud Dancer's left leg. They hurried up to the top of the castle. Bleddyn stood on the walkway facing toward Rimsdale. He spoke in strange words and chirping sounds. As he lifted his arm and sent the great eagle on its way, he called out the one word the others understood.

His voice soared to tumble in the building clouds.

"*Meghan*!"

CHAPTER 21

Meghan!

She heard her name whirl and dip with the wind and glanced furtively around. A deep canopy of leaves rustling above turned the day dusky. Alert to every sound and sight, she noted the voice of a raptor. Heavy gusts of wind parted the green ceiling, giving her glimpses of the eagle that followed in the wispy clouds.

Cloud Dancer. No other but he could soar and swoop with such grace. As faithful as Guardian or Ugsome, he followed her. She hid a smile, not wanting to alert the warriors around her.

Rolf kept up the hard pace to Rimsdale, his eyes lit with sparks near bursting into flames, the stony set of his jaw at war with the furrows in his brow. Each time she glimpsed his face, she tried to judge his thoughts.

Uncertainty? Determination? Despair?

Was that guilt that flashed in his eyes, then quickly changed to anger? What hidden reflections roused it?

Soon they arrived at Rimsdale, and Rolf vaulted from Luath.

"Dinna move."

To her mind, his tone was too demanding. "To hell with ye." Flinging her leg up and over Storm's head, she slid off him as Rolf reached her. Cold and silent, he grasped her wrist and hauled her into the castle.

Heat and tension radiated from him, feeding her own distemper. She did not believe Rimsdale was blameless for

Blackthorn's forays. Damron was too honest and loyal a man to do aught that would cause her dismay. If 'twas true that he ordered the missing men taken, then he had good reason.

Rolf slammed the solar door and turned to her all in one swift movement.

"Never call me vile names again." So loud did he shout the words that their force fairly shook the bed hangings. He paced in agitation, putting distance between them. "Had you not been ill afore, you would now wear my hand's print on your arse."

"If ever ye try to leave yer *print* on my arse, ye will find a brazier across yer thick skull," she shouted back.

"Dinna tempt me. Ill or not, I will take no more from you."

"Ha. And why not? Ye have taken all else from me. Ye took my dirk, my right to defend myself." Her gaze shot daggers at him.

"With good cause." His fist thumped the table beside him. "You tried to wield it against me."

"Aye. And had *I* not good cause?" Disgust radiated from her. "Ye deny me the right to fly Simple in the hunt, my right to ride Storm where I will. Ye refuse me the clothin' I favor and hamper me with skirts about my legs." She jerked off the rose tunic she had worn to please him and tossed it to the floor. The temptation almost overwhelmed her to stomp on it like a bad-tempered bairn.

"Dinna dare." His eyes narrowed to hot, silver slits.

"Hmpf!" She picked up her right foot and stamped on the edge of the tunic.

"Pick it up!" The words barely escaped his clenched teeth.

She brought her left foot over and slammed it down beside her other. Heaven help her! This dominating man called out her worst impulses. She could not believe she had done such a childish thing, but she could not back down.

Ever since he had captured her in the forest, he had compelled her to his will. Day by day, as he tried to force her into the role of a foolish, servile woman, he stripped her of her identity, her pride. She *wouldna* have it.

Planting her hands on her hips, she glared defiance at him. "Meghan!"

She folded her arms across her chest and lifted her chin in stubborn determination.

With a savage growl, he lunged for her. Quick as a hare fleeing a falcon, she slipped sideways from his grasping hands. He lunged again. She spun away and sprinted to the other side of the room. He near trod on her heels.

She somersaulted over the bed, putting it between them. His lips drew back in a wicked smile.

"'Tis a bedding you wish, Meghan?" His voice purred as he stalked her to the foot of the bed, just out of reach.

He inched his heavy belt through the pewter clasp. When it was free, his tartan slipped to the floor with a whisper of sound. While he coiled the leather belt around his hand, he watched her every twitch.

Never had he known a woman with such strong will. Though her breathing quickened, no fear flashed in her eyes. Not even Alpin would dare defy him so when he was angered. He took a deep breath and tried to calm his racing blood.

By the saints, the woman had to be daft. She couldna know he blustered with the belt. Never would he strike her with it.

She leapt to the edge of the bed. He launched himself at her like a giant cat, and they landed together in the middle of the featherbed with Meghan on her stomach beneath him.

Where she belonged.

"Since you are so anxious to rid yourself of clothin', I will gladly aid you."

She fought like a maddened, hissing cat, trying to twist in his arms to claw him. He raised up enough to allow her to breathe but kept a hand on her back so she could not wrestle free. Ridding himself of the belt, he grasped the hem of her smock and tugged.

"Dinna dare, ye rutting boar."

"Dare? Oh, I dare, Meghan. You are mine. My possession." He grunted with the effort to control her as he burrowed an arm under her waist and lifted her enough to pull the smock free.

She bucked so violently it caught him by surprise and near toppled him, reminding him of a time years past when she had interrupted his tryst with Connor's favorite dairy maid. She had come upon them in the stable and whacked his heaving arse with a stout branch.

He had chased her down, ready to thrash her. When he lunged and grabbed her around her waist, they had tumbled to the ground. Though she had been all gangly arms and legs then, her form as yet lacking the soft curves to entice a man, for the first time, the power of her scent had overwhelmed him. It had taken him by surprise to feel a stirring of lust for her.

That same lass could now entice him with but a fleeting glance, the echo of her laughter across a room or her teasing scent when she walked past. All his anger at her challenging him afore his men dissolved.

"Lout, get off me." Meghan tried to twist to her side.

He did not let her. "Um, Meghan mine," he whispered. " 'Tis a game I like well, this cat-and-mouse chase, but I wish for a gentler coupling," he purred in her ear. When she started to surge forward, he nuzzled her neck and gently mouthed her shoulder for several heartbeats, much as a stallion stills a mare.

"Shh, love. Quiet." He had no need to hold her still now as he aroused her passion. He made gentle love to her, and in the doing, his body strove to show her all the tender emotions he could not allow himself to speak of. When she shivered, he kissed and lapped her flesh, caressed his way down every inch of her velvety body, and stopped only to whisper how much he had always needed her, how only she could call forth every emotion 'twas possible for a man to feel.

Slowly, his hands feathered over the velvety flesh of her supple hips, her quivering thighs, then reached between them to caress her hot flesh. He murmured with satisfaction, feeling the slippery opening there. His eager tarse nudged, then entered. He caressed her, enjoying the feel of his slick tarse as it entered and retreated. 'Twas a contact that never failed to heighten her pleasure.

Heat radiated from her body, much as if she had risen from a hot bath. He felt her tension build, and she began to quiver. He rubbed her pleasure spot and sent her into an explosive frenzy.

They fought each other as they climaxed. Pillows and sheets fell to the floor. By the time her body wrested the last drop of his seed from him, she was half off the bed.

He gathered her close in his arms, kissed her forehead, and murmured against her neck. "Meghan mine, why do you fight me from sunup till sundown on every issue? Yield to me in other things as you do in this."

"Never will I be as other women. Ye know it well. I will accept no man as *master* o'er me. 'Twould take the very pride from my soul."

The quiet resolve in her husky voice stabbed wider the rent in the vengeance that surrounded his heart. His soul ached with love and anguish, knowing how much pride he had already stripped from her without her knowing.

Meghan walked about the battlements, stealing glances at the sky. She came to an open embrasure between merlons where she was far enough from the lookouts that they would not see her. Cloud Dancer circled and waited. She wrapped the edge of her cloak around her left arm and braced her hand on the warm stone of the merlons, anticipating the eagle's weight.

Cloud Dancer glided ever lower, floating on the wind as if he hunted for his prey. When he had drifted to the right height, he swooped down.

Meghan did not flinch, for she knew he would not hurt her.

"Ho, Cloud Dancer. What a beautiful sight ye are to my eyes," she cooed to him as he landed on her braced arm. He ducked his head and allowed her to run her hand over the glistening white feathers of his head, down his shiny, brown-feathered back and down his leg to the parchment tied there

as he shifted onto the stone merlon. She wasted not a breath
of time to untie it and read the words there.

*If you have caught a male chauvinist pig and wish to
throw him back, join the birds in your nest.*

Lusty laughter escaped her. Unfortunately, the eagle had
not gone unnoticed. People shouted below, and footsteps
pounded up the stairway to the walkway. She quickly tied the
message to his opposite leg and coaxed him back to her wrist.

"Hurry, now. Away with ye afore they think ye meant me
harm," she urged and lifted her arm to send him on his way.
The eagle was still within an arrow's range when she heard
racing footsteps behind her. She whirled around.

"Nay, Jamie!"

She struck his arm at the same time he released the arrow,
sending it wild. Cloud Dancer called as if to assure her he was
safe. Arrows flew from other directions, only to reach their
peak and drop to the ground.

"Lucifer's fiery eyes, Meghan! I thought to see that great
winged bird tear your throat. Are you hurt?" Rolf's frantic
gaze searched over her, his face devoid of his usual healthy
color. "What caused him to attack and then leave you un-
scathed?" His body shook as he hugged her tight.

"He was but curious. Mayhap he thought me a great mag-
pie with my black cape?" She pulled back in his arms.

"When I caught sight of you, he had your arm in his
talons," Jamie said, his look suspicious.

"Aye." Several others nodded their agreement.

A superstitious lot, the men's eyes were wide, their look
wary. She could not let them think it so unusual, else they
would deem her a witch.

"Mayhap his eyesight is poor. He must have thought me a
bird worthy of his attentions." Their eyes widened, looking
like spilled eggs, and caused her to chuckle. "Then he saw I
was a strange creature that lacked wings. I disappointed him

so much, he flew away." Rolf's searching gaze narrowed. He would not fall for such a tale.

"Go about your duties," he said to all in sight. To her he had one word. "Come."

He halted midway down the spiral stairwell. Placing a hand on either side of her head, he stared at her and waited.

"What?"

He wanted answers she did not want to give.

"You well know what. Dinna think to give me that pap you fed my men."

"Always have I had a way with beasts and birds. Ye know it well."

"Aye. But that raptor was not Simple. Someone has trained the eagle, and it was not you." His jaw firmed in a hard line.

"Why do ye question it? Because Simple is so foolish? I doubt even the great Rolf could train my wee hapless bird. Sparrowhawks are noted for being gowks."

"Tell me of the eagle, Meghan."

"I canna be sure, but I think he is the same one that oft comes to Blackthorn. Our head falconer Simon treats him as one of his own charges and throws treats high for him to capture." She saw he was not satisfied with that. "I was forever around the mews helping Brianna and Netta learn the art of falconry. Perchance he remembered me."

"Aye, that could be." His body relaxed, and he drew back to fix her with stern eyes. "Mayhap I should warn the men to keep watch and bring him down."

"Nay! Dinna harm him. I will never forgive ye if anythin' happens to that noble bird." She grasped his shirt and tugged on it. "Please, Rolf. Let him be."

"It means so much to you?" He frowned as he studied her. "Promise me you willna do anythin' foolish with the eagle again."

"Aye. I willna," she promised easily. 'Twas no lie, for she knew being with Cloud Dancer was never foolish.

Rolf nodded, satisfied, and turned to clatter down the steps.

Leaning against the cool stones of the wall, she listened as his footsteps faded in the distance.

She covered her mouth as a gurgle of laughter threatened to erupt. Brianna had written the missive, for 'twas in her hand. The *male chauvinist pig* was as good as her signature, for no one else heard of it until Damron brought her to Blackthorn.

When first the two met, they had many robust arguments over her strange use of words. He had thought she referred to a "shovingist" pig and demand she explain, for he had never seen the animal act in such a way. So, that part of the message told her if Rolf became too domineering or caused her unhappiness, she had but to leave. Someone would watch for her.

Join the birds in your nest. Nest? Ah, in a tree, of course! They well knew her liking for climbing trees. Guardian must have led them to the tree where Rolf found her sleeping. Her belt would have left its marks around the bark.

Calm spread its warm mantle over her. Were she to become unduly distressed, she had a way to escape.

Rolf had no doubt about his disappearing men. What puzzled him was why Damron of Blackthorn had neither demanded ransoms nor slain them.

If a skirmish ensued during the laird's forays into Rimsdale lands, the wounds inflicted were not life threatening but done solely to take that man out of the fighting. Did Damron know the truth of it all, no doubt he would not be so courtly.

When he stepped out into the bailey, he spotted his cousin at the laundry room door. "Ede, I would speak with you." He led her beneath a shady tree where they could talk in privacy.

"This morn, Meghan sickened at the sight of blood," he started, but stopped when Ede rolled her eyes at him.

"Mayhap not so much the sight of blood as being the cause of it?" Ede nodded to where Alpin worked with Dougald. "He told me how she defended him. Hmf! Most women would have spewed at the very thought and stood by useless as a babe while that man skewered Alpin."

What if Meghan had yielded to her softer side and it was the cause of her sickness? Disappointment nagged at him. The thought of her increasing with his child was a heady one, and his instinct told him she carried his babe.

"Nay. Meghan of Blackthorn wouldna blink at killing a man if she did so to protect another. If she sickens again, tell me."

Never afore had Ede looked at him with such distaste. He squared his jaw and walked away from her.

Days passed without any untoward happenings. Rolf took every opportunity to be with Meghan. His greatest delight was hearing her throaty laughter when he would catch her unaware and swing her around in the air like she was naught but a wee lass.

Her eyes sparkled whenever he came into sight. She would quickly glance around, and if they had privacy, she would tug the hair at his temples until she could reach his lips to kiss him, all the while, her greedy hands roved over his bare chest.

'Twas on a bright cloudless day that Rolf planned ahead to please her. He had his warriors search the woods on the mainland, then patrol at a discreet distance from a clearing carpeted with heather. In the center of the clearing stood one lone, magnificent oak tree. Beneath it, he stashed a thick blanket, a flask of sweet wine, apples, a thick wedge of cheese, and a loaf of freshly baked bread. Dense oak and beech trees surrounded the clearing, giving added privacy.

When Rolf returned to the bailey, he spied Meghan about to enter the stables. Afore she knew what he was about, he swooped down and grasped her about the waist and up into his arms. He grinned at her startled look, then kissed her soundly.

After several moments, he pretended to struggle from her grasp and eyed her sternly. "Come, woman, enough. Where is your shame to kiss me so afore all?"

"I did no such thing, oaf. 'Tis ye who accosted me," Meghan

huffed and punched his shoulder before sliding from his grasp to the ground. "What do ye here?"

"Ah, your puny woman's sight does not see Storm waitin' patiently for you? Nor Malcolm with Simple?" He delighted in the eager look she cast up at him. "Aye. I thought mayhap you would like to exercise Simple in the woods."

Afore the last word was spoken, Meghan was seated on Storm's saddle, holding out her bare wrist to welcome her sparrowhawk.

"Don the wrist guard first, Meghan," Rolf commanded, then watched as Malcolm handed it to her. Once it was on her arm and Simple was settled there, swaying back and forth as if excited, Rolf flashed a smile at her. "Last one across the bridge must grant the other's wish."

People scattered like leaves afore a summer's gale as they galloped through the open barbican and onto the bridge. Rolf held Luath back until the last moment, then urged him on. He flashed her a grin when Luath's hooves were the first to strike land. She raised her brows in question, and he winked at her.

"Later, Meghan mine, you'll grant my wish later."

Meghan smiled with pleasure on seeing the clearing. When they stopped beneath the tree, she threw her head back to look up at the thick canopy of leaves fluttering in the wind with sunlight peeking through like flashing gems.

The scent of heather surrounded them, and from the wicked look in Rolf's gray eyes, Meghan knew he had selected this spot because of it. When he flared his nostrils, lowered his head, and snorted like a randy boar, she shrieked with laughter and scrambled up the tree. He came after her, always allowing her to escape him up to the next fork in the branches. Finally, they settled near the top, one on either side of the heavy trunk.

Simple hopped from one spot to another, cocked her head, and looked as if they were the simple ones, not she.

" 'Tis beautiful." Rolf took a deep breath of air and exhaled slowly. "Were that life could be as peaceful as the scene around us."

"Ye would grow bored within a sennight." Meghan studied
the wistful expression in his eyes, then he blinked and sighed.
"Come, if I dinna go below, Simple will think she should
build a nest here, foolish bird that she is." She was gratified
to hear his bark of laughter.

Rolf swung down, insisting he be below in case of a
mishap. She scoffed at the idea, but allowed him his way.
Once again, as he had in the forest when she had escaped
him, he caught her about the thighs when she left the tree. He
nuzzled her stomach, her breast, her neck as he lowered her,
lifting her skirts all the while. She was naked when he set her
feet on the ground.

Soon after, they lay on the blanket with the sunlight flashing across their bare flesh.

"Mmm, Meghan mine," Rolf murmured in her ear, "do you
like the breeze betwixt your legs, the sunlight warming your
breasts?" He lapped her straining nipples, first one then the
other.

For answer, she wrapped her legs around his hips and urged
him to take her.

"Nay, love. You lost the race." Folding his arms around her,
he rolled onto his back so that she was astride him. " 'Tis my
wish you ride me as you would Storm."

Which Meghan did, with great fervor. She leaned forward,
her hands beside his head, and urged him to suckle the breast
she offered him. Later, after both were sated, they nibbled the
bread and cheese and drank the wine while they watched
Simple hunt.

The sparrowhawk spotted a young hare streaking across
the heather and pursued it. The hare led Simple on a merry
chase, first going right, then left, then circling around and
heading in the opposite direction. When the fleet animal
ducked beneath a bush, the hapless raptor dove beak first
right into the center of it and flailed about, stuck.

"Hold, you foolish bird," Rolf shouted as he raced to aid her.
He reached her afore Meghan, and she stood back and watched.
Rolf took long moments to soothe Simple, murmuring gentle

words and lightly caressing the little head with the backs of his fingers. When Simple calmed, he carefully freed her from the bush and held her to his chest while he checked her for injuries.

Meghan watched, and her heart surged at the gentle expression on his face. This was the Rolf who had carefully nurtured a forsaken Ugsome as a pup, who took the time to chew food and feed it to him. The same man who took steps to make his young brother feel loved, worthy, even seeking revenge for the boy's injuries. She could not fault him for that.

Too soon, the waning sun warned them 'twas time to return within the castle walls.

One rainy afternoon, Rolf greeted another messenger. He was not from Blackthorn, though Rolf would much have preferred it after learning that three days hence, Ailsa would ride across the bridge and into the bailey. Cold dread washed over him.

Never had he been so torn. Too late, he knew his vengeance would destroy Meghan and himself a great deal more than it would Connor. When she had come so close to death during the battle with the varlets who had raided his crofters, his heart had stopped beating. When it resumed, it near leaped from his chest.

Now, guilt consumed him for what he was about to do. He was no stranger to guilt. When Ingirid and his child had died, guilt near destroyed him because he had not been there to defend his home.

He shoved his somber thoughts aside and smiled with a more recent memory. His blood leapt with joy believing Meghan was carrying his bairn. He watched her carefully. Though too early to note any physical changes, his instinct told him his seed had taken. In another fortnight, no doubt her breasts would begin to ripen, their nipples turn a rosier hue.

A fortnight? Would she even bear him in her presence at that time, much less let him test the weight of her breasts? That icy thought washed all feelings of elation from his mind.

With a heavy heart, he went in search of Ede and found her in the kitchens.

"Have Cook prepare Meghan's favorite foods and chill wine in the well. Have them brought to my solar for our evening meal. I would be alone with her this night." He spied Meghan with Storm in the horses' exercise area. He could see she talked to the gelding as she brushed his mane.

He strode over to her, needing to spend as much time with her as he could cram into the rest of the day.

"Come, Meghan, the water lures me. I would wash the sweat from my body." His heart quickened when a look of pleasure crossed her face. In a short time, they were astride their mounts and racing across the bridge and into the forest.

When they reached the pool, he was off Luath and at her side afore she could dismount.

"Ye have no need to help me, Rolf. I am no helpless lass."

"Aye, you are not. But dinna deny me my pleasures." He held her close against his body, letting her glide slowly down his length. Her eyes smiled when she noted his avid state.

"Mmm, do I sense eagerness, my lord?"

"Mmm, do I sense need, my lady? You have learned well all I have taught you of pleasure. Now, indulge me. I would sit and watch you about your water play." He turned her toward the beckoning water and urged her forward. She did not disappoint him as he made his way to the rock and stood waiting, expectant.

Laughing, she stepped to the water's edge. She threw back her head and pretended to ignore him as she lowered her hands to the hem of her tunic. He held his breath while she inched the cloth up, revealing the sheer smock beneath. When the cloth came to her head, she held her arms high, hiding her face behind it for a moment.

His hot gaze swept over her. The sun outlined her exquisite form for his eyes, stirring him as no full nudity would. She seemed to sense that. She propped her foot on a rock, pulled the smock up to the joining of her legs, and untied the ribbon holding her stocking in place. As she peeled it down her right leg, he thought he could not swell any larger or he would burst with need.

He was wrong.

When she lifted her left leg and started undressing it, he couldna tear his eyes away. Not so his own clothing. His shirt ripped as he whipped it over his head, afraid he would miss one heartbeat of time in watching her. Her plump mound and its pink flesh were exposed to his eyes.

His belt clattered to the rock; his plaid slithered beside it. He was naked. His tarse was as hard as the steel of Beast. Her chuckle was as wicked as sin. He pulled his gaze from her pink flesh for seconds and was sorry for it. She lowered her leg, gave him a teasing glance, and slowly walked into the water.

The hem of her smock floated atop the water, allowing him a glimpse of the dark curls between her legs. How could cloth excite him so? Bending forward, she took handfuls of water and splashed it over her breasts.

She faced him, her lovely breasts jutting their pink, pebbled nipples at him and begging him for his lips. He reached down, encircled his tarse, and stared into her eyes as he rubbed his hand up and down, his body tensing with the pleasure of it.

Seeing what he did, her eyes widened in surprise.

It did not daunt her. Smiling, she raised her hands. Her fingertips fondled her nipples while she dampened her parted lips. Watching his hand now, when he stroked himself upward, she pulled gently, extending her nipples.

Rolf growled with delight; Meghan moaned with desire.

He launched himself off the rock in a dive that took her beneath the water with him. By the time they surfaced, he was deep within her hot center.

Their love play did not end until the sun began to dip. They lay upon the rock, her head nestled on his shoulder and her leg thrown across his warm belly. As they watched the shadows lengthen, they wished for more hours to dally. When they donned their clothing at last, Rolf didna want the day to ever end.

If he could hold back time, he would do so now. He cursed the fleeing hours as they returned to the castle. He grasped her hand and hurried with her to his solar.

Servants had pulled back the bedding the way he had ordered, and a peat fire burned, warm and inviting. Cook's helpers had brought succulent trenchers of hot food when they had spotted their master coming across the bridge.

Nay, Rolf could not ask for a more delightful setting than this.

Still, he could ask that it never end.

Yet it would.

His heart lurched sickeningly.

CHAPTER 22

Rolf fed Meghan her favorite meat, savory morsels of roasted boar. She lapped his fingertips after each offering. Not to be outdone by her sensual teasing, he held the dew-wet goblet of chilled wine for her to sip, then kissed away each glistening droplet that lingered on her lips like sparkling red jewels.

They dined slowly, and Rolf tempted her with soft touches and slow kisses that fired his own blood till he was ready to devour her.

With each kiss, he eased a garment from her body, slowly, worshipfully. Her eager hands soon had his belt beneath the table, his plaid crumpled on the floor. From that first night together, she had equaled him in passion. Never had he known a woman who flamed so hotly at his lightest touch.

A heavy fur rug covered the floor in front of the fireplace, and it was there he coaxed Meghan. He placed her on her back, fanned her silky, chestnut hair around her head, and hunkered back on his heels to savor the sight of her golden body. Her firm arms and muscled, long legs were finely proportioned, but it was her lovely breasts and taut stomach that drew his gaze.

The cook had provided a tray of fruits, cheese, and hot bread, along with jellies made of plums and peaches. When Rolf reached up to search the top of the table, his fingers dunked into the small bowl of plum jelly.

Grinning like a fool, he straddled her and waggled his purple-smeared fingers close to her lips. Her tongue flicked out to lick the sweets from his thumb, but he pulled back and smeared her nipples with a streak of the fruit instead.

"Ah, love, what a tasty sight," he whispered as he lowered his head.

Eager as any bairn awaking from sleep, he suckled at each breast. After all the sweetness was gone, he reached out and filled another finger with the jelly and trailed it down to her navel. She shivered with anticipation. He raised his brows and shook his head.

"Nay, Meghan mine. Not yet."

His hot tongue flashed out to lick and tease, setting her to squirming as he neared the dark curls low on her body. To hold her still, he sat on her calves, supporting his weight with his legs. His sac seemed filled with hot sand, heavy and heated.

This time, he dipped his thumb deep into the jellied fruit. His smile wicked now, he tapped her lips. Heat built in her eyes as she licked and teased his thumb, then drew it deep into her mouth to suck. With each strong pull of her hot mouth, his pulse pounded heavy through his groin as his lust built. His rod throbbed and swelled till his skin stretched so tight he feared it would burst. He trembled with anticipation.

Loud in the quiet room, his breath rasped and mingled with the sounds of her greedy sucking. He started to pull his hand away, but she drew on his thumb all the stronger. His tarse bucked, and with an eager cry, he spread her legs and entered her with one powerful surge. Her legs gripped tight around his hips, and she mimicked the same strong rhythm with her hot mouth as he deepened his thrusts.

Only when they climaxed together did she release his thumb.

"Ah, Meghan mine." He grasped her tight to his body and rolled over, bringing her atop him. "Ne'er have I felt the need for a woman as I have for you." His voice broke.

"Love, I will always be here. I wouldna deny ye, for my need for ye is as great," Meghan whispered.

Rolf's heart ached at the words, and his chest could not

hurt more even if an anvil rested on it. He blinked his eyes, masking the tears there. Meghan straightened her arms and lifted above him, grinning mischievously. Bending her head, her hair flipped forward to form a curtain around their faces. Long years past, he had once pinned her against a wall and whispered to her of a dream he'd had where she had made love to him with her hair. When he had freed her, she had blackened his eye for speaking such wicked thoughts.

Now, Meghan made love to him as he had described it. Inch by slow inch, she trailed her warm hair over him, tickled and enticed him as she neared what she sought.

Neither slept but short bursts of time throughout the night. Rolf pleasured her in every way he knew how. He made slow, exquisite love to her as he poured out his feelings to surround her in the warmth of them. She responded with equal tenderness, whispering how much she needed him.

By the time Meghan slept, dawn peeped its red-gold head to lighten the sky. Rolf inched his way off the bed. If she awoke as he left, he could not bear it. Carrying his clothing, he turned to engrave her image in his heart and mind.

Meghan lay on her back, the covers tangled around her knees. She was a vital, golden woman of the earth, one arm flung above her head, the other bent with her hand curled against her cheek. Rosy-tipped breasts beckoned him never to leave her.

Did she carry his bairn? Did she know?

As if to tell him it was her secret to reveal or hide, a faint smile lingered on her lips as he slipped from the room.

Hearing a soft noise, Meghan stirred.

"Rolf?" she murmured, still half asleep.

Hearing no answer, she reached out to feel for him. Nothing but his still-warm pillow greeted her. She forced herself awake, feeling saddened by the loss of his presence. Dread prickled her mind and soul. 'Twas like entering a nightmare, but how could that be? She was awake, not dreaming.

What caused this feeling? She thought of the glorious night. For truth, they had been the most unforgettable hours of her life.

Hours she could never hope to relive again. The memory of his tender and passionate loving gladdened her heart.

Some new emotion had underlaid his feelings as he made love to her. Had there been a note of sadness, of desperation? Mayhap he thought their love doomed because of his stubborn belief that Connor was to blame for his past tragedies?

Surely 'twas possible to overcome if he would relent and allow the two families to meet on neutral ground. Connor and Damron would prove to him they were in Abernethy at the time of the assault on Rolf's wife. Even Mereck had been gone from Blackthorn overseeing the manning of Damron's newly acquired estates from his proxy marriage to Brianna.

Meghan dressed and went in search of Rolf. A heavy blanket of unease seemed to overlay Rimsdale and all its people. He was in the practice field swinging Beast at Dougald like his very life depended on the outcome. Not content when he tired Dougald, he motioned Jamie over to take his commander's place. Sun glinted off their helmets, shooting shafts of light to her eyes.

"Come, lady." Alpin's hand rested lightly on her elbow to turn her to look at him. "Rolf is in a surly mood this morn. He would work it off. 'Tis best you not distract him, or he may do himself an injury."

She looked around at the men and frowned.

"Has something happened? Dinna tell me another man has gone missing?"

"Nay." Alpin flushed and glanced around him. Seeing Garith and Ugsome coming toward them, he called out. "Ho, Garith. I heard you wished Meghan to exercise Simple so Jamie's squire couldna deny you told him true of her clumsy flight?"

Garith tilted his head to the side and eyed Alpin. His brow furrowed, then cleared when he stared at the practice field and saw Rolf. Understanding lit his face.

"Aye, that I do. My lessons with the good priest have near put me to sleep. All that learning of sums and languages make me wish to hide beneath the hay in the stable."

Until late in the day, someone was always at hand to occupy Meghan's time. No sooner did she finish with one person than another took his place. Why this sudden need for her company?

At the noon meal, Rolf didna appear.

"Dougald, does yer lord not wish to dine?" she asked as soon as the stocky commander came to the table.

"My lady, he has ridden out with the last patrol and willna return until this next morn." He rolled his shoulders and shoved a shock of black hair from his forehead. He shifted from one foot to the other. "Uh, Rolf often takes another man's place on night patrol to give that man relief." He sat with a thud on his stool.

"'Tis most generous of him," Meghan said. It did seem something he would do for his men. In her time here at Rimsdale, she had noted he was good to his tenants and kind to all who were under his care. Her shoulders slumped. She sorely missed him this day and had looked forward to nightfall.

The evening dragged by. When Alpin requested a tune on the bagpipes, she was glad to oblige. As she filled the great hall with merry Scottish tunes, men and women laughed and stomped as they danced and vanquished their uneasy spirits.

'Twas lonely when she went up to their chamber. Never had a bed seemed so overlarge. Hours later, she finally slept.

She raced through the forest, fighting off the heavy branches that snagged her hair and tore at her clothing. Cold fingers of fear crept up her neck, and she darted a glance behind her. Seeing who pursued her, she sobbed and ran faster. She must escape.

From him. From Rolf. If he captured her now, she would forever be lost.

Meghan jolted awake. Her heart pounded and her mind filled with dread. She raced to the window opening in hopes that Rolf would ride across the bridge in the early hours afore dawn. A quiet scene met her eye. Other than guards atop the walkways, no one stirred.

When Rolf did return, the day was far gone. He seemed curt and withdrawn, doing naught but nod his head at her afore he went off with his men. Puzzled, she watched him. Even from afar, she could see he was in a quarrelsome mood.

She walked out to the short wooden barrier that separated the practice area from the rest of the outer bailey. She knew he saw her. Why did he turn his head away and motion Jamie, Dougald and Alpin to follow him to the far end of the field? Once there, he kept his back to her.

Seeing his red-haired squire hurry to the armorer's hut, she followed him.

"Cormac, when ye return to yer master, please tell him I wish to speak with him." Meghan's face heated with her awkward request.

"I be sorry, my lady, but he has, uh, ordered that no one disturb his practice this day."

The young man's face flushed bright as his hair, and his gaze barely met hers afore he quickly looked away. Her stomach churned.

Rolf was avoiding her. She could no longer deny it.

Alpin's guest was due to arrive the next day. Ede, her brow furrowed, bustled about from one end of the castle to the other, as she directed teams of workers.

"Ede, how may I help? Would ye like me to see to the bedchamber for Alpin's elderly sister? I know my grandda likes things to be just right. If not, he blusters and grouses that we dinna pay enough attention to him."

"Elderly?" Ede looked up with wide eyes.

"Aye? Is she not?" Meghan frowned. "The chandler said he must have candles aplenty, for *the lady* fears darkness. Cook worries how she can flavor the foods, for *the lady* dislikes spices. She is afeared she willna have enough custards and fruit for soft pasties. The goose girl plans to hide her flock, for *the lady* oft demands she refill her pillows after but a few nights."

Ede gulped so loud, she looked startled. Meghan burst into laughter.

"See? She has even caused ye to race about in a frenzy. Dinna fret. I will see her bedchamber filled with cheerful flowers and sweet rushes, a large, hot brazier of peat to ward off the chill, and candles enough for the most timid of creatures to take comfort." Ede gulped again, and Meghan patted her back. "Which room have ye prepared for her?"

"Uh, 'tis next to Rolf's, of cou . . ." Ede's voice trailed off.

Meghan gave her an encouraging smile and set off to help make the woman's arrival as peaceful and comfortable as possible.

Meghan studied the room and smiled, satisfied. She ordered that peat be lit afore the sun rose the next morn and kept stoked to ward off dampness. Frail bones did not like chilly rooms. Grandda always said his knees ached when the fires were not lit.

The bed, with goose-down pillows piled high and an extra soft woolen blanket added beneath the covers, looked warm and inviting. On the morrow, servants would bring fresh flowers to brighten the bedside table.

Why did everyone avoid meeting her eye? All seemed uneasy, oft rubbing their arms or their necks. Did she not know better, she would have thought she detected a note of pity in their behavior.

Leaving the room, she spied Cormac following Ede down the hall. She startled, for in his arms was the trunk of female clothing from Rolf's room.

"Ede, where are ye movin' my things?"

"To my room," Ede murmured, but did not turn.

Far from her normal cheerful manner, the sprightly woman's shoulders slumped, and her walk was slow. For what reason did she appear so saddened?

"To yer room? I dinna ken the reason." Cold chills gathered

in the pit of her stomach. A shudder coursed through her as she followed them into Ede's room.

"Because of our *guest*," Ede whispered.

Blessed saints. Ede had tears in her eyes. Was something amiss? A new thought dawned. Her tension eased. Mayhap the woman didna approve of a handfast. Of course. Knowing her pride would suffer a blow if the woman deemed her a slut, Rolf wished to protect her.

"Ede, please dinna fash yerself over this. I dinna mind hidin' my relationship with Rolf while she is here. 'Tis kind of him to be thoughtful of her feelin's and my own."

Cormac grated out a curse and dropped the trunk on the floor. He shoved it back against the wall and muttered to himself. He hurried away, his face red and scowling.

Ede all but ran after him, swiping at her eyes. Meghan took but a single step after her to ask the reason for her distress, but her unease built so strong she feared she knew the answer.

It needed no great mind to ken the reason. Rolf. After their weeks together, had those days of frenzied lovemaking tired him of her? She slumped down on the side of the bed, thinking over their last days together afore he became so distant.

Never had he shown he didna want her. He had sought her out at every turn, impatient with wanting her. In its need, his lovemaking had been ardent. Frantic even. That last eve, more than any other, she had sensed his deep caring for her. Was it all a lie?

At the evening meal, Rolf was already seated when she entered the room. She blinked when she saw him. She did not believe her eyes, for the torchlight behind him lit strands of silver hair at his temples where there had been none afore. Never had she seen anyone's hair turn overnight! She reached to touch it, but he flinched away. His eyes were darkly shadowed, their expression much as an injured pup's.

Dougald and Alpin sat to Rolf's right, but on his left where she was used to being placed, Garith sat with Ede next to him.

"What goes here, Rolf?" Meghan motioned with her head to the new seating arrangement.

" 'Tis needful that you sit apart from me now," Rolf said, his voice raspy. His gaze did not linger on her face.

Alpin rose and took her by the elbow to lead her to sit beside him. As they passed Ede, Ede raised red-rimmed eyes filled with sympathy and anger. Not wanting to cause her more distress, Meghan said nothing more. As she passed behind Rolf, she heard his sharp intake of breath and saw his body become so taut he looked made of stone.

Throughout the meal, she could not have had a more attentive partner than Alpin. His face took on a glow that brought out the beauty there. As he sought to make her meal pleasant, the more devoted he became in seeking her comfort, the more Rolf glowered. At the meal's end, Alpin leaned close to put his hand on her wrist and ask what she would prefer from the jellies, slabs of cheese, layers of wafers, and cut fruit.

"Eneuch." Rolf's voice cracked sharp and cold. 'Twas apparent it was meant for Alpin.

Though it was the middle of the night, Meghan could not sleep. Ede had looked so upset when they went to bed that Meghan had not pressed her for an explanation on the evening's happenings. She listened to Ede's soft breathing as she lifted the covers and got out of bed. She stripped off her night shift and threw a mantle around her shoulders. Easing the door open, she went out onto the landing and made her way to Rolf's room.

Inside, she saw him sprawled on a chair beside the window opening. He bolted to his feet.

Meghan braced her hands on the hard wood behind her and backed up to close the door. The green mantle she had slung with such haste across her shoulders slithered down her body to land at her feet.

A beam of moonlight washed over Rolf's face and glinted off the streaks of silver at his temples. She saw him clench his teeth as he stared at her naked body. Praying he would come to her, she held out her arms.

He did not. His body stiffened, his hands fisted, and the muscles at his jaw twitched. Through narrowed eyes, his gaze raked over every inch of her.

Shocked, she grabbed his circular shield propped aside the door and held it to cover her breasts and hips.

Why did he stare at her as if she were a stranger? The air around him radiated tension. Earlier in the evening, she thought him like stone. Now, 'twas more than that.

Rolf had become cold, hard granite. The man who had ignited into a blazing fire every time she came into his presence for these last weeks now showed naught but chilly indifference.

Neither uttered a single, audible word. Gathering her pride close, she tossed the shield aside. Its clatter filled the room. She whirled and yanked the door open to return to Ede's room.

Rolf let out the breath he had held since Meghan exposed her lovely body. Never afore had he needed such iron control to mask his feelings.

The confused look on her face made his heart yearn to comfort her.

The shame in her eyes when she grasped his shield to cover her nakedness shred his honor that he had treated her so.

Had Meghan known how much he wanted her, loved her, he would have been helpless to deny her. He scooped up her mantle and swallowed back a moan, then returned to his chair. He buried his face in it and inhaled deeply. His shoulders slumped.

Soon, she would know all.

He would do anything if he could deny the sun's rising on this next morn.

CHAPTER 23

Darkness faded into gray, but Meghan had still not closed her eyes. What had brought about Rolf's startling withdrawal? Was it because of the guest expected to arrive this day?

She would do all she could to make the visitor welcome. If the saints were with her, the lady would not stay for an extended visit. At the bottom of the trunk, she found a sea-green smock and a deep-green tunic and donned them. She noted the colors brought a glow to her sun-kissed skin. Taking her time, she braided a small section of hair on each side of her temples in the same manner as Rolf wore his. She brushed the rest of her hair and let it fall freely down her back. He would be pleased that she took special care of her appearance.

She wended her way through the sleeping bodies on the great room floor and, careful not to make noise, picked up the bagpipes from beside the hearth. At the cookhouse, she selected freshly baked bread, a wedge of cheese, and an apple. Nibbling on the bread, she went atop the barbican and made her way over to stop above the portcullis that protected the gateway below.

She greeted the guards and settled down to wait. From this vantage point, she would see the riders as soon as they left the wooded path on the mainland. 'Twas a dismal morning. Feelings of dread invaded her like the dreary, dark sky that promised rain.

Just as the first rays of the sun broke through building clouds, she spotted riders and packhorses leaving the woods. Her eyes opened wide, and she stared in dismay. She had hoped for a short visit. It didna seem likely. It appeared the lady brought most of her possessions with her. Swallowing disappointment, she brought the air-filled bagpipe to her lips and started a merry *Ceol mor* tune of welcome that had never failed to bring a smile to the lips of visitors entering Blackthorn.

As the horsemen approached over the long bridge, she noted a woman seated on a dainty palfrey. Surprise near caused her to miss a note. On either side of the horse rode men who grasped wooden poles to hold aloft a canopy of heavy linen. She could not see the woman's face or form but kenned she was frail.

She played her joyful welcome until the last horseman rode into the bailey.

"Ye did Rimsdale proud with yer playin', lady," the guard standing beside her said.

"Aye. 'Tis much more than anyone else would ha'e done," the warrior stationed at the top of the stairs added. Strangely, he patted her shoulder as she carried the bagpipe past him and made her way down to greet their company.

By the time she reached the steps to the castle, Rolf had assisted the woman from her horse. He and Alpin were leading her inside the great doors, followed by Ede. Meghan gripped the bagpipe close to her side and hurried after them into the great hall.

All she could see of their guest was long silvery hair, near identical to Alpin's, who stood beside her. They were of the same height and slender build. Meghan's heart began to thump.

"Rolf, could you not find a piper skillful enough to play a proper welcome? I have heard better from barn cats fighting over a scrap of food." Though her words were harsh, the sound was melodious.

"Leave off, Ailsa. I thought the tune well-played," a voice rough with irritation answered.

Heartsick, Meghan realized 'twas not Rolf who defended her, but Alpin, who had once professed to be her enemy.

"You have neither ear nor eye for beauty, brother, and canna judge." Ailsa's chin lifted high, and she stretched her shoulders back, thrusting out her breasts. She ran her hands over her body and preened for Rolf's eye. "Has not everyone said I was born with not only the beauty, but also the keen mind in the family?"

When she turned her head to look at Alpin, Meghan drew in a sharp breath. 'Twas no elderly dame needing special comforts and care who stood there, but Alpin's twin.

The woman's face was exquisite with creamy white skin, blond shapely brows, and lovely ice-blue eyes fringed with lush, ash-blond lashes. A perfect nose rested above full rosy lips and beautiful white teeth. Meghan reached out to steady herself and felt a comforting arm brace her waist. 'Twas Jamie who helped to steady her. Dougald hurried to her other side.

"Lady Meghan, let me hold the pipes for ye." His voice soft with kindness, Dougald took the heavy pipes from her.

"She may ha'e been born with beauty, but she also was born with a meanness that puts a mad boar to shame," Jamie muttered.

He proved his judgment when Ailsa demanded, "Is it too much to ask for comfort after my long journey?"

"We prepared a chamber for you, and all is ready. Would you care to refresh yourself afore we break our fast?" Ede asked, and went over to stand beside the beautiful woman.

"Do you suggest I do not look lovely enough for this hovel?" Ailsa's nostrils flared.

"I am sure Ede didna mean anything of the kind, Ailsa." Rolf's words were soft and gentle.

It fell like a pail of icy water over Meghan's soul.

"Have you not been able to bribe a suitable man to husband Ede? Though with her unseemly red hair, 'tis likely no man desires her." Ailsa tossed her head, causing her long hair to ripple down her back like a silver stream.

" 'Tis a witch she is," Jamie muttered; then he spoke loud enough so everyone could hear. "Lord Rolf has no need to bribe any man to ask for the lady's hand. He has had so many offers he doesna know which to honor."

Ede's face turned as bright as her hair. Jamie's words also brought Ailsa's regard to them. She had her mouth open for

what would surely be a sour retort when her gaze met
Meghan's face.

"Why, 'tis the unskilled piper." Her gaze raking over Meghan
was as scornful as if she examined a cesspit. "I thought the figure to be a man, so uncomely was she atop the barbican."

Rolf stood immobile, his face blank of any expression.

Ailsa turned her back on Meghan and placed her hand on
his chest. "Rolf, must I stand all this day?"

As the spectacle had been unfolding, the cook and her
helpers had carried in huge trays of food. The servants
arranged all manner of prepared eggs, cold meat, pigeon pie,
cheese, hot scones, porridge, butter, cream, jellies, fruit pas-
tries, and other tempting foods on the table—a feast fit for the
finest lords.

"I am most sorry, Ailsa. Please, let me assist you to the
table," Rolf said, and escorted her to sit beside him.

Meghan remained motionless. Alpin hurried over and
glared at Jamie, who still supported her. Jamie's arm dropped,
and Alpin held out his wrist to escort her.

How could Rolf allow this mean-spirited woman even to
enter his castle? Her fist curled with the need to strike him on
the jaw. He should have turned her skinny arse around and
dumped her back atop her palfrey, prodded the poor beast,
and sent them galloping on their way.

While she seethed, Alpin led her to sit beside him. He
poured a tankard of ale and offered it to her. She controlled
the urge to grab it and throw its contents over the hateful
woman's head. That wouldna be enough, she decided.

"'Tis best you take a sip, Meghan. My sister can be charm-
ing with men, but she isna so with women." His mouth,
pinched in at the sides, showed his irritation at Ailsa.

As he spoke, a loud shuffling and struggle at the doorway
caught their attention. Ugsome fought two guards who tried
to hold him back. He snarled and pulled his lips back in a
menacing grin that showed every tooth. His nose wrinkled as
he snapped at the nearest ankle and broke away. Eyes intent
on Ailsa, he snarled and made a dash toward the table.

"Stay, Ugsome," Garith shouted, and jumped up from his seat.

Ugsome did not break his stride.

"Ugsome, stop!" Rolf commanded. The beast came on.

Meghan stood and waited until the dog was but a pace away from the table.

"Ugsome," she said quietly, and put her right forefinger on her chin, signaling him to stand and follow her.

The homely beast skidded to a halt at the sound of his name from her lips. He looked at her and saw what she wanted. For the first time, he hesitated about obeying her and turned eyes full of hate at the woman beside Rolf.

"Come." Meghan smiled when the dog looked back at her. As if disappointed she would not approve of his taking a nip out of their visitor, he shook his head. Quiet now, he padded over and plopped down on the floor by her feet.

Rolf's brows shot up. For the first time, he must have realized Ugsome had never been a threatening guard over her.

"You should kill that ugly, horrible dog," Ailsa shouted. "Did you not see he was going to attack Garith?"

"Nay! He wouldna hurt me. He was looking at yo . . . uh, something on the floor," Garith said, indignant.

"No one is going to harm Ugsome, Garith. I will ne'er allow such. But from now on, he willna be allowed inside the castle." Rolf's stern voice angered Ailsa, for she frowned. She opened her mouth, but when he turned a cold look on her, she snapped it shut.

Throughout the meal, though Alpin tried his best to tempt Meghan with savory offerings, she could not eat. Waves of nausea roiled through her. She was not surprised, for she had not slept the whole night. It did not help that Ailsa was Alpin's twin, not a frail, elderly lady. What reason brought her here? For certes it was not because she favored Rimsdale or anyone residing in it.

Except Rolf.

Ede looked as ill as Meghan felt. Their gazes met, and Meghan smiled encouragement to her. Later, she would try to soothe the sweet woman's tattered feelings. Knowing she needed to quell her uneasy stomach, she took the hot scone Alpin proffered. She broke off a piece and ate it, then took another and reached down and offered it to Ugsome. Her hand brushed the hilt of the dagger strapped to Alpin's boot.

The mood in the room bristled with tension. Even more so than the day Rolf brought her to Rimsdale as a captive. She shrugged, for 'twas easy to understand why. The woman made it plain to all she thought Rimsdale inferior. Meghan wished Alpin would ease in his attention to her, for each time he leaned close to offer her a tidbit, she felt Rolf's disapproving regard. She didna want to cause trouble between the two friends.

After Alpin brushed her lips with a juicy plum, Rolf slammed his goblet on the table and bolted to his feet. Offering his hand to Ailsa, he helped her rise and led her to the center of the room. He turned, so they faced the high table.

What did he intend? She had not long to think on it afore Rolf began to speak, his voice calm and firm.

"My people of Rimsdale, most of you have met the Lady Ailsa on earlier visits." His shoulders twitched. He hesitated a moment, then took a deep breath. His jaw hardened, and his body stiffened.

"She has come today not as Lord Alpin's sister, a visitor, but as my bride, your future lady." His gaze met Meghan's.

"Lady Ailsa and I will wed on the morrow."

CHAPTER 24

"Nay!" Shock and horror stabbed through Meghan. *She could not have heard him aright.* He had handfast with her—had vowed to keep himself to her.

Ugsome growled and snarled. She reached down to calm him, and as her hand came back up, she secreted Alpin's knife in the folds of her green tunic. That very tunic she had worn to please Rolf. She rose to face him.

Should a hair fall from Ugsome's head, it would be heard in that unearthly quiet room. Rolf waited, rigid as the trunk of a giant oak.

"Ye are handfast with me, Rolf. Everyone at Rimsdale heard yer pledge to me and mine to ye for a year and a day."

Rolf's jaw twitched, the lone sign that he was in any way upset. "My pledge to you wasna for a year and a day, Meghan. My true words were, 'I, Rolf, the MacDhaidh of Rimsdale, pledge myself to Meghan, a Morgan of Blackthorn. I keep myself only to her for as long as we are one.' As of three days past, we are no longer *as one.*"

Horror prickled over her like a thousand nettles. She used all her strength to keep from trembling. These weeks gone by were but a lie. Rolf had deceived her.

Rolf had made her love him. For vengeance.

Rolf had made her believe she was his handfast wife. For vengeance.

She could barely breathe. Hot fury roiled deep within her, realizing what more he had done to her.

He had trampled her pride in the muck of a cesspit. All those days and nights of love were not love. They were vengeance.

She walked slowly around the table. Ugsome followed. He protected her and kept so close he brushed against her legs. His eyes stared at Rolf as if he hated the man as much as the pale beauty at the man's side. Meghan halted ten paces from them.

A new feeling, foreign to her, pulsed through every inch of her body.

Hate. A hate so great it crackled the very air around her.

"Ye are right, Rolf. When I refused to be yer leman, ye did pledge 'as long as we are one,' while I vowed a year and a day. That doesna change the fact that our handfast is legal."

"Nay, not legal, Meghan. I signed a contract for Ailsa over a year hence. It is to that vow I must keep." His words were slow and distinct. Everyone in the hall could hear him.

Meghan's soul screamed in agony. She had been what she had sworn she would never be.

Any man's leman.

All her scorn for him flashed in her eyes as she stared at Rolf. Without a blink or a moment's hesitation, her hand whipped out and light flashed off the speeding blade of Alpin's knife.

Thunk!

The honed tip embedded in the floor between his feet where but two fingers' width separated them. It landed with such force the haft vibrated back and forth and brushed against his boots.

Ailsa screamed and scurried behind him. The men who had come with Ailsa found their arms grasped by Rimsdale warriors. No one uttered a word or moved to touch Meghan. Rolf's people had grown to know the Pride of Blackthorn and her depth of honor. Had she meant harm to their lord, he would now be dead.

"Aye! That blade disavows my own *year and a day*, Rolf. We *are one* no longer." Contempt rang in her voice as she spoke loud and clear. "I vow afore all that I owe the MacDhaidh of Rimsdale naught. No part of me will ever be his. Should I be breedin', he has no rights since we were never legally handfast by his own words. I owe him no loyalty. No respect. Naught."

Meghan looked at Ailsa quaking behind Rolf, and then met his gaze. "Ye are well met in yer choice of a life-mate, Rolf. A harpy befits a liar."

She had to escape this room afore her rage led her to do something she would later regret. She strode with regal dignity toward the doorway. Ugsome placed himself between Meghan and anyone they passed on their way from the room.

Rolf did not try to detain her.

Every muscle in Rolf's body turned rigid. As Ailsa rode in on her palfrey, he had longed to send her away. In all honor, he could not break a signed contract.

Lucifer's hateful soul! Had he any thought that Meghan planned to play a welcome tribute atop the barbican, he would have hidden the bagpipes so she could not. She had unknowingly paid a salute to the woman who came to usurp the place that should have been hers. When Ailsa scorned her beautiful music, his hand had twitched, so great was the urge to slap his bride's mouth.

His heart died as he had watched the emotions that flashed in Meghan's lovely eyes. Hurt that he ignored her; disbelief when she spied Ailsa; horror when he exposed what he had done to her.

He had lived in fear that when she learned what he had done, it would kill her spirit. He need worry no longer. Hatred throbbed through her every pore. It would keep her strong.

"Rolf," Ailsa shrieked at him. "Imprison that crazy woman. She meant to murder me! Had you not been so swift to protect me, my life's blood would now be flowing through these rushes."

Rolf ignored her as he bent to retrieve the knife. He recognized it as Alpin's and held it out to him.

"That woman is brainsick. You must have her whipped

until her flesh hangs in ribbons," Ailsa insisted as she tugged the tunic at his shoulder to get his attention.

"Alpin, see Ailsa to her room," Rolf said without looking at her. Knowing he would spend the rest of his days with this woman made him wish to mount Luath and ride until they dropped.

"She meant to kill me. I am certain of it," Ailsa argued as Alpin led her from the room. "Had she not been so unskilled, that blade would now be through my heart."

"Enough, Ailsa," Alpin muttered as he urged her up the stairwell. "Even the youngest child at Rimsdale knows the skill Meghan used to place that blade in such a wee spot."

Turning to Dougald and Jamie, Rolf gave his next orders. "See that every warrior at Rimsdale knows Meghan isna allowed to leave."

Dougald spoke so none but Rolf could hear. "Lad, do ye no' think ye should let the lass return to Blackthorn? Ye have yer revenge. To keep her here, where she will be forced to see ye both each day, may well destroy her."

"She is not to leave," Rolf shouted. He knew 'twas wrong to force her to remain, but he could not bear it if she was gone, never to see her again. "By rights, her life was forfeit once she drew a blade on me. I dinna seek her death, but she will remain a 'guest' at Rimsdale."

Seeing Dougald would speak again, Rolf's anger grew. "Eneuch! Or would you prefer I place her in the dungeons?"

His words echoed off the walls of the emptying room. He knew why everyone was leaving. Many had not attempted to hide their displeasure in the day's events, for they had come to admire and love Meghan of Blackthorn. Her honesty and willingness to help the lowest of them had made her a welcome addition to Rimsdale.

Years ago when Ailsa had come to the castle to attend his marriage to her cousin Ingirid, all knew the moment she spied him that she coveted her kin's mate. After that, she visited often. His wife was not fond of the pale beauty and looked ill at ease each time she arrived yet again with Alpin.

Rolf had been aware of Ailsa's lust for him, for she took every opportunity to confront him alone, to brush against him and offer herself wordlessly. After she became open in her pursuit, he had told her outright that he would remain faithful to Ingirid. From then on, Ailsa's visits were infrequent and lacked even a show of pretended warmth for her cousin.

When he knew he must wed again, he wanted to avoid a bride search. Alpin, knowing his sister was in love with Rolf, suggested Ailsa. Rolf had agreed. 'Twas easier to take a wife who desired him than to contract for an unseen stranger.

Never had she revealed this side of herself he witnessed today. He did not like it. Was she two women? One soft and eager to offer him anything, the other sharp and demanding? He would soon put her in her place. If he could not have the woman he loved, he would have one who served him well, gave him sons, and helped make his life comfortable.

He sat on the nearest bench, shoulders slumped and elbows rested on his knees, and held his head between his hands. What devil had possessed him to avenge Ingirid and his son's deaths in such a way? To contract for Ailsa's hand, when love for Meghan had smoldered in the depths of his soul? 'Twas like he had cut out his own heart and fed it to Ugsome, were that possible.

He sighed. Never again would he be happy and look forward to each morn as he had these many days with Meghan.

Meghan entered the stable, knowing Jamie noted her presence but did not intrude. She was grateful for his kindness. That Rolf had not thrown her into the dungeons surprised her. He had every right, for she had drawn a blade on him afore his people.

Storm nickered in welcome, giving her the comfort she so sorely needed. From this moment on, she would expend all her energy finding a means to escape. As great as her love for Rolf had been, she now loathed him with equal vigor. He had forced her to live a lie. Had shamed her afore everyone.

Each day she would wait atop the castle and watch for Cloud Dancer. With an aching heart, she tore a strip of cloth from the hem of her green undertunic and secured it to her thigh. The eagle would come again, and she would tie it to his leg to let Blackthorn know she planned to escape. Truly, 'twas not necessary. She knew someone would always watch close by the tree.

Ugsome stood outside the stall. If anyone ventured near, his angry snarls sent them scurrying away. All but Garith. When he sought her out, she had not the heart to ignore the young man. He looked sore at heart. He was torn between the brother he worshiped and his own sense of chivalry.

"Garith, dinna fash yerself. Yer brother never hid the fact he wanted revenge on my family. 'Tis the reason he hunted me down and brought me to Rimsdale."

"Aye, I ken that. Still, I knew he signed a contract with Alpin for his sister's hand. He forbade anyone to mention it. I am shamed for I was too cowardly to tell you." His voice quavered. He stared at the tip of his leather shoes. "Rolf has been so happy these past weeks. Like a dimwitted gowk, I believed he rethought the idea and that you would wed at the end of the year."

"What yer brother did will not cause me to think less of ye. Ye are honor bound to obey yer lord and couldna go against his command." Rage and heartbreak made her voice huskier than usual. "If ye would, Garith, I must needs be alone this day. Would ye take Simple out for her exercise? I would deem it a kindness. I trust her with no other man than ye or Malcolm."

Garith nodded solemnly and left her alone. Meghan knew Rolf would give orders to thwart her escape. Now it would be more difficult than afore, but she had to escape Rimsdale.

She brushed and groomed Storm. Soon, Ede approached carrying a square of linen. It was well past the noon hour, and Meghan had not eaten but that one bite of bread to ward off sickness.

"I knew you would be hungry. You have not eaten this day," Ede said, her voice soft with sympathy.

"Thank ye, Ede. Ye are most kind to think of me."

"Nay, not kind." Ede started to cry as she handed Meghan the bundle of food. "If I was, I would have ignored Rolf's commands and told you what I suspected. When he suggested the handfast, I thought it the whole of his revenge to wait a year to marry you. I never believed he could be so cruel as this."

"I know. Dinna fash yerself, Ede. Ye have been a good friend to me since I arrived." Meghan sat on a bale of hay and patted the spot next to her for Ede to join her. "I willna ever again sit at table with Rolf. I would take it as a kindness if ye would help me as ye have done today."

"Aye, I will see you dinna lack for food." She clasped her hands in her lap until the knuckles turned white. She stared down at them and rocked back and forth. "My husband's uncle lives in Perth, a few leagues from Abernethy. I have told Dougald I wish to send him a missive. I would find if he will take me in. I canna live here any longer."

Meghan opened her mouth to protest, but Ede held up her hand to stop her. "After meeting Ailsa, do you dream we would deal well together? She would see me married to the lowest serf to rid herself of me."

Ede returned to the castle, and Ugsome plopped down at Meghan's feet. Seeing a new wound on his snout, an idea formed in her mind. Of an evening, the beast would always be within the castle grounds when the barbican was closed. Yet, the next morn he would pad across the bridge from the mainland.

Every castle had a bolt hole. After dark, she had but to follow Ugsome, and the dog would show her the where of it. Avoiding the guards would be the difficult part. Mayhap Ede could help her with that.

Late that evening as everyone assembled in the great hall, Meghan returned to Ede's room. Since that morn, she had forced all feeling for Rolf from her mind. He was now *Mac-Dhaidh* to her. Never again Rolf. When once more on Black-thorn lands, she would release her emotions. Until then, she would think only of a way to escape him.

Soon she heard Ede's voice outside and opened the door wide for Dougald to carry in a large tray of steaming food. Seeing the commander of the Rimsdale warriors doing such a duty surprised Meghan. She thanked him for his kindness afore he left.

After eating, Meghan went over her plans with Ede and asked her help. It was much to ask, for in a sense, she bade the woman to disobey her lord. Ede did not hesitate to offer her aid.

She donned the men's clothing Ede brought her and covered herself in a brown mantle. She opened the door a crack to be sure no one lurked on the landing. She padded from the room and kept to the shadows as she made her way out into the bailey. The moon was full, but clouds chased across the sky to mask its bright glow. In the shadows of a thickly leafed tree, she folded the mantle and laid it close to the trunk, where she covered it with leaves.

She didna need to search out Ugsome. He came to her. No one paid much note to the figure of a slender man and the dog walking beside the castle walls. Meghan followed him and sought a way to tell the dog what she needed.

"Ugsome, leave," she commanded. It did not work.

"Out, Ugsome." Nothing.

"Hunt, Ugsome." Still, no response.

Then she pictured the small strip of land outside the castle walls. If he went through a bolt hole, how did he reach the bridge to cross to the mainland? He could not. Though a man could lower a ladder to the land where they worked on the outside walls, a dog couldna climb up the sides of the bridge. However, he could swim to shore!

"Water." No flicker of interest. Then she thought of the times she, Ede, Garith, and Ugsome spent enjoying the lovely pool of water just inside the forest.

"Swim, Ugsome."

He twirled in circles, his tongue lolling out. Trotting ahead, he turned often to see if she followed. He stopped at the south wall where dense shrubs as high as her head grew against the stone walls.

A guard paced above where Ugsome disappeared. She stepped but a pace into the open, but of a sudden the clouds passed. 'Twas bright as day.

"Ho, there," the guard called out.

Meghan lowered her head, raised her arm, and waved quickly. She turned her back on him, approached the nearest tree, and pretended to open her breeches and relieve herself as a man would do. He said no more, but she knew she could go no farther tonight.

She retrieved the cloak and returned to Ede's chamber. No sooner had she closed the door behind her, than she heard MacDhaidh's footsteps approach his room.

Shame scorched her soul, knowing she had been used as a common leman. So much did it affect her, that bile surged up her throat, burning it until she felt it was afire. She barely made it to the basin afore she spewed her meal.

CHAPTER 25

Today was the MacDhaidh's wedding day. Meghan awoke as the sky lightened in the east, and she ate the stale bread she had secreted under her pillow. Once she knew her stomach would not rebel, she eased herself out of bed.

She was no coward. She wouldna make it easy for herself or for the MacDhaidh. He would marry afore her eyes, killing the dreams she had fostered in her heart these many years.

She dressed in the rose outfit he preferred, brushed her long hair until it crackled, and placed a shining silver circlet around her forehead to control it. She studied the face in the polished metal square.

Wiser. She looked wiser, by too many years. Hmpf! Why not?

No dreams were left to make her eyes guileless.

No hopes left to make them expectant.

Nay. The woman who peered back at her knew the worst. Her eyes were like stone.

She waited atop the castle and calmly watched people scurrying to prepare for the big event. Dougald and Alpin brought Luath and the palfrey to the foot of the castle entrance, and she went below. Ugsome followed close beside her skirts. Everyone made way for her and the beast. Some smiled shyly. Others hung their heads, shamed for what their master had done.

The MacDhaidh emerged. He had shaved his face smooth, and someone had trimmed his hair. The silver streak at his temples was twice as wide as the day afore, making the braids there glisten in the sun. He was resplendent in a black silk tunic. Across his shoulders rested a black silk cape covered over with fine stitches depicting beasts and trees of all kinds done in brightly colored threads. The silver lining seemed to ripple with changing shades.

His ceremonial sword rode at his hip, its scabbard glistening with emeralds of all hues. Silver hose met black leather shoes, their garters red silk.

He wore but one ring. The ring that proclaimed him The MacDhaidh of Rimsdale.

She knew the moment he saw her. His jaw twitched, then firmed to granite. He did not meet her eye, nor did he need to. Her appearance at his wedding told him he was now as nothing to her.

Alpin helped Ailsa mount her palfrey. She wore a gown of white, glittering with yellow roses done with gold threads. At the center of each was a pearl. A veil covered her silvery hair. Alpin also wore white. Together they looked like two beautiful silver twin angels come down to grace Rimsdale's bailey.

Father Mark held the ceremony outside the chapel door so all could hear and bear witness to the wedding. Meghan swallowed bile as she heard Rolf swear to "worship thee with my body." While he spoke the words, he glanced up and his gaze met hers.

Had she not been staring so coldly at him, she would have missed the emotion that flashed through his eyes.

Pain. Not of the body. Of the soul.

At the end of the ceremony, he lowered his head to kiss his bride. Meghan melted back through the crowd.

She returned to the highest part of the castle as Ugsome followed closely. She was there but a short time when she heard a tumult on the stairway. The MacDhaidh's curses recoiled off the stones as he burst through the doorway, Dougald and Jamie behind him.

The sun's light glinted off his jeweled scabbard like a crystal, flashing beautiful streaks across her tunic. As soon as he spotted her, he jolted to a halt. Had he thought she could disappear at will? Nay, 'twas not that. He gave his thoughts away when he looked at the open spaces between the merlons.

"Dinna flatter yerself, MacDhaidh. Ye are as nothing to me." She let all her feelings flash from her eyes.

Betrayal. Hate. Scorn. Distrust.

He stiffened and stared a moment, then acknowledged her with a nod before he turned and disappeared down the stairway. Her hands curled into fists.

Meghan watched the sky and prayed Cloud Dancer would soon come. She remained atop the castle and avoided all the festivities. In the bailey below, they had set tables laden with food. Off to the side was a large roped-off area where the men competed in games of skill. 'Twas that sight that drew her attention. She watched as the day marched on. Finally, the archery competition pitted one man against the other.

None could best Rolf. Once they ran out of men to challenge their lord's skill, Dougald approached him. Soon, a crowd gathered around the two men. They appeared to argue over some point. After much urging from the crowd, Rolf nodded. What were they about? Garith pointed to the top of the castle. She knew. Men began wagering coins into two helmets, and excited voices reached her ear. Rolf shrugged his shoulders, and Garith took off at a run.

"Meghan!" His voice sounded breathless as he pounded up the stairs and hurtled through the doorway. He stopped but long enough to tug Ugsome's ear and thump his sides. "None has bettered Rolf's aim, but Dougald has bet everyone that you can."

"Nay." Meghan turned to face toward Blackthorn and willed the great eagle to come gliding through the clouds.

"I know 'tis not to your liking, but that witch who is now my sister-by-law laughed and sneered when Dougald said you were a worthy opponent. The chandler, the baker, the tanner, even the falconer's lad put coins in the helmet for you as winner."

"See Dougald returns their hard-earned money. I dinna wish to be in yer brother's presence."

"Ailsa has made a special bet. She said she noted your *ugly* silver band." He frowned, adding, "She lies, for 'tis beautiful. She pledged the gold circlet with a sapphire at its center that Rolf gave her for her betrothal gift. She said if Rolf's wh— uh, if you can best him, the circlet is yours."

"Nay. I dinna care what she pledged. It interests me not."

"Please, Meghan," he pleaded. "She said you would know you were too unskilled, and if you refused, the coins collected should go to her." His face became agitated, but she still did not move. "The men agreed. If you dinna, they will lose all."

She glanced down at the stillness below. They all waited quietly as they shielded their eyes from the sun and watched her.

"Lucifer's poxed tarse." She whirled toward the stairway. Garith ran over to the open area, raised a fist high in the air, and shouted a war cry.

Meghan gritted her teeth to keep from screaming curses as she hiked up her skirts and stalked from the castle. The crowd parted as Garith led her and Ugsome to the waiting men. She noted Dougald held her bow and quiver of arrows, an excited grin splitting his face.

"One arrow each. The MacDhaidh will shoot first," Meghan ordered. Not once did she look at Rolf.

Pandemonium broke out. Everyone argued 'twas not fair to her that she have but one chance to beat him.

Meghan turned steely eyes on the crowd, and they quieted. She faced him and allowed her contempt to show in her face.

"One try. If I win, ye will return my clothin', and Garith will take Storm to Blackthorn under a flag of truce. Ye will give back the wagered coins. Yer *wife* may keep her circlet. I dislike baubles."

"Aye. One shot. If I win, you will vow not to escape."

Meghan uttered a sound deep in her throat. Her lips stretched and lifted in a snarl to equal Ugsome's.

If looks could render a man impotent, he wouldna be fit to perform his marital duties this night.

* * *

Rolf's soul flinched at the look of revulsion flashing in Meghan's eyes. From the moment he had announced Ailsa would be his bride, all hope for happiness slid from his heart like melting snow off mountain tops in late spring.

He forced his features to a stern rigidity, afeared his dread of the future would show. He glanced at the rose tunic that accented her beauty tenfold. Ailsa was the moon's shadow. Meghan was the earth's energy and the sun's warmth in one golden form.

"Will your clothin' not hinder your aim?" He eyed her flowing tunic.

"Will yers?" She looked pointedly at his own fancy attire. "Then let us settle this."

Dougald's men pushed the crowd back to the far side of the rope. Only Rolf, Dougald, Meghan, and Garith remained inside.

Taking an arrow from Dougald, Rolf aimed for the dead center of the target. He could do no less, since 'twas there he had landed more oft than not this day. As he expected, but not as he had hoped, he struck true.

"Since my strength is greater than yours, take five paces forward afore you shoot."

"I need no concession from ye." She eyed him with disgust.

Rolf prayed she would not shame herself. His face felt taut as leather as she borrowed two ribbons at the neck of Garith's shirt. She pulled the sleeves of her tunic up to her shoulders, and Garith helped tie them there with the ribbons.

Taking her bow, she tested its tautness, for in these many weeks at Rimsdale she had not the use of it. Satisfied with its familiar feel, she held her hand out to Garith for an arrow.

With fluid grace, she raised the bow, notched the arrow, and sighted down its length. Smooth and leisurely, as if she was alone on the field, she arched the bow till he marveled how her arms stood the strain. She let the arrow loose. It flew toward the target, its whoosh of air audible in the silence.

Time slowed as Rolf watched it soar through the open space. It made a sharp, snapping noise as it struck. Not at the edge of the target. Not at the center of the target beside his own. His arrow fell to the ground. Split in half.

Involuntarily, a shout left his lips. His heart pounded with pride for her. He caught himself, shrugged, and feigned boredom.

"Garith will deliver Storm to Blackthorn on the morrow." His gaze scanned her comely form. A grimace flashed over his features as he added, "Afore the sun sets, your boyish garments will be sent to your chamber."

Meghan nodded and turned her back on him. Ugsome again cleared a path for her return.

As he watched her leave, naught was left for him but the raw misery of an aching heart. He clamped his jaw shut. From the corner of his eye, he saw Ailsa seize the gold circlet and secret it in the folds of her finery.

Gray mist shrouded the mountains to the north and crept over the land, making the waning day appear near nightfall. Ugsome padded beside her as Meghan paced the parapets. She studied the shoreline where she must swim ashore when she made good her escape. The forest was closest there, leaving but a small open stretch of land for her to cross afore gaining the line of ancient rowan trees.

Satisfied that she would have no difficulty even on the darkest night, she waved at the alert guards and went below to Ede's chamber. Spying the returned clothing folded neatly upon the bed, she nodded grimly.

The MacDhaidh had kept to worthless promises, but the one that mattered as much as her life and death, he broke without a qualm. She stripped off the lovely rose outfit and tossed it into the peat fire burning in the grate, then dusted off her hands as if ridding herself of trappings meant to please a man. Ugsome looked up at her and back at the fire. They watched together as flames licked the edges of the cloth, then consumed the garment. Satisfied, she dressed swiftly in the familiar breeches and open-necked shirt.

After she wrapped the belt twice around her slender waist, she untangled her windswept hair with a carved comb. An idea struck. 'Twas a long comb, slender at one end. She turned it around in her hands and studied it. Was she to break off the last three teeth, a sharp thin edge would be left. Could she pick the lock on the MacDhaidh's chest where her dagger rested?

With efficient speed, she soon had what she needed. She checked the landing afore she slipped from her room to the MacDhaidh's. A few heartbeats later, she had picked the lock open, delved within the chest, and brought forth her dagger and sheath. Small pieces of parchment caught her eye, for her own handwriting was visible on it.

Her missives to Connor, telling him they need not worry for her! Her heart cracked wider with this latest deceit. No wonder Blackthorn warriors had picked off his men. To question them of her safety, no doubt.

Gritting her teeth to keep silent, she locked the chest and secured her weapon beneath her shirt, then left the room and slipped through the shadows on her way to the stables.

On the morrow, Garith would turn Storm over to a Blackthorn patrol. She took special pains to groom her steed and check his equipment. Never would she have Connor think she willingly neglected her mount.

Night spread over Rimsdale. With the creeping dusk came the awareness that the MacDhaidh would soon bed his bride. Pain struck, near felling her as she grasped Storm's neck and moaned. After kissing and giving him one last, long pat from his forehead to his withers, she turned and fled through the night.

Meghan could not sleep in Ede's room. 'Twas so close they could not fail to hear the wedded couple across the landing. She would lose herself deep in the castle. As she passed the great hall, she spied the bagpipes resting outside the doorway. She grabbed a candle from a holder nearby, flint, and the bagpipe, and went down one stairway to the next. She lit the candle, and finally, she was in the bowels of the castle.

She shivered, for she was in the dungeons, a place she had

hated and feared since the blacksmith's cruel son locked her in the depths of Blackthorn. Filling the bagpipe with air, she started to play. 'Twould chase her memories away.

Not a soft lament. Not a lively tune to set her foot tapping. The sounds coming from the bagpipe were meant to make a man's heart race. To stir him to a killing mood.

'Twas Blackthorn's battle cry that rang out. The sound crashed against the stone walls, drifted through the door cracks and up the stairwells, softening as it traveled.

Rolf's feet lagged. Way too soon he stood outside his chamber door. He hesitated and took a deep, shaky breath. Though he had downed enough wine to dull the ache in his mind, his heart cried out that it was Ailsa, and not his love, who awaited him.

His wife sat propped against white silk pillows, the sheet resting at her waist. Her naked body was as pale as her face, and she had artfully spread her silvery hair around her head. All but invisible on her breasts, her nipples were a muted pink. She saw him in the doorway and waited several moments afore she clutched the sheet to her neck in pretended shyness.

Rolf sighed and wondered how he could coax his limp tarse to enough eagerness to consummate his marriage. Even his ballocks seemed to shrink away from his thighs. From the listless weight of his sex, he knew he must needs nip out the candles' flames and douse the fire. If he couldna see his bride, could he pretend 'twas his golden lass who was eager to welcome him? At the thought, his tarse stirred.

Still without speaking, he closed the door and started to darken the room. No sooner had he pinched out the first flame than he heard the sound of boots pounding toward his door. With a sense of reprieve, he opened it to find Dougald, breathless and ready to rap his fist against the sturdy wood.

"Forgive me, Rolf, but I kenned I had best seek your wishes," he said as he nodded toward the bed.

Rolf stepped out of the room and closed the door behind him. "What has happened?"

"The stable boy became alarmed when Meghan fled after cosseting Storm. She has disappeared. Sounds of Blackthorn's battle call float about as if drifting on the fog. The men are edgy, wonderin' if she could have called forth their warriors."

Rolf darted past him and raced up the stone steps to the top of the castle. Once there, they listened, holding their breaths. True to Dougald's word, the call to war sounded ghostly. They could not tell from whence it came. He saw warriors had crossed the bridge and were returning. They hurried below to meet them.

"Not from land," Jamie blurted, out of breath. "You canna hear the sounds past the front bailey."

Rolf issued his orders, and soon the castle and all its grounds teemed with men carrying torchlights and swords. After a time, the music faded into the mists.

'Twas Rolf who found her. The dawn would soon be upon them when he descended to the dungeons, a place he never thought to look until they had searched each inch of ground. Walking quietly, he looked inside each dank, musty cell. He came to the farthest corner and stepped past the iron bars, holding his candle aloft.

Crowded against the damp rear wall, Meghan lay curled into a tight ball, her head atop the bagpipe. Ugsome lay backed up against her as if he sought to share his warmth with her. The dog's lips drew back in a soundless snarl as he protected her.

Meghan had come to a place she feared. To hide. Dark circles shadowed her eyes, and there for him to see were the tracks of the many tears she had shed afore she slept. His Meghan whom he had never seen cry from despair. Not even after the shame he heaped on her when he brought her roped like a wild mare to Rimsdale.

A burning ache invaded his soul. He blinked moisture away and swallowed the lump in his throat. Finally, he returned to the great hall and called off the search. While all believed he went to his marriage bed, he slipped below.

He stopped where Meghan would not see him, but near enough to be there if, when she awakened, she feared someone had again locked her in the depths of the castle with no way out. He slid his back down the rough wall and sat on the cold damp stones, not caring what damage it did to his fine garments. Pinching out the candle flame, he set himself to watch over her.

Hours later, Ugsome made soft greeting sounds, and Rolf heard Meghan's voice, husky from sleep, tell the beast what a sweet dog he was. He soundlessly rose and went above.

So as not to humiliate Ailsa, Rolf kept to the shadows and used the rear stairwells up to his solar to change his clothing. He straightened his slumped shoulders upon entering his room.

His eyes snapped wide in disbelief. The room was in shambles. Ailsa had yanked his clothing from the wall pegs, tossed others from his chest and scattered them about the floor. Atop one heap was her wedding smock, ripped asunder from neck to hem.

By the looks of things, he knew she had stomped on the pile.

His roar of rage jolted her to her feet. Naked, she eyed him as if she would kill him if she could.

"Look at you," Ailsa screamed at him. "You spent our wedding night swiving that whore in filth like the animal she is. You spilled seed that belongs to no one but me."

"I will tup any woman I wish to offer my favors to, be it Meghan of Blackthorn or any to whom my tarse leads me. You have no say in where I spill my seed."

"I willna allow your leman in my castle."

"Heh." He snorted in disgust. "For you, there is no *my castle*. Rimsdale is mine alone. Should I die without a son, it will pass to Garith. Naught here belongs to you but your clothin', and that only if I deem you will have them."

By the time he finished venting his anger, Ailsa's eyes glinted with malice. He did not care. He had no need for her affection, merely the use of her body to carry an heir. Though at the moment he did not know how he could work up enough lust to accomplish that task. He yanked off his clothing, then grabbed a tartan from the floor. After belting it around his waist, he turned to leave the room.

"When I return, this room will be as I left it last eve. Dinna try my temper about it." She flinched under his glare.

After Meghan refreshed herself in Ede's room, she avoided contact with anyone. Passing the open door to the lord's solar, she heard Ailsa bragging to the servants.

"Last eve he was so eager to take my maidenhead that he tore the gown from my body. He was like an animal, tossing his own clothes about the room in his haste." She sniggered when the maids giggled. "He is as big as a destrier and so savage he near split me in two. 'Tis why blood stains the sheets and still drips down my thighs."

"Oh, me lady, ne'er have I heard such from the lasses he—" The sound of a vicious slap cut off the girl's words.

"Never speak to me of sluts. Should any try to lure him to their beds, I will see they are sent to service swineherds or sold as slaves."

Meghan swallowed hard, striving to keep from spewing onto the rushes. Wrapping her arms around her chest, she fought the shudders that the overheard words caused. In all his eagerness to bed her, never had he been so lustful as to lose control. Not even after their first time had she continued to bleed the next morn.

She darted down to the great doors leading outside and thrust them open to escape into the cool morning air. She wanted to give Storm one last hug and spied Garith entering the stable. As she neared the doorway, she halted on hearing the MacDhaidh's voice. Though he but praised Storm and gave Garith his last instructions to safely hand over the horse to a Blackthorn patrol, anger flew through her. She could not bear to see him now. Turning, she sprinted across the bailey and hurried to the top of the barbican.

As Garith rode out through the gatehouse, she noted he had attached Storm's lead to the belt at his waist. The gelding trotted behind him.

"Dinna fret, Meghan, I will see no harm comes to him," Garith shouted up to her and waved.

She nodded and lifted her hand in a brief gesture. She trusted him. Unlike his brother, he lacked deceit. Her nape tingled, for the heat of a man's gaze caressed her back like ardent fingers. Fury stiffened her shoulders. After spending a night swiving his wife as often as Ailsa had claimed, how dare MacDhaidh eye her with lust. Turning, her lips curled with disgust as she took extra care not to brush against him. Every muscle twitched and throbbed with the urge to strike out at him. Below, she sought comfort with exercising Simple. The laughter of the children at the sparrowhawk's antics helped comfort her mind.

The rest of the day passed in a sickly blur. Ede seemed to take every opportunity to escape the castle and its new mistress. She brought food from the noon meal, for herself and for Meghan. They sat beneath an apple tree and enjoyed a cool breeze as they ate. Once done, Ede was reluctant to return inside.

"Ailsa has done naught but scream at everyone this day. Not one service has she praised, but carped over the least thing. She demands changes of all kinds. Rolf says not a word but ignores her as if she isna there."

Meghan shrugged. "Mayhap he will get more than he kenned by taking her to wife." It mattered not what happened within the castle. All that concerned her was that Garith return to tell her Storm was delivered to Blackthorn's warriors. That and her need to find the bolt hole Ugsome used.

She spent the rest of the day atop Rimsdale in hopes she would see Cloud Dancer floating through the clouds. Night fell, and she stayed in their room until she forced down enough food to keep up her strength. She was sure she carried a bairn, but she would keep it secret. Did the MacDhaidh know, her chance to escape would be gone.

Dressed in black leggings and black shirt, she slipped from the castle. Ugsome trotted in front of her, seeming to know she wished him to lead her to where he took his nightly forays. Luck was with her, for she evaded the guards atop the walkways. The dog shoved between the bushes at the south wall. She followed close behind.

Had Ugsome not been with her, she would have missed the old wooden door covered with vines. In the darkness, Meghan felt all along the door, wondering how the beast could have escaped through it. The lock and metal hinges felt well oiled. Ugsome's wet nose shoved her hand aside. Placing her fingers on his neck, she felt him flatten against the ground. In a short time, he wriggled and pushed with his back paws and was on the other side of the door.

At the bottom, the door had begun to rot away. The dog had scratched away enough of the wood, and then had dug a small trench to finish the opening. Disappointed, she sighed. Perhaps a child could pass through, but not a full-grown woman.

Ugsome stuck his nose back inside, whining and snuffling at her hand, inviting her to join him. She patted him, and when she did not follow him, he padded away.

She again felt the lock. Concentrating, she noted the size, shape, and keyhole. Could she pick this lock as she had the trunk? She grasped the altered comb and tried until it broke in two. Mayhap it would take a while, but in the end, she would find a way to open it.

'Twas well past the noon hour when Garith and the men returned. As he rode across the bridge, she saw he studied the skyline of the battlements until he spied her. He flashed a grin and nodded slightly, letting her know he would seek her out when he could.

Below, Rolf's long strides took him across the front bailey to await his brother at the barbican. Garith rode through and vaulted from his horse. Rolf grasped his shoulders and scrutinized him in a worried manner, and then embraced him in a quick hug.

Did the fool think the laird of Blackthorn as false-hearted as he himself? Garith had ridden under a flag of truce. Not a warrior at Blackthorn would betray that. She watched as he motioned the men into the castle to question them. Meghan sighed. It would be no little time afore Garith could come to her.

"Meghan! I got away as swiftly as I could, but Rolf had so many questions," Garith said as he burst through the doorway at the top of the main tower. Ugsome trotted behind him, and when the young man stopped, he reared up and put his paws on Garith's shoulders. He sniffed over him from his head to his toes.

"'Tis the wolf Guardian you smell, but dinna worry. I will always love you best." He laughed as he thumped the dog on his sides.

"Did it take ye much time to search out a Blackthorn patrol?" Meghan was anxious to hear of her own people.

"Nay. The strangest thing happened," he answered, excitement making his voice crackle. "You know the fork in the path where one leads to Rimsdale, the other to Blackthorn?"

"Aye." How could she forget? 'Twas there the MacDhaidh displayed the Blackthorn helmet and plaids as warning.

"The most amazing man I have e'er seen stood in the middle of the path. He wore a marvelous cape. I ken 'twas made of feathers of all kinds. The colors were of such beauty I didna fear his face."

"His name is Bleddyn," Meghan said, and smiled at him. "He came alone, did he not?"

"Aye. How did you know?"

"'Tis his way. He needs no other to protect him."

The young man near fidgeted out of his skin in eagerness to tell her all. "A white wolf stood next to him. A bigger beast than even Ugsome! Just as we drew near, he looked up at . . .

did you say his name was Bleddyn?" Seeing her nod, he continued. "He had but to nod and the beast sat back on his haunches. Oh, did you know Bleddyn paints half his face blue, and the other half has a terrible scar he paints red?"

"Aye. 'Tis also his way. He is Welsh and follows the old customs. When not for battle, it is done as an honor. He knew ye would meet him."

"I told Rolf such, for he called me Garith in his greeting. By what means did he know it would be me?"

"He knows many things. The how of it I dinna ken."

"Our warriors were frightened and drew their bows. He had but to look at them and their hands stilled. Meghan, I have ne'er seen such. Storm went over to him and nickered for his touch, then waited calmly by Guardian. We could have returned then, but Bleddyn told us he had prepared a camp and had roasted a small boar in our honor."

"The others didna object?"

"Nay. In but moments, we felt like he knew all about our lives, what feats we had done and even what we liked."

Meghan controlled her face to keep from grinning. Bleddyn would have read their thoughts the moment he saw them. From them, he learned all that had happened at Rimsdale.

"When time to leave, he thanked us for taking such care to see Storm returned." Garith looked at her and twisted his head to the side in question. "He said to tell you to 'toss little feathers on high to join the clouds when the sun dips.' He rubbed his cheek and frowned. "Though I canna make sense of it, that is what he said."

Meghan pretended she didna ken his words, though she did.

"I mistrusted my eyes when prepared to leave. One moment he stood beside me, the next he was astride Storm. Within a blink of time, 'twas as if man, horse, and wolf disappeared into the woods." He smiled at her, his eyes alight with the adventure he had completed.

"Thank ye, Garith. I could rely on no other but ye to see

to Storm's safety. Come, I must exercise Simple and thought mayhap ye would enjoy helping."

She and Garith spent their time together laughing and relishing each other's company until the sun started to dim. When time for the evening meal, she again shunned to dine in the great hall, saying she preferred the clean air atop the castle. No one thought it odd that she took Simple with her.

Taking the green strip of cloth she had tied to her thigh to use once the time came, she secured it around Simple's left leg. She knew Cloud Dancer would soon appear to lead the hapless bird home to Blackthorn. The strip of cloth told Blackthorn to watch for her.

Her eyes scanned the sky, studying each bit of white as the sun began to wane. Finally, she saw that for which she watched. High above Loch Rimsdale, Cloud Dancer soared toward her.

"Ah, my wee birdie," she whispered as she petted Simple from her small head back to her tail feathers. "Pay heed to yer friend. Dinna be foolish and stray to attempt lifting a hefty rabbit from the ground. Simon awaits ye at the mews with a fat morsel of chicken."

Hearing Cloud Dancer's call, she peered up at the sky to see him gliding with the wind above her. Wee Simple cocked her head and padded her small feet impatiently up and down Meghan's wrist. After she kissed the birdie's head, she lifted her arm.

Before Simple could take flight, the door from the spiral staircase burst open.

CHAPTER 26

"Meghan, why have you not joined us in the hall for your meals?" Rolf stepped out onto the rooftop, his voice deliberately harsh. He well knew why, yet he refused to accept that she would ne'er sit at table with him again.

"Why, indeed," Meghan responded, the sarcasm in her voice making him flinch. She raised her arm high. "Begone!"

Instantly angry, Rolf thought she referred to him until Simple fluttered her wings, gave one last, quick look at her mistress, and lifted into the air in graceful flight.

"God's love, Meghan, call her back," he ordered, fearful, as he spied the eagle. "That great bird will take the wee bird as easy prey. She willna have a chance against him." He whistled, loud and shrill, but Simple ignored his command.

"Nay. He will see no harm comes to her." Meghan lifted her face to the sky and watched Simple take ever larger spirals to climb higher into the sky.

"How can you know that?" His every muscle tensed, knowing how Meghan loved the little hawk. He expected at any moment to see the bird seized in the eagle's talons.

"'Tis Cloud Dancer from Blackthorn. He has come to take her home."

Simple leveled off and glided toward the south end of the loch. Cloud Dancer swooped down and maneuvered ahead of the small hawk, guiding her around until she faced north. He stayed close by her side as they followed the line of water. Neither Rolf nor Meghan took their eyes from the two birds until they were out of sight. Even then, she wouldna look at him.

"Why did you release her?" he asked, though he knew she would not answer. His heart suspected the reason. She had ensured he would return Storm to Blackthorn. Now she sent her sparrowhawk on her way. Meghan planned to follow.

He would not let her. He could not. Though 'twas torture not to have her, he could not bear to let her leave.

These last days had been a living hell. Each time he looked at Ailsa, despair surged that she was there. If not for her, Meghan of Blackthorn would be his bride. Were she his wife, seated beside him for meals, he would eat heartily. If she were close of an evening, he would take pleasure in her company.

He could not bear to think with what eagerness he would go to his bed if Meghan awaited him there.

His tarse, so listless and shrunken of late, surged to frenzied life. He suspected that only a glimpse of Meghan's shadow could cause it to spring upward in eagerness.

"You will take your meals in the great hall where all at Rimsdale dine." He steeled himself, knowing when she turned to him, naught but her loathing of him would show on her face. Her body vibrated with it.

"Nay. I willna. Did I not make myself clear afore?"

She turned, and her feelings hurtled at him as he had expected. He did not flinch but nodded, solemn.

To be able to see her, he must yield a concession. Tomorrow, carpenters would add a smaller table to the dais at the end of the high table. Ede, Meghan, and Jamie would sit there.

"Aye, you did. I willna insist this eve. Come the next noon hour, you will dine with us." Before she could protest, he held up his hand to halt her. "You need not sit at table with me, but with those you wish by your side."

Rolf feared she was not eating properly, for her face had thinned overmuch. He had watched her these last days, hoping to spy signs she increased with his bairn. Did she do so, he could never let her go. Before she could offer yet another argument, he whirled and left.

The day he wed, he had held little hope he and Ailsa could deal well together, and he had felt the future held naught but stark, lonely pain for him. The next morn, her jealous rage ended that fragment of hope. At day's end, he had told Ailsa that should he wish her in his bed, he would send for her. Even so, she pressed herself against him at every chance. Though not wed to Ailsa a sennight, nor even bedded her, he felt strangled by her presence.

He shook off his gloomy thoughts and went to tell the carpenters how he wanted the table built. After that was done, he would find Dougald. Together they would work off his black mood.

When Rolf went to his bed that eve, Meghan did not go above with Ede. To hear Ailsa's moans of pleasure were more than her mind could stand. In truth, her stomach roiled at the mere thought of it.

Misty fog aided her to reach the postern gate unseen. She swiped the moisture from her hands and labored to trip the tumbler on the monstrous lock. Never again would she take a lock for granted but would learn the secrets of each one.

Half the night passed. At last, she gave up her quest and returned to ease herself into bed with Ede. What was left of the night she spent in a restless dream where she escaped Rimsdale only to have Ailsa lead a lawless band of warriors to her treetop refuge. The ruffians clutched her ankles and yanked her to the ground. Ailsa laughed and promised purses of gold as she urged them to use her so roughly the Mac-Dhaidh would scorn her.

At the sun's rise, she awoke sweaty and sick. Bread calmed her revolting stomach, and she donned dark brown trews and a saffron-colored tunic.

Missing Storm, she sought out Luath and took comfort talking to him and brushing his mane. Upon hearing the MacDhaidh's voice, she cursed and stalked out the rear door.

Having further witnessed her skill during the wedding entertainment, Rimsdale's warriors sought her every suggestion to aid their own improvement. Whenever she felt their lord's presence, she ceased what she was doing and sought the opposite direction.

If the MacDhaidh trained in the far field, she worked with the archers. If he strolled over to inspect the archers, she went to another area, whether it was the quintain or where squires practiced with short swords. All trusted her now, for they knew her honor would not allow her to harm any one of them.

The sun had risen high when Alpin sought her out.

"I would deem it an honor to share a trencher with you."

Never had Meghan seen him look so unsure of himself. As if her answer truly mattered to him.

"I thank ye for the askin', but I willna break bread with the MacDhaidh." She smiled at him to soften the refusal.

" 'Tis easy to see you have not noted the change on the dais this day." He grimaced and added under his breath, "Nor has Ailsa, for that matter."

"What can be different? The high table still requires we dine there."

"Come." His eyes danced, and he grinned as he captured her elbow and steered her toward the castle. "On my honor, I vow you willna be close to Rolf."

As they entered the doorway into the great hall, Alpin smiled down at her with a thoughtful look in his eyes.

"What is it?" Meghan frowned and studied his face.

He laughed, surprising her. "After your arrow pricked my pride, I ne'er thought I would seek your company at the board." He wriggled his blond brows at her, and his eyes crinkled at the corners. "Had I known then of your skill, I would have deemed it an honor you didna place the arrow betwixt my, uh, eyes."

Meghan could not hold back a chuckle, but it soon died in her throat. Unease settled around her shoulders like a mantle adorned with thistles. She looked up to see they stood at the left end of the dais. A new table, large enough for four people, stood there. Ede and Jamie smiled up at her. Not from them did she feel this unease.

Glancing aside, she noted Garith and Dougald at the end

of the lord's table. Several knights and their wives graced the other end, but 'twas not they who caused her discomfort.

At his usual place, Rolf slouched, dull misery turning his eyes to murky gray. A scowl covered his face while Alpin handed her up to the dais and helped her to sit.

But 'twas his wife's eyes that caused her spine to chill. She read in them the hate and jealousy that promised Ailsa would see her life taken when she could.

Throughout the meal, Meghan tried hard to ignore them. It did no good. Ailsa took every opportunity to make snide remarks to the other wives about the "graceless, overgrown leman who strives to be a man."

After all had dined, servants cleared away the food and brought in fruits and cheeses. Jamie asked for her to play a tune on the bagpipes. Alpin added his own plea, stating they had much need of a happy note to end the meal.

"I do believe my head will burst if I hear that dreadful screeching," Ailsa's voice rang out. Placing the back of her hand to her forehead, she sighed.

Jamie snorted and then muttered under his breath, "Good, 'tis settled. I will fetch the pipes."

He was back in a trice. "I e'en filled the bag for ye to save time." He flashed a sheepish look at Alpin.

"Play loud, Meghan," Alpin urged, his face mischievous.

She hefted the pipes, thinking of the merriest tune she could remember. 'Twas Connor's favorite, other than the call to Blackthorn warriors, of course.

Halfway through the piece, Ailsa flounced from the table looking like a bad-tempered hedgehog and hurried toward the door. As she reached it, Meghan screeched out a note that so startled the woman she shrieked and jumped. 'Twas some satisfaction to see her scurry through the doorway.

Over the next days, Rolf grew more surly by the hour. His stomach cramped to a burning ball as he ate less and less, and his hair whitened even more. He took every opportunity to ensure Alpin stayed within his sight. Away from Meghan.

In turn, Alpin sought every opening to be with her.

Mealtimes became laden with tension for Rolf. 'Twas annoying when Ailsa thought to entice him by rubbing her leg against him under the table. Now her hand stole across his thigh to seek between his legs. He almost shot from the bench.

Her forward actions pricked at his mind. Had Alpin not assured him she was yet a virgin, he would have thought her well versed in tempting a man's appetites. She acted much like a woman accustomed to bedsport and too long deprived of it.

On the day following their wedding, he was at first startled when his warriors baited him about the bloodied wedding sheets. Ailsa had faked the consummation, but he did not fault her for that. She had reason to be offended that he had not claimed his marital rights.

Alpin's growing desire for Meghan made Rolf grind his teeth and fist his hands with the need to pummel his friend into the mud. 'Twas often he noted the man's tarse strained against his clothing, raging to be satisfied. That Meghan appeared unaware of her admirer's increasing lust eased his mind somewhat—until she smiled and he heard her husky chuckle over some quip.

Lucifer's fetid teeth! Did Alpin's hand inch its way around her waist?

Rolf's legs tensed to spring up and declare 'twas time they sought their beds, but Meghan swatted at the invading hand and scowled at its owner. Rolf's muscles relaxed. An angry hiss turned his gaze to his wife. 'Twas obvious she had noted his reaction to her brother's attentions. She glared at Rolf, her hand clenched tight to her eating knife.

"Ne'er think on it, woman. Try it but once and you will find yourself confined to an abbey till your heart grows too ancient to beat."

" 'Tis not seemly your slattern resides within the castle with your lawful wife," her angry voice hissed at him.

"Ne'er has she been my *slattern*. She came to me intact of

her innocence. Not until she believed we were legally hand-fast did she come to my bed." He stared at Ailsa in stony silence until her gaze sidled away from his. She picked at the food on their trencher and again spoke, annoying him that she dared.

"If she was as virtuous as you claim, you have ruined her." She watched him from the corner of her eye. "Even common men will deem her fair game for their attentions."

Rolf scowled at her. That some ruffian might expect Meghan to serve his needs made his breath catch with sudden rage.

"No decent man will seek her to bear his children." Ailsa, with a sly look, added, "If she is for truth not the slattern everyone believes, you must see her settled and safe."

"I willna return her to Blackthorn."

"Nay. Still, would it not add flavor to your revenge to see her wed without her brother's knowledge?" Appearing indifferent about the situation, she drew patterns on the cloth with the tip of her eating knife.

"Didna you just say no decent man would seek her hand?"

"If you held a contest of strength where men for leagues around could attend, and offer *her* as prize, mayhap—"

"A contest?" Rolf shouted and surged to his feet. "Are you brainsick?"

Dougald slammed his goblet down so hard it sloshed ale across the table, drawing Rolf's attention. Garith's cheeks were red with anger, and feeling angry stares from the men nearby, he noted the downcast eyes of their wives. They had overheard.

"What is this? A contest, Rolf?" Alpin's eyes were alight with curiosity.

Meghan tilted her head, looking as inquisitive as her wee sparrowhawk.

"Every available male within twenty leagues would fight to the death to win that match," Dougald muttered.

Ailsa, with a sly smile, started to answer Alpin. Rolf grasped her shoulder and hauled her to her feet.

"Eneuch! Not another word."

Sparks flew through his body, as though lightning was

about to strike. Anger coursed through him. Nay, not just anger, 'twas more like battle fury. He imagined Meghan being dragged away to some dingy castle by a sweaty, hairy giant of a man. The lout would likely toss her on a grimy pallet and force her legs apart.

The vision of a swollen shaft ramming into her sweet body made him wish to spew his meal onto the steps as he shoved Ailsa up the spiral stairwell and into her bedchamber. How had she dared put forth such an obscene suggestion?

Night had fallen and all was in deep shadows in the room. Ailsa scurried over to the bedside table. Keeping half-turned from him, she took a small container and sprinkled its contents into the pitcher of wine waiting there.

"Linger a moment, husband. Ede prepared sweet spices that I added to the wine," she explained as she stirred. " 'Tis said to enhance the flavor. Have but a drink with me." She poured some into two goblets and offered one to him.

'Twas not too much to ask of him. He would down it and leave. Ailsa gulped her own as he sipped, cautious. Did she think to entice him with wine? Swirling it around in his mouth, he tested the taste. Sweeter. Fruitier.

"Why have you not come to my bed, Rolf?" She caught her breath, and her eyes opened wide. Then, coyly, she lowered her gaze. "I have heard of men who canna perform their marital duties. They take a lowly woman who is skilled in pleasing warriors into their bed to use her wiles till she entices him to excitement."

"What? How came you by such a brainsick notion?" When had she discarded her red tunic?

"You have gone to your bed each night alone." She grasped the hem of her pink smock and slipped it over her head to drop at her feet. "We have been husband and wife these past ten days, but you have yet to consummate our vows."

He gulped down the rest of the wine. Already he could feel the effect, for his appetite had been poor of late. He shrugged and gestured for more. Were they to talk of his marital duties, he had need of it. She refilled his goblet, then propped herself up against the tall pillows of her bed. She stared at the juncture of his thighs in an appraising way while she lifted one slender white leg and began to peel down her stocking.

"Alpin has oft of late shown an eagerness to swive, while you remain shriveled, without even a hint of manliness."

Letting the silk stocking slide through her fingers over the side of the bed, she spread her legs wider as if to balance. Bit by bit, she rolled down the other stocking and disposed of it.

His wife thought him a eunuch?

A shaft of moonlight worked magic on the gleaming silver thatch guarding her exposed flesh. Her pink nether lips glistened with feminine dew. Her hands cupped her breasts, offering them to his view. He stared, then blinked and gulped down the rest of his wine. He swayed on his feet. What caused such dizziness? His blood pulsed harder through his veins. Why did his body flame as if he were suspended over a roasting pit? He plucked at his stifling clothing.

Watching him, Ailsa pinched her nipples till they were erect. She sighed with pleasure and smoothed her hands over her softly rounded belly, then stopped to rest on the insides of her thighs. She lifted her hips in invitation.

Rolf's groin ached and his tarse thrust outward, ardent and turgid. Stumbling, he looked down to scowl at the obstacle. Clothing littered the floor. When had he ripped his own off?

He rubbed his eyes and tried to see through the hot haze. From the bed, the scent of heather and spices floated up and surrounded the air around them. Silver hair darkened to rich brown, and pale flesh turned to sun-kissed gold and lured him.

Meghan mine? 'Twas his love there who welcomed him with beckoning arms and legs spread wide. Uttering a frantic groan, he tripped over his feet in haste to reach her. As he fell on her, she locked her legs around him.

Twitching with impatience, his lips searched her breasts. Through the flaming haze, he puzzled that they were smaller. Her body leaner. He coaxed a nipple into his mouth and suckled, noisy with greed. Filled with urgency, he felt he would die if he did not have his Meghan. A groan of agony welled up from his heart, and he angled his hips to thrust into her.

Afore his world went black, he cried out.

"Meghan mine!"

CHAPTER 27

Rolf's mind clawed awake well past dawn the next morn. Lucifer's cloven hooves stomped a sword dance on his head, turning it to porridge. Just as he believed he could bear it no longer, the accursed torturer set his brain to burning over a cook fire.

The faint scent of heather teased his memory, as did the certainty that a warm, female body lay curled against his back. Heather? 'Twas Meghan!

With a glad cry, he turned to her. When his hands touched the woman, his arms that had been eager to pull Meghan into his embrace, recoiled. Pain near blinded him.

"You." The word tore from his lips. His heart plummeted in despair when he looked through slitted eyes at the woman beside him. What did he here? In Ailsa's bed?

She was naked. As naked as he.

"Good morn, husband," her voice purred while she stretched and preened her pale body like an elegant white cat.

If she thought to entice him, she failed. He felt only disgust. He was about to demand that she explain what had happened the night just passed, when her servant opened the door. With an appreciative glance down Rolf's body, she grinned and hesitated.

Rolf rose up and balanced himself on his elbow. "Get out!"

The maid jumped back through the doorway and near knocked Meghan off balance. Meghan caught hold of the doorframe and steadied herself. While her startled gaze took in the scene, her lip curled with disgust.

Ailsa, her eyes lit with hostile glee, slung her leg over Rolf's groin, as if to shield his sex from his lover's sight.

Rolf sensed rather than heard Meghan's sharp intake of breath, afore she blanketed her face with cold indifference. For a moment, he met her gaze. Revulsion stared back at him afore she squared her shoulders and turned away. Her footsteps faded.

Wanting only to hold his head and close his eyes to the piercing light, he forced himself to stand and welcomed the shock of the cold floor beneath his feet. Faint shadows of memory plagued him.

"How came I to your bed?"

"Do you not remember, husband?" She gestured to the rumpled bed and the clothing strewn across the floor. "You were in such heat to swive me, you tore the clothes from your body."

"'Tis not possible. Ne'er have I been so needful."

"Oh? How do you explain their shredding and yourself in my bed? Do you not remember ramming your monstrous tarse into me throughout the night?" She glanced down coyly and gave a little shudder. "You were like an animal. Never satisfied."

Rolf remembered nothing of the sort. After splashing cold water on his face, he noticed the empty chalice. Suspicious, he picked it up and sniffed.

"Mayhap you drank overmuch. You were beyond reason. Each time I pleaded for rest, you allowed me but moments of sleep afore you woke me again."

He snorted in disbelief. 'Twould take more than a dozen cups of wine to make him ready to swive his wife even once with any degree of success. Even more suspicious now, he glanced at where he had lain and then down at his own body. He saw no evidence of a night of heavy swiving.

Bellowing for Cormac, he yanked the door wide. He had no need. The squire waited there, fresh clothing over his arm and a mug of foul-smelling liquid balanced gingerly in his hands.

"After hearing yer yell a bit ago, Dougald said ye might have need of this to kill the devils in yer skull." Cormac avoided looking anywhere but at the middle of his lord's chest.

Rolf scowled and motioned for him to follow. Thankfully, no one was about to see their naked lord grimace and groan with each footstep. Once inside his room, he grabbed the proffered remedy, held his nose, and swallowed as fast as he could. After the third gulp, he thrust it back, slapped a hand over his mouth, and made a mad dash for the window opening.

"Dougald said ye would do that, but I was to be sure ye finished the rest," Cormac said, and handed him a wet cloth. After Rolf wiped his face, Cormac shoved the mug at him again.

Rolf reluctantly took the mug of odious liquid and downed it. He grimaced, though not from the potion. Lucifer's puckered arse! His squire looked at him as if he had found him cheating on his wife. His soul shuddered. Why did he feel as if he had?

"Dougald said ye were to keep it down else he would come and see ye drank another," Cormac all but shouted.

"Dougald said, Dougald said," Rolf mimicked. "Know ye not somethin' else to speak of?"

"Aye." Cormac eyed him warily. "The Lady Meghan was up at sunrise. She is teaching Garith the skill of riding bareback."

Rolf grasped the sides of his head, having the fearful fancy that if he did not, it would split apart.

Cormac eyed him warily and continued. "She showed how a man could be seated then rise to stand on the horse's bare back. She rode around the ring, her arms in the air. I know not how she guides him. As she passed beneath a tree, she grasped a branch and pulled herself to the top of the tree while the horse continued. She said a man can escape pursuit by doing such."

"What?" Rolf bellowed. "Ahh!" Pain shot through his skull. He waited a moment for his thinking to clear. "The lady has no horse. Tell me she uses that old swaybacked Plodder, Garith's first nag?"

"Nay, Lord Rolf." Cormac shifted about on his feet, watching as his master began throwing clothes on his naked body. He waited as Rolf tried to shove his head through an arm opening thinking it was the neck of the tunic. "Dougald says she could ride the devil's back and not be thrown."

Through muffled curses, Rolf demanded, "What horse does she ride?"

"Luath."

Riipppp! Rolf's head cleared the fabric. Fortunately, he had already donned leggings, for he pulled the torn clothing from his head and slung it behind him as he ran.

Meghan had returned to her room earlier to get her bow and arrow, and 'twas then she saw Rolf and his wife abed. Sickened by the sight, she wanted nothing more than to be alone. She could not, for the men had clamored and reminded her of her promise to show them this last trick.

Now, holding an arrow between her teeth, she took one last swift circle around the field and concentrated on watching her prey. Luath's gait was smooth as the sea on a windless day. In the center of the ring, a warrior twirled a small target in the air much like a falconer would tempt a raptor. Foreseeing where the target would be on its highest arc, she notched an arrow and let it fly. It struck, causing the lure to plummet.

"Get you here," the MacDhaidh roared.

She could not speak to him now. Not after spying his naked body next to his wife but a short time ago. The hurt was too deep, and she feared she could not mask it.

"Meghan. Obey me!"

She would as soon obey Lucifer. Guiding Luath toward the far side of the bailey, she made for the stairway leading up to the walkway. 'Twould be easy enough to slide off the horse and be away in a flash.

She did not have a chance. His demanding whistle split the air. Meghan fought for control of Luath and thought she had succeeded, until an even louder and more insistant command shrilled. She could not break Luath's years of training. He turned. Drat the man! By the time the steed galloped over to the MacDhaidh, she wanted to strike out at him with her feet.

'Twas good she had no other arrows, else the temptation would be great to embed it in his fickle tarse.

'Twas fortunate for her that the excited men gathered around their master. Before Luath's hooves settled, she slid off his back and turned toward Dougald.

"If ye train the men in such a way—" She got no further afore a heavy hand grasped her shoulder. She need not smell his scent to know who it was. Her body stiffened with rage.

"Take yer filthy paws off me, MacDhaidh." Gathering all her strength, she slammed her right elbow into him. Staggering back, he released her. She spun around to face him. "Ne'er put hand to me again. Ye have not the right."

"I have the right. All at Rimsdale are under my protection and control." The hard look in his eyes warned her not to speak. "If you dinna wish me to shackle you, ne'er act so brainsick again! What if somethin' had startled Luath? He could have killed you." He winced and rubbed his temple. "What possessed you to allow such?" he shouted as he glared around at his warriors.

So violently did the vein in his forehead swell, she feared it would burst.

Dougald frowned in displeasure, for he had been most pleased with her instructions. Alpin raised his brows, and Jamie scratched the side of his face. Garith's jaw stuck out in a mulish way.

"Meghan of Blackthorn is more skilled than our best riders, Rolf," Garith said. "We could learn much from her."

"Aye. And you could also have learned how to scrape up her remains and bury her afore dusk," Rolf bellowed. "Leave us."

Gauging his rage correctly, the men took to their heels faster than a flock of red grouse scattering on finding a hunting dog in their midst. Meghan folded her arms and ignored him.

He would not allow it. He grabbed her shoulders and gave her a slight shake. "Have you no thought to your own life? What if ye are carryin' my bairn? Ye could easily lose it."

She looked down at his hands in silence until he released

her. "*Yer* bairn? Ye have no right to claim a bairn as yers. Ye gave up that right the day ye took another as bride."

They glared at each other like two rabid foxes, neither wanting to be first to look away.

Meghan sucked her teeth. "I have done the riding often afore. I was ne'er in danger from Luath. The perils to my life have all been under yer hands. Especially now."

"Nay. Why think you such a thing?"

"Why, indeed? Are ye not the same man who last eve spoke of a contest of strength with me as prize? Ye would bestow me on another like a common slave?"

Meghan watched shame steal across his face.

"What will ye do to excite their interest, MacDhaidh? Will ye strip the clothin' from my body and describe how ardent a lover I was? Or do ye think the sight of my flesh will be enough to stoke their desire?"

"Dinna speak such filth."

"Your wife spoke such filth."

"In kindness, she sought to find a man to husband you, since you are no longer virgin."

"Kindness? Are ye blind as well as a fool?" Meghan wanted to smash his nose. "I need no aid to find a husband. Once I return to Blackthorn, I will wed a man I choose to father my children."

"Are ye carryin' my bairn?" His teeth grated together.

"When ye have a son, ye will learn of it," was all she would reply. Looking up, she spied Ailsa hurrying toward them. "Yer wife craves another swivin'. She charges toward ye like a bitch in heat." While he hesitated, Meghan strode toward the stable. Luath followed close behind her.

The next days saw tensions within Rimsdale tighten near to the point of an explosion. Ailsa's voice became waspish and shrill. Rolf turned coward and spent most of his day away from the castle, leaving everyone else to bear the brunt of her anger. Though the servants tried hard to please their new mistress, they could do nothing right for the woman.

Of an evening, Alpin sat to Meghan's left to shield her from

Ailsa's spiteful stares. One night, after Alpin was especially attentive, Meghan felt the MacDhaidh's eyes scorch her back. She glanced up and jerked with surprise. Ailsa's glare of hatred was directed on her husband and not on Meghan as was usual.

How quickly love turned to hate.

Not for the first time this day, Rolf fought to control his temper. Time and again, Ailsa carped at him. After he refused her idea of a contest, she demanded he force Meghan to marry.

He refused every name Ailsa put forth, saying Father Mark would never perform a wedding ceremony over a woman who was bound and gagged as Meghan would likely be.

Tonight Ailsa ventured a name he tried hard to find arguments against. 'Twas Alpin. Her claim that he loved Meghan was true. Anyone with half an eye could see Meghan made the man daft. The chance was high Father Mark would be in favor of it, for he had lectured Rolf long and hard on the sin he had committed by despoiling Meghan.

Though Alpin was his lifelong friend, the thought of him cradled between Meghan's thighs made him want to kill him in an ungodly way. How could he feel such emotion about a woman he had set out to ruin? He shuddered and watched his friend. Alpin's face softened with an inner glow whenever he looked at Meghan. 'Twas love. Rolf didna doubt it.

Pain shook him. His eyes blurred. He could never have her. His revenge had turned to bitter defeat. Wrenching dishonor shredded his soul. He had done the unpardonable. He had heaped shame on the one woman he had ever truly loved.

Rolf was unaware of the tears that tracked their slow way down his sun-browned cheeks. Ailsa was not, though. Fury sparked from her. All those years she had planned and prepared had been for naught. Aye, her love for him had been fervent, as fervent as the hate that now roiled through her.

The fool! He had not seen how useless Ingirid was as a wife. A weakling. She wouldna have birthed a worthy son.

Could he not see that she, Ailsa, could give him a son to rival all others?

On a visit to Rimsdale as a girl, she had spied Rolf's father secreting the postern gate key behind a loose stone in the great hall. It had been easy enough to steal it and have another made.

Years later, it took little persuasion for her lover to pilfer clothing from Blackthorn while Connor and Damron were at Abernethy. Damron's leman had been more than obliging, for she and Ailsa shared lovers. Two brothers. One who rode with Eric MacLaren, the other with Alpin. After a frenzied night of coupling, the Blackthorn leman had given her lover a helmet of Connor's and a tunic.

The fools at Rimsdale thought Blackthorn's men had climbed the walls to gain entrance. They had no need. An accomplice inside Rimsdale used the key to give them easy access. Her man made sure the lout didna see the next dawn. The one failed part of her plan was that Garith yet lived. He would cause no problem now.

Alpin remained an issue. Her twin was weak. Too tender. She should have been the male. She must needs assure he suspected nothing, yet she would gain Rimsdale through him. Meghan must be first to go. Then she would see Rolf and Garith soon followed.

Ailsa was certain she was increasing with her lover's child. No one would suspect. She had made certain the servants had passed on the story of the bloodied sheet after her wedding night. When she had drugged Rolf a sennight earlier, she'd had unforseen fortune when the servant opened the door the next morn and saw them naked together.

She had one regret. Rolf had collapsed afore he could ram his magnificent shaft into her eager body. Not one to do without pleasure, she had spent long, luxurious hours licking his body and marveling over every inch of him.

After accomplishing her plans, she would persuade Alpin to take over Rimsdale for the sake of what he would believe was Rolf's child. That the babe was not Rolf's made her triumph all the sweeter!

* * *

Meghan oft visited the blacksmith and the armorer, and it was not long afore she spied a short sword that would fit her needs. The blade had nicks that needed honing, and the wooden hilt had begun to crack. The weapon had been left there for many moons. No one would miss it. As darkness fell, the men had yet to return from their meal. Like as not, they reveled in the ample charms of the scullery maids. In less time than it would take to count to five, she secured the weapon beneath her clothing.

Each night she spent time with Luath, avoiding Ede's chamber until sure the MacDhaidh would have left Ailsa's bed. This night, on hearing two people stealthily enter, whispering, she went quiet as a feather landing on a frozen loch. She backed into a dark corner of Luath's stall.

She had no need for caution, for the pair was too concerned with their own mischief to be aware of her. 'Twas Ailsa and an unknown man she heard entering a nearby stall.

"My rutting stallion, you serve me well. You relieved Rolf of his nithing of a wife and made way for me to be his bride." Ailsa's voice sounded breathless in her haste to disrobe. "I have brought the love potion."

"I ha'e no need for such. Am I not as massive as Luath when he services the mares?"

The man's voice sounded familiar. Meghan rolled her eyes toward the ceiling and prayed they would hurry with their love sport.

"Umm, aye, you are as great around. Ah, so hard. Like a wild beast." Her words sounded slow and disjointed as if she stroked him while speaking. "After Rolf drank the love potion in his wine, his tarse swelled near to bursting as the crone promised. His eyes deceived him into thinking 'twas the slut Meghan who lay under him." Her voice turned peevish. "The potion was too strong. He passed out afore I could enjoy the swiving."

"What need had ye o' him when I service ye often?" the voice asked.

"Ah, but he is even more massive than you," she said with a spiteful tone. "After he passed out, I stroked his tarse so he remained rock hard. I straddled him to take my pleasure, but the bastard rolled to his side afore I could guide him in. I couldna turn him."

"Ow! Dinna squeeze me ballocks so hard," the man complained.

"You like pain. See? You have swollen near to bursting."

"Bitch. On yer knees," he ordered to the sound of a hand slapping bare flesh.

From the sounds of it, Ailsa seemed to take great pleasure in pretending she was a mare in heat and her lover a stallion. Her cries of pleasure sickened Meghan as much as the man's hoggish grunts while laboring to please her.

If they did not soon finish their unholy rutting, Meghan feared she would be sick. She concentrated on breathing slow and deep and near missed their whispered words once they were done.

"Be there enough mandrake to bring down a man of Rolf's size and his brother too?" Ailsa asked.

"Aye. Ye need but a drop or two in their ale each day. They will quickly sicken. 'Twill look like a common ailment pesters them."

"Like a dutiful wife, I will tend them myself." Ailsa's voice sounded wicked. "My pleasure will be to watch his pain. I will allow no other into the room. His own filth will soon cover him."

"Mayhap ye should dose others to make it appear a common ailment?"

"The Blackthorn bitch must be first. I will give her but two days to live, and then put it about that she shared her sickness while swiving with Rolf and his brother." Her laugh was more a quiet cackle. "Rolf will believe she spread her legs for Garith and the men she pursued."

"I near had her that night here in the stable. Had I spread her virgin's blood o'er her, that crazy Ugsome would have ripped her apart," he said with disappointment in his voice.

Meghan's lips pulled back in a silent snarl. So, it was the lout Fergus whom the MacDhaidh had thrown out of Rimsdale.

"Leave now. I will return to my chamber and smear your seed on the sheets. The servants will believe Rolf and I swived the night away," Ailsa gloated. "I canna come to the gate with you. Leave the key in the hole as afore."

Keeping to the shadows after they left, Meghan watched Ailsa slip away toward the castle, then she followed Fergus. Several times she despaired he had heard her, for he turned and she felt his eyes search the darkness. He came to the postern gate and scurried behind a large bush. He knelt, and within moments, he was back out with the key in his hands. After unlocking the gate, he returned the key to its hiding place, eased the gate open, and disappeared into the night.

No doubt, Ailsa would return the next day and retrieve the key. Meghan knew she had to escape tonight. Yet she could not without first warning Rolf what his wife planned. No matter how much she now hated him, she could not allow Ailsa to follow through with her evil plot.

Minutes later, she eased his solar door open and slipped inside the dark room. She had not moved a step from it afore a hand clamped over her mouth and an arm of steel pulled her back against rock-hard flesh.

CHAPTER 28

The MacDhaidh's familiar scent and the soft rustle of his breath in her ear made her quiver. Rough fingertips caressed the side of her cheek as he growled low in his throat. Fighting a relentless urge to melt back against him, she twisted her head and bit the tip of his middle finger. He squeezed her cheeks hard in warning, afore he removed his hand and spun her to face him.

"Ah, Meghan mine. What do you here?"

"I dinna come to rut with ye, MacDhaidh. I came to warn ye. Yer beloved wife plots with Fergus to kill ye and Garith. So that it will appear a sudden sickness, she plans to poison others as well." She jerked away from his hold.

"Lucifer's rotted guts!" He shoved her ahead of him as he made his way to the table beside his bed. "Dinna move." In moments, he held a candle aloft and studied her face.

In the soft light, she saw he wore naught but a damp pair of leggings that hid nothing from her eyes. Seeing his arousal, her gaze flashed to his face. Disbelief was reflected there.

"I overheard Ailsa meeting Fergus this eve. They whispered of some potion she will slip into the wine. A drop at first. Enough to cause malaise. When others sicken, she will add enough to yer and Garith's wine to finish ye."

"What addle-pated scheme have you thought up, Meghan?"

"Brainsick lout. 'Tis what they plotted, not I." She wanted to take him by the neck and shake him like Ugsome would did he come upon a hapless hare.

"Fergus isna here. He wouldna show his face at Rimsdale."

She could not tell him of the postern gate, for he would secure it in an instant with but a shout to Jamie.

" 'Twas Fergus. I would ne'er forget his voice. He has gained entrance and met with her in the stable. He brought the potion, and she plans to begin using it on the morrow."

"Meghan, ne'er did I believe you would yield to jealousy. My wife would not gain by ridding herself of me and Garith. She would have nothing. The castle would revert to a distant kinsman."

"Not if she is increasing with child." Becoming angrier by the moment, she near hissed the words at him.

"Ah. There is the flaw. Ailsa couldna be carryin' my bairn."

"She is carryin' a babe rightly enough. After ye perish from the poison, she will convince Alpin 'tis yer son. She plans to have Alpin take over Rimsdale for the sake of yer heir."

His face turned cold as a death mask. The hard look in his eyes warned her not to utter another word.

"Mayhap Ailsa is right," he said in a voice dead of emotion.

"What are ye talking about?"

"She seeks to find a suitable man to husband you." His jaw clamped together, but the jerking muscles in his cheeks showed with what strain he held himself. "Alpin is a good man and will treat you with kindness. I will see it done on the morrow."

"Fool! If ye think I built a tale out of jealousy, ye are not worth savin'." Afore he could speak again, she spun on her heels and was out the door.

The MacDhaidh had not believed her, but when she slipped into the sleeping chamber, she had no trouble convincing Ede.

"You must leave at once, else Ailsa will see you dead afore Alpin even learns of Rolf's marriage plan," Ede said. "Dinna worry. I will find ways to spill their wine so they willna swallow a drop, except what I offer them."

"I will seek help at Blackthorn," Meghan whispered as she secured her dagger and belted on the newly sharpened short sword. She threw a black cape around her shoulders, then turned to hug Ede. Keeping to the shadows, she made her way below. Creeping past the pallets of sleeping men and women, she decided a band of ruffians could move amongst them without being heard above the snores, belches, and blasts of breaking wind that echoed through the great hall.

The soft breezes floating over Loch Naver held a hint of rain. She glanced up to judge the clouds in the night sky, hoping they would not spill their bounty until she was safely aloft in her tree hideaway. She took a deep, steadying breath and stealthily made her way to the postern gate. As she eased it open and slipped out to freedom, she thanked all the saints in heaven that Ailsa had not yet returned to lock it.

She waited until a cloud covered the full moon, then dashed across the stretch of land to the loch. Dropping her cloak, she dove into the water. The cold shocked the breath from her, for 'twas like plunging naked into melted snow. Gasping, she swam in the protective shadows of the bridge. By the time she reached the shore, she fought for breath. When next she saw her brother and cousins, she would bless them for insisting she increase her stamina by pulling one of them with her as she swam.

No sooner did she enter the woods than she sensed danger. Her heart lurched. She stood motionless, near hugging the trunk of an oak tree while her eyes probed the foggy shadows. She darted from tree to tree, going deeper into the woods. What man lurked nearby? 'Twas not someone from Rimsdale, else he would sound an alarm. 'Twas not a Blackthorn warrior either. He would make his presence known.

Before each move forward, she stopped to listen. A horse snuffled. Her eyes sought movement in the darkness. Not a leaf stirred. Was she surrounded? Nay. Her instinct said not. Cautiously, she crept toward a tall pine tree. A burly arm whipped around her neck and snapped her back against beefy flesh.

"I got ye now," gloated a gravelly voice in her ear. "I knew ye follered me to the gate." He sniffed noisily and chuckled. "Yer scent told me. The high and mighty Pride of Blackthorn wants what I been pleasurin' Ailsa with, eh?" He pinched the side of her breast.

Meghan faked a whimper and ceased struggling. She drew in a deep breath and let every muscle go limp, sagging slightly, letting him think her terrified. With an ugly chuckle, he loosened his hold. She grabbed his wrist, bent her right leg parallel to the ground, swiveled her hip toward the right, and pivoted on her left foot. Swiftly, she snapped her leg down and struck his bare shin with the hard sole of her boot, ripping his flesh all the way to the top of his foot.

Fergus roared with rage and released her. Her short sword sang as it whooshed from its scabbard. Screaming curses, he clutched his dagger in his beefy fist and lunged. Meghan turned her short sword sideways. His blade ripped into her left arm but inches from her shoulder. Her sword slid between his ribs. He fell, his scream echoing through the still night as her weapon left his body. Darting a glance at him to be sure he could not pursue her, she dashed toward where she had heard the horse.

Lucifer's cursed horns! The fires of Hades burnt in her arm. Though she bled like a gutted pig, she had no time to tend it. Clasping her hand over the wound, she ran so fast she all but collided with a horse tied to a dying oak.

Meghan tore the reins loose with her blood-soaked hand. She put her foot in the stirrup and grasped the pommel, but a wave of dizziness swept her. It took two attempts before she gained the saddle. 'Twas then she heard the sound of horsemen tearing across the bridge. An eerie wail floated on the cold wind and caused chill bumps to scamper like a thousand fleas over her body. Needing no further encouragement to escape, she kicked her mount into a gallop.

More than once, she was not sure she could elude them. The sound of the MacDhaidh bellowing, "Find the lass. She is injured," drifted to her. The pain in her arm was as nothing to what she felt in her heart.

Join the birds in your nest, Brianna had written. She headed for the tree.

Hooves thundered close behind. Splashing through the water, she spied the tree and its overhanging branch ahead and slowed her mount. Waves of dizziness swept through her, and she swallowed bile that surged to her throat. Fighting for balance, she cautiously knelt on the horse's back.

A few short paces from the tree, she gritted her teeth and sprang to her feet. Stifling a cry, she grabbed the branch and near let go when fiery pain ripped through her arm as the terrified horse bolted away.

She no sooner climbed to the highest branch than warriors thundered past, some on land and some in the water.

"Ahead! A giant brown horse entered the woods," one man called. "'Tis a Blackthorn raider!"

"Nay! Over here," came another shout. "A huge white shot through the trees to the right. 'Tis Laird Damron's mount."

The sounds of horses crashing through brush came from all directions. Utter confusion reigned. She knew Blackthorn's warriors divided the Rimsdale men and drew them away from her.

"Rolf! I have searched to the right of the stream. She isna here," Dougald's voice shouted beneath her tree. "Ye are all wrong. I see them just ahead on the left."

Meghan held her breath as Dougald looked at the ground below her at the red splotches barely visible from moonlight filtering through the leaves. Tilting his head back, he stared straight into her eyes and winked. "Take care and bind that wound," he whispered loud enough for her to hear, then pranced his horse around, scattering the leaves to hide the telltale blood.

"To me, you lackwits," he bellowed at the men. "A Blackthorn raider on a gray horse is but a short distance ahead." Dougald spurred his mount and led the men away.

While Meghan waited for their sounds to fade, she tore off the hem of her shirt, made a pad, and tied it around her wound.

Close by in the woods, a horse moved with near-silent steps. She stiffened. Held her breath. Had one been more canny than the rest? If so, she would hurl herself down on his back and put her blade to his throat afore he could draw breath.

"Meghan, lass, 'tis me," a deep voice whispered. "Dinna pounce on me and slit my throat. Netta would ne'er forgive you."

"Ah, Mereck, I thought 'twas M'Famhair the men spied. He is the only giant brown in the Highlands," she whispered back as she made her way down to a low branch. She sighed with relief when Mereck's strong arms plucked her off the tree like a dainty flower he feared to bruise.

"Damron and the men will lead them on a merry chase," he said as he wrapped her securely in his black cape. "Rest now. Soon we will be home. By the morrow, Bleddyn will have you back to rights."

After Meghan had stormed out of his room, Rolf thought long and hard. He was wrong. Meghan's honor wouldna allow her to create such a tale. If she said Ailsa planned to kill him, then 'twas true. He stiffened his jaw and bellowed.

"Cormac!" The lad raced to him. "Awake Dougald and bid him come to Lady Ailsa's chamber. Then find her brother and do the same."

Not bothering to scratch on the wood and seek entrance, Rolf slammed open the door to Ailsa's chamber. "Where have you hidden it?" Rolf's angry voice bounced off the walls.

Ailsa knelt on the floor, rustling through her clothing chest. She jumped to her feet and spun around. All color drained from her face leaving it the waxen hue of a body whose soul had quickly departed. "My lord husband? Hide what?" She reached behind her, gripped the lid, and slammed it down, then stepped back to press her legs against it.

"You know well of what I speak. I want the vial Fergus handed you earlier. Did he also supply you with the love potion?"

"Love potion?" She threw her robe open, exposing her lithe body to him. "What need have I of love potions?"

His glance slid over her body trying to discover if the woman had come to him already with child. His fists convulsed in fury. As blood surged and heated his face, his heartbeat slammed in his ears. 'Twas fortunate Dougald came to his rescue.

"You asked for me, Rolf?"

"Aye." He ordered Ailsa, "Cover yourself, woman!" His nails dug into his palms as he spun to Dougald. "When Alpin arrives, search this room. You may have no need to go farther than the clothing trunk she seeks to protect." Even to his own ears, his voice was bitter.

Tears streamed down Ailsa's face as she flung her arms around him. "I have nothing to hide, husband. If aught is in my trunk, your slut placed it there."

Rolf thrust his arms wide and recoiled, feeling like a snake had wrapped around him. "If ye value your life, ne'er touch me again."

"Rolf, what goes here?" Alpin's voice rang with alarm. "Why do you strike out at my sister?"

"You will see soon enough. Seat her and dinna let her rise." Rolf stabbed his hand toward the chair by the window and grabbed deep breaths to calm his rage. As twins, Alpin and Ailsa were closer than most, but she had hidden her treachery well from her brother. Rolf nodded to Dougald.

Dougald rummaged through the chest and quickly found the vials. One was larger than the other. He withdrew the cork on the smaller one and sniffed the contents. Rolf recognized the love potion. The other had an odor unknown to him.

He handed it to Dougald. "Take it below and find a fowl not worthy of the cook pot. Use a twig to put a drop of the potion on its tongue. Be careful you dinna spill it, and dinna touch it with your hands. Report to me what happens." Dougald nodded and hurried below.

Ailsa screamed at Rolf. "Last eve, I found Meghan in my room. Fetch her. Beat the truth from her. 'Tis she who placed mandrake there."

"If you knew naught of it, how did you know 'tis mandrake in the vial?" Rolf crossed his arms and stared at her, his lip curled in contempt.

A short time later, Dougald burst back into the room carrying a chicken's carcass by the feet. Alpin turned ashen. Groaning, he lurched to the window and spewed, then stared at Ailsa as if she were a stranger to him.

"It took but a few heartbeats, Rolf. 'Tis a heavy poison, to be sure." Dougald looked unsure of what to do next.

"Weakling," Ailsa shouted at Alpin. "The Blackthorn slut has ruined all my years of planning. From the first, Rimsdale should have been mine." She turned on Rolf, her eyes gleaming with madness. "That whining Ingirid was not worthy to be your wife. She didna fight but blubbered like a bairn when Fergus dragged her to the stairs and shoved her. Garith was too much the weakling to fend him off. All mewling cowards. I would have rid you of them. Our bairn will be strong. Look! I carry your son."

She tried to wrench her robe open again, but Alpin put his arms around her to restrain her. Distraught, tears streamed down his face.

Jamie burst into the room, his face twitching with anxiety.

"What has happened, man?" Rolf asked.

"We heard a man's screams inside the woods. We found Fergus." He stopped and looked at Alpin. "Dead. Stabbed. A trail of blood leads away from him." He gulped and handed a bit of cloth to Rolf. "We found this on a branch but ten paces away."

Blood splattered the fabric. Rolf's heart ached as the faint hint of heather reached him. 'Twas from Meghan's shirt. She had avenged herself.

Ailsa shrieked, "My love! The slut murdered my love!"

Rolf clutched the fabric to his chest. He longed to throttle his wife. "Alpin, dinna allow her to leave. We will settle this when I return."

He galloped across the bridge with Jamie. If Meghan died, 'twas his fault. He had suffered grief and regret aplenty over Ingirid's death. Now, the choking fear that gripped him was nigh unbearable.

With each drum of Luath's hooves, his conscience, his

honor, beat at him. Connor, Meghan, Laird Damron—all at Blackthorn were innocent of foul deeds. But not himself.

He had sought revenge in a most vile way. He had used the woman he loved, had ripped her pride from her and stomped it in the cesspit.

He had treated Meghan's honor as being of less value than a lowly man's nod.

He had taken her love and forged it into hate.

Had he also caused her death?

A wail of pain welled up from his heart to rent the air. Luath whinnied and reared up to paw empty space, near tossing Rolf from his back.

Rolf's stomach revolted, and he swallowed hard, fearing he would shame himself in front of his men. He took a deep, steadying breath.

The Rimsdale warriors were hard-pressed in their search, for Blackthorn's men scattered them for leagues around. They hunted far and wide but failed to find Meghan. Near dawn, Rolf returned to Rimsdale in defeat. Anxiety weighed his shoulders and pained his chest. Though certain now that Laird Damron's men had protected and rescued her, he suffered, wondering how severe were her wounds.

He tore his fingers through his hair knowing he must now deal with his traitorous wife. He could not throttle her, no matter how his hands ached to do the deed. 'Twould be best that he confine her to an abbey for the rest of her days. For ample funds, they would provide a cell where she could not escape and do another harm.

Although all was quiet after passing through the barbican, he sensed something was amiss. In the middle of the front bailey, Garith stood with his arms bracing Ede's shoulders. Tears streaked her face, swollen with bloody scratches. The imprint of a hand blazed red on the right side.

"Ailsa near felled her brother with an iron candleholder," Garith said in a wobbly voice. "Ede went to his aid, but Ailsa attacked her like a wild animal. Alpin and I were barely able to fend her off so we could get Ede out of the room." His eyes showed horror at seeing the strength of the crazed woman.

"Has he calmed her?"

"She is gone." Garith's ashen face twitched with stress.

"Gone? How could she have gone?" Rolf's gaze darted around the bailey as if seeking her.

"Alpin had to take her away." He gulped and patted Ede on the shoulder. "She screamed and ranted 'twas not safe here. Even claimed you couldna mate with her. She vowed when the moon was high, you became a horned Lucifer, your shaft larger than a bull. She said you could swive none but the witch Meghan. She broke everything in sight. Her room is a shambles. Alpin couldna calm her till he promised to take her back to MacKean Castle."

He lifted Ede's face to examine it and sucked in a deep breath. "Take Ede to the women and see her tended to, Garith." He squared his shoulders and turned to study his men. "I must needs have you with me, Dougald. Pick enough warriors to defend Rimsdale should Damron of Blackthorn attack." Sickness filled him, recalling Ede's words that Rimsdale would pay for what he had done to Meghan.

"We ride to MacKean Castle?" Dougald asked.

"Aye. Jamie will be in charge here with Garith. Every man we can spare must gather weapons and provisions for a battle, should Alpin not give Ailsa over to me."

"That sheep's patoot! When we get hold of Rolf, I'll give him a kick in his overactive ballocks he'll not soon forget," Damron's Brianna promised as she and Bleddyn scrubbed their hands at Blackthorn Castle. She cleaned Meghan's wound and stood back for Bleddyn to take over.

"Rolf believed what they told him, little one," Bleddyn said. "Even Alpin didna know 'twas Ailsa and Fergus who were responsible for Rolf's tragedy."

"Well, damn and blast," Brianna muttered as she watched him stitch Meghan's arm. "I still say we should give him a healthy kick or two." She stood at the ready with a salve to spread over the stitches and cloths they had boiled in water and then dried in Bleddyn's herbarium.

"I plan to snatch a bald spot on his knotty-pated head," Mereck's Netta added, nodding all the while.

"I will let my Dougall spew his milk down the neck of his shirt," Elise, Connor's timid wife ventured. Her young son was famous for spurting his milk farther than any of his cousins.

"Meghan, lass, if ye birth a son, do us a boon and name him with somethin' not startin' with *D*." Damron grinned and shook his head. "Netta's Donald, our own Douglas, and now Elise's Dougall—mayhap somethin' like Ian or Eric?"

"Aye, I will think on it," Meghan said through gritted teeth. "I have the feelin' it will be a Mari for mine own mother, or Aldyth for Grandda's love." She drew a slow, even breath, waiting for the stitching to end. "How soon can the men be ready to ride again? We must needs hurry. 'Tis a chance Ailsa could put too much of the potion in the first dose and kill them all."

Connor burst into the room, followed by Mereck. "You are not going, Meghan. That is final," he shouted at her.

"Ye willna leave me here. I am ridin' with ye, and *that* is final." Meghan glared at him as she spoke. "Tell them, Bleddyn. Am I not hearty enough to ride? I willna have the three of ye chargin' up to Rimsdale and causin' turmoil. They will know 'tis in peace we come if I ride with ye."

"Meghan speaks true. And if she rests well this night and does not take with a fever, she will be fit enough if we ride close by her side to aid her. Even so, we will not be heading to Rimsdale," Bleddyn answered.

"If not to Rimsdale, where do we go?" Damron long since learned Bleddyn knew things no other mortal could.

It took the Welshman but a short time to apprise them of what had happened after Meghan left Rimsdale. It was close to the noon hour the next day before they could leave, for the men nearly had to lock their wives in Damron's solar to keep them at Blackthorn.

They clattered over the drawbridge with Blackthorn's army at their back. Damron led with Mereck, and behind them rode Connor and Bleddyn with Meghan between them, her arm heavy with bandages bound close to her chest.

Late the next day, when they finally galloped through Rimsdale's lands, people scattered in fear. Not so much from the sight of Damron and his army but for the man who rode at his side.

He wore a hide tunic that came to just below his knees. Wolf skins covered his massive shoulders, and leather arm-bands circled his wrists up to his elbows. Long hair flew wild and free, baring piercing green eyes peering from a wolfish face. One side of that face he had painted with blue woad.

'Twas Damron's half-brother Mereck, known as Baresark, a warrior feared by men throughout England and Scotland for his ferocity.

CHAPTER 29

Rolf stood at the portcullis of MacKean Castle and grieved for the heartsick look on Alpin's face. "Ailsa is my wife, Alpin. 'Tis for me to say what needs be done with her."

"You would lock her away. Like some crazed beast. I canna allow it." Alpin swiped a hand across his eyes, shamed at the moisture there. "The madness has left since I brought her here. Mayhap 'twill take hold for good, should she be caged."

"Ailsa's schemes killed not only my wife and son, but other good men. 'Tis fortunate Garith is regaining the use of his arm, thanks to Meghan's help."

He paced, slapping the safety shield on Beast. He could not allow Ailsa to roam free. She was a danger to all within her reach. By rights, he could hang her for what she had done and had planned to do. None would question him, not even King Malcolm.

"I will give you until the morrow to open your gates. If you dinna, I have no choice but to enter by force." He stared hard at Alpin. "I vow to you, together we will find the proper abbey to secure her." He turned on his heels and strode to join his men.

Out of reach of Alpin's archers, Jamie had directed men to set up a village of tents while others sectioned off an area to confine the horses.

Rolf prayed his friend would not thwart him on the morrow, though he feared he would. Ailsa had brought enough grief. He wanted no more widows and children left crying. With Dougald and Jamie, he formed a battle plan that would cause the least bloodshed.

* * *

As the first rays of dawn lightened the sky, Rolf rode Luath to the portcullis. Alpin's trusted commander stood beside him atop the barbican. As Donnall studied the city of tents and the line of warriors waiting there, his brow furrowed. He turned and seemed to argue with Alpin, to no avail.

Alpin, his face ravaged by sadness and a sleepless night, said but two lone words that gave Rolf his decision.

"I canna."

Rolf had no choice but to take the castle by force. He squared his shoulders to keep them from sagging over the anguish he felt for his friend and returned to the far side of the clearing. His men waited, their weapons at the ready. Warriors with newly acquired crossbows would be first to move up, followed by archers, and then lines of warriors with axes, double-edged swords, and spears. When his army approached, mayhap Donnall could reason with Alpin before any blood need be spilled.

He raised his arm, spun his hand in a circle, and pointed forward. They began to move. Rolf's reluctance kept Luath at a slow pace as they neared the castle.

The sound of his army's approach was drowned out by the roar of thunder in the distance. The sky had not a cloud. The skin across his shoulders and down his back prickled. Acid welled up from his belly, filling his mouth. Dread filled his soul. He swiveled in his saddle and stared eastward toward the growing din. In the blinding rays of sun, the advancing army looked like the heavens had opened to send horsemen down on beams of light.

At the lead rode the most impressive warriors in the Highlands. As they came ever closer, Rolf made out Connor on the far left. To his right rode Laird Damron of Blackthorn, the fearsome Mereck at the center. Next to him rode a slender figure covered in chain mail and helmet. Last came Bleddyn ap Tewdwr. Rolf knew 'twas he by Garith's description of the Welshman's many-colored great cape and scarred face.

To Rolf's front, the battlements of MacKean Castle bristled with warriors; the might of Blackthorn gathered at his back. He was tightly boxed in.

"Halt," he bellowed to his men before they were within striking distance of MacKean Castle. "Dougald, hold steady. We canna fight back to back. We have not enough men to carry it off. Naught is left for me but to offer single combat to a man of Laird Damron's choosing."

"Aye, Rolf. Have a care." Dougald rubbed the back of his neck and squinted his eyes as he stared at the advancing army. "If the laird offers you choice of your opponent, Connor is your best match. 'Twould not be seemly to select the youth beside the mystic."

Rolf led Luath through a path opening between his men. He rode out into the open area until he came face-to-face with Blackthorn's might. The slender youth seen from afar was no longer a mystery.

'Twas Meghan. No one had more right than she to see to his defeat. He had shredded her dignity and torn her pride from her before trampling them through the slimy mire of his deceit.

He had destroyed her.

Tearing his attention from her, his gaze met cynical green eyes on either side of the laird of Blackthorn's gold-plated nose piece.

"I must seek a boon from you, Damron. Single combat with a man of your choosing. I would save the families of Rimsdale and Blackthorn further grief."

"For what you have done to Meghan, Lucifer will freeze from his dwelling afore you may seek a boon from Blackthorn," Connor blurted out.

"Hold, cousin." Damron held up a quieting hand. "Rolf, by what right do ye ask a favor of me after what ye have done to the Pride of Blackthorn?" Damron's gimlet stare did not leave Rolf.

"Aye. You have much to bring me to account for. I will—" He got no further, for Meghan approached him on Storm.

"Enough of this blather. We have not come to destroy ye

but to see to yer well-being. Ye took none of the mandrake? Garith? He is well also? What of Ede, is she safe?"

Shame flooded him. Instead of berating him as was her due, her concern was for his own people.

"Nay. We have taken none of it. Garith and Ede are well. After you left my chambers"—he hesitated, wary as he eyed Connor—"Dougald searched Ailsa's room. We found two vials of potions." He shifted in his seat, hoping she would not ask of the other potion. "One bore a strange scent. Dougald tested it on a hapless fowl. 'Twas laced with the mandrake.

"Ailsa is brainsick. None but Alpin could calm her. I told him I would confine her in an abbey for the rest of her days to assure she harms no others or herself. I returned after searching for you and found they were gone."

"Alpin will not agree?" Mereck's deep baritone asked.

"Aye. He refuses to allow it."

"Ailsa is within the great hall of yon castle thinking all is well," Bleddyn said. "For the moment, she is sane." He moved his huge mount Thunder forward a pace. "Come. Alpin will speak with me."

He startled Rolf. How could the man know someone so distant would wish to address him?

In moments, Bleddyn stood alone in front of the barbican entrance. His great mantle whipped about him in the breeze, the brilliant-colored feathers adorning it shimmering in the sun.

Clasping a large talisman hanging from a heavy chain around his neck, he called out to the man waiting above.

"Alpin MacKean. Listen to me." Alpin's tormented gaze met Bleddyn's, and then lowered to stare at the talisman. Bleddyn continued. "Our armies will stay without. We must decide what needs be done together. We will not play you false. Open your door to us." Alpin hesitated, looked behind him, then back down at Bleddyn. He tore his fingers through his hair and nodded, then whirled around and disappeared. The iron door beside the portcullis screeched open, wide enough for one person to enter at a time.

No one spoke as they followed Alpin across the bailey and

into the castle. They entered the great hall and saw Ailsa, who waited calm and serene at the high table.

Damron and Connor were first to enter. She stood and swept them a low bow. "Welcome to my home, sirs." With her golden hair agleam and the flowing white dress she wore, she appeared a sweet angel. Rolf had not seen her look thus since she was ten and seven.

Meghan stepped through the doorway.

"Out! Out of my sight, murdering slut," Ailsa screeched. She darted toward Meghan, her hands outstretched like claws. Alpin grasped her shoulders, and with soft, shushing sounds, soothed her. Meghan moved aside, out of the mad woman's view.

As Mereck came forward, Ailsa stiffened. "I know of you," she said to him. "You are Baresark." She tried to jerk away from Alpin's grip. "You come to take my head as trophy for your belt." She turned to stare at Bleddyn and calmed but a moment. "You are the Angel of Death waiting to carry my soul to the afterlife."

"Nay, lady, I come to help you. Look into my eyes and you will see the truth there."

Ailsa looked everywhere but at him. With a mad burst of energy, she tore from Alpin and dashed to the corner stairwell. As fleet as a doe, she dodged them all as she seemed to fly up the stairs.

By the time they caught up to her, she stood balanced in a crenellation on the battlements. A brisk breeze whipped her hair and clothing about her. Beautiful still, though madness peered from her eyes, she waved a small vial.

"I will prove 'tis naught but a love potion." Her gaze wild and darting about, she removed the stopper with her teeth. She looked at Rolf and then smiled at Alpin.

"Nay, sister, dinna." Alpin's voice filled with horror. " 'Twill be your death!" He raced toward her, but she tilted the vial and drank it all. Alpin reached her. She clutched at him and in a frenzy, pulled him onto the open crenellation. In but a heartbeat or two, spasms shook her body. She began to froth at the mouth. Alpin struggled to pull Ailsa back onto the rooftop.

Horror clutched Rolf's throat in a strangling grip. He lunged for Alpin's arm. For naught. As Ailsa toppled her brother over with her, Alpin's gaze met Rolf's. A wealth of sorrow shone there before they plummeted into space. Ailsa's shrieks were as nothing to but one scream torn from Alpin's lips.

"Meghan!"

Love. Passion. Heartache. Sorrow. A plea for forgiveness. All sounded in that one word. Meghan.

Late that evening, Donnall carried out his lord's last wishes.

"Lord Rolf, Alpin ordered that I hand ye this should the time come that he couldna." Donnall cleared his throat as he held out a parchment sealed with the MacKean crest. "Ye will see all is legal and proper. The priest will witness that last eve my lord wrote that which is here."

Rolf broke the seal and unrolled the scroll. There in Alpin's familiar hand was a document stating that should MacKean Castle fall to the MacDhaidh, he prayed that Rolf would heed his last wish. He asked that Garith be given MacKean Castle and lands and that until he was ten and eight, Rolf would train his brother. The document was brief. He also asked that Donnall retain his post as commander of the MacKean warriors and act as advisor along with Rolf. 'Twas obvious Alpin had expected to die in battle and had thought to make amends for the grief his sister had caused the youth.

"I would gladly honor Alpin's wishes. Though mayhap I dinna have the right, Donnall." He passed the parchment to Laird Damron and waited, knowing he must needs settle with Blackthorn for what he had done.

"I for one dinna object," Meghan's husky voice broke the silence. "Garith will make a fine lord. His arm grows stronger with each sennight. Donnall can take over his physical training."

"I will speak with King Malcolm in favor of it," Damron said quietly.

"I agree with Meghan." Connor turned to glare at his sister. "Were ye not carryin' Rolf's bairn, I would happily spit him over a fire in place of a boar. That is, after I had Damron blister yer own hide."

"Ahem."

The harsh sound from Mereck's throat came out as more of a bestial growl than a bid for attention. The people of Rimsdale quietly awaiting to learn what was to become of them jerked with worry and looked at the man known as Baresark.

"Speakin' of bairns"—his face hardened as he looked first at Meghan and then at Rolf—"what is to become of this newest child of Blackthorn?"

"Meghan, forgive me." Rolf burned with misery. "What I have done to you can ne'er be undone. I have taken your pride and shredded it. I have taken your person and treated you indecently. You gave me your vow with honor. I gave you my vow in deceit, for I didna mean to keep it.

"Though I claimed I would take the bairn from your breast, I knew I couldna do it. Ne'er fear. You are free to choose whether to return to Blackthorn never to see me again, or to allow me to be a husband to you and father to our child." Rolf's shoulders slouched in defeat.

Rolf's eyes beseeched Meghan. Watching him, all the misery and scorn melted from her soul and slid from her shoulders. Never did she think she could fully forgive him. Only time would tell. She could meet him halfway, though. She squared her shoulders and cradled her throbbing arm against her chest.

"I will return to Rimsdale to assure myself all are well." At the look of hope in his face, her expression hardened. She threw her next words at him. "I will remain there, but I willna be a wife to ye. I no longer wish it."

"You canna mean it," the startled words burst from his lips.

"I can. I do." Meghan glared at him. "Where ye believed I was but good enough to be yer leman, I now believe ye will not be a suitable life-mate. Ye will be my lover. Not my husband."

"You will not live openly with him, Meghan," Connor shouted.

"Dinna tell me what I can and canna do! None can force me to wed where I will not." She eyed Damron, half afraid he would forbid it. When he spoke, she relaxed. Being married to Brianna, a woman with a will as strong as her own, he understood.

" 'Tis Meghan's life to do with as she wills."

EPILOGUE

Meghan busied herself seeing that all was well at Rimsdale Castle. Ugsome was her constant companion. Sensing the rift between Rolf and Meghan, when Rolf was near, the dog placed himself between them.

Careful to give her the space she needed, Rolf saw to her every need and was cautious not to go too quickly with her.

At times, he felt she tested him. Like that first sennight after her arm had healed. 'Twas a lovely Monday morn, and knowing Meghan would prefer to be out of doors, he had sought her company. He found her in the solar sitting next to Ede, scowling at something in her hands. So heavy was her concentration, the tip of her tongue peeked between her lips. Silently, he padded across the room to stop behind her and peer over her shoulder.

His Meghan was sewing?

She sensed someone there, and her hand jerked, stabbing the needle in her finger.

"Lucifer's beady eyes! Dinna sneak up on me, Rolf, else ye may well feel my blade in yer flesh," she grumbled.

"Here, love, let me help afore you stain the bairn's wee garment." Rolf knelt and placed her finger between his lips to suck away the blood. "Come, the day is yet fresh and the apples are ripe." Her face lit. He was still on his knees by the time she reached the stairway.

"Hold, Meghan mine." He scrambled to his feet and chased after her. "I would aid you down the stairway."

He heard her explosive huff and did not catch up with her till she reached the great doors of the castle. When he snaked his arm around her to open the door, she rolled her eyes at him.

Two juicy apples later, when she started to climb high atop an apple tree, he became wise to her ploy. His hands reached to grasp hold of her shoulder and his mouth opened, ready to say nay. He spied her watching from the corner of her eye, stepped back, and kept his tongue behind his teeth.

That Wednesday, she resumed training his horsemen to be more agile on their mounts. Rather than roar and forbid her the activity, he bit that same tongue.

Bit by small bit, she began to relax in his company. He had asked Ede to see to the removal of all that had been Ailsa's and distribute it among the women of the castle. All else the servants were to cart away. Nothing went to waste, for he bade them keep what they wished. They scrubbed the room from ceiling to floor. Carpenters built a new bed and room furnishings. The softest linens covered the pallet stuffed with down feathers, and weavers made a colorful yellow, leaf-green, and brown coverlet for the new bed. Brown fur rugs lay about the floor. All was done by the time Meghan's belongings arrived from Blackthorn. If not at her side, her sword rested on a wooden stand close by the bed. A clothing chest holding soft, female garments stood against the wall beside a smaller one stuffed with Connor's outgrown breeches and tunics. The room was as she liked it.

'Twas hers to do with as she chose.

To share. If she chose.

She didna.

Rolf courted her as he had dreamed of doing so many years ago. He did not send men afar to find trinkets of gold or give her jewels. Neither did he lay silken ribbons on her pillows to surprise her when she retired, nor did he ply her with flowers.

He bade the armorer and blacksmith to fashion a sword whose weight and length suited her. The fletcher made ten and five of the finest arrows, and the tanner sewed a new leather quiver. He had Ede and the women fashion tunics and breeches that would suit her expanding body, all in the earth

tones she favored. Meghan's back was to him the day Ede
gave them to her. His heart lightened, for she gave a pleased
cry and rubbed a light green tunic of the softest wool against
her cheek.

What delighted Meghan most of all was the arrival of her
own bagpipes, along with Simple and Storm. Each day, Rolf
took her out to ride along the waterfront. Whenever Simple did
some foolish thing, he gloried in Meghan's husky laughter.

After a month of this, Rolf ventured to take her to the pool
to swim. For the first time, he saw her changing body, though
'twas through a thin smock.

Had he thought Meghan lovely before, she was truly more
beautiful now. Her face glowed with an inner light that caused
everyone near to smile at her. Her breasts were fuller, their
pink tips rosier than before. What struck his heart as the most
beautiful change of all was the soft roundness of her stomach.

His bairn nestled there.

Under and around her he swam in ever-closing circles,
watching her reaction. At first, she shied away. He did not stop.
He kept up his water play, courting her with his wet body.

A short time later, his heart quickened when he broke from
the water and saw her avid eyes on him. Pretending not to notice her regard, he swam with slow, easy strokes over to the
flat rock. Slinging his head to rid his hair of water, he took his
time as he lifted his slick, dripping body onto the rock. He
could feel her gaze like hands fondling his buttocks.

Slowly, he turned to face her. His tarse sprang to attention.
Upright. The thought that it searched the sky for clouds made
his lips twitch as he stifled a grin.

Meghan held her breath. No man had the right to be so
finely made. She watched as he flowed effortlessly around
her. The water currents from his gliding body caressed her.
Each time he moved closer, she caught her breath. When he
shot up into the air like a playful fish and made his way to
leave the water, she felt forsaken. She watched as he pulled

himself up onto the rock. How she wanted to grasp those sleek buttocks and place kisses on them, to slide her hands up over his wet back and shoulders!

Rolf turned. She caught her breath. Seeing his arousal, a shock of hot desire shot to her core. He stood there and let her have her fill as her gaze roved over his body. His tarse bucked.

How much longer could he wait?

Lucifer's pointy ears! How much longer could *she* wait was the question. She needed him. Now. Taking her time, she gave him the same slow show as she moved through the water toward him. As her head broke free of the water near the rock, she saw his toes balanced on the edge. She looked up at him. Slowly. Inch by enticing inch. She noted his ballocks, swollen and heavy beneath his tarse that began to seep with need.

Her gaze roved over his flat stomach, his corded muscles, his massive shoulders. Till she met his eyes. Love and eagerness shone there. In slow moves, he bent and lifted her from the water. As he brought her against his sun-warmed body, his arms locked around her in eagerness. He buried his face in her neck, and she felt his breath catch in a suppressed sob. Then she heard his whispered words.

"Ah, Meghan mine. I love you more than life."

Five months later, Rimsdale Castle seemed ready to burst with people. All Meghan's loved ones from Blackthorn were there. Brianna would see her through the birthing with Netta's help. Should there be any difficulty, Bleddyn would take over. Had it not been for his skill, Brianna would have been lost after her first birthing.

The men lounged back on their seats, sipping wine chilled in the well. Now and again, they would grin between themselves, for Rolf paced and near pulled the white hair at his temples from his head.

"She still refuses to marry me," Rolf said for at least the thirtieth time in the last four days. "Each night for the past five months I have asked her. I have e'en thrown my pride out yon window, gone down on my knees and begged her. Each time she has answered nay."

He paced back and forth and stopped in front of Connor.

"You are her brother. Tell her 'tis not seemly her child is to be born a bastard."

"Huh! Not me. From the sounds of it, Meghan's temper is short. She may well take that fancy new sword to my arse."

Rolf huffed and raked his fingers through his already wildly disheveled hair. He eyed Damron and Mereck. Bleddyn had gone to see how the women fared. Choosing Damron as the head of the Blackthorn family, he besought him. "Damron, you are my last chance. You can order her to marry me. She will listen to you as her laird."

"Uh huh. The way she listened to me for the last ten and more years? Ye know better than that, Rolf. She will decide in her own time. Wait and see."

"Is our new baby here yet, Da?" Serena hollered as she burst into the room. She raced over to pull on Damron's tunic. Ede and Elise hurried after her, each carrying a babe. Never had Rimsdale had so much laughter and giggling and little ones crawling and toddling about.

"Nay, my sweet. Still, ye must all be very good if ye wish to see the bairn today." Damron hugged her spindly little body to him and nuzzled her neck.

"Rolf," Bleddyn spoke softly from the doorway. "Meghan asks that you be there for the birthing as is Blackthorn's custom. The time is short now. Father Mark awaits outside the door. Be wise and do not tell Meghan of it."

"Now? 'Tis time? Now?" Rolf felt panic for the first time in his life.

"Aye. If ye dinna wish yer ears boxed, ye had best go as soon as she calls for ye. We can all tell ye our wives become ragin' boars when they are a birthin'." Damron laughed, for at that moment Meghan added her own command.

"Rolf!" Her scream turned Rolf's legs to porridge. He tripped over his feet in his haste to get to her.

Meghan knew she had no time to lose. Rolf flew through

the door and knelt on the floor beside her bed. He looked affrighted out of his wits. She scowled at him. "Dinna tell me
ye will faint like Mereck did when Netta birthed."

Rolf looked desperate on hearing the news. His eyes
widened. 'Twas evident the men had not told him the feared
Baresark had fainted.

"I willna. Meghan mine." Unthinking, he clasped his hands
together in a prayerful way and begged, "Please dinna deny
me again. Wed me and let me be a husband to you. I know
that which I denied you, you have denied me. You have pun-
ished me aplenty. Dinna punish our bairn. I will do anythin'
you ask—"

"Will ye halt yammerin' at me, love, and call the priest? I
willna have our babe born a bastard." She took quick panting
breaths like Brianna had taught her. As the pain ebbed, she
added, "Dinna scare the good man by the look on yer face
into thinkin 'tis the last rites ye want." She could not resist a
chuckle as Rolf scrambled to his feet and raced out the door.

"Father Mark," he bellowed, "hurry! She has agreed!"

Meghan knew the good father had to be right outside the
door for him to arrive so speedily. At his heels were the men
of Blackthorn and their wives to bear witness to the vows. She
knew if they didna soon get on with it, it would be much more
they would witness. She took a slow breath and tried not to
scream, for poor Mereck would likely land on the rushes again.

Never had she heard a priest speak the wedding vows so
quickly. His eyes looked straight up at the ceiling of the room.

"I pronounce ye husband and wife," was as far as Father
Mark got afore he fled the room. He collided with Mereck,
who she had seen backing toward the door moments earlier.
Thankfully, the room cleared like magic just as she felt the little head begin to force its way from her body.

"Look, Rolf. Your bairn's hair is as dark and lush as
Meghan's," Brianna's happy voice informed him.

Meghan clutched his arms. "Ahh, dinna move if ye value
yer life," she gasped the words at him. "Hold me, husband."

With a glad cry, Rolf leaned over and placed his arms

around her shoulders. The warm, solid form of her love surrounding her helped her give that final great push that brought their daughter into the world.

A short time later, once Brianna and Netta had seen to the happy chore of bathing mother and daughter, and the servants had freshened up the bed with clean linens, Rolf gazed down at his love. Though he had sought Meghan as a means to his revenge, he vowed he would happily spend a lifetime proving to her his everlasting love.

He cuddled wee Mari to his chest after having shown her to all and sundry, who made over the little babe with a powerful cry. They were properly impressed.

"Ye are in for it now, Rolf," Damron had said. "If Meghan does not have her riding astride and wrestling with her cousins by the time she is four winters old, my name isna Damron."

Rolf looked down at his beautiful wife and almost hesitated to speak. He eyed the small chest in the corner of their room where she had placed the babe's clothing.

"Meghan mine? You dinna have tiny breeches tucked away in yon chest . . . do you?"

Meghan's husky chuckle gave him hope. In but a moment, she dashed it.

"We will see, love. We will see."

Author's Note

"Swings by his thigh a thing most magical. . . ." This is an old Anglo-Saxon riddle Meghan told which upset Rolf. The riddle was translated by Michael Alexander, and taken from "The Old English Riddles of The Exeter Book," Craig Williamson, Chapel Hill, University of North Carolina Press.

When I read these riddles, I imagine a cold winter night in the Highlands. Stormy clouds hide the moon as icy rain falls on a medieval keep. In the crowded great hall, rowdy men have staked out a trestle table near the fire. While a sotted man composes his riddle, his hand flashes out to steal a pinch on a buxom serving lass's derriere. Can you picture the other men cackling and buffeting each other off their benches when he challenges the listeners to solve his racy rhyme?

I have tried to keep "modern" words out of the manuscript dialog, but if an author truly used words suitable to this period, it would have to be in Old English. I doubt that telling a medieval tale would be possible, for how could anyone but a scholar in old languages interpret it?

Visit me at www.sophiajohnson.net.